Whatever
MAY COME

A JAMESON FAMILY NOVEL BOOK 1

TRACEE LYDIA GARNER

Interior Format

ALSO BY TRACEE LYDIA GARNER

FICTION
Family Affairs (All That & Then Some anthology)

Love Unchosen

Anchored Hearts (Book 1 | Cole Parker's Story)

Deadly Affections (Book 2 | Dexter Parker's Story)

Fatal Opposition (Book 3 | James Parker's Story)

Whatever May Come - (Tish's story)
Jameson Family Book 1

A Current Affair - (Dean's Story)
Jameson Family Book 2

NONFICTION
Pack Light: Thoughts for the Journey

DEAR READER,

Whatever May Come is the reissue of a book I first wrote almost seventeen years ago. Can you believe that I've been in the business for that long? I can't. I'm excited to update this story and revisit the wonderful Jameson Family. If you read it back when it was titled *Come What May*, I hope you'll enjoy this new version. It's very special to me as this was only my second story published, way back when, with BET Books.

The story has changed: it's been updated in a way that reflects my current writing style. The story now includes inspirational, faith-based elements without compromising the suspenseful elements that I hope make my stories intriguing. The second story in this family series is coming soon, as well as two more books to complement this first story from 17 years ago. A very special supporter of us authors asked me about finishing the storyline (she really asked about "Jojo") and I thought: *wow, I wasn't sure anyone would want the rest!* At the time, I admit the task seemed daunting. The series is four books long so far. You can always write me and tell me if you see someone show up in these tales that you want to know more about and I will certainly see what I can do. In any case, hearing a kind word from any of my readers means the world to me, now more than ever. So always, I encourage every reader to write his/her favorite author.

Until then, please enjoy, whether this is your first or second time around.

Thank you for continuing to support my work.

With love,

Tracee

To God be the glory for the things He has done.

ONE

———

*P*AT, PAT, CLAP, CLAP...
  "Elephant."
  Pat, pat, clap, clap...
  "Flamingo."
  Pat, pat, clap, clap...
  Pat, pat, clap, clap...
  "Come on, Thomas, you can do it."
  "Giraffe!" Thomas called out enthusiastically before joining back in with the beat. *Pat, pat, clap, clap...* "Hippopotamus," the next voice chanted. *Pat, pat, clap, clap...* "Iguana."
  "Wonderful, Cathy!" Tisha Jameson praised, beaming at the child before glancing at her watch. "But sorry you guys, we've got to stop now. It's about time to get ready to go, okay?"
  Tisha smiled as the students let out audible groans of regret that the day was over, bringing an end to their favorite game.
  "Where's my carpet-squares helper?" she yelled.
  "I'll do it, Ms. Jameson," Thomas piped up, bending to stack the squares.
  "Thank you, Thomas," Tisha said with a fond smile. She raised her voice to address the entire class as they raced around for their backpacks and coats. "Remember, spelling test on Monday, and we'll do – hmm let's see... an out-

doors theme for our alphabet game."

Tisha got up from the floor as the rambunctious kids hurried around the room in anxious anticipation of the weekend that lay ahead. As she began wiping the whiteboard clean, she turned for just a moment to take in the sight of her second-grade classroom. It still filled her with pride and gratitude. Only a month had passed - though it seemed much longer - since she had moved to Macon, Georgia, jumped into her new job and begun her new life. It seemed so far away from her old Virginia home and its problems.

Coming to teach at the recently-built private school had been a good choice. For once, she felt optimistic about a decision she'd made: that of taking the position of lead teacher and head of second-grade curriculum. But this new school held other significance for Tisha. For one thing, its students came from well-to-do families that took care of their children.

Tisha began to pack items into her tote bag as she looked around the almost-empty room. The chatter died down as everyone left to catch buses and meet their parents.

Removing her glasses, Tisha rubbed her tired eyes. Taking out a sheet of paper, she scribbled down the various school supplies and decorations she wanted to get for her room, along with a few notes for themes she might incorporate for Black History Month.

A knock on her door brought her head up quickly from her task. A short, dark figure stood in the doorway.

"Hi," she said cheerfully to the blur standing at the door, groping blindly for her glasses. Locating them at last, she hastily secured them to her face and the child came immediately into focus. "Thomas, honey, come in. How are you?" Thomas was one of the reasons she loved her job. He was bright, pleasant and mannerly: a thoroughly sweet kid. Incidentally, he was also one of the few African-Americans in Glen Dale Academy.

"Hi, Ms. Jameson. I came to tell you..." He hesitated a moment before leaning in closer to whisper: "My dad is coming. He... he wants to talk to you." A note of warning entered Thomas's voice.

"Well, okay, sweetheart. That's fine," Tisha replied gently. "Do you know what it's about?" she asked, although she knew what it was most likely about: the note she had recently sent home. In it, she'd asked that Thomas's lessons be reinforced just a little bit more outside the classroom, so that he wouldn't fall behind in school.

She'd never met Mr. Alton personally, but she'd written similar notes to a few other parents and could take an educated guess at his "type". This would be one who thought the teacher was supposed to do all the work. The type that would charge in to see the teacher at the drop of a hat, not at all shy of showing how disgruntled and offended they were by her note. She knew that letters from the teacher were never viewed as the aid for parents they were meant to be. For the recipients, it inevitably seemed like a personal dig at something they weren't doing right, or a criticism of their child-rearing skills. It was a shame, because the letters were intended as simple notifications to assist parents in working on the problems outlined and tackling them before they got out of hand and the child started to lag behind.

Before Thomas could say another word, heavy footsteps shuffled close to where he was standing.

"Here he is! Hey, dad, this is my teacher," Thomas said enthusiastically, as if his father wouldn't know. Then he turned back to his teacher. "My dad used to play pro football. He even made most valuable player — *more than once.*"

Thomas glowed, sounding for all the world like an enthusiastic sports announcer, so proud was he of his father's accomplishments.

"Wow," Tisha replied politely. Her eyes left the boy, traveling slowly up from his face to that of his father. All at once, thoughts of handling the situation with the utmost professionalism went sailing out the window. He was tall, dark and bearded. Tisha looked from the man back to the boy and instantly knew exactly where Thomas's thick, long, beautiful eyelashes had come from, not to mention his height: Thomas was tall for a second-grader, and that attribute clearly came from his father as well.

"Good afternoon, Mr. Alton," she said, smiling up at him. She knew from his stiff back and piercing gaze that this wasn't intended to be a pleasant visit and that he had indeed taken issue with the letter she'd sent.

TWO

———◆———

"M S. JAMESON," HE SAID HESITANTLY, assessing her. She was a little on the fragile side, Chase thought silently. What a tiny little woman. She apparently hung around kids too much: from the black tights to the red jumper ending just above her knees and a colorful mock turtleneck, her outfit featured every color most likely to be found in a Crayola crayon box, right down to the rainbow rims of her glasses. She looked somewhat cute, he supposed - harmless enough, but he still didn't get what his son saw in her. Thomas couldn't stop talking about Ms. Jameson this and Ms. Jameson that, every single day after school. What the boy saw was either hidden from Chase's eyes or was so silly that it could only be appreciated by a second-grader.

In any case, it was her letter implying that Thomas needed additional help that had sent him stomping over to the school, wondering if she could truly know what she was talking about. In confusion, he noticed that as he continued to gawk at her, the head of steam he'd been building up for this meeting was rapidly deserting him.

"I received your letter about Thomas - " he began tersely, but halted his prepared speech abruptly as her hand lifted.

"Mr. Alton, before you begin, I just want to say what a wonderful student Thomas is." She paused, watching Thomas stand just a bit straighter, lifting his chin and inflating his chest with pride in front of his father. She winked at him.

"The letter isn't a new thing, Mr. Alton," she continued calmly. "In fact, it's standard: traditionally, all my students receive periodic progress reports. With this school being so new, though, I'm afraid we're just now implementing it here. Of course, the reports are not intended as personal attacks on the parents," she assured him.

"I see," Chase Alton replied as his jaw dropped to the floor. *How had she read him so quickly and completely?* Truth be told, the letter had indeed brought him up short, making him realize he needed to spend more time with his son and stop expecting the housekeeper to double as Thomas's tutor - but the accuracy hadn't made the letter any easier to digest. What the diminutive woman before him was saying made sense, but he didn't plan on telling her that. For one thing, she looked as if she hadn't been teaching more than a few years at most. The fact that she was new to the town and possibly the entire education system was not in her favor.

Chase stammered just a bit before continuing, searching in vain for the best words to explain that he didn't know just how to help his son. "Well... can you give me some pointers on where exactly his problem areas are?" he asked skeptically.

Thomas looked from his father to his teacher, wrinkling his nose in distaste. This was going to take longer than he had expected. He rolled his eyes in boredom before skulking off to the back of the room.

"Of course," Tisha replied. "I can give you a few things that will certainly help for right now. First things first, the kids have a spelling test on Monday. But I can write up a specific plan in more detail over the weekend and give it to Thomas to bring home next week."

Tisha sat down, smiling to herself. Whenever parents could get past their injured pride and bring themselves to ask for guidance from teachers, her view of them went up several notches. She'd offered the same explanation to other parents only for them to leave in a huff without asking how they could best help their children, and it was always the child who ultimately suffered. Yes, she reflected: some children paid dearly for needing just a little more patience…

She shook her head to clear the encroaching memories and tried to refocus. Clearing a space on her cluttered desk, Tisha wrote down a few helpful exercises for Thomas, explaining them aloud to his father as she wrote.

As Ms. Jameson slid her glasses back up her nose, Chase caught a brief glimpse of her eyes. They were hazel, with flecks of gray: confirmation of his suspicions that she was something other than African-American, though he couldn't guess exactly what. It didn't matter, anyway: after all, he was a B.W.O.B.: Black woman only brother. *But… why was that? Wasn't that a silly way to be?* The thought snuck up on him as he continued to look at her. Regardless of any intellectual positions on who he'd date or consider as a mother figure for his child, the attraction he felt toward her couldn't be denied.

There had been a time when he would go for just about anyone. Being a single parent seemed to have made him more attractive to all sorts of women, that was for sure. But he had a certain kind of candidate in mind now that Thomas was his sole responsibility. He had to make the right choices… *And why on earth was Ms. Jameson coming to mind when he thought about this?*

He remembered making fun of a young girl in elementary school because of the thick, nerdy-looking glasses she wore. If that poor girl had turned out anything like his son's teacher, Chase reflected, he would be thoroughly chagrined.

He took the paper from her gratefully and called to Thomas, who'd stationed himself at the computer center in the back of the room. When there was no response, Chase turned, noticing how engrossed his son was in the game on the monitor. The headphones covered his ears, shutting out all other noise. As Chase walked over briskly to tap his son on the shoulder, Tisha resumed packing her things, rooting through her bag for her car keys.

A light-skinned guy entered the room, diverting Chase's attention. He was dressed in khaki pants, with thick-soled oxfords and a royal-blue sweater with stripes across the chest and biceps. The two men's eyes met, and Chase stiffened involuntarily. He noticed the pigment of the man's skin. The face was almost pink, but the hands were like his own, the color of cocoa. Chase wondered who the man was.

The man took his gaze from Chase to address Ms. Jameson, who still hadn't noticed him enter.

"Tee-Tee," the man said, clearing his throat as he remained at the door.

Tisha looked up and let out a squeal of delight as she launched herself into the big stranger's arms.

THREE

DEAN JAMESON BENT TO SCOOP up his little sister. Her feet dangled inches from the floor as he held her tight and landed a sound smack on her honey-toned cheek before releasing her and setting her down securely. He glanced briefly at the man at the back of the room, silently wondering who he was. A child sat at the computer, engrossed in the animated action on the monitor.

Tisha followed her brother's gaze, remembering Mr. Alton, who had yet to pry his son away from the computer. She stepped away from Dean, remembering where she was, and introduced the two.

Chase finally got his son away from the computer, and father and son made their way to the front of the room. The men acknowledged each other briefly before Thomas spoke up. "Are you Ms. Jameson's husband?" he asked pointedly.

"Nah, little man," Dean laughed. "I'm her brother." His gaze moved to the boy's father. "She's a cool teach, ain't she?"

Thomas nodded in confirmation. "Yeah. She's the coolest," he replied, turning to beam at his dad, whose face indicated he wasn't quite ready to agree, considering he didn't know her all that well. "Thank you, Ms. Jameson." Placing a hand on Thomas's shoulder, Chase ushered his chatty son out of the room. He raised his hand to tip an imaginary hat before leaving.

"Have a good weekend, guys," Tisha called after them. She turned to face Dean, scowling at the mischievous face he made at her before grabbing her coat and tote bag. "What?" she exclaimed, innocently running a finger through her hair.

"Umm-hmm. You barely been here a month and already stirring up trouble." Dean said, the laugh lines around his eyes crinkling. "That man likes you, but he's big... and dumb. Don't fall for him."

"Dean, don't be so mean!" she exclaimed incredulously, knowing full well that her brother never sugarcoated anything.

"Well, I noticed the sigh of relief when I said I was your brother and not your husband," Dean said matter-of-factly. "Then he looked a little shocked, like me and you being related was impossible - and you know what that means."

She knew exactly what it meant. No matter how she'd tried to fix her skin and bring back her brown tones, they were gone forever. As a woman, she insisted on using makeup to give herself an even complexion and cover the scars as much as she could, but Dean had refused such superficial remedies. The only color that hid the scars was a foundation lighter than her original skin tone: very different to the coloring of her siblings.

After the accident, still young and in school, she had felt out of place having such light-colored hair when her other family members had jet-black locks. She had come by her hair color naturally, inherited from her grandmother, but the accident had left both she and Dean with drastic physical changes. At first glance, many thought she had the skin condition vitiligo, and the way her skin had peeled from the grafting and the burns did suggest that. The make-up gave her an even complexion, at least, and her wig was flattering, if itchy. At times, she felt even the wig was just too dark to go with the rest of her.

While many stole curious glances at her skin and hair, most were polite enough to simply ignore her. It took close attention to notice that some of the bumpy skin on her neck and fingers didn't match the shade on her face. Occasionally, someone would inquire hesitantly about what had happened. She wasn't shy about informing them when they asked directly, but when people just stared at the inconsistencies or made rude comments about them, she let them remain ignorant. Chase Alton, it seemed, would be one of those who remained ignorant. *Well, who cares?* she said to herself.

"How's Momma? Is Daddy okay?" she asked her brother. "Did Jojo come with you? What about Jina and Tony? Oh, I miss you guys so much." The thoughts of her large and close-knit family brought sudden pangs of homesickness. At times like this, she wondered if the move had really been for the best.

"Nope, just me, but we want you to come home. Momma says she can't believe you've gone so far away. Oh, and Jina's pregnant."

He looked at her sideways as they reached the end of the hall and stepped out of the door to the parking lot, anticipating her astonished outburst. He held up a hand. "But you can't tell anyone I told you. She wanted to do it herself, but, well, I saw you first so that's just too darn bad." Dean's eyes twinkled mischievously. "You gotta act surprised when she calls you tonight."

"Jina's pregnant?" Tisha exclaimed. "Oh, that's so wonderful. She's gonna know you told me, though. I can't keep anything from her. How long have you known? Why didn't you tell me?"

"Shush. I just told you, didn't I? - and I haven't known that long." He bent down to speak with her as she got into her car. "Are you doing all right, Tisha? I mean, really all right?"

"Yes, Dean, I'm fine." She eyed him warily. She knew

what he meant: to this day, her family was constantly expressing concern because of that tragic incident so long ago. She knew they loved her, but the very reason she had left was to find herself and discover what she wanted out of life without their incessant sheltering.

"You can follow me home, we'll order pizza, and you can move all my furniture around until I decide if I like it," she joked, trying valiantly to change the subject.

"Is that supposed to make me feel better? How about your eyes? When's the last time you've been to the optometrist?" he quizzed, refusing to be so easily put off.

Tisha turned the key in the ignition, pushing his hand away. "Would you stop it?" she said with some irritation. "The last time I saw you was before I left home. Now, can we please just go? When we get to my place, you can do your little search on whichever one of the countless gadgets you no doubt brought with you and find the perfect eye doctor for me to see here in town. Okay?"

"Okay," he said reluctantly, walking to his own car, "but you're not getting out of it."

On the drive home, Tisha reflected on the reasons she had left. She remembered the family, whom she loved dearly but who had always expressed their concerns over-abundantly and had ultimately smothered her with their constant protection. Then she thought about the other reason she had left: the little girl. *If that child had had even half the love that she herself had had growing up, she'd be alive and well right now, and Tisha might still be living at home…*

The beep of her brother's car horn from behind her brought Tisha back to the present with a jolt. Taking her foot off the brake, she turned at the now-green light, trying once again to rid herself of her grief and guilt.

———◆———

"You like Ms. Jameson?" Thomas asked his dad as they

rode home in the black Navigator that Chase loved so much.

"She seems nice enough, son. But I just met her." Chase gave his son a don't-go-there look before returning his focus to the road ahead. "What's important is that you like her and that as your teacher, she's a good one."

"Oh, she's the best," Thomas chanted.

Chase rolled his eyes, concentrated on the road and geared up for another of Thomas's Ms.-Jameson-themed promo sessions.

"She never yells and always takes time to help everybody. Everybody loves her, Dad. She doesn't even get mad when we make a mess. Man, she's real cool." Thomas sighed, awestruck.

"Well, cool or whatever, we've got to work on your spelling - so no b-ball until we get that squared away. Understand?" Chase braked for the stoplight as his eyes met his son's incredulous gaze. "Sorry, son. I mean it."

Thomas merely nodded in reply, surprising Chase with a sudden flash of maturity. His son was in second grade, and there was a time Chase couldn't have imagined being a single parent. But that was his life now, and he was doing his best. Over the years, he'd watched as his wife gradually usurped his own former "player" role, and with time, Chase had found he rather liked the identity he'd gained in return. He was rewarded each time he looked into his child's eyes. Fatherhood was special to him, and he reckoned that he was measuring up to the task quite nicely.

When they arrived, Thomas sprang out of the SUV quickly, eager for the after-school snack waiting in the house. Angie, their part-time housekeeper, met him at the door. Angie was kind, did her job well, and they all got along great. She kept things running smoothly. If it weren't for her, Chase reflected, he and Thomas would probably have died of starvation - if his own pathetic attempts at cooking hadn't killed them first. Angie minded her own business, took detailed messages, and the meals she cooked were not just edible but downright delicious. She tolerated Thomas: didn't try to fawn over him but wasn't mean to him either. Just as well. One snide remark from any employee under Chase Alton and they'd be gone in a wink.

"Mr. Alton, Malika keeps calling here. She says it's urgent," Angie announced.

Malika... Malika who? Then he remembered: his ex-wife had changed her name, thinking somehow it would get her an acting gig quicker than plain old Teresa. She called every so often, supposedly to ask about Thomas, but always stopped short of asking to see or speak to the boy directly. No: her usual reason for calling was monetary, or to root around after the name of some producer or other bigwig Chase had met while playing pro football in Los Angeles. He never provided the hoped-for contacts, always wishing she would just give up the whole game.

As well as being short on acting skills, the fact that she couldn't decide whose bed she wished to sleep in always sent his blood boiling. The part he'd hated most of all of their rocky marriage were all her affairs. More than once, the bitter doubt had even entered his mind that perhaps Thomas wasn't his, pushing him so far as to get a DNA test to confirm his parentage. Then, when Thomas was still a baby, Chase cleaned up his act, changed his own lifestyle and took her to court, winning full custody after Teresa-Malika's half-hearted attempt to pretend that she wanted their son at all.

"Thanks, Angie," was all he said. He didn't care what his ex had to say, so probably wouldn't return her phone calls. Chase knew she kept calling only because she knew that Angie would diligently answer her calls and write down what she said to report back to him. Everyone else reached him on his cell phone, or via e-mail, but leaving a message directly with Angie probably made her feel better, despite every one of her notes ending up in the trash can. Chase held out hope for his son's sake that one day Thomas's mother might call asking to speak to him, but Chase was glumly pessimistic about that.

Before tossing his coat over the leather office chair, he dug through the inside pocket for the papers he'd received from Ms. Jameson, trying desperately to decipher the scribbled notes. The words she used weren't in his everyday vocabulary. *That, and he'd been concentrating on* her *and not* her words. If he had her phone number, Chase reasoned, she might be willing to explain in greater detail what she was talking about regarding phonics, comprehension, vocabulary building… and then of course he could be lulled by that husky voice, in that petite body…

Her skin was rather light. He'd always thought that he preferred darker women – but suddenly that sounded like the dumbest statement ever. Thinking about her skin, he recalled noticing some scarring on her neck. He wondered what on earth could have happened to her. There was just something about her, and those delicate hands of hers she that she constantly moved while she talked…

Chase stood too abruptly and winced at the spike of pain in his injured knee. His mind reeled, wondering where such intimate thoughts about his son's teacher were coming from. Why on earth was he even thinking about her at all?

He walked quickly up the stairs to his son's room. The blinking and bing-bonging of animated characters on the screen had his son captivated, while his little hands worked frantically on the controller.

"Say, T, wanna go out for pizza?" Chase walked into the room and took a seat on the end of the bed. He gazed around his son's immaculate room. Thomas was way too neat for a seven-year-old.

"Sure, Dad." Shutting down the game, Thomas jumped up to locate his coat, which was folded tidily on the edge of the bed, but paused as he was putting his hands into the sleeves.

"Dad, won't Angie be mad? She gets mad if we go out when she's already cooked," he asked hesitantly.

Chase waved his hand dismissively. "I'll let her come in late Monday. She'll be cool."

"She comes in late anyway, Dad," Thomas said, reminding his father that despite the tough-employer-guy facade, he really was a big old lenient softy.

"Well… she won't know," Chase countered lamely. "We can reheat it tomorrow. C'mon."

FOUR

———

DEAN BROUGHT THEIR SOFT DRINKS to the back of the restaurant where his sister had reserved a table. It was Friday night and the place was packed.

"This place is kind of cool, huh, Dean?" Tisha shouted over the din, gauging her brother's reaction. He hated crowds, but she knew that wasn't the reason for his mood. He had been more than a little perturbed since she'd casually mentioned that one of the deadbolts on her door had broken mysteriously last week, and that the landlord's promised replacement had yet to materialize.

Between the two sisters in their family, the stubbornness was about evenly matched - but unlike Jina, Tisha was innocent. It sometimes annoyed Dean just how naive and sweet she could be. While it was undoubtedly genuine, he needed her to look out for herself more. If he went home and told Mom or, God forbid, Jojo about Tisha's current situation, they'd most likely send him marching all the way back to Georgia the same day, with orders not to return until she was set up with a steel door and three extra locks.

Dean didn't mind looking after his sister - he loved her, naturally - but it was the tongue-lashing he would get on her behalf that annoyed him. In his opinion, Tisha trusted the wrong people. She had faith in people who didn't deserve it and ultimately she was always the one to get hurt. He understood her decision to leave home, but if she was serious about her new endeavor, she had to learn to be cautious.

Dean took a deep breath and blew it out, eyeing her. "I just want you to take care of yourself, Tisha. Mom and Jojo are going to kill me if they find out you don't even have a double lock. I can go to Home Depot and get one – your landlord will likely use low-grade locks. You can give him a receipt."

"And how would Mom ever know I don't have some special kind of lock here?" Tisha challenged.

"Don't even think about it," snapped Dean. "You know they're going to call me asking for a report, if they haven't already." He pulled his phone out and scrolled through his texts. "For goodness sake, Tisha. How long has it been broken?"

"It's fine Dean, I've talked to Momma and Jina myself – not about the lock, but, uh, you know…" She shrugged guiltily, avoiding his gaze. "Anyway, it's fine. You should meet my landlord. He is the cutest little old man – oh, and his wife…"

"Wait a minute, old man and his wife? You're *friends* with them now? You'll never get anything, you're too nice, Tisha."

Dean didn't know why he bothered. If there was one species he knew nothing about, it was women. He threw up his hands in resignation as the waitress approached with a hot dish of pizza, the spatula hidden under the steaming crust, and placed plates in front of each of them.

"Thank you," Tisha said to the woman's retreating back. The smells wafting past her nose made her stomach rumble hungrily. Lifting a single slice, she deposited it onto Dean's plate before piling two slices onto her own. Dean looked at her questioningly and she stuck out her tongue at him, feeling some of the tension ease at last when he hooted with laughter.

"What am I gonna do with you, gal?" Dean shook his

head at his sister, playfully snatching the spatula from her and helping himself to another slice. Tisha suppressed a giggle as she filled her mouth with gooey, stringy cheese. Just then, a little boy ran up to her.

"Hey, handsome," Tisha said thickly, quickly chewing the huge bite she'd just stuck in her mouth.

"Hi, Ms. Jameson! Hi, Mr. Jameson!" Thomas said, acknowledging Dean as if they were old buddies.

"Hey, shortie," Dean replied, reaching for a napkin to wipe his mouth and looking pointedly at Tisha, subtly indicating she should do the same. She grabbed one and patted her greasy mouth.

"What's up? Here to get your grub on?" she said to Thomas before noticing Chase as he neared their table, clearly embarrassed that his son had gotten away from him. "Mr. Alton."

"Yep," Thomas said enthusiastically. He grabbed a chair from the next table, politely asking if it was taken and dragging it noisily across the wooden floor before the young couple could completely answer, plunking himself down beside Tisha.

"Uh... hi." Chase found his voice, realizing belatedly that his son had just invited himself to join his teacher's table. Clearing his throat loudly, he glared at Thomas. "Thomas, how 'bout we get a pizza and take it to Grandma's? I'm sure Ms. Jameson wants to spend some time with her brother. *Alone.* She'll see you Monday." His voice was cheery, but the tone brooked no argument.

"Ah, Dad..." Thomas whined.

"That's all right, sweetheart," Tisha said firmly. "You're welcome to join us. It's pretty crowded tonight – might be hard to find another spot to sit."

Reaching for a couple of napkins and the spatula, Tisha served a slice to Thomas. "Here you go," she said, smiling warmly. She asked the passing waitress to bring more plates, glasses, another medium pizza, and a pitcher of soda.

Thomas grabbed the slice Tisha held out to him and shoved half of it in his mouth, smacking loudly. He finished the slice and burped.

"Excuse me." Thomas covered his mouth, averting his glance from his disapproving father.

"That's the way I like my men to eat," Tisha laughed.

Chase had sat down rather reluctantly; he watched Ms. Jameson in amazement. What kind of teacher encouraged vacuum-style consumption of food followed by *burping*? She hadn't acted the least bit offended when Thomas had plopped his little tail down at their table uninvited, either. Most of the teachers he knew couldn't wait to get away from the little runts they taught day in and day out, and sure wouldn't encourage an impromptu dinner date with a student.

As his son reached for seconds and thirds, Chase had little choice but to settle in himself. He took off his jacket and crossed his left leg over his right knee, limiting himself to two slices of pizza rather than the five or six slices he would normally have put away. He didn't know why the amount he ate should be concerning him. He wouldn't have given a second thought about eating like a pig in front of his wife back when he was married. Why on earth would he care about what this Ms. Jameson thought of his eating habits now?

He watched his son and Ms. Jameson chat amicably about anything and everything, as if the two had known each other for years. He secretly hoped he and his son would some day enjoy the same type of easy banter. Witnessing Thomas and Ms. Jameson's closeness had him thinking that perhaps his own relationship with his son was in need of a little work. He felt a tug of jealousy.

"Say, do you know the owner of the Village Apartments?" Dean was asking Chase, breaking into his thoughts. "Tisha here has a real geezer for a landlord. Her lock's busted and the old man's been promising to replace it forever and a day."

Tisha eyed Dean disapprovingly. "I am fine," she said, gritting her teeth and giving him a look before continuing. "It's just... something's wrong with the door. My landlord couple are very nice, Dean." She smiled sweetly. "I told you I'd handle it. Who asked you to—"

"Well, I know someone who could look into it," Chase cut in. He wanted to laugh at her sudden mean gaze. Her big, beautiful eyes had narrowed into slits that were strangely alluring. He also noticed she'd changed her glasses and her clothes. These lenses were smaller, revealing more of her eyes, and she was wearing a pretty peach sweater and jeans.

"I don't need anyone looking into anything for me," she said to him shortly. She picked at the elastic-like cheese on her pizza, wrapping a long strand around her finger and popping it into her mouth. "I can take care of myself just fine," she finished, casting an end-of-discussion gaze at Chase and an even meaner look at her brother.

Stubborn woman, Chase thought. What was wrong with her? Teresa would be whining right about now, complaining about living alone, not having a housekeeper, the small size of her million-dollar condo in LA. She'd no doubt be asking for help she didn't need to complete the simplest of tasks. If he could or wanted to help Ms. Jameson, that was his business: all she had to do was sit tight and let him handle things - but nooo, she was one of these so-called independent women. *Gimme a break,* he thought in disbelief, looking away and then back at her. There was such a thing as being too independent, he mused, and she must've been that type.

For years, Chase had wished Teresa would grow up, act her age and start functioning on her own. Just once in a while, he wanted her to be one of the I-can-take-care-of-myself types - but there was Moneybags Chase, as the guys on the team always called him, available to wait on her hand and foot. If Tisha Jameson had something to prove, why the heck should he care? And didn't she know it was rude to lick your fingers? Why couldn't she pick up a napkin instead of pursing her gloss-covered lips and using her slender, delicate fingers to clean them of red tomato sauce?

"So for Black History Month..."

Chase tried to focus on what she was saying, sitting up a little straighter as she continued: "Langston Hughes, maybe, or Thurgood Marshall. I was thinking about writing a play or skit. A series of their powerful speeches, taking the audience through a sort of time line of our rich heritage," she said, addressing everyone at the table as she became excited, waving her hands to express herself. It was clear there was a torrent of ideas running through her head.

Chase was stone-faced as he saw her try to get everyone excited. It was working on his son, that was for sure.

"Some of the historical events are done to death," Tisha opined, glancing at Thomas to include him in the conversation, "so our class should try to pick out something not quite so typical: something few people know about or have heard before. We could do something totally different!" She took a sip of her drink, eyes dancing.

"Oh, cool, we never did plays in my old school," Thomas said.

Tisha's excitement didn't go unnoticed by Chase. The woman who already occupied his mind a little too often was certainly beginning to intrigue him more and more. But she was... well, how would *she* know about the struggles of African-Americans? Perhaps the lone paragraph on Black history from the white-dominated textbooks of his own school days had been expanded somewhat by now. He always knew there had to be more, but none of his teachers ever encouraged further research, and as he got older, he hadn't bothered to look for himself. Thomas's teacher certainly talked like she was one of the few who did a little off-the-clock digging - but it wasn't personal to her, so how would she really know?

He spoke up. "And what major events would those be? Rosa Parks and the bus scene, Abraham Lincoln signing the Emancipation Proclamation? Or let's go for broke and make a huge production to depict Dr. King's March on Washington. Tell me, Ms. Jameson, are you really the best person to help the kids with this? Shouldn't you include – ah, *other parts* of your ethnicity? You know, to be inclusive and to please the school personnel and all that? I'd be interested to see if the school even cares about this huge production you seem so overly excited about making. Don't use my son to check some Black History Month curriculum box!"

FIVE

———◆———

THE SILENCE THAT FOLLOWED CHASE'S outburst seemed to stretch on and on. Chase should have been deeply embarrassed by his comment about her heritage. Expressing so much consideration about any minority group should be a point in her favor, regardless of her roots, but the truth was that her whole enthusiastic attitude just irked him. Why, exactly, was she singling out Thomas and Black folks when it looked pretty obvious to him that she had other types of heritage running through her veins? It was all just… *odd* to him. Chase wasn't about to let her use his son for some kind of Black Lives Matter crusade. What exactly was her goal?

Chase wasn't sure of the exact point when he'd become so easily offended, but he stoked his own anger by telling himself that she'd probably targeted him with that little note just the other day because of his ethnicity. Now here she was again, insinuating that he and other African-American parents hadn't taken the time to teach their children about their heritage!

Deep down, it dismayed him how right she was, even if unwittingly. It was true that he, along with many Black people, didn't really talk to children about their history. He hadn't ever said much of anything, not even talking to his son about how to conduct himself at an upcoming sleepover despite having heard a famous couple talk to

Oprah about that very subject just the other day. He was so behind… and he didn't need this Ms. Jameson to tell him just how far.

Tisha stood slowly, swiping her mouth with the napkin before crumpling it and tossing it disdainfully onto the table. Chase stared back. He was suddenly consumed by embarrassment, desperate to take back his words and rewind the last five minutes. There was another feeling, too: sheer regret. He'd clearly hurt her. Instead of using his new and uncomfortable feelings to get to know more about just who Ms. Jameson was, he'd done nothing but give her more cause to dislike him. For the last few minutes, he'd disliked himself, too. This wasn't who he was.

"Thomas, honey, I'll see you in school Monday okay?" Tisha said. "I'm sorry - I ate way too much pizza, now I - I have a belly ache. You have a good weekend, OK?"

She reached down to give him a quick tight hug before grabbing her coat and clutch and heading for the door. Chase couldn't be sure, but he thought he saw glassy tears in her eyes as she turned.

Dean stood too. He threw three twenties on the table - more than enough for two pizzas and drinks. "I'll see ya, dude," he said to Thomas, then turned to Chase with a withering glare.

"Open your eyes, partner. Look before you speak. You better have an apology ready next time you see her." With that, he followed his sister out into the night.

Thomas looked at his dad as if he were about to cry. "What'd you *say?*"

Chase didn't answer. Half of the second pizza remained on the table, but he was no longer hungry. He'd messed up big time, and no matter how much he wanted to be mad at Tisha and Dean for leaving before he could apologize, he knew he was the only one to blame. She'd even made a polite excuse to leave rather than blame him in front of Thomas. He bowed his head.

"I said something I shouldn't have. I'm... I'm sorry, T."

"Did you know that Ms. Jameson was burned in a fire?" Thomas spoke up. "She told us all at school. It made her skin lighter and she's very self-conscious about it."

Chase looked heavenward.

"I'm sorry, Thomas. I didn't know that." Chase watched his son, now mournful that his teacher-friend was gone: a very nice evening was ruined. The boy picked sadly at the cheese on his pizza before pushing it away and shrugging into his coat.

"Ms. Jameson said sometimes adults act really weird and say stupid, hurtful things," Thomas continued. "That's what bullies do sometimes, too. Are... are you a bully, dad?"

Chase shook his head slowly, feeling sick. He didn't want to be anything less than a hero to his son. He cleared his throat. "I'm not, son. I just... didn't know. I'm going to apologize to her the first chance I get, okay? I'm sorry."

Removing his coat from the back of his chair, Chase pulled out his wallet to put more money on the table, just to make himself feel a little better. At least the waitress would have a good night, he thought resignedly. "We all have the crazy moments, son. Keep living - you'll act weird one day, too."

Chase vowed to apologize to Tisha first thing Monday morning, not just because he'd told his son he would and not because her big brother had told him to, but because he was desperate to erase that hurt from her eyes. He really wanted to see her again - and the next time, he resolved to get it right.

SIX

THE WEEKS WERE PASSING BY pleasantly enough for Tisha. The new classroom assistants were godsends to most of the teachers. Tisha's own assistant was an athletic Caucasian woman who at first glance seemed better suited to sports coaching than to helping in the classroom. She was one of the tallest women Tisha had ever met. The woman could play basketball with men and give them a good workout. She was strong, solid and exerted an endless amount of energy with the children.

Through talking to her, Tisha learned that the woman, whose name was Andrea Robinson, had only recently moved to the area, just as she had. Although they got along well enough, a couple of subtle signals showed Tisha that Andrea didn't always care for her enthusiastic teaching approach. Tisha refused to complain. It was her classroom, after all, and maybe Andrea just didn't get as passionate about teaching as Tisha did. She wasn't surprised: there were few who got as excited about their work as she did. She just cared so much about teaching that she really tried to make learning more fun for the students, assessing each of their learning styles carefully and adjusting her lessons accordingly. That's just who she was.

Tisha thought back to her own kindergarten teacher long ago: Mrs. Sampson, whom she had loved so much. If Tisha was doing even half the job her former favorite teachers had done, then she was satisfied, no matter what anyone else thought.

"I cut out the flowers the girls made for the calendar," Andrea said, as Tisha sat plunking away on her laptop.

Tisha looked up. "Thanks so much, Andrea. I appreciate it."

Andrea nodded as she came around to stand behind Tisha and peered over her shoulder. "Whatcha working on?"

Tisha relaxed her fingers at the keys, feeling awkward as the imposing woman towered over her. "I was, er, just putting together some last-minute changes for the play next week. The principal wanted to know more when he read my proposal, so I'm updating some things that I've fleshed out. The kids are so excited about the play - especially Thomas, he's got his lines down pat," she said excitedly. "The parents should really enjoy the performance. They'll be so proud of their children's hard work."

"So, Black History Month, right?" Andrea said casually. "Something with Martin Luther King, Malcolm X, and Rosa Parks, am I right? That should about cover it. I wouldn't waste my time putting too much effort into it if I were you. That's a lot of work you don't have to do." She turned to clean up the art station.

"In most cases you'd be right - for most people, anyway." Tisha wanted to make clear that she *wasn't* 'most people'.

"There were a lot more people in our history than those three, Andrea," she continued. "Plenty more people." She tried to keep her tone light and educational, fighting to keep the hostility out of her voice and wondering if she was succeeding. "Those you mentioned are just the ones most people have heard about." Tisha clicked the command to print out the pages with her changes, saved her work and then exited the system, bracing herself for the inevitable next comment.

"Well, you know, it's not up to *us* to explain it all. I mean, what's left for these kids' sorry parents to do, anyway?"

Andrea replied flippantly, shrugging.

Up to us who? Tisha wondered. She had once asked Andrea to go over some lesson material with the children, but Andrea had stated that wasn't in her job description. An assistant did not a teacher make, according to the gospel of Andrea Robinson. *So to whom could she possibly be referring?* Tisha wondered wryly.

"That is where some of the problem is, yes." Tisha nodded thoughtfully as if she could see Andrea's point, but she was determined nonetheless to teach this ignorant woman a little more about Black history. Another recent encounter, not as blatant but ignorant just the same, came to mind: Chase Alton.

She should probably let it go, she knew, but she ploughed on. "The other problem lies with the people who keep saying we can stick with the bare factual minimum, never trying to do more, inform more, teach more."

"Hey, whoa, whoa." Andrea held up her hands in mock defense. "If you want to spend a lot of energy digging up all this stuff and doing a whole lot of work for a bunch of second-grade brats, be my guest." A small frown had appeared on her forehead as she rolled her eyes, giving the paintbrushes she was washing a flick and spraying tiny droplets over Tisha's papers. "Oh, and some of the kids were talking about you and those fire safety classes you were so bent on having," she continued in a soft, dangerous tone. "I guess you were as brown as a Georgia pecan before that fire, huh? Now, well, of course that's why you're so touchy about all this race stuff. Hey, I'm sorry. I—I just... well, no wonder you're so damn worked up. You did a good job of covering yourself though. They have a lot more shades of makeup now. I'll bet it was a chore to match you just right, wasn't it? I've seen some burn victims, skin all discolored and shriveled up. Pretty gross."

Andrea shook herself as if shaking off a chill. "You look so light-skinned-white. But you're mixed or completely

Black, aren't you? Anyway, being half Black or whatever you are, I guess you gotta get that side of you in the lime- light somehow, huh?" Andrea said, leaning in to take closer inspection of Tisha, her eyes roaming unashamedly over her face and then lower, to her neck.

Tisha ran her hands over her head. She hated to be reminded, but she could never forget what had happened to both her and Dean as children. It changed her life. *This woman was really mean*, Tisha thought. *And how on earth did she know?*

"Save it, Andrea. And if you consider these children brats" - she ignored the spiteful, hate-filled things the woman had said about her personally and responded only to her remarks on the children - "perhaps you're in the wrong profession."

Tisha was alarmed that Andrea had uttered any such thoughts aloud, even if there were just the two of them in the room. The comments about her skin had stung a bit, but she would never let on how they affected her. She'd survived too much to let this woman tell her otherwise.

"As far as race goes, I am African-American," she per- sisted with dignity. "To summarize, you thought that I was white, or mixed, and as such - as only *half* African-Ameri- can - that I shouldn't try to teach various histories equally? I shouldn't go 'out of my way', as you put it, to find infor- mation that's not in the standard textbook?"

Tisha fought to keep her voice calm. She was very aware that by refusing to let this discussion drop, she might well be putting their whole working relationship in jeopardy.

"You listen up, bitch." The teaching assistant's word rang out like a dropped fork in the quiet classroom. "You aren't to tell me nothing about what I thought. You better shut your stupid mouth or I'll hurt you," Andrea hissed. "I lost my last job because of some - some know-it-all just like you. I won't let anyone tell me what I should and should not think about – or do."

A knock sounded on the door and both women turned. Tisha watched, stunned, as Andrea immediately arranged her face into a sunny smile and was the first to speak, as if nothing of note had just happened, when Chase Alton walked into the room.

"Mr. Alton, right? Hello, hi. Um, can we help you?" Andrea said, walking over to Chase and extending her hand.

Tisha watched as Chase took the proffered hand briefly, then continued toward Tisha. He glanced at Andrea, who evidently recognized him. "Hi... sorry, I'm here to speak to Ms. Jameson."

Andrea remained rooted to the spot near the door. She looked a little starstruck.

"Alone, please," Chase said firmly, watching as the woman managed to tear her gaze away and leave the room.

"Mr. Alton," Tisha said, attempting some semblance of cheerfulness. She felt a little dizzy, and as if sensing her inner turmoil from her voice, Chase moved closer and searched her eyes.

"What - ? Uh, did I just walk in on something? Are you all right?" he questioned, using a tone she recognized as sincerity.

"I'm fine, thank you," she said tightly. Truth be told, her nerves were ragged. She was quite scared by the outburst she had just witnessed from Andrea - especially the threat at the end. "It's fine," she said again.

Chase made a mental note to ask Thomas about the day's events later that evening and about the new teaching assistant lady in his class room. Wrongfooted, he fumbled for a moment. He had prepared what he wanted to say, but even as he'd rehearsed it on the walk from car to classroom, he still wasn't sold on its believability. What could he possibly say to excuse his own ignorance? And the fact that it had taken his seven-year-old son to explain something to him that he should have been more observant about? It was clear to him now that he should never have uttered such awful words in the first place.

Chase smiled awkwardly. He wished Tisha wouldn't look at him with that searching gaze: it put him on the spot.

"I've been meaning to apologize, but time has gotten away from me, and traveling, and, well... I'm here now, I guess," he finished lamely. He ran a nervous hand over his hair.

"It's really okay, Mr. Alton. I understand," Tisha said crisply.

Chase nodded. He could tell she really didn't feel like dealing with anything or anyone else for the rest of the day. "No, no, I don't think you do — please just let me explain," he pleaded, and waited a beat. When he saw that she wasn't going to interrupt him further, he continued. "You're certainly different than any of the other teachers I've known."

As she gazed at him in astonishment, he cast his eyes down, staring at the desk, smoothing his hand over the surface, wiping away imaginary dust and crumbs. "My son is very taken with you, too, and it's obvious that the two of you get along very well. He's got good taste, and I just wanted to let you know his father is beginning to see the light. I made a major mistake about not only your race but your motives, and I'm sorry, Tisha. I assumed - I shouldn't have - and even if you were something... other than what I thought, I should have recognized your sincerity."

Chase shook his head at the question on her face. "Yes, okay, so your brother is... well... but he's only slightly darker than you. He looks a little, ahh... a little less than you... oh, I don't know." Chase threw up his hands in frustration. This was so uncomfortable and awkward. He walked around to where Tisha was standing.

Tisha had turned from Chase to wipe the board. As she turned back around, she brushed up against him, not realizing he'd closed the distance between them. "People make that mistake all the time, Mr. Alton. I didn't — I don't expect you to be any different."

Tisha tried to retreat, but the holder for the dry erase markers, pressed into her back. Chase knew he'd cornered her, but it was those eyes that drew him in... he had to see more closely and make sure she really understood how sorry he was. He was determined to prove that he was no bully, as his son had all but called him.

"Thomas asked me if I was a bully and it hurt," he said softly. "Your hair - and your face - and the... this - " he touched her neck, which he knew was bold...

"Please don't," Tisha said softly. Alarm bells were ringing, but still she didn't pull away. "M-my hair is a wig, in case you're wondering. It's – it's all fake."

"But you aren't," Chase replied. "You're sincere and caring and even when you could have blamed me for the other night, you covered for me in front of Thomas... and that made me feel even worse."

"As you should have," she returned. A smile of victory tickled her lips, but she tried to maintain a straight face.

"Ms. Jameson, I'm not done apologizing. Rather than try to get to know you, which I very much want to do, I've been inventing all sorts of wrongheaded ideas to force myself to run from you."

"I'm certainly not able to run right now, myself - there's this big dude in my way," Tisha quipped.

"Do you want to?" he breathed.

She hesitated, then shook her head as he reached out to touch her hair. It didn't feel like a wig. Her eyes, hazel and large through her thick glasses, made everything feel euphoric. He rubbed a tendril of her hair gently between his fingers. He was so close they were almost touching, and still she didn't flinch.

"I'd like to start over somehow," he said.

She nodded, smiling. "Okay. I'm Ms. Jameson."

"I'm Chase Alton... but I was thinking, I would like to

call you by your first name, so I can show my son I have more pull."

She laughed. "I'm not sure you have pull. He's way cuter."

"Really?"

"Um hmm."

"I'm not cute?"

"I didn't say that. I said he's cuter."

"So you think I *am* cute. Hey, that's a great start, but remember, I have a much bigger... vocabulary."

"Really? Well, who's fault is that?"

"Yours."

She laughed and it was music to his ears. Something had been made right between them and he knew he should just leave it at that, but he was so happy and relieved to see her smile. "But I'm up to helping him," he continued, "so we're gonna fix that vocabulary issue at home."

"That would win you major points," she replied.

"Then I should get started."

"You should."

"Can you come over and help us sometime?"

Tisha hesitated again. "I don't think that's a good idea."

Chase raised an eyebrow. "You were pretty on board before."

"You will do fine. I'll give you all the supplemental lessons I can."

Chase took a deep breath. "Can I at least have a hug to restart our new and improved relationship?"

Without waiting for an answer, Chase moved closer and his arms enveloped her, planting a quick kiss on her mottled cheek.

"My son thinks you're wonderful and I'm starting to see why," he said, smiling at her as he headed for the door.

SEVEN

———◆———

TISHA'S SENSES WERE REELING. THE memory of Chase's sheer size lingered through her entire body and his subtle cologne tickled her nostrils. In all her life she'd never been hugged like that - never before had she felt this overwhelming physical attraction.

Tisha loved big men. Her father and brothers were big old teddy bears, and despite only being about five foot three herself, she wasn't at all afraid of them. She packed a lot of pint-sized power, her friends and brothers often teased. The thick-soled boots she loved to wear gave her just a little more height, but could also give a mean kick if she so chose.

Chase's gentle touch, kind eyes and sincere apology had made her feel safe in his arms. His fingers on 'her' hair had felt curious, rubbing the strands back and forth, marveling at the fact that she'd told him the truth about it. The fact that it was fake didn't seem to bother him. Real enough were her hazel eyes - another gift from her grandmother.

Chase really seemed to care, she reflected. What his son had implied about him being a bully had truly brought him to his senses. In stark contrast to her new classroom assistant, he'd swiftly apologized to her for words spoken in anger and really did seem to want a fresh start - even if this process happened to involve turning up his charming sex appeal. Granted, she mused, he had the looks and the impressive muscle to do so. Plus, Thomas was a good kid, and at least a portion of that must be credited to his father.

There was no denying that all these little details meant something to her; but still, she reminded herself sternly, she couldn't get involved with him. No matter what. She was his son's teacher and that was it: she needed to end all notions of getting involved - no matter how much the last few tense yet fantasy-inducing moments had told her they both wanted to. And that kiss... how dare he!

She smiled in spite of herself, remembering the lips that had brushed across her cheek so soft and smooth. Tisha closed her eyes. The contact, as brief as it was, had sent a tingle to every nerve ending in her body. Still, she'd do best to tuck that memory away, because that was about all that was going to happen.

As if to signal the end of her time for private thoughts, Tish heard Andrea's whistling approaching from the corridor. She needed to leave anyway, and with the added motivation of getting well away from Andrea she was sure she would make record time.

"Well, well, well," Andrea said as she waltzed dramatically back into the room. Tish looked up to acknowledge her but said nothing.

"Oh, don't pretend, darlin'," Andrea drawled. "I think Mr. Alton has got some designs on you."

Tisha rolled her eyes. She hated gossip with a passion. She also certainly hadn't forgotten their previous exchange, despite the fact that Andrea was now smiling as if nothing had happened at all. Tisha shrugged, trying to appear unflustered by this woman who only minutes before had been taunting her, calling her names and even threatening her.

"Mr. Alton and I are just friends," Tisha replied, turning away from Andrea's cynical gaze. She really did need to leave, and she prayed she could avoid another incident with Andrea that would force her to report her unpredictable assistant. She remembered her brother's remark, about her being 'too nice'. Tisha wasn't always nice - not any more.

She reminded herself that she'd known Andrea for all of a few weeks, and moreover, Tisha got along with just about everybody. She loved people... yet something about Andrea Robinson just didn't sit right with her. Changing her mind, she made a mental note to talk to the principal as soon as possible about the woman's threat.

Walking slowly down the hall, Tisha glanced in the direction of the principal's office. Chris Jeeter was a nice man to work for, and she'd been surprised to discover he was African-American when she came face to face with him after a few phone conversations. The two of them got along great. Chris often said that as long as the students were performing well and parents were happy, he hoped to stay out of the way of his teachers and let them implement the curriculum as they saw fit, and that set-up worked just fine for Tisha. She admired his ability to always seem low-key, even approachable, when he was alone with some of the teachers. When dealing with parents and school officials, by contrast, he was all business, even putting on a slight air.

"What's happening, Tisha?" Chris asked as he came out of his office.

"Hi, Chris. I was just passing by, so I wanted to drop off the amendments I made to the play," she said, handing him the printed papers.

Chris took the papers from her, grimacing. "Oh, you didn't have to do that, Tisha. I got the gist of the play from your first draft: you can surprise me a little. I've seen nothing but the best from you. I'm glad I went ahead and got you signed up for this trial run teaching before I even received your paperwork. It was one of the wisest decisions I've ever made," he added, displaying a mouth full of teeth.

Tisha smiled but looked a little hesitant. "But you did eventually get my paperwork, didn't you?"

"Oh, sure." Chris waved his hand, noticing her worry. "But I just had to get you, you know?" he continued, holding the papers in his hand like evidence, "I wouldn't want anyone else to snap up one of my best teachers. I can't wait for that play next week. Tell you what - I'm gonna get the *Macon Weekly* to do a little story."

"Well, that's great — but, I mean, it's no big deal, you know," Tisha responded modestly. "I just wanted the kids to put on a little production and also use my creative juices a little more."

She hadn't known he would make such a big deal about the play, and such thoughts made her a little nervous. Then again, the small local paper didn't have a particularly huge circulation, and maybe there wouldn't be much room to discuss the play. At most, perhaps a small paragraph at the bottom of a page that most people wouldn't give more than a cursory glance.

"Well, sure the kids get that opportunity, but let's draw a little attention to it," Chris chuckled. "You know, being a new school and all, we've got to make a name for ourselves as inspiring and innovative with our approach. We are one of few STEAM schools in the area — and now we can advertise the fact that we don't just have Science, Technology, Engineering and Math, we truly have the arts too! This could really make people sit up and take notice. Well, keep up the good work and I'll make sure your name gets a little mention, too."

"Well, actually, there was something else I wanted to talk to you about as well, Chris," she began - but then his words about her name being mentioned in the paper registered. "Wait - no," she said, flustered, "putting my name on it is really not necessary, Chris - what's most important is — "

"Mr. Jeeter, it's the *Telegraph* on the line," the secretary called over, looking excited as she motioned him back to his office.

"The *Telegraph*, too? Tisha!" he said, nearly jumping up

and down in excitement. "Make me look good," he called over his shoulder, waving the papers in his hand once more as he jogged back to his office and shut the door.

Tisha walked in a daze to her car. This was getting just a little out of hand. She hated attention more than anything, but she supposed the play being promoted in the paper was great for the children and of course the school. That being said, it sounded like Chris was going to be making a huge production out of it all, and that had to mean he was after some of the attention for himself. *Maybe it's not such a big deal,* her mind whispered. *A couple of local papers talking about the new school and its first play — now then, it shouldn't be a big deal at all.*

Once inside her car, Tisha took out her date book and flipped through, checking whether she'd forgotten anything that she might need to pick up on the way home. She checked off her list: the props for the set had all been obtained, the kids had painted them, and everything was just about ready for the play.

Tisha scanned farther down the list. An entry she'd jotted down weeks ago caught her eye: *Find the names and numbers for the foster homes in Macon. Get any abuse history.* There was no checkmark beside this particular item. Pulling out a pink highlighter, she marked the entry to remind her of its urgency. Despite all she'd done to start a new life, she still maintained one old personal mission she'd been working on since Virginia. Having been through all that she had herself, she was determined to continue her work; but right now, the pain was still too fresh to tackle it.

EIGHT

C HASE ENTERED THE DIMLY LIT auditorium just
in time and opened the program that had been thrust
into his hand upon entering. He'd been held up getting
an interview for his weekly newspaper column, then finding a place to park had been difficult. A pint-sized usher
promptly led him to an empty seat with a little flashlight,
which she shone happily into his face in her enthusiasm.
He breathed a sigh of relief as he folded himself into a
rickety metal chair. A Black woman seated beside him
smiled, and Chase responded in kind.

Once his vision returned, Chase read the small paragraph summarizing each of the segments to be portrayed,
his eyes hunting for Tisha's name. He tucked the program
into his suit-coat pocket as the first child came out.

"Ain't I a woman ..." the child said, imitating Sojourner
Truth. The little girl moved her body, rolled her neck, and
stuck out her hands, waving them and placing a fist on her
hip as she leaned forward, speaking to the audience.

A second child came out, stomping. *"I'm sick and tired of
being sick and tired!"* she said, quoting the words of Fannie
Lou Hamer, and then clapping her hands and tapping her
foot. After sharing facts about the civil rights leader, she
broke into song with "This little Light of Mine." Hamer,
the program noted, was known to have lifted her voice
often in song throughout marches and sit-ins, rallying the

group together, united in their cause.

Now other children came out. The first was a little girl in tennis shoes and a little white outfit, a tennis racquet in her hand: Althea Gibson. A little boy came out next, as Jesse Owens, the Olympic champion runner. Chase knew there were only a few African-Americans in Tisha's class, but all the children took part and related something unique to them, participating as all of them should.

Chase sat there, forgetting his discomfort at being perched on the little folding chair. He was taken on a journey, truly fascinated by how Tisha had managed to take a very serious subject and project the complexities to the watching adults without pushing the material beyond the children's understanding. As he watched what she'd planned so carefully all come together, it was so much better than he had imagined. He was mesmerized and impressed.

———

Backstage, Tisha coached the little children, reinforcing their parts, building self-esteem here and confidence there, giving praises for a job well done. As she lined up the kids in order of appearance, though, Tisha noticed that Thomas was nowhere in sight. He was on in a few minutes, and she went in frantic search of him.

She hurried up a flight of stairs to a small covered balcony, where a small figure was cowering in the corner. "Thomas, honey, what are you doing? What's the matter?" she asked in concern. The lone shaft of light illuminated tears running down his face.

"I can't do it. I'll mess up. I'm too dumb," he said with a sob.

Tisha moved forward to hug him close and kissed his cheek. "Don't ever say that. You are the smartest boy I know." She was angry that he would think such a thing, and surprised that this insecurity seemed to have bubbled up out of nowhere. He'd been fine and excited earlier. Something must have transpired just this evening for him to begin doubting himself.

"Who told you that?" she questioned.

"Nobody… nobody told me," Thomas said, hastily bolting from Tisha to stand near the stairs.

Tisha viewed him skeptically. He looked almost panicked when she queried him, when she knew he'd been so excited about the play right up until now. Someone must've said something.

"Nobody told me, okay?" Thomas said again. "I just… don't think I can do it."

"Well, okay," Tisha said to him, though in fact it was anything but. Getting up to walk down the stairs, she turned to him, standing on the top step. She smoothed the wrinkles in his clothes and gently wiped the streaks from his face. "Listen to me," she began softly. "I believe in you. I think you are smart and so very special. We've been practicing, and you are the only one who has had his lines perfect every time. I *know* you can do it – but if you don't want to," she concluded sadly, "I'll understand. But, Thomas, don't ever let anyone tell you you're stupid or dumb, 'cause that is not true. Do you understand? *I* believe you can do anything, and even if you mess up, it's not the end of the world. No one will think badly of you. Hey, we all mess up sometimes."

With cautious hope, Tisha watched the spark slowly come to life again in his eyes. Thomas perked up, taking a deep, cleansing breath. He gave Tisha a hopeful smile before rushing down the steps to take his place.

Tisha gave her own sigh of relief before following him down. She resolved to find whoever had planted such distressing notions in his head, and she knew exactly who she'd question first.

Chase sat forward as Thomas walked out slowly onto the stage. His head was held low before he gradually raised it, carefully drawing out the dramatization.

"By any means necessary..." he began, raising a closed fist toward the ceiling. Then he went on to depict two other African-Americans in history and finish the play.

The entire class came out to stand behind him, and together they danced to a South African song while the background showed slides of Nelson Mandela and children of all ages rallying behind him. Then came a picture of Colin Kaepernick with the words: *Still, we will do even more.*

Tisha stood on the edge of the stage as she listened to Thomas's lines. Despite his earlier doubt, the final ones were so powerful and delivered with such emotion that Tisha felt even more concerned over whatever - or whomever - had made him feel the way he did.

As she walked onto the stage to take her bow, Tisha noticed a fellow teacher, Mrs. Wellington, clasp her hands together and use a crumpled tissue to dab at a tear. As the lights came up, she got an unexpected glimpse of Chase, too, who was cheering and clapping loudly along with the rest of the crowd. She hesitated and faltered a little, but quickly signaled for the children to take their final bow as she ushered them all backstage.

When she got backstage, Mrs. Wellington pulled her into a bear hug, catching her off guard. Tisha laughed, knowing the woman was just as excited as she was. She liked Mrs. Wellington very much. The older woman, who would soon retire, was something of a mother figure to her, reminding her of her own mother whom she missed dearly.

"Honey, amazing, just amazing!" the woman said, clasping her frail hands in front of her. "I'm telling you, what a wonderful job you have done." Tisha smiled back at her.

"Thank you for your encouragement, Mrs. Wellington. It did turn out nice," she said, relieved.

The older woman nodded, beaming proudly. "Nice is an understatement." She moved on, loudly praising the children as she went, helping them get out of their costumes and back to their waiting parents.

Tisha felt good, but her celebration was short-lived as that brief incident with Thomas weighed on her mind. One thing she was sure of: she needed to find Andrea Robinson as soon as possible.

NINE

THOMAS RAN THROUGH THE CROWD of wait-
ing parents to meet his dad. Chase was so proud of
Thomas. Impulsively, he scooped the boy up in his arms
to hug him before setting him quickly back on his feet,
remembering too late not to embarrass his son. Those dis-
plays of affection were for kids, according to Thomas, and
at seven years old, he assured his father he wasn't one of
those any longer.

"Dad, can I go for pizza with Jason, please please please?"
Thomas asked, tugging his dad in the direction of Jason
and his mom and dad. Jason George was a year older than
Thomas, in the third grade.

Chase hesitated in agreeing. He rarely let Thomas spend
time with any of his friends without him there. Then again,
pizza with Jason seemed harmless enough, he decided,
reminding himself again how much his son was growing
up.

"All right, but I'll pick you up in about an hour," Chase
relented. He pulled out a ten-dollar bill and handed it to
his son.

"There's no need for that, Chase. We're cool," Jason's
father said, walking over to him. Jebson George was tall,
dark and slightly on the skinny side. Chase had heard via
Thomas's chatter that Jebson and his wife were getting a
divorce. Whenever Thomas and Chase went out for pizza,

Jeb George was always there, at the bar.

"Say, man, you ever think about going back to football?" Jeb asked, too casually.

Chase looked up. "No," he said curtly. He'd been asked that question a million times.

"What a waste. I mean, you got some serious talent…"

"Thanks." Chase shrugged. He supposed there was a compliment in there, but shrugged it off.

"Listen, I can bring Thomas on home later if you want. Got Jase for the weekend, you know?"

Chase wasn't so sure about how this plan was shaping up. "Nah, that's okay." Chase paused. "Thanks, though," he said, remembering to be polite. "I'll pick him up in about an hour." He gave Thomas a warning look. He didn't take the money back, but trusted that his son would put it away as he'd been told and at least have it in case he needed it for anything. The arcade adjacent to the restaurant was probably where it would end up being spent if he didn't use it for food. Chase smiled as the group made their way out.

As Chase turned, Tisha exited the backstage room, chatting with an older African-American woman. She slowed when her eyes met Chase's as he stared intently at her and walked toward them.

"Hi," Chase said, looking pointedly at Tisha. Thrusting his hands into his pants pockets, he suddenly felt rather awkward. He had wanted to ask her out, but every time he'd seen her at the school she'd been all business. He didn't want to pressure her, but seeing her every day and enjoying their light banter made him want to know her better. She seemed nothing like Teresa, and that intrigued him even more.

Tisha nodded in greeting as he drew closer and she turned to the woman beside her before speaking. "Mrs. Wellington, this is Mr. Alton - Thomas's father."

"Hello, I'm Sharon Wellington," the older woman said, extending a hand. "Yes, Thomas. He's such a wonderful boy," she smiled, looking back and forth between the two of them. "I'll wait for you at the car, honey," Sharon said to Tisha. "Nice meeting you, Mr. Alton."

"Um... yes, you too," Chase said, trying to think of something more conversational to say to the woman but coming up empty. "Uh, do you need a ride?"

"No, no thanks. Mrs. Wellington has already offered," Tisha replied. "My car died just as I was about to leave the house. Luckily, Mrs. Wellington lives just a few blocks from me, so I got a ride from her." Tisha smiled at her companion. "This lady is going to retire in just a couple of months. I'm going to miss you so much."

"You will do fine, dear, don't worry." Mrs. Wellington looked up at the two and Chase smiled again.

"Would you two like to spend some time together?" she asked knowingly.

"Well, uh, I was thinking I could give you a ride home, if it's okay," Chase repeated. "It's no trouble," he insisted, looking at Mrs. Wellington, who nodded and winked, while Tisha continued to look at him like he'd lost his mind. He smiled at her, too.

"Well, if you insist. Such a nice man," Mrs. Wellington said, turning around to them and delivering a not-so-concealed eyebrow raise. "We women need a fine man around to look at things like cars and such when they break down. I don't know nothing 'bout such things myself, but my Herby, he's so wonderful. Hey now, I bet you could take a look at the car, couldn't you, dear?"

She smiled at both Chase and Tisha. "I'll see you Monday, honey. You did a wonderful job tonight!"

She patted Tisha's hand and left, a huge grin on her face as she moved hurriedly to the exit.

TEN

———◆———

TISHA'S MOUTH DROPPED OPEN IN astonishment and she turned to Chase, narrowing her eyes with a grin.

"What's the big deal? It's not like we don't know each other," he protested, as if he could read her mind.

Tisha shrugged and started to walk. "Yes, that may be true," she whispered to him when he caught up, "but I'd rather not start people's tongues a'wagging." She moved forward and exited, using a different door than the one he held for her. "And… people talk, is all. I hate that. I'm sorry, where is Thomas?" she asked, scanning the parking lot for Chase's truck.

Chase walked up behind her, sliding an arm around her waist as he pulled her in the direction of his truck. "He's going out for pizza with Jason and his family." He could feel her stiffen in his arms.

"We, uh, we'll be alone?" she said hesitantly.

"Is that okay, Tisha?"

"Yes, yes - fine," she said and continued walking, pretending that nothing was wrong. She wanted to talk to Thomas more too, but that would be difficult considering the circumstances. She still had Andrea on her mind, but that little matter would likely have to wait until the weekend was over.

The parking lot was almost bare but Chase must have

been late: his truck was clear across the lot, almost at the end.

"You know, Tisha," Chase said thoughtfully. "Since I left the NFL and moved to a small town – yes, I agree, people talk, but you never lived in the fish bowl I lived in before. Here, I've gained a new kind of freedom."

"Really? And why would you need that?" Tisha returned. She immediately resolved to soften her tone and listen to what he said. Of course, she already knew he was an ex-NFL player: one Sunday afternoon – okay a couple, after church - she'd seen him in action on TV, talking and quoting stats with the rest of his commentator friends: Howie Long, James Brown and Michael Strahan. Each of them was funny in their own way, and each of them, including Chase, was always impeccably dressed for primetime television. They just articulated the game infor-mation in a way that she found herself liking to listen to on Sunday evenings while she worked around her house. Listening had been one way to get to know him, albeit unbeknownst to him. She doubted he knew she watched – she'd never mentioned it.

"I went through a lot with my ex-wife, and the media covered everything when we lived in Los Angeles," Chase continued. "It's a big city, but the news and TMZ were relentless in chasing my family business. You'd think that in such a large place, all the murders, robberies and polit-ical scandal would be enough to talk about, yet they still found time to discuss my marital issues every single day. They rooted everything out, including her infidelity and my son's paternity."

They had reached the SUV but Tisha didn't make a move to get in; she simply turned to look at him. "Chase, I'm - I'm sorry."

The last thing she'd expected him to do was to spill the beans like this about such a painful time in his life. She felt embarrassed for trivializing their conversation by comparing her small-town issues to the real, large-scale sensationalism of his private life that he'd experienced. That made all her own issues seem small. Back in Virginia, reporters had eventually moved on when more pressing matters came up, but every now and then there were still developments that mentioned her name. Certainly it was difficult, but to question Thomas's paternity? That sounded unforgiveable. Considering Chase now had custody, the outcome of that case was evident.

"Sorry about that." She touched his face, and before she could remove her hand, he held it there a tad longer, rubbing her hand in his own before gently letting her go. Tisha stepped back as he courteously opened the door for her.

"Despite those times, I know you're nothing like my ex," Chase stated. "Every day, you're the same - and I want to get to know you better."

"I appreciate that, but - "

Before she could finish her sentence, Chase closed the door and put a hand to his ear, waving his hands in question and pointed at the window. "I'm sorry," he yelled, "I can't hear you."

She smiled and laughed as he came around and got into the truck. Inside, he repeated: "You're way different than my ex, Tisha, and I know that in my heart. There is something very special about you."

She smiled reassuringly at him and didn't voice her own hesitant thoughts as they pulled out of the parking lot. She navigated, and within minutes they were at her apartment.

———◆———

Tisha was silent as she unlocked the door and entered her small apartment. She was about to turn and thank Chase when she noticed he'd closely followed her, indicating he was coming in as well. She hadn't invited him in, but she certainly didn't want to be rude. If she was anything, she was honest with herself, admitting and acknowledging the twinges of desire that had made her long for his company.

"I'll make some tea," Tisha said, disappearing hurriedly into the kitchen.

Chase nodded, closing the door behind him and noting as he did so the two locks that were in place. Rather than test them, he made a mental note to ask her. He walked down the short hall to the living room and surveyed the space. It looked lived in: only a few boxes remained, indicating that she only had minimal unpacking left to do. It was a neat place: simple, cozy and cute, just like her.

She loved art, a fact evidenced by the varied collection of work that covered her walls. The pieces were nice too, mostly African-American; and he spotted a large Kaepernick jersey thrown over her sofa arm. Tisha had even taken the time to frame some pictures that were evidently drawn by children - most likely her former students, he guessed.

He couldn't remember the last time Thomas had drawn something. His son was getting too old for such activities, but when he was younger, Chase recalled that Thomas had created various family portraits and other happy scenes. When it had become apparent to Thomas that Teresa wasn't coming back, he'd started drawing pictures of just the two of them: himself and his dad. The absence of a mother figure in those new depictions had saddened Chase a bit. Thomas seemed to remember Teresa, though she'd left when he was barely three years old.

Looking at Tisha's pictures, Chase thought of what it would be like had there been three people in more of Thomas's drawings. He wished he'd kept more of his son's artwork, too. Being around Tisha was somehow making him think deeper, care a little more. Her mere presence reminded him that something was missing from his own life. Maybe, he reflected, that something was simply... her.

Chase shook off such thoughts as he continued looking around her place. A cushiony sofa and huge armchairs provided an area to sit down. At the entertainment center, where in most homes the television would be, he saw only an old portable CD player and an abundance of music CDs.

Chase discovered the phone on an end table, nestled under a heap of newspapers. Picking it up, he held it to his ear for a second, glad to hear the dial tone humming loud and clear, before setting it back in its cradle. Dean had also mentioned some issues with her landline, and although most people no longer used one, he liked it: he still had one himself. It just made a home feel more secure.

Chase continued looking around. Everything in Tisha's place was functional, compact and neat – everything, that is, except the cluttered desktop. There sat tons of family photos, picture frames and to-do lists, piled haphazardly one on top of the other next to a big binder, with pictures, papers and clippings of newspaper reports spilling from its bulging covers.

He picked up one small tattered newspaper clipping that caught his eye. The headline was faded, but he was able to make it out before scanning the rest of the article: CHILD DIES AT LOCAL FOSTER HOME.

"What are you looking at so seriously?" Tisha asked, entering the room with a small wooden serving tray and two steaming cups.

"Uh, nothing," Chase said, startled. He quickly put down the clipping, sliding it under other papers. "Just... looking at your family photos, that's all." He walked back over to the couch and took a seat beside her.

They sipped tea and talked a little about the play and about Thomas. Chase tried to concentrate, but his curiosity had been piqued by the headline he'd found. He wondered how to broach the subject. There wasn't a doubt in his mind that Tisha Jameson was a great teacher and beautiful person. Still, the girl in that article had to have meant something to her at one time, or why would she have saved it? He tried to forget about it for now.

"The play was great, Tisha," he said, noticing that she'd removed her glasses to relax her eyes.

"Thank you. Thomas was fantastic, wasn't he?" She paused for a moment. "He practiced so hard, and I – uh…" She turned to face Chase. "Actually, there's something I wanted to ask you about."

Chase moved forward and set down his tea. "Okay?"

"I feel like… like someone shook Thomas's confidence, right before the play. He was so worried, he almost didn't perform. I found him hiding up in the small balcony, very upset, with his confidence badly shaken. Do you know what could have happened?"

Chase was thoughtful. He always tried to reinforce his son's self-esteem, but although Thomas's performance had ultimately been so confident, Chase knew that kids could be masterful at hiding things.

"All children get a little discouraged from time to time, though," he said eventually, casting his gaze toward her.

"I know," Tisha replied, "but I was wondering if he had mentioned anything to you about... about doubting that he would do a good job? Feeling that he wasn't good enough?"

Chase cocked his head quizzically. "Thomas? That kid was so excited. He couldn't wait for tonight. It was all he talked about." *Other than you, of course,* he thought. Even if he wanted to forget about her, which he didn't, his son was always there to remind him. "I think he's okay," he continued. "I mean, what do *you* think could have happened between this afternoon and this evening?"

"I... I think someone might have said something to him. I'll talk to… that person about it."

"Who?" Chase asked. Kids were mean to one another all the time, but his son having a bully to deal with at school hadn't crossed his mind.

"I'll get it straightened out," Tisha said, sitting up. She stretched her arms over her head.

"You can't at least tell me the person's name? Is it a kid from his class?" Chase said incredulously.

"I will handle it. Okay?" Tisha stood and began pacing nervously in front of him.

A thought struck Chase. "Wait a second. Does that new teacher's aide have anything to do with this?"

Sitting up straight, he braced his arms on his knees, watching Tisha keenly. He now remembered Thomas saying that the new classroom assistant, whatever her name was, was a mean person, but Chase had taken this assessment with a pinch of salt: at Thomas's age, he'd reckoned that more teachers seemed mean than nice. He frowned in concentration.

"That day I walked in, she..." Chase couldn't think of her name right then but wracked his brain to come up with more details. "That woman had said something to upset you just before I came in, hadn't she?"

"I said I'd handle it." Tisha stopped pacing to look at Chase. "Did... what else has Thomas said about her?" She implored him with her eyes.

"Look, Tisha." Chase stood. "I get the whole Ms. Independent thing, but if she upset you, why can't you at least tell me? Why is it you can't let anyone help you? I can help - and this does involve my son, after all."

"Yes, I know and I'm sorry, Chase," Tisha breathed. "God, it happened right under my nose. I should have seen it... I should have seen it then, and I should have seen it now. I can fix it. I'll make it right. Oh, and I'll fight my own battles, thank you very much." A steely edge returned to her voice. She blew out a breath, and Chase was actually concerned about how haunted she looked: as though something, perhaps her mysterious past, was coming back to her.

He wanted to help her, that was all. He would do anything he could to help her. Seeing his face, Tisha's shoulders sagged, and her voice softened.

"I'm sorry, I just... one time something happened, and I just felt... powerless." She took another breath. "But things are different now. *I'm* different - wiser..."

Chase was standing right in front of her when she finally looked up at him, seeming almost startled to see him so close. He knew by the look in her eyes, by the stopping of her pacing, that she wasn't there with him. She was in another time, another place in her life. Maybe it had something to do with the little girl in that newspaper clipping. He couldn't be certain. Maybe he just needed to ask her outright. Placing his hands gently on her shoulders, he spoke just above a whisper.

"Is it something to do with Melinda, Tisha? The little girl who died, in Virginia?"

ELEVEN

"WHAT ARE YOU TALKING ABOUT?"

She couldn't have heard him correctly, and her body began to shake as the emotion of reliving the ordeal overwhelmed her. *How did he know? Who told him? Would he blame her, too?* She moved away from him to begin pacing the room once again.

"The little girl, Tisha - the one that died at that foster home. I saw the article you kept. What happened to her? You can tell me. I can see how much this pains you."

Tisha's eyes flashed. "Why were you looking through my things? You weren't there, you don't know what happened." She stared at him, her eyes filling with tears. "It wasn't my fault."

No matter how many times she had said that, how clear it all was on a rational level, or how many times others had said it to her, she still felt as if it were indeed her fault. Protesting her own innocence was just automatic: she still didn't believe it to be true, despite repeating it so many times. None of it took away the pain: it didn't bring back that innocent child, or ease her gnawing guilt.

"I'm just asking you to tell me what's going on. I want to help. I want to understand," Chase said, watching the war of thought and emotion play out on her face.

"And just how in the world am I supposed to help you understand something that doesn't even make sense to me?" she asked, tapping the side of her head. "And I was *there*. You can't help someone else understand what you don't know for yourself."

"Well, just tell me what happened - the facts," he said beseechingly.

"What happened? What *happened*? A child died, that's what happened, and if it hadn't been for me she might still be alive," Tisha snapped. She was yelling now, as a tear escaped down her cheek before she could wipe it away.

"I don't believe it was your fault," Chase said doggedly. "I can see you blame yourself for whatever it is that went down, but regardless, Tisha, I just don't think you had anything to do with it. I've seen you with the kids in your class. I've seen their response to you. You can't fake that."

Who the heck is this man? Tisha thought. He didn't truly know her. She thought she knew people, and then when she least expected it, they turned. She moved back a step when he moved toward her, staring intensely into her eyes. If he tried to embrace her, if he held her, she knew she'd break.

"I know you already," Chase continued softly, the worry clearly visible in his eyes. She resisted his outstretched arms, his large comforting presence that suggested if she would just allow herself to let him into her life, he could comfort her into releasing all the pain she still harbored inside her.

But maybe that pain was for her to learn to cope with, day after day - and maybe she deserved that.

"Let yourself out," Tisha said shortly. She turned from him and ran up the stairs.

———◆———

Chase felt defeated. He let her go without reaching out to stop her. Looking at his watch, he realized he had to go pick up Thomas. If Tisha thought it was over between them, though, she had another thing coming.

On Chase's way out to his truck, a thought occurred to him and he stopped to check out her car. He popped the hood and used his keychain flashlight to survey the inner workings. There, even in the weak little beam of light, he could see that one of the electrical cords was severed – almost as if it had been deliberately cut. In alarm, he looked around him, checking the lighting and wondering if there were any cameras around.

He also noticed her tires were low, and he could sense that a whole host of other regular problems were most likely just waiting to happen. He made a mental note to have his mechanic look at her car over the weekend.

He wasn't sure why he was bothering at all anymore, as she obviously wanted no part of his friendship or his help… but the stubborn side of him replied that that was just too bad, because he wanted to help her and he didn't plan to stop trying. After all, his heart wouldn't let him.

TWELVE

———

DESPITE THE WAY THINGS HAD ended with Chase the other night, Tisha thought about him constantly. While he continued to be kind and understanding, she made an effort to avoid him every afternoon when he came to pick Thomas up. Still, just to satisfy her wonderings, she reviewed the section of the school's handbook about teachers dating the parent of a child. While it appeared that it might be a breach of social etiquette, the guide didn't specify that it was against any explicit rules.

She put the book aside and gave herself a little shake, trying as hard as she could not to think about Chase in that way. At this point, she just wanted to apologize - not to accept one of his many invitations for pizza or dinner at a local restaurant. Granted, she *was* eager to know more about her new city. But she did sort of want to show Chase her own skills in the kitchen with a meal at home, too...

Sadly, all of that would have to wait. Maybe in the summer, when she wasn't teaching; though she'd planned to go home for a month while she was off.

The initial impression she'd given him the other night was weighing heavily on her mind. She hated it. She should just let him continue to think that she was a nut job – then, she thought wryly, she could introduce him to the second of her overprotective brothers just to reconfirm that image. Jojo was even worse than Dean in that regard. He would really send Chase Alton packing… and that thought too saddened her.

Ugh, I can't win.

She sat in her room alone, going over lesson plans. Her past experiences with men had been nil, thanks to the combined efforts of her siblings. Jojo and Dean were the worst, well-meaning or not. She smiled sadly. Despite their irritating protectiveness, she missed her family terribly.

She shrugged. Perhaps she, Chase and Thomas could just go bowling, or some other fun familial activity. That didn't imply dating, right? There shouldn't be any real rules against that, and they could even take separate cars to get there. *Yeah.* Tisha congratulated herself for the turnaround in her thinking. *That should work, right?*

Tisha's emotions were all over the place. She already trusted Chase enough that she knew she could eventually tell him what had happened in her past. Then he could judge for himself. *Even though there's nothing to judge,* she reminded herself once again, trying to push away the usual nagging guilt.

Distractedly, she pulled at one of the yellow roses he'd given her. He'd insisted on a belated Valentine's gift, because she'd refused to have dinner with him and he had wanted to do something. Sniffing the bloom, she thought of the sender, and how patient he had been not to take her 'no' as a final answer.

Replacing the stem in its vase, she sat down at her desk once more and continued cutting out letters for the March calendar, glancing once more at the Black History month items she'd soon be taking down. The month would be over in just a few days, and she thought excitedly of the upcoming Cherry Blossom Festival, held every year here in Macon. The festival sounded even more involved and spectacular than those she had attended back in D.C., where her whole family used to take the metro into the District to witness the Cherry Blossom Parade. With any luck, this small town wouldn't have that gridlocked traffic. Something about that smallness charmed her, and she was intrigued to see what this Georgia version was going to be like.

Picking up a copy of the *Macon Telegraph,* she read of exhibits, dances, rides, and concerts. Because even here she guessed the crowds would be large, she would feel comfortable enough agreeing to that particular outing with the two wonderful Alton men. She hoped they'd ask her… or, if she would just get over herself, perhaps she could even be the one to casually suggest that they go together.

As Tisha replaced the scissors in her drawer, the recent newspaper article that she'd saved caught her eye. Retrieving it, she reread it proudly, skimming through the list of accolades and commendations the school had received as a result of her own contributions:

Teachers at Glen Dale promote innovation while remembering the struggle of African-Americans. Their eye-opening Black History Month program connects the past to the hard-won present: a first for the new school that opened just one year ago.

Tisha smiled, remembering the staff reporter who'd written the wonderful article about the play and the school as a whole. Other teachers in the school, who had rarely spoken to her when she was a newcomer, finally begin recognizing her as an equal. The play and its rave reviews reflected well on all the school personnel, reminding them that they were a team and should act as such. Now, when Tisha walked through the halls, people acknowledged her, smiled, even asked her with a newfound respect about the detailed curriculum she insisted upon and the other contributions she was trying to make to the school.

Tisha folded the paper and stuck it back in the drawer as the sound of frantic footsteps echoed down the hall.

Although kids ran through school all the time, she was a

tad alarmed. She grabbed her glasses as Thomas burst into the room, yelling.

"Tishaaa! Tisha!" His face was smudged with dirt and his eyes were filled with tears while he stammered and tried to form comprehensible sentences.

Tisha would have to get after him about calling her by her first name – but judging by the look on his face, now was clearly not the time.

"Thomas, sweetheart, what's the matter?" Tisha asked, placing her hands on his shoulders.

Thomas grabbed her hand and began pulling her toward the door. His words came clipped and sporadic.

"It's Ms. Robinson," he sputtered breathlessly. "She's hitting Marina. I—I tried to get her to stop, I really tried, but she wouldn't."

Tisha picked up her pace as she and Thomas ran to the back of the school where the playgrounds were located, racing through the fifth- and third-graders' playgrounds before finally reaching the younger children's playground.

Tisha looked around in earnest, her eyes searching for any sign of something wrong. It wasn't recess, so why would any children even be outside? she wondered. None were, she confirmed as she scanned the grounds.

Thomas's eyes were moving just as frantically around the playground. "But I saw her..."

Finally he spotted them, just seconds before Tisha did. Andrea was close to the edge of the playground, where the fence stretched around the perimeter and the woods grew thick behind it. Thomas's grip tightened on Tisha's hand.

Tisha kept up with Thomas. His hand was slick with sweat, or was it hers? She didn't know for sure. Her blood was already boiling with adrenaline and dread about what she would find. As the heat rushed to her face, a strong breeze whipped through the air, raising the hairs on her bare arms and chilling her skin.

As Tisha moved close to Andrea, her heart fluttered and

the color drained from her face. In her arms, Andrea Robinson held a child whose left eye was swollen shut and beginning to turn hideously brown. The child looked as if she didn't have an ounce of fight left in her. She simply lay still, her body limp as her one good eye rolled toward Tisha, silently pleading to be rescued.

Tisha stepped forward slowly, fighting against the disbelief that had temporarily rendered her limbs leaden and stiff. Gently but quickly she managed to take the child from Andrea's arms.

She had seen nothing like it, since... since she left Virginia. Back then, when she had arrived, it had been too late... This was too much for her to bear. As she looked at the little girl here in her arms, Tisha saw another girl's face instead, and she felt dizzy as the entire episode came rushing back to her.

Marina was flaccid in Tisha's arms as she turned from Andrea and laid her carefully on the ground to inspect the extent of the abuse and the injuries. "What have you *done?*" she breathed to Andrea.

"What have I done?" Andrea repeated sardonically, as she watched Tisha kneel on the ground with the child. "I was doing something that should have been done long ago, obviously. These damn kids don't get enough discipline. I was just picking up where the parents decided to leave off." She placed her hands on her hips, looking positively proud of her actions.

Tisha turned back to Andrea. "You are crazy!" she hollered. *Why was this happening?*

"I am not crazy!" Andrea replied indignantly. "*You* are! And everybody will know after today."

She looked on with a twisted, ugly smile as Tisha spoke soothingly to the child; then her face transformed in an instant into an expression of mock horror and sugary compassion. Her voice dropped low and dangerous as she spoke:

"How could you beat this poor, innocent child? Look at her! *You* did this," Andrea continued, pointing a finger at Tisha. "The nice teacher. The one everybody loves. It's just a cover-up for the abuser you are. *Everyone* will know."

Andrea bent closer to look Tisha in the face. "You take children from their poor, loving parents and… well, now look." Her face became a mask, her eyes glassy, and she smirked when a look of recognition came over Tisha's face.

The acidic taste of bile rose in Tisha's throat and she felt sick to her stomach. This woman somehow knew her, knew what had happened all that time ago, only her facts were terribly twisted.

"That's not true - *you* did it!" a shrill small voice piped up. "You're the mean one. Ms. Jameson's the nice teacher. It was *you*. I'll tell them it was you!" Thomas yelled at Andrea. It was clear that he didn't fully understand what had transpired, but he knew that somehow Andrea was twisting things.

"Shut up, you stupid little…" Andrea rounded on Thomas, staring at him as if he had magically appeared out of nowhere. She hurled herself at him. Her hand swung back and a fist landed against his beautiful cheek. She drew her arm back, about to strike him again, when Tisha grabbed her arm.

"If you touch him again, I swear I'll kill you," Tisha said softly. Everything that was unfolding before her eyes seemed unconscionable – as if she'd somehow stumbled into the worst nightmare imaginable. But Thomas - oh God, not Thomas. Andrea Robinson would have to bury her alive before she would allow her to hurt Thomas.

Turning toward him, Tisha spoke as calmly as her racing heart would permit. If she could just get him away from this scene, at least he'd be safe. Then she'd get Marina to safety as well, if it weren't too late…

"Thomas… honey, I need you to run and get help, okay? Ask Mrs. Wellington in room ten to call an ambulance and to get the principal." She watched Thomas, his concern and reluctance to leave her evident on his little face. She didn't know anything for sure, least of all what further damage this woman would do either to her or to the child, but she spoke encouragingly anyway. "I'll be okay, Thomas. I promise I'll be okay. You have to get me some help, though, baby."

Thomas nodded hesitantly before he slowly stood. He cast one last baleful and terrified look in Andrea's direction before he took off back toward the school.

Andrea watched Thomas leave. As soon as the boy disappeared around the brick wall of the building, she pulled back her free hand, curled it into a fist and smashed it against Tisha's face.

Tisha abruptly let go of the woman when she was propelled back from the blow. She grabbed her cheek, feeling the skin break inside her mouth, and everything around her blurred. She tried to refocus and moved her hands through the mulch and grass, searching frantically for her glasses which had been knocked from her face. She tasted the blood on her teeth and swallowed several times.

Andrea came toward her, standing to her full six-foot height, and then kicked Tisha in the leg. When Tisha screamed out in pain, Andrea just smiled devilishly.

"Kids are placed in your care and you let them die. Just like then, isn't it? You're just doing it again."

Tisha saw stars from the unadulterated pain the woman was causing her. She swayed from the second blow to her side, but quickly righted herself. Andrea kept coming toward her. Tisha scrambled back in a vain attempt to put some distance between them while she racked her brain for a plan.

"You had to go and open your big mouth about me to Mr. Jeeter, didn't you?" Andrea went on. "I'll teach you a thing or two. Always blowing your horn. Well, it's time someone taught *you* a lesson. Then maybe you'll learn to keep your mouth shut."

Uncurling her legs from underneath her, Tisha used her right booted foot to kick Andrea in the shin, watching her fall to the ground. But the madwoman was only temporarily put off. Shaking off the wood chips and dirt, she moved slowly toward Tisha on all fours like a deranged and rabid dog. She was the predator and Tisha was the prey.

"I lost my job and my dignity - you took all of it," Andrea snarled.

Tisha could only make out the silhouette of Andrea coming after her: with her glasses gone, she could hardly see. She laid on her back and prepared to use her legs.

Andrea smiled triumphantly as Tisha turned over on her hands and knees. "You're a coward - that's right, lay there and die."

Andrea's words were cut off abruptly when Tisha's foot connected with her leg. When Andrea fell, she struck her again in the chin. Tisha's leg hurt, but she had swung it as hard as she could. The force of it sent Andrea backward, knocked unconscious. She landed in a heap, on top of the child she'd beaten so brutally.

THIRTEEN

—◆—

MOVING QUICKLY, TISHA SUMMONED THE strength from every part of her body to roll Andrea's dead weight off Marina. She had to get the girl to the building and safety.

Thanking God, Tisha noticed that Marina was conscious; but her frail, whimpering cries frightened Tisha, and the child's little body convulsed and shuddered violently. She whimpered as Tisha tried to move her carefully and slowly. The procedures for moving injured persons deserted her as she tried desperately to remember what could possibly result from moving someone who might have any degree of internal injury... She knew she really shouldn't move the girl at all, and the what-ifs ran through her mind: What if something was broken? What if moving her caused further damage? What if Andrea awoke and the injuries were made far worse?

Andrea. Her body lay face down and unmoving in the dirt, but Tisha knew the blow she'd delivered to Andrea was only a temporary put-off. She had only bought herself a little bit of time by knocking the woman unconscious; Andrea would eventually wake up, and what if she and the girl were still on the playground waiting for help? Tisha wasn't sure whether she could do a second battle with someone twice her size. She had to move. She prayed that when Andrea did wake up, the police would be present

to place her in handcuffs and cart her off to jail. Tisha
couldn't worry about her right now; there were more
pressing issues at hand.

As she stood, Tisha tried not to squish Marina, but her
own immense anger and fear caused her muscles to tremble
with adrenaline. With the child in her arms and without
her glasses, Tisha looked around but found everything out
of focus: the route to the school doors was a blur.

The sidewalk. If she could locate the concrete and remain
on the path, she would be okay. The sidewalk to the playground wrapped around the entire back of the building.
She limped in the direction of the door, as fast as her
injured leg would carry her.

As she moved nearer, she made out a silhouette she recognized as Thomas. He was waiting for her at the door and
held it open as Tisha made her way inside, holding Marina
protectively close.

Sharon Wellington rushed over to them. "What happened? I couldn't get anyone to watch my third-grade
class - Ms. Robinson just took Marina to the bathroom a
few minutes ago, and..."

Sharon stopped, stunned and horrified by what she saw.
She brought a hand to her mouth. She rushed over to
Tisha, seeing that her eye was also swollen and black.

Tisha moved awkwardly through the doors of the building carrying Marina Stamos. The sweet little Latina had
special needs – and here she lay bloody, her entire face
swollen and red.

Tisha breathed a sigh of relief at the fact that Sharon
Wellington, the first woman to befriend her when she'd
moved to Macon, was now involved. She let go of the child
reluctantly, already feeling an all-too-familiar misplaced
responsibility for Marina's condition. Tisha felt helpless,
although she reminded herself hurriedly that the child's
name was *Marina*, not Melinda. Tisha wondered vaguely
who had called the ambulance, as she heard its faint wail

from outside. Thank goodness someone had called them. She felt sick to her stomach and no longer had the strength to remain standing.

A flood of relief came over Tisha, then her legs buckled and she felt herself collapse to the floor. Then she saw Thomas. His eyes were flooded with tears and his face was drawn in concern. She wanted to be strong for him, but the worst headache she'd had in her entire life now pounded her skull. *He looks every bit like Chase* was her last thought as her eyes closed. "I'm all right, Thomas," she whispered as she felt his hand touch her shoulder – then her head gave an almighty throb and she collapsed into an unknown darkness.

Chase knew that something was wrong the moment Thomas met him outside, before he could even exit his truck. On a normal school day, Chase would enter the school to retrieve his son and often, to his delight, chat with Tisha while he was at it. He looked forward to seeing her every day - only on this occasion, he could tell that something was badly amiss.

"Dad, Dad, we gotta go... hospital. Ms. Jameson... she fell... Ms. Robinson…"

"Well, what, son? Is she all right?"

"No, no!" Thomas shook his head frantically, clambering into the cab. Chase immediately noticed Thomas's red puffy eyes and the swollen abrasion on his cheek. "What the heck happened to you, son?"

The name *Ms. Jameson* and the word *hospital* in the same sentence sent his blood pressure skyrocketing. He'd get the information on the way, but for now he faced forward, cranked the ignition, put the car in gear, and pressed his foot to the accelerator.

The extent of the damages would be the determining

factor in choosing the hospital. It could be North Macon, or they could be headed to the bigger ward in Forsyth. "Do you know which hospital, son?"

"I don't know, Dad. I don't know," Thomas said, as he grew still more agitated.

"Okay, okay," Chase responded. It was best, he could tell, that he just let Thomas tell him what he knew, instead of asking for information the boy clearly did not have. Questions seemed only to distress him more.

"Just tell me what happened. It'll be okay," Chase assured his panicked son.

During the twenty-minute trip to the hospital, Thomas went over the entire school day, repeating some parts where he got so worked up he couldn't gather what he wanted to say. Chase still didn't know what to make of anything he'd heard; after all, he'd never heard anything like it.

From what Chase was able to gather from Thomas, Ms. Robinson had tormented the kids since she began working at the school. It started with her calling them names. Soon, rough games started, where the children would be the ones to get hurt. Either in kickball or tag, a subtle shove or push would be enough to hurt them, but never so much that any unsuspecting adult would think it anything more serious than the usual nicks and scrapes kids got while playing. And to think Chase had been grateful to find a school that got the kids outdoors by reinstating recess.

At the stoplight, Chase turned to his son, his gaze intense and unwavering. "That day you said you fell, son… did she push you? You've got to tell me the truth."

Thomas's hesitation gave Chase his answer. His blood boiled.

"Why didn't you tell me?" he exploded. "And did she – did Ms. Robinson discourage you at the play that night?" Chase tried to keep the anger from his voice: it was directed not at Thomas but at the situation in general. He realized he wasn't doing a very good job: Thomas's lower lip began to quiver and his eyes filled with more tears.

"She always asked us who our favorite teacher is... She told us that one day she'd hurt Ms. Jameson if we didn't keep our mouths shut. So I didn't tell, Daddy. Nobody did." The tears spilled over and cascaded down the boy's cheeks.

"It's all right. It's okay." Chase patted Thomas's shoulder. He wished he could believe that it was going to be all right, but if something had happened to Tisha, he wasn't sure it would be.

When Chase got to the hospital it seemed extra busy. He held his son by the hand and they moved through the hospital with a single purpose: to find Tisha. If there was one thing Chase hated, it was hospitals. Every single one seemed exactly the same: in looks and, to Chase's particular revulsion, in smell.

At the nurses' station, a group of people were gathered. A young man and woman held each other close while a young doctor talked patiently with them. Thomas broke away from Chase and took off running in their direction. "Mrs. Stamos, is Marina okay? Do you know where Tisha is?" he questioned. Chase searched for any sign of Tisha, but his frustration at not seeing her anywhere was beginning to make him angry.

The Spanish woman noticed as Thomas stopped in front of them. "Oh, *Tomas*—"

Her eyes were bloodshot. "What happened, who, why do this to my baby, *Tomas*?" she questioned him in broken English, pleading with Thomas as if he were the one who had all the answers. She stooped low, looking Thomas in the eyes, and started crying.

Chase came up, standing behind Thomas. He managed a concerned look, realizing that if the tables had been turned, as Thomas had indicated they almost would have been if it hadn't been for Tisha, his own child could've been hurt as well. Still, right now he had to find Tisha. He had to know that she was all right. He addressed the woman calmly.

"Mrs. Stamos, I'm Thomas's father, Chase Alton. I'm very sorry to hear about your daughter. How is she?" His eyes did a quick sweep of the hallway before returning to the young woman.

"No good," Mrs. Stamos said. Her accent chopped her words, and Chase listened carefully, but she only wrung her hands together, looking at the man who Chase surmised was her husband. Her fingers worried a tattered tissue. Small pieces of it sprinkled down onto her wool winter coat.

Mrs. Stamos continued, waving her hands about. "I don't know what happen. *Tomas,* you see what happen?" she asked, bending again to implore Thomas tell her more. "I need to know, you tell me, yes?"

Thomas looked up at his father for permission. When Chase nodded, Thomas looked at Marina's mother. "It was Ms. Robinson," he said, beginning to relay the entire ordeal, much more calmly now than when he'd first told the story to his father.

When he finished, Mrs. Stamos looked around the room. "Where this Ms. Robinson? Where she now? Why she hurt my baby?" Mrs. Stamos questioned when Thomas finished. Her voice was high-pitched with anxiety. Her eyes moved quickly and expectantly around the hospital, as if the culprit would suddenly materialize among them.

She looked back at Thomas. "Where this Ms. Jameson? She help my daughter? What happen to her?"

FOURTEEN

———

S TARTLED, CHASE LOOKED UP. "WE thought she would be here. You don't know her? You haven't seen her?"

Chase tried to keep the alarm out of his voice. Thomas looked up at him as if he were about to cry again, so Chase immediately shoved down his own rising panic and replaced it with a tenuous patience.

The man that Mrs. Stamos had kept looking to for help, who was also largely silent, came to stand beside his wife. He addressed his wife in Spanish – something that sounded like: "The doctor needs to speak with us" – and ushered her away. As they left, he did manage to say in English: "I'm sorry, I don't know where this Tisha is - you can speak with the nurse."

Chase's eyebrow rose. He was wondering what to do next when he noticed a uniformed officer holding a note-pad making his way in their direction. Chase felt a rush of relief to see that the police had arrived.

"I'm Officer Davis," the man began. "You all family members of the victim?"

"No, we're not family. We came to see Ms. Jameson. Would you know where she is?" Chase asked.

"Jameson? Jameson?" Davis repeated the name, flipping back a couple of pages in his steno pad to search for the name. "Yeah, okay, here we go... mixed race female…"

"She's African-American," Chase corrected, tight-lipped.

"Well, this Ms. Jameson - Tricia Jameson, is it?"

"*Tisha* Jameson," Chase said impatiently.

"Well, she's in custody. We got a woman by the name of *Tisha* Jameson in police custody downtown." He closed the notebook with a snap. With his stiff stance and closed-off look, Officer Davis couldn't have indicated more clearly that he cared nothing about Tisha Jameson and that until he had information otherwise, she was just another suspect.

Chase's calm demeanor was nearly shot. He spaced his words evenly and slowly. "Why on earth is she in police custody? She didn't do anything wrong."

"She is the last person seen with the rescued child," the officer returned, with a slight air of arrogance.

"But that's wrong," Chase spoke quickly. "She was the one who made sure the child got here. She *saved* Marina Stamos *from* the woman you *should* have in custody."

"Another woman?" the officer asked. His eyes indicated renewed interest as he licked his thumb and turned to a new page to scribble down the information. "What's her name, you say? Her role in this is... what exactly?"

Chase's mouth dropped in complete astonishment. If the officials didn't yet have the correct person, there was no telling what kind of panic Tisha was in. He was clearly in the wrong place, and he knew he had to get going.

"Andrea Robinson," Chase said. He spoke more forcefully than was strictly necessary: he was not happy that no one even knew of the guilty woman. Why weren't these officers at the school interviewing the kids, or at minimum seeing how they could help there?

"Andrea Robinson is a teacher's aide at the school," Chase continued hurriedly. "She's the one who beat up the little girl. According to my son here, she's been tormenting the children for some time." He didn't hesitate a moment; he recounted the story as if he had been there to witness the event for himself. It didn't matter that a seven-year-old had been the one to relay to Chase what happened. Chase believed his son, thus he spoke confidently about the events of the day.

As he spoke, he remembered Tisha voicing concern about exactly this possibility with Andrea. He understood now, and he was sorry he'd dismissed her concern at the time.

"Tisha Jameson is the one who helped the little girl get *away* from Ms. Robinson. Officer, from what you're telling me - or not telling me - you don't know where Ms. Robinson is, and you have Ms. Jameson in custody, no doubt being thoroughly interrogated?" Chase spat, his chest rising and falling with each breath. He glanced at Thomas and, with an effort, brought himself under control.

"Well, this is our first time hearing anything about a Ms. Robinson. Perhaps my partner can..." the officer replied reaching for the radio on his shoulder.

"You do that," Chase snapped. "See if you guys can get a communication plan going at some point during this entire day." Chase grabbed Thomas's hand and set off toward the door. His son kept pace, both of them simply anxious to get to Tisha.

"Wait - you need to make a statement." The officer rushed to catch up with them. "Son, did you see anything?" The officer directed the question to Thomas, who stopped immediately. The officer bent down to stare at him expectantly.

Chase stepped forward and answered loud and slow, enunciating every syllable: "We'll give a statement when we get to the station and not a moment sooner—and certainly not until after we see Ms. Jameson. *Okay?*"

The officer stood to his full height, and still he had to look up at Chase. He nodded. "We'll get your statement sooner or later." Without further acknowledgement, Chase and Thomas left the hospital.

———◆———

In the truck, Chase addressed Thomas. "I'm going to call Angie and ask her to stay with you while I go to the station," Chase said. He wanted to appear firm, but his entire tone lacked conviction. Chase was beginning to see how much his son loved Tisha. He, too, prayed she was all right. He hoped she'd at least called her family, although he guessed she probably hadn't. She was all alone, here in her new town, determined to make it without help. Whatever Thomas's feelings, though, Chase reasoned that the boy had been through enough, and there was no telling what other things he would witness if he came along to the station.

"No, no, Dad, I wanna go too," Thomas whined. "You gotta let me go, you gotta!"

Chase hesitated. "Okay… but listen." Chase maneuvered the truck out of the lot and set off for the station as he continued: "Sometimes, son, there are bad people at a police station. Criminals - people on their way to jail for the bad things they've done - have to wait there, so I want you to stay with me. Do not, I repeat, do *not* run off." Chase raised his voice slightly, hoping to scare Thomas into obedience. He was satisfied when Thomas looked somewhat terrified and nodded slowly. "Put your jacket on," Chase said, securing his lightweight topcoat as they pulled into the station.

Thomas jumped down from the truck and started to run toward the station, but didn't get more than a couple of paces before he turned to look at Chase. Slowing his gait, Thomas tightly gripped the hand his father held out as they made their way to the entrance together.

"And you are?" the officer behind the desk asked. "Chase Alton," Chase repeated for the third time. The man took his time writing it down while hunting around the large desk for other information, periodically interrupted by a ringing telephone. He turned to the computer.

Trying to be discreet, Chase peered at the ledger sitting on the desk. Finally he made out the words T. Jameson near the bottom of the page, and strained to read the officer's name beside the ledger entry.

"Officer... Cantrell?" he said. "Where is his desk?" He needed to confirm with his own eyes that Tisha was all right. He'd go through the entire station and question every officer until he located her.

"Oh, you know Officer Cantrell?" the man asked, surprised.

"Yeah, we go way back," Chase lied, hoping Officer Cantrell wasn't some pimply young kid who had just recently joined the force.

"Hey man, you're Take-out Chase Alton!" the officer exclaimed, finally looking at Chase long enough to recognize him as a retired pro football player and breaking into an appreciative smile. "Man, you were somethin' when you played. M.V.P. twice! Pro-Bowl! Hey, why'd you quit, man? You were at the top of your game. I mean, for real, they sure could still use you out there!"

Chase nodded. That's the way it always was when someone retired at their peak. The fans took it personally, almost resentful that a top-performing player would leave the sport simply because his heart was no longer in it. They couldn't fathom any reason other than injury or age as cause for retirement: they acted like their heroes should just play forever. Even for himself, Chase reflected, it had taken divorce and fatherhood to put everything in perspective.

He nodded cordially, hoping just a little more nice-guy chitchat would get him the information he sought.

"Yeah," Chase shrugged adding a fake smile. "Sometimes it's just time to let it go. I'm just plain ol' Chase Alton now: a different person leading a totally different life. Hey, listen man - uh, my buddy Cantrell's desk — where is it?"

Standing, the officer smiled, becoming friendlier by the minute. He leaned over the desk and jerked his thumb toward the back of the station, where men stood around, some uniformed and others not.

Chase tightened his grip on Thomas's hand and led the way.

———◆———

Tisha's head hadn't stopped throbbing as she sat beside the desk of Officer George Cantrell. Her stomach growled from a combination of painful hunger cramps and her bruised ribs. The officer had finally offered to get her a drink of water, but if he ever returned from what she thought should be a simple task, she doubted she'd be able to hold the water down.

Her hunger and tiredness were second only to her fear and anger. She had never been inside a police station in all her twenty-eight years, and to return within another twenty-eight would be too soon. The officer had refused to tell her what was going on, so her mind overcompensated, making up all sorts of tragic and negative reasons. She thought of Thomas and prayed he was okay: that this entire ordeal hadn't forever marred his childhood. Then she thought about Chase. At this moment, she wanted nothing more than his strong arms around her. But mostly, she thought of Marina. She silently prayed that this time she had intervened in time.

As if one of her prayers had been answered, Tisha swore she heard Thomas calling her name. Wondering if she were simply so tired that she had begun to hear things, she looked around to find the source of the voice… but a headache and the loss of her glasses rendered everything a noisy blur. The clicking of fingers on keyboards, the orders from officers to their suspects, the humming of machinery, the scraping of chairs across the wooden floor and harsh, foul language from the mouths of disgruntled arrestees all echoed around and merged into a single mass, clashing in her ears.

The officer had questioned her repeatedly: it was more than apparent that they thought she was the one responsible for the child's abuse. She hadn't been treated right, even as she told them the truth repeatedly.

Holding her stomach, Tisha doubled over from the pain inside her head and the equivalent pain inside her heart. She would never comprehend why people chose to harm innocent children. There was no excuse: no explanation could ever make her understand. Such brutality was simply unfathomable.

Raising her hands to rub her temples, she closed her eyes. Then she felt cool air rush past her as a pair of small, sweaty palms touched both her cheeks. Tisha opened her eyes. "Oh, Thomas," she breathed.

She didn't want to cry and she promised herself she wouldn't, but tears were the only emotional release she could muster. She grabbed Thomas around his neck and hugged him tightly, nearly squeezing the breath out of him. Her eyes wouldn't focus, but her hands roamed over his face, and she drew her thumb tenderly across the small raised welt on his cheek.

Thomas smiled back at her, brushing her hand away gently. "I'm okay," he said proudly, as if the mark symbolized a rite of passage all little boys went through.

"You are so brave, Thomas," Tisha said before leaning to plant a peck on his cheek. She tried to stand, feeling the pain announce itself in her upper thigh and throb throughout her body. Then she felt a heavier hand on her shoulder. She didn't need to see anything to guess that the large figure before her was Chase. Before she could step forward, his arms enclosed her upper torso, lifting her up off the ground.

"Hey. It's all right now," he soothed. "It's all over."

Chase held her tightly until her trembling subsided. He brushed back the hair that fell over her face and kissed her cheek, then set her down but didn't let her go. He wiped away her tears, but more soon came. Relieved, Tisha leaned against him, hoping her nightmare would end soon.

FIFTEEN

"YOU TWO DONE?" THE OFFICER asked as he returned to his desk. Without waiting for a response, he continued without otherwise acknowledging Chase or his son: "Now I'll finish taking your statement." Holding Tisha's hand, Chase stepped in front of her as Officer Cantrell placed a cup of water on the edge of his desk.

Chase sized up George Cantrell in a matter of moments. Chase's late father had also been a police officer, and a very good one at that: thus, Chase could tell straight away that Officer Cantrell took pride in his work. At the same time, however, Chase had learned to spot someone with something to prove a mile away.

Cantrell was an older man. His hair and his beard were completely gray. He moved casually, as if he owned the station and all the men in the place were under his thumb. Chase knew better: he knew full well that this type of posturing was all an act, a silly intimidation tactic. Chase had no plans of letting the officer do anything out of order, whether he had something to prove or was just another bully with a badge and a gun. Chase knew he was not in LA anymore, but some rules still applied.

"Thank you, Officer, but you won't be taking any more statements from Ms. Jameson because Ms. Jameson won't be giving any until her lawyer is present." Chase moved completely in front of Tisha and looked pointedly at the surprised man. He knew Tisha was innocent, and he also knew that if the police department believed she was a victim, they would have let her leave a long time ago. She needed to rest, and he wouldn't sit by and let the officials interrogate her without legal counsel.

"And just who are you?" the officer questioned, regaining his composure. "This is my jurisdiction, and you can't just come in here and tell me what I'm going to do."

"My name is Chase Alton. I'm a friend of Ms. Jameson," Chase replied curtly. "Tell me, George, have you found the suspect yet? A Ms. Andrea Robinson?" Chase stepped closer to the man, daring him to meet the implicit challenge.

"We're, ah, searching for her," stammered the officer. "I was just going to get a description from Ms. Jameson before you – "

"You can contact the school or use your handy-dandy databases for that," Chase interrupted. "Her school badge should be on file; you should have had that a long time ago. She is a threat. I'm concerned for Ms. Jameson's and my child's safety."

He turned back to Tisha. "Let's go," he said, shrugging off his jacket and putting it around Tisha's shoulders. She smiled up at him. It was all he could do not to scoop her up and carry her out of there. They turned to leave. He held her hand again, just comforted by her presence, however fragile she looked.

"Now you wait just a damn minute! I'm not done here," the officer exclaimed. "You can't just walk out of here!"

Chase looked the man over, his eyes turning a shade darker. Again, the officer reminded Chase of his old man. Samuel Alton had been a tough man, who drilled that same toughness into his son. He'd never raised his hand to Chase, but he'd pushed his only child hard, with unrelenting discipline, constant scrutiny and harsh criticism. As a result, Chase had a tendency to square up to everyone who reminded him of his father. Cantrell pushed all Chase's buttons.

"No, *you* wait." Chase surprised himself by how calmly he said it. "People have rights, you see," he continued, knowing that Cantrell was likely bridling at being defied. Few probably had the gall to stand up to the man.

Chase knew that Tisha Jameson was kind-hearted and didn't deserve to be there. He knew she'd cooperate with the police with very little fight - not only because of her kindness and because she was innocent, but because she was the type of person who believed in the law as a protector and a symbol of justice. She had an endless optimism about people in general and their motives. But Chase knew she needed a lawyer. The police wouldn't do any extra work if they didn't feel they had to.

"Do you have enough evidence to arrest Ms. Jameson?" Chase asked bluntly.

"She was the last person with the child," Cantrell replied obstinately.

"That is not what I asked you. Do you have enough evidence to detain Ms. Jameson any longer?" Chase repeated. "Do you have other witness accounts? Shouldn't you get those and then get a warrant?"

When the officer didn't respond, Chase turned silently around and led Thomas and Tisha away from the cubicle.

"Look at that - another Lite Brite taking a fine man off the market," a woman's voice sneered. "Can't you stick to your own kind, boyfriend? You so fine!"

Chase stopped short when he heard the comment. His back immediately stiffened. He was about to turn when Tisha clamped both her hands around his arm, firmly tugging him toward the exit.

"Come on, please. Let's just get out of here," she pleaded, looking up at Chase.

Chase shot a quick look at the woman who had uttered

the comment. He was shocked anybody would say something so ignorant; but he kept walking as Tisha pulled him. He looked into her beautiful eyes: she struggled to see him properly without glasses. One of her eyes was dark and swollen, and the corner of her delicate mouth was bruised. Chase muttered something he could not repeat and placed his arm more firmly around her as the trio kept moving.

Back in the car, Thomas clambered over the front seat to sit between Tisha and his father. The cab of the truck had more than enough room, but both Thomas and Tisha sat closer than Chase was used to. It was fine with him. Back in the safety of the truck, he realized things could have been much worse today, and that perhaps they all needed this closeness to assure themselves things were okay. Neither of them were in the hospital clinging to life like poor little Marina, and for that alone he was thankful. They were all safe, and that was all that mattered.

"When I get home I can call the hospital and see how Marina is doing," Tisha said, breaking the silence. "Did you guys already go to the hospital? The officers at the station refused to give me any information - they just badgered me with one question after another about the incident. Is she okay, you guys?"

"She's alive," Chase offered, "but we don't know much of anything, honey. We don't know... the extent of the damage."

Tisha looked away again to watch as the cars drifted past her window.

"Maybe I shouldn't be teaching," she mused sadly.

"You're the best teacher," Thomas interjected.

"Yes, you are," Chase put in.

Tisha smiled sadly and Chase hurt for her. "Thanks..."

Chase could tell she was thinking about a lot of things, and he wanted to reassure her because of the little he knew about her past. That said, he wanted to talk to her without Thomas present, so he managed to keep silent for the moment. He drove at a normal pace, picturing the lawyer he'd call for her as soon as they got home.

Thomas pulled something out of his pocket and handed it to Tisha. "They're broken," he said apologetically. "I tried to fix them."

Tisha took her glasses from his small hands.

"They are perfect. I can see better with broken glasses than I can with none at all. Thank you, Thomas. Hey - you were so brave today, you did such a good job. Thank you, sweet pea." She looked down at him, trying to keep her voice clear.

Chase listened intently. He hadn't thought to encourage his son this entire time, but once again, she had. She'd been through a lot, and still she was cheering others up. It tugged on his heart.

She put on her glasses after trying to clean the lone intact lens. She smiled down at Thomas and caressed his face, careful of the new bruise.

It could have been worse. That's all Chase could think about – that and the fact that Tisha Jameson was a beautiful angel he could grow to love just as much as his son had in the last few months. He wanted to protect her, and shadows from her past didn't faze him at all. He'd find out what happened, but it was clear that would happen in her time. In his heart, he knew she'd done all she could. Chase tried to recall any private detectives he might know, considering that Tisha would need some protection if this Andrea Robinson woman wasn't found, and soon.

Tisha's glasses were crooked, but at least she could see now. She looked out at the road ahead then back at him. "Um, Chase? Where are we going? Why aren't you taking me home?"

Chase glanced at her, barely taking his eyes from the road, and shrugged. The truth was that he really didn't want her staying at that dilapidated apartment alone. He wanted her somewhere he could be near her, at least until

Andrea Robinson was apprehended. That said, he really didn't want to start an argument with her, knowing her independent spirit, so he considered his words carefully before he spoke.

"Andrea Robinson hasn't been apprehended, okay," he began. "When she is, I'll take you home... but until that happens, could you please just come and spend some time with Thomas and me?"

"Well she had to be found soon – how hard can it be?" Tisha asked incredulously. As soon as the police had a chance to talk to Principal Jeeter and some of the other teachers, Mrs. Wellington for one, she was sure they would find Andrea in a matter of hours. They had to. This whole situation was unreal.

"I agree," Chase replied hurriedly, "but let's not, uh, take chances, okay?"

"I can take care of myself, you know," she said quietly.

Chase nodded. He wasn't angry – rather, he wanted to smile at her determination. "Of course you can, and Thomas and I want to take care of you, too. Isn't that right, T-boy?"

"Yes, yes, you shouldn't be by yourself," Thomas piped up from the back seat. "Ms. Robinson is so big – almost as big as dad."

Tisha smiled. "Yes, she is big, isn't she? Were you scared, honey? You sure didn't show it, brave boy."

Thomas blushed and smiled shyly. "Yeah, I was. For sure."

"Tisha," Chase said calmly, trying another tack.

"Yes?"

"I'd, uh, I'd *like* you to come stay with Thomas and I until Ms. Robinson is caught. If that's all right with you."

Thomas looked back and forth between the two.

Tisha relented. "Okay, I'll, uh, stay with you guys... but just for a little bit, okay?"

Thomas nodded excitedly and she gave him the best smile she had, considering the circumstances. "I was very scared too, honey," she whispered over her shoulder, as she reached for Chase's hand and squeezed.

Chase said a silent prayer of thanks that she'd finally agreed. He was all too aware that he'd used his own son as helpful reinforcement to coerce her into staying; but little did she know that he wouldn't let her out of his sight until Andrea Robinson was confirmed under arrest and in jail. He'd help plaster that woman's picture all over the United States until that happened, if necessary.

As the three finally pulled into Chase's driveway, Chase felt a jolt of dread as he noticed a little red sports car already parked there.

Teresa. Thomas hopped out quickly and Chase went around the truck to help Tisha down, all the while racking his brain for some way to welcome Tisha in while getting his ex-wife off his property without delay.

SIXTEEN

———◆———

A NGIE MET THEM AT THE door before Chase could get his key into the lock. "Hi, Angie," he greeted her as he entered. "Will you please run a bath for Tisha and put fresh towels in the guest room?"

Thomas was close behind, pulling Tisha with him excitedly to show her the guest room. Angie nodded and closed the door behind them all. Chase grinned at the pair as they hustled past him.

"Thomas, leave Tisha alone after you show her to her room, okay?" he reminded his son. Thomas nodded, excited to have his favorite teacher over at his house. Ms. Jameson was about to get the grand tour: not only of the guest room, but likely every other room in the house as well.

Chase was relieved that Angie had always been trained with strict instructions about what to do in case of a "Teresa invasion". The first step was always to text him, although he'd missed this one: Angie had in fact texted him thirty minutes ago warning him that Teresa was there.

Step two: put Teresa in Chase's office until he got there. The office was a fairly neutral space: there wasn't anything terribly personal there, and it was private enough that they could talk.

He moved quickly down to the lower level, hoping this wasn't the one time she'd decided to go rogue about his house.

Opening the office door he saw her there, sitting cross-legged on his leather sofa and thumbing through the sports magazines.

"Gosh, where you been all day? You don't have a real job," was her opening gambit.

Chase rolled his eyes. As usual, he knew he'd only have to say no a couple dozen times to her requests before she eventually got bored and left. Tisha wouldn't even have to know she was there.

"Teresa-Malika," he said, to be funny and to annoy her. "How are you?"

"I'm great," she responded airily, ignoring his little name game. "We're shooting a short film in Atlanta. Thought I'd just come by and say hello."

"Great. Hello. Goodbye," he said shortly, opening the door for her to leave.

"What is the rush? You got some new girlfriend or something?" sniffed Teresa-Malika, setting down the magazine. "Well, it better not be Angie. She is not your type," she added pointedly.

Chase pasted a neutral look onto his face. He sat down as if he didn't have a care in the world and looked casually through his phone to locate his lawyer Leland's information. He'd call the man as soon as Teresa left.

"Would you like to see Thomas?" he asked, with a flicker of hope. "I can get him for you."

"Aw, you know he's so over me." She waved a hand.

"No, I don't... pretty sure it's the other way around." Chase took a deep breath.

She rolled her eyes. "Look, can you just give me some money for this film I'm making?"

"What?" Chase said incredulously. "When you make a film, *they* pay *you*, right? I thought that's how it worked."

"Well, look, this one's a bit low budget - an indie flick, if you must know. It doesn't have any real backers, and as you know I'm trying to get my name out there. I just… I need some spending money. Please."

Chase didn't budge. After trying a bit more groveling and a bit more whining, she grew tired of begging as she always did. He was getting tougher: he was proud of himself. All too often in the past, he'd grown so exasperated with her performance that he'd given her any amount of money she asked for just to be done with it all.

It wasn't even the money; it was that she never even said hello to Thomas. Chase often didn't even mention to him that she'd stopped by anymore: it would just hurt him. It hurt Chase too. She'd birthed him, for God's sake: did she feel nothing?

Perhaps that was why Tisha intrigued him so much: she was Teresa's opposite. She obviously cared so much, perhaps even too much, and Thomas talked about her every day. The boy clearly cared for her almost like a mother: like the kind of mother he should have, not the collagen-loaded, fake booty, fake boobies, fake teeth, Brazilian-hair-wearing (he knew all these details from the charges that used to litter his bank statements) woman standing in front of him - whom he once knew, and had once thought he loved. Teresa didn't even need all that, he reflected; but that's what L.A. and all the people she followed on social media demanded of her. She was so obviously insecure, and it irked him.

Tisha, on the other hand, had reservations even about allowing herself to stay at his home for one evening, in her own room with a door that locked and a private bathroom. She clearly had morals, even now that times had changed and social norms were so far gone that such notions were barely there at all.

"What on earth are you thinking about?" Malika-Teresa snapped.

"Nothing," he returned evenly.

"Whatever…"

She got up, not without her usual huffing, and headed for the office door. He was almost home free. She reached the top of the stairs… and it was there that she bumped into Tisha.

"Oh," Teresa said. "Well, hello there. Who are you?"

Tisha was somewhat startled. She smiled hesitantly and greeted the woman. "Hello, I'm Tisha Jameson."

Teresa's smile froze. "Oh, you're Thomas's teacher, right?

"Yes'm, I am – and you are?"

"His *momma*," Teresa said forcefully.

Chase caught up with his ex. "She was just leaving," he said, giving her a pointed glare. "She… dropped off some stuff for Thomas."

"Oh, okay," said Tisha hesitantly. "I was just gonna get some tea in the kitchen…"

"I'll have Angie get it for you. It's no problem."

Chase moved closer to her. He was hating the way it all looked, and he was angry that Teresa had picked this day of all days to drop by. It had almost been six months since her last unexpected visit, the longest she'd ever been absent, and he'd enjoyed every minute of it. He still felt bad for Thomas's sake, but he'd be there for Thomas himself. His son didn't need the drama, he didn't need the drama – and Tisha *definitely* did not need the drama – of Teresa. He was thankful when Tisha went up the stairs again, looking exhausted.

"Nice meeting you, dear," Teresa called melodramatically after her.

"Same, thank you," Tish said cordially and smiled before she turned to continue up the stairs.

As soon as Tisha turned, Chase marched Teresa to the door and didn't let go of her arm until they were safely on the other side of it. He closed the door firmly and maneuvered her over to the wrap-around porch.

"Are you kidding me? Let me go." Teresa raised her voice and yanked her arm away from Chase's grip. "You're going to let *her* stay here, in the same house as my son?" Her skirt strained and rose high on her thighs, exposing plenty of flesh as she crossed her arms. Considering it was still winter, the Macon evenings were cool and her skimpy outfit just wasn't enough to keep her warm.

Chase grew uneasy. "What are you talking about? She was in an accident today – they're looking for someone who attacked her. She's not safe in her home."

"Yeah, right." Teresa rolled her eyes. "*I* heard the news reports."

Chase was wrong-footed. "What news reports?"

Teresa gave an affected little laugh. "Um, it's *all* over the news."

"Real news or fake news? As I recall, the only news you tend to read is about so-called celebrities."

"Well my tastes have matured," Teresa replied demurely. "I look at the local news now, and I use my phone to get alerts about my son's neighborhood." She stabbed at her cell with a scarlet fingernail. "There - see - this alert right here: 'Teacher harms innocent child at - the school Tommy goes to…' So, Mr. Alton, are you harboring a criminal?"

Chase snatched the phone from her lacquered claws, leaving her grasping at air and gaping at the maneuver. She gasped.

"This is a lie. She's not - Tisha is not - guilty," Chase snapped.

"Really? Were you there?" she taunted. She took her phone back and he didn't try to stop her. He'd heard enough: he needed to get Leland over to his house, because the report was clearly all wrong. Chase was suddenly so worried he could hardly see straight.

"According to this report, Chase, honey, an innocent child got hurt today, and Ms. Jameson - a Tisha Jameson - is listed as the last one with the child," Teresa drawled. Then her tone became steely. "If she touches my baby I am going to - to…"

"Ms. Jameson saved Marina, Mom! What are you talking about?"

Neither of them had noticed the door swing open and Thomas walk out onto the porch.

Chase closed the door again to ensure Tisha didn't hear them, but he wasn't about to let Thomas stay - unless Teresa finally decided to talk to him. That's the only way his son was staying out there with her, he resolved. They could even go back to his office or his room… but his guess was that the three of them would only be out there a little longer, even as a part of him still held out hope.

"Hey Tommy, look at you," Teresa began awkwardly. "Y-you are getting so big. Mommy's little man!"

"I'm not little," Thomas replied, quietly but clearly.

"Oh, well, of course. I was just trying to - to set up a time with Daddy to come pick you up." She smiled a smile chock full of too-white teeth.

"You were?" Thomas asked, guarded but maybe a little hopeful. "Well… what were you saying about Ms. Jameson just now?"

"Oh, nothing, honey - just some fake news, you know. All those reporters are saying such mean things about your teacher…"

"They are not true." Thomas was stalwart. "You should meet her. You'd like her."

"Oh, well, you know, so long as she's nice to you, that's all that matters," said Teresa brightly.

Chase's jaw twitched. Ms. Jameson was nicer to his son than his own mother was. Tisha cared; Teresa didn't. He'd just stood there and listened to her lie about what they were speaking about not five minutes ago – lie like she always did. How she did it so easily was beyond him. The lies just rolled off her tongue.

"Thomas, you gotta get ready for bed," Chase cut in. "We'll have some dinner, but go get into your pajamas please. We'll check on Ti – Ms. Jameson in a bit, see if she's hungry." He said it mainly for his son's benefit, but he was curious about how Teresa would react to the comment.

Thomas left and Teresa exhaled a dramatic breath.

"Oh my God, that child is *so* your child," she exclaimed. "He's so intense - so straitlaced! He really likes that Tisha teacher woman, though, doesn't he?"

"She's very kind," Chase answered coldly.

"Well, you know, you picked *me* at one time and you seem to think *that's* such a mistake," Teresa retorted. "Don't go choosing someone so *not* me that you... miss things." She gave a stagey wink.

"I wish I missed you."

She gave another gasp. "That hurt, Chase. I...I..."

He prepared for the final act. It was always the same from her. He prepared his usual tirade to fire back at her.

"You know, Teresa, what you do hurts too - do you ever think about that? You just told Thomas you were talking about scheduling something with him. You know why he doesn't say anything about that? Because he doesn't believe you! This whole thing" - Chase waved a finger between himself and Teresa - "this thing between me and you ain't happening. I've said as much many times, but it's obvious that it's just not registering. You are not welcome here, Teresa."

Night had fallen and so had his emotions. Chase was tired, but he had to make sure that Tisha didn't look at the news - and soon. His thoughts were now focused on getting back to her, and the sooner he got rid of Teresa, the sooner he could do so.

"You don't mean that, Teddy Bear," Teresa pouted, as she moved closer to Chase.

"Look, I'm through, Teresa. We're *divorced*. I don't know what you're up to this time, but I don't have time for it."

He watched Teresa closely, observing her racking her brain for an alternative approach.

"Oh, come on, sweetie," Teresa said, batting her long fake

eyelashes. "I just want some monetary support to get my career off the ground, and don't want to do it through Leland. Psh – lawyers! I have to use a dictionary just to communicate with that man. Can't you meet me for breakfast and we can talk? Just a minute or two, please," Teresa wheedled. She closed the distance between them and placed her hands on the collar of his shirt.

"No, Teresa, we can't. There is nothing to discuss." Chase wasn't sorry for his harsh attitude. He didn't know what else to tell her other than the truth. If it didn't involve time with Thomas, for which Leland could work out some sort of visitation contract, a fair schedule, even compensation so she had no excuse not to do fun things with him - then there wasn't anything. He'd moved on.

He continued to watch her carefully. Life to her was nothing but a stage: a performance in which she held the lead role. Nothing about her roused a single shred of desire within him. Every last penny she'd wrung from him thus far was worn somewhere on her person: various parts of her were either enhanced with silicone or reduced by liposuction. Chase had stopped trying to guess which part and for what purpose her latest alteration had been under- taken. Her self-esteem, or lack of it, and her constant need for money were just two of the many weights that had taken the final toll on their marriage.

"I messed up big, but I... oh, Chase. Nobody loved me like you. I want you back, honey," Teresa said. She moved away from him and paced the length of the top step, flex- ing her hands and looking agitated.

Part of what she said was true - Chase knew that much. She probably did want her family back. She had indeed messed up big, as she put it, and maybe now she finally realized that he had sincerely tried to make something of their marriage, back in the day, and that it was she who hadn't made any effort at all.

"I miss my family... and, Chase, I want another baby. I

regret everything. I'm ready to be a mother to Thomas, and take care of him… and his daddy." She stopped in front of him.

"You want to be a mother?" Chase was incredulous. "I find that hard to believe. Thomas was just here a few minutes ago, and did you even see him? No: instead of really talking to him, you're already spewing lies about someone he cares deeply about."

Teresa bit her lip. "Oh God, Chase, you know, I'm sorry. I just - I saw the news, it just popped up on my phone, I didn't know he -"

"You didn't *know* because you don't know anything about your own child," Chase interrupted. "You have no idea what he likes, who he cares about, how his day was."

"Excuse me, I know I messed up… but you hardly know that woman, do you? Seriously?"

Chase was too tired for this. "Look, I care a lot about her, and yes, I've gotten to know her," he whispered. "And anyway, it's too late for you and I."

Chase felt a twinge of guilt as he watched Teresa's expression change from disbelief to hurt. However, there was no forgiveness in his heart for her – not after all that had happened.

After Thomas's birth, Chase had tried to hold onto his marriage much longer than he should have. As a man who had lost his own father at an early age, he didn't want his son to go through having only one parent in the home. Teresa had bailed before he'd even had a chance to quit football, but after her shock departure he'd made moves quickly to give his son a real home, away from her and all her drama. He shook his head: he couldn't revisit that time with Teresa, ever.

As far as Tisha was concerned, he was realizing more about his feelings for her than he wanted to relay to his ex-wife. Whatever he felt, and he was still working that out, those were very private thoughts. Chase rubbed the back of his neck and sighed in exasperation.

"Look, if you want to build a relationship with Thomas, we can talk about it and make some arrangements." He didn't tell Teresa that Thomas had often asked about her years ago, but that when it had seemed his mother wouldn't be coming around, he had finally stopped. Even his coming outside but not lingering was an indicator that he didn't know her and didn't have a desire to get to know her. He hoped he hadn't projected that on to Thomas. He always tried to talk decently about Teresa no matter what: it was what his mother had done for him about his dad, even though as he aged he'd learned the truth about his father and the way he'd died.

The only threat Teresa had on her life was the stupid decisions she made and the crowds she chose. It was all angled to bring her no good. He didn't wish her any ill will, but she'd likely move on eventually in any case.

"I respect you as Thomas's mother, but you've got to get it out of your head that we're going to get back together. It's over."

Chase stepped back through the door of the house and closed it in Teresa's face.

Teresa stared at the door in disbelief. She heard the lock click as the porch light was turned off, leaving her in darkness. She continued to stare at the door.

"I ain't done yet, you got that?" she murmured to herself. She looked back to her phone and reread the news story on her way to the car. In the seven years of Thomas's life, there'd been no other woman that had stayed under Chase's roof. This Tisha Jameson was... a threat.

That girl is history. In the driveway of the large house that should have been hers, she did a search on Tisha's name, her eyebrows knitted as she read the small text. She revved her engine and backed out of the driveway, looking back at the house once more and pounding her steering wheel with the heel of her hand. "*You're my man, Chase Alton,*" she whispered into the air as she pushed her foot to the floor, loving the speed and the feeling of being out of control as she sped away.

SEVENTEEN

———

CHASE QUICKLY REMOVED HIS REGULAR clothes, trading them for a pair of cotton shorts over his boxers and a long-sleeved undershirt before heading to the guest room.

"Tisha..." He tapped on the door lightly, whispering her name.

Tisha sat up abruptly when she heard Chase's voice. She was still in the tub, and the water sloshed as she moved hastily to get up. Even though the bathwater was tepid by this time, her apartment's tiny shower couldn't compare to this huge tub - with massaging jets, too! The bubble bath that Angie had given her was calming, with notes of mint that soothed her sinuses after all the crying. The onslaught of tears threatened to return, but she pushed them away. She asked God for strength: she would get though this, somehow. She was eternally grateful that Chase had offered to let her stay at his place for a bit.

The knock sounded again and Tish stood from the tub at last to reach for the stack of towels and a white terry robe that still had the tags on it.

"Yes, Chase?" she said.

"Are you okay? Do you need help?"

"No, I'm coming. I'll be out in a minute," she replied. His voice, gentle but tinged with concern, tugged at her heart. She took off her wig and wrapped the towel tightly around her head. She didn't have any of her own things, not even the night cap that she always wore to bed. Here she was, at the home of a man she didn't know that well but who clearly cared for her. It was all so surreal. Tish bent to pull the stopper from the tub and opened the bathroom door. The guest room was dark, but she remembered where the bed was located and walked slowly toward it. "Chase..." she whispered, wondering where he'd disappeared to so quickly.

He came back into the room just as she located her glasses and put them on. She smiled more assuredly at him, thankful she could see. "Hi." She smiled, noticing a small tray in his hands that held a silver teapot and a lone porcelain cup. He set the tray on the bed and moved to her side, a move which both surprised and comforted her.

"Are you all right?" Chase said.

She nodded. "The bath was nice. Angie is your – uh...?"

"Housekeeper," Chase supplied.

"No, I know; I just meant that she's, um, great - and she's very attentive. Does she live here?"

"No, I just asked her to stay a little later tonight. She made some food and she's gone already," answered Chase. "There's no one here but you, myself and Thomas." He paused. "Do you want to come down and have something to eat?"

"Oh no, thank you. I'm just relieved to stay here: this room is so gorgeous and quiet. I love your house."

"You can stay here as long as you like," he answered.

She looked down. "I can't do that, Chase."

"Why not?" He leaned down and placed a gentle kiss on her forehead. "Are you hurting anywhere?"

Tisha thought for a moment, glad for a second question to ponder as she came up with a response for the first. Her side was somewhat irritated, but the ache was tolerable. She shook her head. She didn't want to talk or think about anything else, but she didn't want Chase to leave her just yet. She reached for his hand.

Silence surrounded them for long seconds. She wondered whether Chase would run if she never said a word - and if she told him everything, whether he would run even faster. She took a deep breath and began to whisper. "Chase... I need to tell you some things... some things about... about before I moved to Macon..." she began.

"You don't need to tell me anything," Chase responded softly.

"No. No, you're going to hear some things about me right now. I want the truth to be out, before... before someone misconstrues everything," she protested.

"No," Chase repeated firmly. "I don't have to hear a thing, Tisha."

Tisha scrutinized him. She could tell that the situation irritated him, but she didn't feel that anger directed at her. How could it be, when he sat so close and his hand held hers so firmly?

"I'm sorry about whatever happened back in Virginia - but it all sent you here to me, for a reason," Chase continued.

"Don't say that," she breathed. "It was tragic, it was hard... but it wasn't my fault.

"I *know* it wasn't your fault. I'm saying I believe and trust you with my son. While I don't have the entire story, I have the pieces that I need. The things that preceded your moving here sent you into my life, for this moment and this time and to protect my son. That's what makes me know and feel what I do."

Chase drew a deep breath. "In fact... OK, you can tell me everything - but I want to get my lawyer here first, so you can tell him too. That way, we can ensure the police officers that kept you and the doctors that dismissed you know that you are not responsible." He squeezed her hand. "I can't imagine never having met you."

Tisha laughed, disbelieving how honest he was being. It

was a little scary, yet so endearing.

"Here, this is getting cold," he said, passing her the cup. "Angie said it would help you sleep."

"Is this really happening?" she asked. "I'm spending the night?"

"Your door locks. Heck, you can borrow my Taser if you want," Chase smiled.

"That's ridiculous. I'd probably tase myself, accidentally," she laughed.

Chase returned her smile, his seriousness at their conversation never wavering. "Anyway, I look forward to seeing you smile as much as Thomas does," he continued. "I'm not telling you I don't want to hear about your past. I'm just telling you that whatever it is can surely wait till tomorrow, after you've had some rest and when Leland is here to record what happened - so you only have to tell us just once. Plus, you know what else?"

"What?" He didn't know the relief she felt.

"Thomas told me that you sent him away. He wanted to try and protect you and to help; but he told me that Andrea struck him, and it sounds as though by sending him away, you prevented Andrea from harming him more. I don't need any other information than that to know what kind of person you are. You protected my son. She's going to pay for what she did. I don't believe you would ever hurt anyone. Tomorrow we will work this out, but now you need to rest - unless I can bring you a plate up here. Are you hungry?"

Tish was amazed, but she shook her head. She didn't have a single thought about food.

Chase nodded. "I called my lawyer and he'll be here in the morning. Can you try to get some sleep and call me if you need anything? You gotta let this go for now. Just for now, okay?"

Tisha was relieved at all he said. It gave her the time to process what happened earlier that day and, for the moment, the pressure was off to relive and recount her past. That would help keep her tears at bay for now.

"Thank you," she said to him as she reached up to touch Chase's face. He leaned into her palm, then removed her hand, held it in his own and leaned in to kiss her. Tish turned her face up to his and his lips met hers. Fleeting, warm, barely there at first, then she leaned forward for more.

They broke away and he handed her back the cup of tea. She sipped, her face a mask of emotion: no longer about the dramatic events of the day, but about him.

"I was really scared today" she murmured, "but now I feel…"

"What?" Chase said as he moved closer to her.

"Safe," she concluded.

His arm encircled her shoulders. "I won't let anything happen to you. I promise."

He said goodnight and she thanked him again. He told her where his room was and that there was a phone in her room on the bedside table. He backed away and she wondered if he was just as sad to leave her as she was to be left.

He left the door slightly ajar and she settled back into the pillows with her tea. One night to get herself together and be ready to face the world tomorrow… Just then, it didn't seem as lonely as it once had. Chase was there, and something told her he meant what he said.

She finished her tea and drifted into a restless sleep.

EIGHTEEN

———◆———

"WHY HASN'T JOJO CALLED ME yet, Jina? I called him on base - they don't relay messages very well, but he usually calls me right back."

"I know, Momma," Jina Jameson King said, trying to reassure her mother. "I had them page him, so he should be calling me any minute. Are you *sure* they're talking about Tisha's school?"

Jina seldom doubted her mother, but the thought of a national news report about school violence in Macon, Georgia, at the very same private school Tisha just happened to teach at just didn't seem plausible. Her poor sister had been through enough, but as she listened to what her mother said, she had to admit it was becoming more and more alarming.

"Sure, I'm sure!" her mother exclaimed. "What are you talking about? I'm looking at this evening news man talk about it right here, and I even used my recorder to run it back. Turn to the channel, I told you to turn to the channel!"

"Yes, Momma, you did, but I'm at work right now and I can't – remember? I'm putting the paper to bed, OK? Let me look online." Jina smiled at her mother's insistence. When Alfreah Jameson asked you to do something, you better do it.

"Oh yes, baby. I'm sorry. But now, about your sister…"

Jina grabbed a cell phone from a surprised colleague and pulled up a news app. She scrolled through the reports and quickly saw it: the name of Tisha's school, two children beaten and Tisha's own name there as well, in black and white. Jina's heart sank. Her mother was right to be concerned.

"Momma - I'll call you back."

"What?"

"I found the article. Jojo and I will get on the first plane to Macon, okay?" She prayed that her mother would be placated to know that at least they were doing something tangible.

"Oh goodness, what do they say? Did you find something more, or anything different to what I told ya?"

"No, no, Momma," Jina lied. She wouldn't tell her mother that her youngest child's daughter and face was there plain as day on a local CNN station affiliate.

Jina couldn't be stressed at a time like this, but her sister's antics seemed to stress everyone out, including this move to Macon. They'd all been hoping that things might work out better for her in that small suburb.

Jina reviewed the situation and quickly formulated a plan of action. She'd go home, get an overnight bag and get on the next plane as soon as she got in touch with Jojo. She'd tell her husband, too: after she got to Macon, that is, because he was out of town and wouldn't be able stop her by that time. She'd be with Jojo, so her husband would know that her big brother would be looking out for her.

"Oh, and Momma?" she said as she grabbed her purse. "Tony's out of town for a few days, so just don't mention it until I talk to him, 'kay?"

Jina heard her mother sigh through the receiver. Jina hated it when Tony had to go away, too, but with the morning sickness taking up most of her mornings, she was actually glad to have the time to work most evenings on the paper while he was gone this time around.

She'd made senior editor recently, and the adrenaline of the extra work that came with the promotion had been perfect: right up her alley. Sadly, with the baby coming, she'd have to reduce the scope of her role at work - but it was for a good cause, of course, and it was only temporary.

She'd wanted so badly to get pregnant, and they'd tried for almost a year before it finally happened. She'd be back to the bustling life of the newspaper in no time. After all, up until the pregnancy her work at the paper had pretty much been her life. Now, though, her goals were expanding: she would soon give Tony the child he'd always wanted and complete her family.

Despite the reservations her mother had, she was sure all of her siblings would eventually settle down in a similar fashion and find love like she had. Jina was confident that as soon as it happened for them, they'd each decide they wanted a family of their own, too. A few years ago, a family wasn't what she thought she'd wanted either; but she'd changed, and something told her the baby would change her even more. Just the thought of another life developing inside her had Jina feeling excited and completely petrified all at the same time. What really weighed on her mind of late, however, was the fear of another failed attempt.

She put those thoughts aside and concentrated. She had to get away from her mother so she could call her brother, Jojo.

"Lord, Lord. Just so long as you're taking care of my future grandbaby. I'm telling you, Jina, looks like that'll be it for me. Tisha gonna get herself killed out there, and I don't know what I'm going to do with Jojo and Dean. Don't nobody listen to me! I told your sister to keep her tail here, and now she done gone down there and I just do not know what to do."

"Listen Ma, Tisha is a big girl, she'll be fine," Jina soothed. "Hey, Momma, someone's calling me, it's Jojo. I gotta go."

She didn't actually know if it was Jojo or not - the number was unlisted - but her mother didn't need to know that part.

"Momma, please don't worry. I'll have Tisha talk to you as soon as I get to her, okay?"

"You tell Joe I want TT here this weekend," her mother said firmly. "I'm going to fry him if he don't bring my baby home."

"Yes, I'll try, Momma, but..." Jina said, realizing she was talking to no-one as the line clicked abruptly in her ear. She looked at the phone like she'd been slapped by it. That was her mother all right: always telling you what she wanted, you'd better deliver, and there wasn't room for further argument.

Jina pressed the button to accept the next call and spoke to her brother, relaying everything she knew plus all that had been conveyed to her by their mother. When she finished, she took a deep breath. "So, I'll be ready. Pick me up."

"You must be trippin'. No way," Jojo snorted. "Jina, I'm not about to answer to Tony for taking you on a spontaneous road trip while you're pregnant. I'll go down there myself and see what's up, and I'll call you when I get there."

Jina huffed and reminded him that just because he was older didn't really make him in charge. "Yeah right, Joey!" she blared into the phone. She could just see her brother rolling his eyes at the pet name. She only called him that when she was trying to bully him. Her husband Tony seemed tough, but in reality she knew he was as nervous of her two brothers as they were of him. None of the parties knew the other's feelings, however, and the knowledge came in handy to her whenever she wanted something.

Anthony King had turned into 235 pounds of overprotective mush since his wife became pregnant. He was away on business this week, and it was understandable that Jojo didn't want to be the one left holding the bag if the man returned to find his delicate wife off on some trip without visiting a single doctor to okay her travel.

"I'll tell Tony," Jina snapped. "Just get over to my house and pick me up and stop being so dramatic. See you soon." Jina quickly hung up before he could argue, smirking at how her mother had done the exact same thing to her just minutes earlier. She prayed for her sister and left the building, wondering what on earth little sister, more affectionately known to everyone as TT, had gotten herself into this time.

———◆———

Her time spent at The Village Apartments having been a total waste, Andrea Robinson proceeded to her next plan. Now she stood unobserved in a well-guarded neighborhood of a much higher level of class and money. She looked up, plotting the best way to gain access to the second floor. Considering the circumstances, she knew if she simply called up and asked him to let her in, he'd likely refuse this time.

She'd been here numerous times before; the person she sought knew her well, and while he wouldn't be happy to see her considering today's events, he was the only person that could help her out of this mess. Whatever his decision, she wouldn't go down alone.

Andrea walked slowly toward the building. She checked the profiles of those that came and went. Of course: a bunch of uppity professionals were the only ones who could afford to live in such a place. People like the Jamesons, no doubt. Why Ms. Jameson chose to live in a moderately-priced apartment building was beyond her. No one ever got rich being a teacher - but Andrea had no doubt that Tisha Jameson's nerd doctor of a brother, her newspaper hack of a sister, and last but not least her eldest brother, a top-ranking military officer, could more than afford to put her up nicely.

That woman was just... different, though. Challenging her character, Andrea was realizing, might have been a mistake. However, the Jamesons had everything Andrea Robinson longed for but would never have. People like them needed people like her in their lives to take them down a notch or two, she reckoned.

She continued to watch the entrance of the building, waiting patiently.

"Oh, let me help you," Andrea said as she sprang up to help an elderly lady with her groceries. She bent down to pick up the brown paper bag the woman had dropped near the door.

"Oh, thank you, dear," the woman said absently as she opened the secured door with her key fob, and walked through, with Andrea right behind her. Andrea smiled, handed the old lady her bag back and waved a hand as the woman shuffled on her way.

Casually, Andrea moved to the stairwell and took the steps slowly, one at a time. In her previous visits to the same place, she had used the elevator, but this visit was different.

Chris Jeeter sat watching the local news in disbelief. One hand clutched the remote while the other held his cell phone to his ear, allowing him to listen to the advertisements for Decker, Dobson and Thompson drone on and on. When the automated ads stopped abruptly as the phone was picked up at the other end, he didn't wait for an introduction.

"Where the hell have you been? I've been trying to call you and get a real voice since this whole mess ensued. Have you seen the news?"

"Sir, sir! Please calm down. I'm sorry, but your party cannot be reached at this time. I'll gladly take down your name and number and see that Mr. Dobson gets your message."

"What the hell? Why the heck was I on hold for so long? Why wasn't I connected to his voice mail?" Chris snapped.

"Sir, please calm down. Mr. Dobson's mailbox is full. I'm just the answering service. I'll gladly—"

"Oh, the hell with you," Chris shouted. He was turning the volume up louder on the television in irritation when three loud raps sounded on the door. He quickly moved to answer it, wondering who would bother him at this time of night. As he yanked open the door, his heart sunk. He tried to close the door, but she was stronger than he was, and in the next minute Andrea Robinson had forced her way into his apartment.

NINETEEN

———◆———

CHASE AWOKE TO WHAT SOUNDED like someone trying to beat down his front door. He'd slept through the motion-sensing alarm, but he looked at his security camera to see two people standing in the cold at his front door: a woman wrapped up in lots of gray wool all the way up to her neck, a big hat, and a very tall man beside her.

The banging stopped for mere seconds before it commenced again. Chase put on clothes and hurried down the steps. He checked his phone again and pressed the button that would allow him to talk to the people at his door.

"Uh, hello, can I help you?"

"Where's Tisha?" a gruff male voice said, before the other figure shushed him. Realizing who the visitors must be, Chase nervously unbolted the locks and opened the door.

Chase didn't know Tisha's second brother, but if looks could kill Chase knew he was a goner. The tall man's bald head was shiny and glinting in the porch light, and he was sporting Army fatigues. Chase quickly wiped the sleep from his eyes and stepped back. By the looks of things, if ever someone needed an escort to meet the devil, this man was probably the one who could take you.

"Where's Tisha?" the man said curtly, again. His arms were crossed over his chest and his stance grew even more intimidating, if that were possible.

A woman about Tisha's height stepped forward and cast

a withering glance at the man. "Would you just stop it, Jojo!" she said before turning to Chase. She smiled sweetly and extended her hand. "Hi. I'm Jina Jameson-King. I'm Tisha's sister. And this, unfortunately, is her brother Joseph. Tisha isn't here, is she? We've been trying to call her cell phone - we heard the news..."

Chase shook the hand Jina offered and relaxed immediately.

"Yeah, sure. Come on in. She's asleep," he said. "Um... in the guest bedroom," he added quickly, when their eyebrows raised. "Please, come into the den."

Chase closed and locked the front door behind them before leading the way to the large living room just down the hall. There were plenty of couches and a large-screen television, and some of his sports memorabilia collection decorated the walls.

Chase tried to relax as Jina took a seat on the edge of the sofa, while Joseph continued to stand. "I'm Chase," he offered for lack of anything to say. *They probably already know that, you dummy.* Despite Joseph's thunderous look, Chase tried to appear self-assured and confident. He thought about giving a mock salute, in reference to the fatigues, or at least telling Joseph that he could be at ease. He wasn't sure, however, whether the man would get his attempt at humor or take offense. Also, he wouldn't know which hand to raise in salute... In the end, he did and said nothing.

He decided that he'd focus on Jina, who didn't look like her sister at all, except for some of the kindness in her eyes and maybe some of her mannerisms. Since the fire, everyone else in the family had darker skin coloring than Tisha.

"I guess you heard what happened." Chase took a seat across from Jina.

"Yes, that's why we're here," Jina began. "Is she all right? What have the police said? We're from Virginia, but heard it on the national news. We got a flight out as soon as we could…" She indicated her brother. "Jojo here looked up where you lived. Tisha has mentioned your name but, uh, I'm sorry we bothered you so early this morning. We did try to call Tisha…"

Chase waved a hand. He looked out the window for a second and noticed that daylight had begun to peep through. "It's all right," he assured her as he leaned forward, bracing his arms on his knees. After taking a deep breath, he began to tell them what he knew about what had happened earlier that day. He discussed his son, Thomas, how he knew Tisha, what had transpired when he went to pick Thomas up from school, and finally the incident at the police station to get Tisha.

Chase finished. Throughout the tale he had tried to look at both Jina and Joseph. His eyes rested on Joseph's and he watched as Jina took a deep, exasperated breath.

"Would you sit down already! You're making us nervous." Jina looked back at Chase, smiled apologetically and continued talking. He didn't dare cast a glance at Joseph, who stood for only seconds after his sister's prompting and then quietly took a seat on the sofa next to her.

"Our sister is very headstrong and stubborn. We've been asking her to come back home, but she's determined to make it down here in this godforsaken place. Oh, sorry - I mean — well, wait… you're not actually from here, are you?" she stammered.

Chase smiled, "No, no. It's fine, I'm not from here. It's okay." Then panic set in as Chase pondered Jina's words and the mention of the possibility that Tisha would move back to Virginia. *Is that why they are here, to take her back home? Does she want to go back home?*

Chase assured himself that Tisha had said nothing about going back to Virginia, but considering what she'd been through, he couldn't blame her if she now wanted to after all.

"Well, uh, the only reason I brought Tisha here is that

they haven't caught the Robinson woman yet. I thought she'd be safer here than at her place," he added.

"And just what do you want from my sister?" Joseph, who'd been a silent observer until now, spoke up, looking pointedly at Chase.

"I... I want to be her friend, and..." He paused, deciding that if there was anyone to convince about his motives where Tisha was concerned, Joseph Jameson was it, and Chase had better make it good. Tisha meant a lot to him, but the fact was that he really hadn't had the opportunity to get to know her just yet. His feelings just kept coming every time he was near her, and that must mean something.

He looked Joseph in the eye. "I care a lot about your sister," he began, addressing both Joseph and Jina, "and I'm trying to keep her safe, just like her own family would do. That's all." He took a breath, hoping that would suffice. That disclosure, however it came across, felt important.

Chase turned his gaze back toward Jina. She nodded to him encouragingly and he felt that at least his answer met her requirement. Jina Jameson-King was a lot like Tisha. In just seconds, he could tell she was friendly. A little more on the outspoken side than her sister, very direct, but still kind.

Having Jina around until Tisha woke up just might ease any encounter with Joseph. Even Dean hadn't seemed as unfriendly and cold as Tisha's older brother. "Uh... where's Dean?" asked Chase.

"We couldn't reach him. We think he's out of town at a convention. But we left messages," Jina offered.

Chase nodded. "Well, Tisha is in the first bedroom on the right. I called my lawyer, he'll be here in the morning..." Chase looked at his watch, realizing it was morning already. "Ah, a little later today," he corrected himself.

"Do you really think that's necessary?" Jina said.

"I didn't want to, but yes. The police kind of interrogated her. I mean, they asked her a lot of questions, and they had nothing to charge her with. The fact that they haven't found Ms. Robinson is alarming and the child, Marina Stamos, is in very bad shape. I only called him so that we have someone here who knows your sister's legal rights and can look at this objectively. I honestly don't know." Chase shrugged. "He can at least make a statement to the press for her and act as a buffer. I also called a doctor friend of mine to look at Tisha tomorrow."

Jina stood, her eyes round with questions. "Is it really that bad? You made it seem like it wasn't that bad!" she accused. "Shouldn't we take her to the doctor now?"

"Well..." *Oh jeez*, Chase thought. He had revealed too much information. Jina Jameson only looked like Tisha: she was obviously nowhere near as calm. "I think the doctor she saw treated her so hastily because he believed she was responsible for the child's injuries," Chase said gently. "He dismissed her, saying she was okay. She was very ache-y, but I'm not that worried. Just another precaution, that's all."

Jina nodded. She sat down and looked at Chase. "My sister, Chase… she's been through a lot."

"I know," Chase nodded.

Jina looked up abruptly. "You know? About everything? She told you?" she questioned in disbelief.

Chase shook his head. *She had tried to tell him.* "Not— not in so many words. I know that she blames herself for Melinda's death, but I don't know any more details. I told you, I care for her, and I've seen nothing to put doubts in my mind about what kind of person she is."

Joseph spoke up. "Big words you're putting out there, Alton."

Chase looked at him. Tisha's brother was getting on Chase's nerves, but he remained polite in the face of what he knew was an insult and a challenge to what he had said.

"I'm a person of my word," he said to Joseph.

"I'm glad she met you, Chase," Jina countered solemnly.

"If she told you about what happened, then that's huge news. It means she trusts you. She's never talked about it to anyone, barely even to us. You're right, though, she has blamed herself and it wasn't her fault - not at all."

Chase nodded. He was glad their sister had come into his life, too.

"Would you like something to drink? Juice or soda?" Chase stood, addressing them both. When Joseph shook his head, he queried Jina.

"Water is fine." Jina replied. "Thank you."

TWENTY

TISHA TURNED ONTO HER STOMACH for the third time that night. Chase had checked on her earlier and he'd stayed with her a long time; she had no idea when he'd left. She kept seeing visions of Marina Stamos and Andrea's imposing stance over her; then the image would shift to Melinda's lifeless body. Each time Tisha awoke, it was with terror and sweats. She fought the urge to get up. Sleep reclaimed her each time, but it was hard-won.

A familiar, soothing voice drifted through Tisha's awareness: "Wake up, Baby girl…" It reminded her of home. *Daddy? No, that couldn't be Daddy. But Joseph… Jojo?* Joseph Jameson Junior could handle anything. But what on earth would he be doing here? And Dean and Jina - were they here too? Was something the matter? *Daddy… is something wrong with Daddy?*

Startled awake by the progression of her thoughts, she sat up suddenly, blinking rapidly to adjust her eyes to the dark. She knew for sure that Jojo was near when she caught the familiar scent of his cologne.

"Baby girl," a husky voice repeated.

"Jojo?" Disbelieving, Tisha felt his big arms come around her and hug her tight. "Oh, Jojo, what are you doing here?"

"You know what I'm doing here, T.T. We're here to get you out of this mess you done got yourself into."

All eyes turned to the bathroom as the door opened,

spilling light into the darkened room. Jina ambled out, fixing her hair and clothes. "What? I have to pee every two hours. This child has a serious bladder problem."

Laughing, Tisha scrambled from the bed to embrace her sister. She hugged her as close as possible given the round baby belly, squinting to get a good look at her in the dim light. "Look at you! You look so beautiful."

"How would you know?" Jina replied. "You're blind as a bat."

Everyone laughed, including Jojo; but Jina's face quickly sobered as she looked at her sister.

"Where's the sucker that hit you, girl? That's why we're here." She cupped Tisha's chin and turned her face to the light, scowling as she took in the cut on the corner of her mouth.

Jojo moved quickly from the bed to turn on the overhead light for a better look at Tisha's face. "Jesus, Tisha. What'd you do now?"

Tisha shrugged away from her siblings and shook Jina's hand away. "I didn't do anything," she huffed. Although she knew her siblings didn't truly believe that she *had* done anything, their questions were bringing back what had happened and the reason they had come to see her, when all she wanted to do was pretend it had never happened.

Tisha looked at Jina and smiled sadly. Placing an arm around her sister's shoulder, she directed her to the bed. "Come sit down," Tisha said. "I can't believe you waited this long to tell me you were pregnant. I'm so mad at you."

"Hey, I knew Dean couldn't keep his mouth shut. Wait till I get him." Jina raised an eyebrow. "And don't try to change the subject: we're not talking 'bout me here, Tisha Tyrell Jameson. Tell me about this heifer that messed with my kid sister."

Tisha took a deep breath. No hiding place would be far enough away to keep her family from finding out and coming to check up on her. She knew they cared, but just once she'd like to be the one to invite them first.

"Look, let me get dressed, then I'll come down and we'll talk. Did you meet Chase?" She looked at Jina, who returned her elated smile, then turned eagerly to Jojo, who merely grunted.

"Yeah, we met him," he growled. "Just what do you know about that man, anyways? You're here looking mighty comfy with him." Jojo cast a dark glance at both his sisters.

"Oh Jojo, gimme a break. I'll have you know he's absolutely wonderful, so just get used to it," Tisha shot back.

"You know," Jojo replied, "Mr. Alton and I couldn't really have a man-to-man conversation with Ms. Talkative here in the room" — he jerked a thumb at Jina — "so I'll just go down and ask him a few more questions now. Maybe I'll ask him about a criminal record, any involvement with drugs, deadly weapons... I can check if he's here legally, and oh, let's see, anything else that comes to my mind."

"What little mind you got," Jina quipped, and Tisha chuckled.

Jojo raised his brows, then headed for the door. "See you two in a minute."

"Jojo, Jojo! You will not, please - don't you dare embarrass me!" Tisha bellowed in frustration, suddenly alarmed as Jojo marched purposefully out of the door.

Despite the number of people in the room, the den was a quiet place, penetrated only by the smooth voice of Leland McGehee, Esquire. With her hands folded in her lap, Tisha sat next to Chase, listening intently. Dean had arrived soon after the dignified lawyer that morning.

Mr. McGehee was a debonair man: tall, with kind eyes that were bright and alert despite the early hour. His clothes were crisply starched, and Tisha could tell by his appearance alone that he'd handled many cases and was more than up to the task of helping her.

She was nervous about speaking to him at all, but Chase persuaded her that it was for the best. Her confidence grew the more he spoke. Leland McGehee was kind enough to introduce himself to everyone. He rattled off a long list of his competencies as a lawyer, as well as an explanation of how he'd known Chase's father, and how after his good friend had died, Leland had stepped in and taken Chase under his wing as the son he never had.

Leland also recounted how he had represented Chase through his divorce and the custody battle for Thomas. Only then did he proceed to the seriousness of the matter Tisha currently faced. It was clear to Tisha that Leland McGehee was not just Chase's lawyer but also a close friend and colleague. It sounded as though Mr. McGehee, who asked them all to call him Lee, had been a fatherly figure for Chase after his dad had died.

Tisha didn't have to wait long before the questioning began. She had her own questions, but before she had a chance to ask them, her brothers bombarded the lawyer with a veritable quiz. Jojo's tone especially was outright offensive; but to her surprise and relief, Leland McGehee continued to address both her brothers calmly and with seemingly limitless patience.

Tisha looked across the oak table at her sister. Jina's eyelids were drooping, and Tisha realized she was struggling to stay awake. Exhaustion came with pregnancy, Tisha thought happily, and resolved that the very next order of business would be to get her sister's stubborn pregnant self back home. Jina was barely two months along, and Tisha refused to put her sister in any kind of danger. If Tisha had to call Tony on her, she would. She shouldn't be staying in Macon anyway, and Tisha was surprised that protective old Tony had let her come alone.

She was snapped out of her reverie by a question from Leland. "I'd like to know about the incident in Virginia,

Tisha." He looked around the room, clearly expecting a protest. He wasn't disappointed.

"What the hell for?" Jojo exclaimed.

Dean spoke up as well. "That's in the past: irrelevant."

Tisha drew a deep breath. The lawyer's question was warranted, of course: Leland needed to know her past in order to help with her present. Chase immediately grabbed Tisha's hand and squeezed it, reassuring her.

"Leland, is that really necessary?" Chase asked.

"Hell no, it ain't necessary! What's the point in knowing any of that?" Jojo continued. "It happened last year and my sister is trying to forget all that crap. We're not going to sit here and rehash it all." He looked at Tisha. "It's time to go, Tisha. There are plenty of jobs back in Virginia."

"Jojo, would you quit it?" Jina sat up, rubbing her tired eyes. She reached for the water, took a sip and replaced it on the table.

"He's right, J," Dean put in.

"Gimme a break, you guys... and stop talking for her, Deanie. He's not right, he just thinks he is," Jina said to Leland.

"I am too right. I said it's time to go and it is. She needs to get away from all this. It ain't doing us no good rehashing the same old mess to yet another lawyer," Jojo said, fixing Leland with a disgruntled stare.

Tisha sat, watching them. It had always been this way: she was used to it. The only people going back to Virginia, however, were her three siblings. They'd come on an overbearing rescue mission with thoughts of taking her home, where they thought she belonged and should have never left. But the truth was that Macon was her home now. Chase watched with raised eyebrows as Jojo, Dean, and Jina continued to argue as if there was nobody else in the room.

Tisha scooted to the edge of her seat. "Just stop it, okay. Just shut up!" She looked at Dean and Jojo and then at her sister. "The three of you can't decide stuff for me anymore, you know, so quit squabbling."

In the old days, Tisha had willingly let her older sister and brothers figure things out for her. Because they did so without her having to ask, it had been easy. Nowadays she realized what a mistake that had been.

She thought quickly. "I need some stuff for my eyes from the store," she said, rubbing her eyes somewhat dramatically. "I don't have any more," she lied. "Dean, you know what it's called. Jojo, can you go with Dean, please?"

"What kind of store is open at this hour of the morning, Tisha?" Jojo replied skeptically.

"The Super WalMart is open 24 hours," Chase put in quickly, earning a deadly stare from Jojo. "I'll write down the directions," he added, moving to his desk to find a notepad.

"Jina, I think you should go lie down in the guest room for a little while," Tisha said meaningfully, when her sister looked as if she wasn't going to budge.

Dean moved casually to the door and took the paper Chase held. He looked back at Jojo, who moved slowly to stand at his side, staring at Chase.

"Why don't you take a ride with us?" Jojo said as he neared Chase.

"Um..." Chase looked uncertainly at Jojo, then Dean, then at Tisha, silently pleading for her assistance. "Okay..." he agreed hesitantly, trying to maintain his confident air.

"No!" Tisha stood and grabbed Chase's arm. "I - I want you to stay with me." She looked up at Chase's face and he nodded.

"What? How does *he* get to—" Jojo replied with outrage, but his protestations were cut short as Dean pushed him out of the room and toward the front door.

TWENTY-ONE

A NGIE VALENTI MADE HER WAY through the auto-matic doors of the WalMart Supercenter. On days like this, she thanked God for such 24-hour conveniences. She pushed the heavy cart awkwardly over the bump at the entrance. Last night had been a rough one, and if the day hinged on the night, she didn't hold out much optimism for its positive progression.

"Ange? Ange?" A little voice broke into Angie's consciousness. She looked down at the small child seated in the cart she pushed along.

"Yes, Cassie?"

She was supposed to be Aunt Angie to her niece and nephew, but they never managed both words in one sentence. They weren't to know that their deceased mother had also called her Ange when they were growing up. Angie wondered whether they saw any small part of their mother in her, and if they might some day call her Mother. Regardless of what they called her, Angie hoped she was doing a good job raising them.

Looking away, Angie concentrated on the numerous boxes of cereal lining the shelves, trying to remember which one they liked best.

"Cass, I said I'd get your cereal - now settle down or you'll wake Casey," she admonished. She looked over the child's head of unruly hair to see that Casey still slept soundly, his little body scrunched awkwardly in the cart.

"Now, which one does your brother like, again? The Peanut Butter Crunch or the regular?"

Angie couldn't remember, but Cassie would know. The child knew anything and everything you cared to ask her. At the age of five, the little girl didn't hesitate to voice the abundance of things that came to her little mind, and when Casey merely grunted his preferences, his sister never failed to translate what he was trying to say.

"He likes the regular Crunch. He got sick on the peanut butter kind last time, remember?" she sang. "He threw up and had to go number two," she said dramatically, then proceeded to hold up two fingers and wrinkled her nose in disgust.

Angie rolled her eyes. "Yes, I remember," she said patiently. "But there's no need to keep talking about it. He got a little sick, was all."

Angie grabbed the box, placed it in the cart and continued along the aisle, trying to remember the rest of the things she needed and berating herself for forgetting her list.

"Kin I please get down now, Ange?" Cassie said restlessly, shifting around in the cart. "Please," she added again.

"Okay, but what are the rules?" Angie asked. Moving to the side of the cart, she lifted the child and placed her on her feet.

Putting a hand on her hip, Cassie tapped her foot impatiently. "No runnin' and behave, don't talk to strangers." She held up her tiny pointer finger and shook it at Angie as if Cassie were the adult and Angie was the child, just as she'd been admonished so many times before.

Angie laughed as they proceeded, slowly, through the store.

———◆———

"Say, what do you know 'bout this cat, anyways? And what about that old ass lawyer?"

Jojo gestured impatiently as Dean marched beside him into the store. "And where the hell you been, anyway?" he added testily. He waited a beat as the electric doors of the store slid open. Without knowing which way to go, he simply kept pace beside his brother.

"I'm supposed to be in Atlanta right now for a latest-in-laser-eye-surgery seminar. I changed my flight schedule when I got Momma's call," Dean replied.

Jojo squinted into the brightness, the stark lights assaulting his own eyes. Once Dean located the aisle he needed, he bent to check out the prices of saline solutions and eye-baths lining the shelves. "I don't know a whole lot about him — about Alton, I mean," Dean clarified. "He's okay, I guess – seems pretty harmless." Dean looked away from Jojo's incredulous stare. "Just calm down," he continued. "She's fine. I admit, I had reservations when I first met him. He thought... he thought Tisha was white, or mixed or adopted or something. I really don't know what he thought, but he was initially rude."

"Jackass," Jojo muttered under his breath.

"It's not unfathomable, Jo. He's cool, he's taking care of her, and she obviously loves him."

"What? She *loves* him? What the hell — we're too late?" Jojo exclaimed in despair.

"Chill out! You are way too uptight, man — s'matter with you anyways?" Dean eyed his brother warily. "You been acting crazy and I don't know what your problem is. What's Tamara been up to, anyway?"

Jojo rolled his eyes. It'd been months since he'd seen her, yet since he hadn't yet told his family that it was over they didn't know not to ask.

"You in the doghouse with her? That why you so uptight?" Dean asked knowingly, when Jojo didn't respond.

"Don't bug me 'bout no females," Jojo snapped. "And what about you? Did you even know that Chyna was back in town?"

Jojo smiled smugly and crossed his arms over his chest, taking on a stance reminiscent of his father. He quickly unfolded them, and not knowing what else to do, he simply let them hang by his sides as he continued to eye Dean in triumph. He'd turned the tables on his brother and he felt satisfied.

Dean turned away at his brother's question. "Yeah," Dean whispered, and then, more forcefully, "I heard."

He took a deep breath. "So what - she's married, ain't she? What the heck that got to do with me?" he continued, before Jojo could answer. "She's the one who skipped town without so much as a word. Think I got time for that? She's moved on with her life and I moved on with mine."

"You're part of the reason she left, Who-Deanie."

"Shut up," Dean replied. "We're not even talking about me, we're talking about you. I repeat: what's got you so uptight about TT and Alton?" After checking the ingredients, Dean selected the product he wanted and turned to face his brother.

"*Nothing*," Jojo replied angrily. He thrust his hands into his pants pockets and backed away. "I'll wait for you in the car." He turned on his heel and left.

Jojo made his way to the doors and decided he was thirsty. The small refrigerators conveniently located at the front of the store caught his eye. He opened one of them to grab a bottle of water when the stomp of feet hurrying past diverted his attention. He would have ignored the child if he hadn't seen a uniformed employee of the store hurrying after her.

"Come back here, you little thief." the woman yelled.

"No, you big fat meanie!" the child yelled back. Her large eyes were puffy and swollen from crying.

In seconds, Jojo was at the child's side, despite his better judgment telling him he'd better not get involved.

"Now then, what's all the fuss?" He squatted before the

little girl and looked into her eyes.

"Are you her father?" the woman inquired angrily as she reached the two of them. Jojo didn't answer. He simply watched the woman as she took a deep breath and wiped the sweat from her brow before continuing: "If so then you need to teach your child some manners, and not to steal." She leaned closer to the girl and spoke low: "People go to jail for stealing, do you understand, little girl? They lock you up and throw away the key, you ungrateful little..."

Abruptly, Jojo stood to tower over the woman. The small amount of hair covering her head was slicked back with shiny goop. Thin in patches, it revealed her weathered scalp and was grayed at the root but jet black at the ends. Her bosom heaved as she straightened back up, noticing for the first time how tall Jojo was. Placing her hands on her hips, she took a deep breath, clearly winded from the run. Jojo continued to stare at her.

"Now you need to just calm down," he began. "I'm sure there's just a little misunderstanding here."

"Don't patronize me," the woman snapped. "Teach your daughter a lesson about thievery and she won't grow up to be a criminal."

Jojo didn't correct the woman about the kid not being his: he was afraid that might somehow subject the little girl to even greater wrath. Instead of becoming angry with the woman for her overreaction in accusing a young child of theft, he pasted on a placating smile and spoke more calmly than he felt: "Look Ms."—he noticed the name tag — "Charmaine..."

"I said I didn't do it. I put the candy back," the girl declared loudly, interrupting him.

Jojo turned to the girl. "You put it back?"

She started to cry again. "I don't want Ange to get mad at me... I didn't take it."

"See, Ms. Charmaine, she didn't take it. Now why are you all in a huff?" Jojo's heart wasn't in his words, but still he reasoned with the woman. What he really wanted to do was tell her to step off. She was probably the same type of woman that beat up Tisha. Women like her hated kids, so they beat them physically or verbally as a way to relieve their anger and unhappiness with their own lives.

"She didn't steal the candy, did you, baby girl?" He looked at the little girl, who shook her head in earnest. "But I'll be sure to talk to her, okay?" Jojo said as he patted the woman on the shoulder. "Thanks so much for letting me know," he finished. The woman looked at the child briefly. Her gaze hadn't softened and her mean streak was still acting up, but thankfully she turned to leave.

"Mean old lady," Jojo said under his breath and winked at the girl, who blessed him with a big smile.

"Yeah, she's mean - and *big*!" she replied with relish.

"So now we gotta find your mommy, huh?" Jojo said.

"Cassie! I told you not to run off, didn't I?" Angie huffed as she ran up to them. Jojo saw the panicked concern on her face as she neared them. She scooped Cassie up to place her safely in the metal cart, beside another young boy who looked the same age.

"I'm sorry, thank you, uh - "

"He's nice," the little girl piped up.

Angie softened when she noticed the puffy eyes and little red nose.

"Uh, okay, but what happened? What's the matter?" She looked to Jojo, not knowing what to make of the situation. "I'm Angie, by the way."

"She just had a run-in with the devil's Auntie," Jojo offered with a chuckle.

Angie looked somewhat bemused and smiled cautiously.

"But she's cool now," Jojo went on, "isn't that right, Cassie?" When Cassie nodded, Jojo reached out and playfully mussed the girl's head of black hair. "Some store employee who's unhappy about life and the fact that her diets don't work was just being mean to Cassie here. She's good now."

He looked at Angie's hair, noticing that it wasn't anything like the girl's. There was some resemblance, perhaps, but the woman's hair was thick, almost auburn, and it looked as though she hadn't taken a comb to it in days.

"All's well, right?" he repeated. The little girl nodded. He noticed that Angie's hair was parted down the middle, wavy as it rested on her shoulders. She was a few inches shorter than he and she wore a loose-fitting jogging outfit, obscuring her voluptuous curves. Jojo drew his eyes away long enough to glance at the little boy sitting in the cart: a silent observer. The boy's large eyes took him in, but he didn't say a thing.

"How are you, little man?" Jojo inquired. The boy only blinked, but kept his eyes on Joseph.

"He doesn't..." Cassie cut in, then trailed off when Angie gave her a warning look. She smiled apologetically at Jojo, letting the little girl's words hang in the air.

"Well, uh... thank you," said Angie at last, and grasped the handle of the cart ready to push it again - away from him this time.

"What's ya name?" Cassie inquired.

"My name's Joseph... but you can call me Jojo."

"Well uh, thanks... Joseph," Angie said. Then she was gone, berating the little girl in a low voice about talking to strangers and for leaving her side.

Jojo watched them go, the little girl leaning to the side and waving him goodbye. He waved back. He forgot about buying a drink and headed straight for the car. He knew now that he needed to get out of Macon and back to Virginia.

TWENTY-TWO

———◆———

CHASE SAT PATIENTLY AS, AT last, Tisha began to describe to him and to Leland the tragic complexities of what had happened to a child she once taught.

The girl's name was Melinda. Tisha had grown to love her as one of her own, and she had of course thought at the time that what she did was the right thing. Tisha had the child removed from abuse at the hands of her parents and got the Department of Child Protective Services to place her into what they had assured Tisha was a very stable, loving and reputable foster home, with an elderly couple. There was an abundance of volunteers who mentored the twelve children in their care there, and who assisted the elderly couple with some household duties.

As Tisha had seen Melinda daily over the weeks and months that followed, she had noticed with growing concern that her bruises weren't healing. Some were actually getting worse. Armed with the connections the Jameson family had in the community, Tisha had begun a long and drawn-out battle to investigate the home and anyone affiliated with it. She explained breathlessly that the foster home had been awful, and that the only solution had been to shut it down.

In the midst of it all, Tisha said, she had even thought to adopt the child as her own - which meant even more time on the case and more obstacles - but she had been too late. They were being relocated one by one; but the rig-marole of politics, red tape, procedures and overburdened case managers elongated Tisha's fight. At the eleventh hour, Social Services managed to find homes for all the kids.

The process for everything had taken too long, and Melinda, as the last child left in that evil home before being relocated, had been punished brutally in retaliation for Tisha's relentless inquiries.

Tisha always felt that maybe if she had just left Melinda with her family in the first place, she might have had a chance. She would never know for sure, but doubt about what she had started constantly plagued her. That was why she had blamed herself when Melinda had been found dead.

The Jameson family was a prominent, well-to-do family in Springfield, VA, and at first the whole community had rallied behind Tisha. But as the trials dragged on, people's support had begun to waver. Some began to whisper that Tisha should've minded her own business, even as others still said she did the right thing and had, after all, saved eleven other children. Still, Chase knew that Tisha still wondered about it herself.

As Tisha told the story, she became overwhelmed with grief. Chase prodded Leland, who nodded in understand-ing, and fetched a box of tissues. Chase dabbed gently at her tears.

The home had finally been closed down, and while only two arrests were made, a small amount of justice was far better than none at all. Chase believed Tisha had done all that she did because she cared about what happened to people, and especially to children. The children in that home had been defenseless against all that they'd suffered, and only one person had risen up to take their tormentors down.

Chase was angry, wishing he knew the right words to say. He knew how much courage it must have taken her to question that foster family. Who would suspect the motivations of a couple willing to take in twelve children? To most, only a saint would do something so noble; yet, as she'd uncovered, they weren't noble at all. Under the veil of all the heartwarming human-interest stories about this old couple and what they were doing to save these 'throwaway' children, greed, abuse and other horrible conditions had been secretly festering.

Her story finished at last, Tisha was crying softly - so was Jina. Chase passed her the tissues but continued to hold Tisha until she was done. At that moment, he knew that she had burrowed so deep into his heart, God help him if he ever lost her.

———◆———

As Dean and Jojo entered the room, Leland shuffled papers and organized the notes he'd taken. Tisha sat up, wiping her eyes. "What now, Lee?" Chase asked.

Leland paused as Jojo and Dean reclaimed their seats. He looked at Chase, Tisha, and then everyone else in the room.

"First, I need the doctor's report," Leland announced.

"He should be here soon," Chase said, looking at his watch.

"He can edify me on some of the medical jargon for my statement," the lawyer continued. "Then I'll send a condensed report to the police. I'll be in touch with the school principal: he may have his own lawyer already. Meanwhile, it's worth noting that the authorities' hastiness in this entire matter has been simply unconscionable."

Leland glanced through some papers from his briefcase. "It seems the media has been all over the Department for some time due to their incompetence. According to a recent article, they lack focus, often miss important information, have improper evidence collection practices, and lack a certain level of general credibility. I'll bring that up as well. I can at least shift some of the doubt created by curiosity about you, Tisha, and redirect it to the Department's own lack of legwork and comprehensive investigation to help ensure that the real culprits are brought to justice. Robinson will be mentioned, rest assured; and I'll dispel any speculation about what happened in Virginia."

Leland scanned his written notes. "I think you should contact this Mrs. Wellington, the teacher that called 9-1-1, and we can see what other teachers have to say about Tisha and Ms. Robinson," he added. "I can approach them. They probably won't take kindly to me without any introduction, but oh well. If you and Mrs. Wellington have befriended each other, then that's one more person on your side. It's abhorrent, really, just how much misinformation has spread in a matter of one night. I gathered many news reports for review and will take them all to task for false reporting and lack of verification."

"Why can't we sue for… for defamation of character or something?" Jojo wanted to know.

"Excellent point, Mr. Jameson," Leland replied crisply. "What I've read is certainly cause for suit, and I can cross that bridge soon. First, though, let's nip these reports in the bud."

Chase was glad: what his old friend Lee said seemed to quell his doubts. "The media is a mouthpiece for the community's thoughts," Leland went on, "and their views generally represent the local majority. Sure, they are supposed to tell both sides of the story unbiased by any personal suspicions, but the fact remains they don't. Hence, it will be important to ensure that Tisha can remain here and have a life. This mustn't be tried in the court of public opinion." Leland sighed. "Someone always sees fit to promote one side with more vigor, and the people begin to buy into that subtle brainwashing, even though they believe they are forming their own opinions based on all the facts presented."

Jojo straightened visibly. "That sounds well and good, but you are a lawyer, after all. Isn't that what you guys are paid to do: *sound* good? No doubt Alton here pays you top dollar."

Before Tisha could respond, Angie entered the room, carefully balancing a tray of steaming cups to offer coffee or tea to everyone.

"No, no coffee for me, thank you," Jina said, patting her belly.

"There's one tea here for you, if you like?" Angie responded, with a motherly smile of understanding.

"Okay, well, thank you," Jina said, reaching out to accept the cup.

Distributing the last two mugs, Angie finally spotted Jojo. Startled, one of the mugs tilted awkwardly in her grasp, spilling its contents on her fingers. She gasped from the burn.

Quickly, Jojo grabbed the cup from her hand. His fingers touched hers as he did so, and she withdrew quickly.

"Thank you for the coffee," he said.

Angie nodded, her face aflame. She wiped her hand on a small towel that hung from her belt. After handing the final cup to Dean, she hurried out. Jojo watched her leave. When all eyes in the room turned to him, he sipped his drink as if nothing had happened.

Thomas appeared at the door, sleepiness mingling with curiosity on his little face at what the room full of people, most of whom he didn't recognize, might be discussing. Curling a finger, Tisha beckoned him inside. "Come in, sweetheart," she said, and Thomas walked slowly to her. His Batman pajama top was a size too small: his belly peeked over the snug shorts.

Chase watched his son walk toward them. "Hey, sport," Chase said.

"Hi, Dad. Tisha," he said groggily. He looked around, recognizing Dean and then Leland. "Hi, Dean. Hi, Uncle

Lee," Thomas said before climbing up onto the sofa and unselfconsciously wedging himself between Chase and Tisha. Chase managed to move over slightly to let him in between them.

"How are you feeling?" Tisha asked him. She brushed the small scar on his cheek with her finger, trying to keep her emotions in check.

"Okay," Thomas replied. He looked at Tisha and noticed her eyes. "Why you been crying?" he asked in alarm, and then looked at Chase. "What'd you say?" he accused.

Chase was taken aback. His mouth dropped open as he struggled to defend himself. Tisha spoke up:

"Your father didn't say anything to upset me, sweet pea. I was just sad because I had to tell Leland a... very sad story. It was about a little girl I once knew, like Marina." Tisha took a deep breath. "I'll tell you about it some other time, okay?"

"'Kay," Thomas replied.

Without further ado, Tisha introduced her family to Thomas. "Honey, I want you to meet my other brother, Jojo, and my sister Jina. You already know my brother Dean."

Thomas gave everybody a half-interested wave before he cuddled closer to Tisha, who rubbed his head and planted a kiss on his cheek before hugging him close. He slouched lazily against her and rested his head comfortably on her bosom. Tisha removed the afghan from the back of the sofa and draped it over them both.

Leland spoke a little bit more about next steps as Chase regarded Tisha from the corner of his eye, wondering what the future held for them. Looking at the pair of them snuggled up together, he wondered if his son really did know what was best and had already picked Tisha out for him. He thought disgustedly of Teresa and her phony proclamations of love, hinting at second chances for motherhood and family. That mess wasn't family. *This* was family. People who rushed to be by your side, to check out who you were with and make sure you were safe.

"So, if there's anything else you can think of..." Leland concluded, reaching for his laptop and closing the lid.

"Were you talking about Ms. Robinson?" Thomas asked worriedly. He lifted his head and looked at his dad.

"Yeah," Chase admitted.

"But I don't want you to worry. The police will get her for hurting Marina and you," Tisha added reassuringly.

Thomas nodded. "She's kinda crazy, you know," he said, looking at Leland. "She made it seem like Tisha hurt Marina, but I knew it was her. I saw her when she dragged her out of the school."

"I heard about that. Sounds like you were very brave," Leland replied encouragingly. "Did you know that Ms. Robinson might have been a bad person even before she hurt Marina, Thomas?"

"I dunno," Thomas said and shrugged.

"Like, what kinds of things did she say to—" Leland stopped when Tisha shook her head frantically behind Thomas's back.

"I don't want you to ask him questions. I—I—" Tisha stammered.

"I understand your hesitations, Tisha," Leland said. "But it could shed light on something, and anything that would give us insight into Ms. Robinson's general character would be an advantage. Perhaps there was some previous incident, before the incident at the play."

"I can answer the questions," Thomas offered helpfully. Chase saw Tisha plead with her eyes to him, but he nodded to her, letting her know it was okay.

"Go ahead, Thomas," Leland said.

"She said that she would hurt Tisha, and that Tisha made her lose her other job because she was a tattletale."

Tisha gasped. She'd forgotten Andrea's taunts about her past. Strangely, Andrea had seemed to know all about what had happened back then. Tisha had simply assumed that she had heard about it from someone else, or read it in the newspaper. Thomas's revelations opened up a new array of very distasteful possibilities.

"You remember something, Tisha?" Leland asked hopefully, seeing her expression change. He ripped off a piece of paper and began jotting down information on a clean sheet.

"I... I uh, she..." Tisha stuttered.

"Maybe she worked there, at that home?" Jina offered.

"Yeah, Tisha was able to get the whole center closed because the officials and the Department of Social Services couldn't be sure who was guilty and who wasn't," Dean offered.

"Or who had a hand in the abuse of Melinda," Jojo added darkly. "All the children were relocated, but only two arrests were ever made."

"So she knows you better than we thought: she has a vendetta against you, some deep-seated enmity. This is personal," Leland said, as he scribbled furiously.

"This is serious, Tisha," Jojo said, looking at her with concern.

"That's why you should come home," Jina insisted. "Just for a little while. A vacation, until things die down."

"Look, I am not going back to Virginia," Tisha nearly screamed, "but you are." She looked at Jina, then at Dean and Jojo. "All of you. Chase is here, the police are here and I'm staying here too. Macon is my home now."

"The *police*, Tisha? They don't even think there's a problem," Jina groaned. "If they did, you wouldn't have been down at the station in the first place. And don't tell us what we're gonna do, Ms. Thing - we're older, you know."

"Yeah, you're older..." Tisha had heard that one numerous times and was growing weary of it. She realized that maybe it was her sister's poor attempt at humor, but at that moment she couldn't find anything funny. She summoned her courage and stared back at Jina.

"That just means you've had more years to get some sense, so start using some of it!"

The assembled family stared at her in disbelief.

"I love you guys, you know that, more than anyone, but..." Tisha looked at Chase for a mere second before turning back to Jina.

"I'm not having you here, Jina - not in your condition." She pointed to Jina's belly. "I want you far away from here. Nothing is going to happen to me and certainly nothing is going to happen to any of you guys. This is *my* battle, and I'll get out of it all right. Leland is going to clear all this up." She glanced at the lawyer, who didn't dispute her statement.

"I will call you guys with reports of what's happening - but I'm sure you'll find out one way or the other and come running regardless of what I do. Regardless, I'm not going to have everyone gathered around me putting their own lives on hold. You got me?"

Chase was thinking she was getting the hang of this blunt independence stuff, as far as her siblings over-protectiveness was concerned, and he liked it. Plus, he didn't want her to go back to Virginia with her siblings any more than she wanted to go herself. He silently cheered her on.

"I moved away for a reason: I am an adult. Also, I have a friend who is going to help me."

She reached for Chase's hand and he got to his feet to take it, as Tisha was already standing up – literally and figuratively - to her family.

"One phone call and I know you'll be here, but I'm going to be fine. I'm going to get through this."

Chase stood at her side as she continued, her courage and determination touching his heart even more - not to mention that she'd called him a friend to her whole family, and clearly planned to count on him. He was there for her, no matter what.

The silence stretched on. Tisha had said her piece, and at last she sat back down. Leland shut the locks on his brief-case and placed the laptop in his computer bag.

"I'll get a list of the people at the center where Robin-son might have worked and see what else I can find out about her past. Seeing as she was employed at Glen Dale School, there should be something in her records there that lists her previous jobs. If it doesn't specify that the last place was closed down, or the reason for it, there'd be no reason for Human Resources to have had any qualms about hiring her."

Tisha nodded her understanding, and Chase moved for-ward to shake Leland's hand before escorting him to the door.

Tisha looked at Thomas and stood again. "I'm hungry, sweetie, how 'bout you?" She chuckled at the rather noisy tummy rumble she heard in place of his answer. "Jina and I are going to go help Angie in the kitchen. You go wash up and change out of your pajamas, okay?"

Thomas nodded and moved to get down from the sofa. Tisha told her siblings they could stay for breakfast, but that they were to get on the first plane back to Virginia and that she'd see them later.

Just as she finished speaking, Angie arrived. "Breakfast is ready. I made enough for Mr. McGehee and Tisha's family, if they want to stay," Angie announced, looking at every-one in the room.

"Oh Angie, I wanted to help you," Tisha began.

"Thank you, Angie," Chase said, reappearing as she left the room. Jojo was the first to excuse himself.

———◆———

Angie showed Jina where that floor's bathroom was located, then began to the set the large dining table adja-cent to the kitchen. She took a deep breath. Since she'd left

WalMart that morning and taken the kids to their babysit-
ter, she'd felt like she'd been running all day - and it was
barely 10:00am. She arranged the table family-style, putting out plates, napkins, forks, knives and spoons at one
end and the buffet-style spread down the center. As she
entered the kitchen to retrieve the last plate of food, she
saw Jojo standing at the entrance.

   "It's Angie, right?"

TWENTY-THREE

———◆———

A NGIE LOOKED UP AND NODDED, absently brushing a strand of hair away. Jojo noticed that she looked
different from the first time he'd seen her. Her fresh-
ly-combed hair flowed longer and straighter, while a nice
snug pair of blue jeans and a Georgia Tech sweatshirt
defined her curves.

"We just – uh — met at the Wal-Mart, remember?"
Well, that was original. He looked away when she looked at
him, as if she had the words *short-term memory loss sufferer*
stamped across her forehead.

"You have some cute kids," Jojo remarked.

Angie laughed. "They're my sister's kids," she replied
automatically.

There is a God, Jojo thought to himself, but looked away
when her eyes examined him more closely. He felt as if she
had read his mind.

She paused in her task of vigorously scrubbing a frying
pan, wondering to herself how much longer she'd describe
her situation like that.

"I... take care of them," she said awkwardly, by way of
explaining things and not explaining them at the same
time. She didn't know why she bothered with any of it.
After being granted legal guardianship, she had loved and
raised her sister's kids like her own. But saying they were
her sister's had become rote, although Angie was all they

had left in the world.

Anyway, she didn't know why she felt the need to explain anything to this guy. They didn't know each other, but she knew people like him and had summed him up in a matter of minutes. He looked like the I-only-date-models type: all dark-skinned tall intimidating stance - and the uniform didn't help. She was unfazed. She had known men like him, and this man lacked patience - that Angie was certain of. He was a good-looking man, but overall it didn't work in his favor as far as Angie was concerned.

She dried the dishes and placed them on a wooden plate rack. Mr. Alton had every gadget, including a soothingly quiet dishwasher, but most of the time Angie preferred to do something with her hands to busy herself.

When her phone rang, Angie answered it without further acknowledging Jojo's presence. "Cassie, what's the matter?" she said, as Jojo looked on. She wished he'd leave. "I told you to call only when there is an emergency. No, I'm not coming to pick you up early... No, we can't go! You know the rules."

She clicked off, leaving a whining child on the other end.

"Do they call you a lot?" he asked.

Man, are you nosy, she thought. "No. I just taught Cassie how to use the phone and am teaching her to read numbers, in case of an emergency."

"She seems like a good kid," he replied.

"Yes, she's very smart," Angie smiled to herself, hoping that she was responsible for most if not all of Cassie's intelligence. She thought of Casey, hoping that he too was picking up some of her teachings, though he never said anything to let her know one way or the other.

"Why doesn't the boy talk?"

How did she know that was coming? She looked at him, not quite sure what to say. "You sure do ask a lot of questions," she replied. Immediately she saw the embarrassment on his face. She almost felt bad for him - almost.

He nodded slightly, smiling. "I'm sorry. It's just that..."

"It's all right. He..." She breathed a sigh of relief when the phone rang again: she wouldn't have to explain. "Cassie?" she said into the receiver. "You what? Where's Ms. Morrow? ... Ugh. I'll be there in a little bit."

Angie clipped the phone back on her belt and reached for her coat. She hurriedly scribbled a note for Chase, who understood such emergencies and wouldn't be upset. She'd be back, most likely; she was good at her job and a damn good cook. She didn't take the job for granted, though: most of all, she was so grateful that her employer was a fellow parent. Only another person with kids, she felt, would understand the constant string of mini-emergencies.

She looked at Jojo. "It was nice meeting you, again. I have to go."

"What's the matter? Are they okay? Your sister - why can't they call her?"

Angie flipped her hair out of the back of her coat. That was another thing she'd soon have to give up, she thought sadly: her weave, the one luxury she'd kept as her budget with two young children to support got tighter and tighter. She'd never bothered with nails, because she cooked and cleaned and they wouldn't last anyway if she was going to be a world-class chef someday... though that dream was slowly waning. Even under all the responsibilities she now had, she tried to keep hope alive.

She could tell by the way Jojo looked at her that he expected an answer. She looked back at him. "My sister's dead," she replied curtly. *Just as she knew Jojo came running for his baby sister, she came running for kids who were not hers.* She grabbed the note she'd hastily written and left the kitchen without another word to the overtly curious Jojo Jameson.

Tisha, Dean, Thomas and Jina sat at the table in the dining room. From just one previous sample of Angie's cooking, Tisha knew that Chase's housekeeper had impeccable culinary skills, but her body simply couldn't get up the energy to eat the amazing amount of food before her, even though she had been very hungry. Dean nursed a second cup of coffee but didn't eat anything, while Thomas and Jina dug in enthusiastically.

When a phone rang, Tisha jumped. Dean handed his cell phone to Tisha without answering it: "You know it's Momma."

Tisha reluctantly took the phone and excused herself from the table. In the hallway, she accepted the call and spoke to her mother, assuring an irate and worried Alfreah Jameson that she was all right. Her mother made no secret of her unhappiness about the fact that she was the one doing the calling, instead of being called with reports from her other three children.

"I'm sorry, Momma, I... I was going to call you, but I'm really okay," Tisha assured her mother, and promised that she'd come home for a visit, when it was evident Alfreah wouldn't be able to get her daughter to move back home for good.

The call wasn't long: likely because her mother knew that her other children would have full reports any day now. Tisha said her goodbyes and hung up. She moved down the hall toward the den, where she noticed that the door was slightly ajar.

"She said she wants her family back, but I can't worry about her, Lee. I really can't."

Clearly Chase was talking on the phone to Leland, who had left just a few minutes earlier, but his voice was agitated and he spoke low. "I'm sick and tired of her games. I'm only mentioning it because I wondered if she had contacted you?"

Chase held the phone to his ear, listening and speaking a

moment longer before he said his goodbyes and hung up. "Hey, come in here," he said to Tisha, who hadn't realized he'd seen her.

Tisha entered sheepishly, hoping he hadn't thought she was eavesdropping. "I'm sorry, I saw you on the phone and I was going to leave…" she stammered.

"It's fine. Come in here and tell me how you're doing."

To her surprise, he took her hand and led her the rest of the way into the room, closing the door behind them. All of a sudden, he embraced her fully.

Tisha tried to smile as she looked up at Chase. "I just wanted to know if you were going to eat," she said. "Angie had to go. She left a note but didn't want to interrupt you."

"I'll get something to eat in a minute. I was just discussing something with Leland, but I'm coming."

With that she nodded and prepared to retreat, but he held her tighter momentarily and kissed her lips. "I don't want you to worry about anything." Chase brushed his lips over hers again. "I'm so glad you're here, and I've enjoyed meeting your family. This is going to be okay."

"How do you know?"

"I feel it in my heart," he assured her.

"Your words can't stop me from worrying," Tisha sighed. "Since I woke up, it seems like things have gotten completely out of hand."

"You remember what Leland said, don't you? It's the spin of the media, to trump up reports and sensationalize everything for their own ratings."

"It hurts," she said softly.

"I know, and it kills me that it's hurting you… but it's gonna be okay, Tisha. I was happy to hear you tell your family that you could count on me."

"I want to think I can…"

"Of course you can."

She nodded. "I wasn't very agreeable when you first asked me out," she said ruefully.

"And now look, you're at my mercy, stuck under the same roof with me," Chase chuckled.

"It's nice here. I feel safe."

"I'm glad. It will always be safe for you."

"I want to trust that, and I, just… thank you so much for everything that you've done."

"You don't have to thank me for anything, everything I have is yours. Anything I can do to help you, to protect you and to show you I care, I will do."

Tisha drew closer, first searching his eyes, until at last she put her head against his chest and rested in his large arms, which shielded and cradled her like no one she'd ever met. She closed her eyes and simply stood there with him a moment longer, shutting out her family and all their bickering and the world that seemed so against her.

She was feeling ready to get on with her life once and for all, with Chase by her side.

TWENTY-FOUR

W HEN TISHA AND CHASE RE-ENTERED the kitchen, Jina was washing the dishes and Dean was on drying duty. Chase made himself a cup of coffee and sat at the island counter on a barstool.

Jojo had left already and Dean and Jina would travel together. "Well, baby cakes, we're just about ready to go now. I know you're all broken up about it," - she winked - "but don't you worry: we'll be back."

Jina grabbed her sister's arm and pulled her closer to the door.

"What do you say to the idea that Tony and I come back in another week or so? Perhaps this whole thing will have blown over by then, and we can do some shopping for the baby?"

Tisha smiled and tried not to cry. Now they that were really leaving, it felt like a final goodbye all over again. When she'd left Virginia, she'd had a job offer, a tiny apartment to move into that she could afford, and so much to look forward to in Macon. She still had something to look forward to here, in Chase, and she was happy about that; but she still couldn't shake the dark cloud of sadness.

She looked closely at her sister. "Love you very much, you know that?"

"Of course, you love me more than your other two knucklehead siblings. I know. It's our secret."

Tisha nodded and laughed at their recurring joke. She knew her siblings meant well and, despite everything, she felt sad that they were leaving. In Virginia, there hadn't been a day where she didn't talk to them or see them face to face, but she felt like she was growing up, as hard as that was. She was only two hours away by plane – or ten by car – from them all… though right then, it seemed more like they would be two oceans apart.

"I'll be fine," Tisha said, a little less confidently than she had planned.

Jina opened the front door and turned to cast a warm smile on Chase, who had approached to stand just a few feet behind Tisha. "Take care of my sister," she said.

Chase nodded enthusiastically. Before he could prepare himself, however, Jina walked back to him and surprised him as she stood on the tip of her toes and gave him a huge warm hug.

"Thanks so much for letting me eat your food."

She laughed as she stepped back and rubbed her belly in dramatic circles. "Angie should be a chef. She can really burn." She patted Chase on the arm, kissed her sister on the cheek, and left – for real this time - through the front door.

"I'll see you, baby girl. You better call me," Dean warned. Embracing Tisha, he pecked her once on her cheek and narrowed his eyes at Chase behind her. A curt "Alton" was the only thing he uttered in acknowledgement. Then he, too, was gone.

Despite the nice weather, there was still a slight chill in the mid-morning air. Tisha shivered as she moved closer to Chase.

"Well, I'm obviously prone to danger," she said, waving her hands to indicate their present situation and the last twenty-four hours. "I've got not just one but two" — she held up two fingers — "melodramatic, overprotective, musclebound brothers." Tisha regarded Chase. "Want to call it quits now before you get any further involved?"

Tisha's smile faded as she quickly realized that her intended joke had gone down like a lead balloon when Chase only stared seriously back at her. She was still exhausted, but she meant what she said.

"Never," Chase said determinedly. He reached over to place his cup on the counter before opening his arms to Tisha. She hesitated a second before walking into them. "That's family, Tisha. I'm an only child, and honestly, the way you guys are is pretty new to me but it's definitely not as bad as you think. So long as you and Jina are around, I'm safe." He chuckled, then grew serious. "They love you and they just want you to be happy. I think I'd act the same way if I had a little sister. But I know once they get to know me they'll be okay."

Tisha laughed. "Can you say that again so I can record it and play it to you later — like around Thanksgiving or Christmas? Holidays are pretty tense times." Tisha realized that despite what she'd gone through, she was still thinking ahead: about knowing him, about being in his life for a long while. *Hey, that was a new one she hadn't considered yet...* The thoughts just kept tumbling along.

"Your mention of the holidays," Chase smiled, raising an eyebrow, "means that you see me and Thomas being around for the long haul. Well, I see that too - and honestly? I can't wait."

With the new revelation between them came a new awareness, and they stared at each other for just a beat longer before he leaned down and sealed the possibility of a future together with a kiss.

TWENTY-FIVE

"HE CAN'T DO THAT... CAN he?"

Tisha looked at Chase in astonishment. Placing the duffel bag she'd recently packed on the floor, he turned to regard Leland, standing near the door, and moved closer as Tisha pressed her cell phone button to replay a message she'd missed and increased the volume as the curt voice was heard:

"Ms. Jameson, Chris Jeeter here. I think it's best under the current circumstances that you take a sabbatical from your duties at the school. Until we straighten things out, you're on administrative leave. Upon review of this case, we will make our decision: we cannot discuss your return until that time. Thank you."

It was so like him to sound all professional even at a time like this, she thought with disgust. Did he think she was guilty as well? Why hadn't he sounded like everything was okay?

"How generic is that?" she cried. "He has to know I'm a competent and caring teacher who would never endanger the lives or safety of her pupils. How could he sound so... so *callous?*" She looked beseechingly at Leland.

"Now, now," Leland soothed, "don't go thinking from that message alone that he doesn't believe you're innocent. Until things clear, he has to sound neutral. Until the matter is straightened out, you most likely won't be permitted entry into the school. Not Ms. Robinson either."

"What?" she cried. "I can't even go there?"

Other messages were continuing to play, including one from the library and another from Chase's friend the mechanic. Tisha pressed the skip button. Her car was a lemon, what a revelation… she already knew that. Then Tisha's ears pricked up as Mrs. Wellington's voice drifted over the recording.

"Tisha, oh… dear heart? Lord in heaven, where are you? Please call me when you get this message. I hope you are all right. In all my thirty years of teaching I've never been a party to anything so awful. I know you'd never hurt those children. I just can't believe it…" The woman paused and her voice became slightly muffled. *"Please call me, honey. Well"* — she was silent for a long moment and a heavy sigh escaped her — *"'bye now."*

"See, there you have it. There's one person, and it sounds like she's with you," Leland declared hopefully. "We'll go visit with her and see what the police have gathered from her."

Tisha nodded, imbued with only slightly more confidence. It was impossible for her to believe that anyone thought ill of her, and in one day – heck, a matter of hours - her life had turned into a complete mess. No-one other than her family, Chase and Leland seemed to be on her side – they and, she hoped, Mrs. Wellington. That said, her family didn't count because they were biased, and Chase… well, she liked to believe he was partial to her. Leland reminded her of her father, calculating evidence as it presented itself, wise and never judging a person unless he had concrete evidence.

"All right," she conceded, with a slight hint of optimism creeping in.

She took one last look around her small apartment. She still couldn't believe she'd agreed to stay with Chase any longer than the two nights she'd already stayed. She could get a hotel, but what a lonely place to be by herself. She felt defenseless. Andrea Robinson was larger than her and had already beat up on her once before. It could have been so much worse. And it might be weeks before she could come home again. She grabbed some of her smaller family photos and held them close to her heart. She looked at Chase. He held out a hand and together they left her apartment.

———◆———

At the older couple's house, Tisha wrung her hands. Leland had knocked on the door of Mr and Mrs Wellington's apartment. When the door creaked open, an old man stood nonplussed as he looked over the three people on the other side. "Kin I help you?" he said, looking skeptical.

Tisha stepped forward, never doubting that the man before her was Herbert Wellington. Mrs. Wellington talked often about her husband, her Herby. What Tisha didn't expect was for him to look so old and worn, despite the agile and dramatic energy Mrs. Wellington herself seemed to exude and despite the way she'd always described the man. Herbert Wellington's frame was slightly bent, his glasses slid off his shiny bulbous nose, and his scalp was weathered and gray.

"My... my name is Tisha Jameson. I'm a..."

"Yes, yes, the schoolteacher friend of my wife's," Herbert cut her off. "I know ya. Shar speaks highly of you. Who're the two fellas with you?" Mr. Wellington asked as his eyes moved slowly up over Tisha's head to examine the two men standing behind her.

"Uh, this is Chase Alton, and Leland McGehee, a friend of ours. Ah - we came to talk with Mrs. Wellington. Is she here? I'm sorry to bother you, but—"

"She went to the store, but she's been gone a while, should be back any minute. You wanna wait for her?"

"Uh, if that's all right. Thank you, Mr. Wellington."

Tisha stepped forward as Leland and Chase followed her

through the door. Not knowing what to do, she stood awkwardly until Mr. Wellington ambled his way through to the living room.

"Have a seat if you'd like. I plan to." With that, Mr. Wellington sat down heavily in the nearest chair available, as if the few steps from the door to the living room had winded him. From his pocket he produced an old rag and wiped his forehead with it.

After taking a seat beside him, Tisha looked around the room, noticing how sparsely decorated the place was. The furniture was old and antique, and the sofa groaned as he sat down.

It looked as if Mr. Wellington had dozed off when a jingle of keys from outside caused his eyes to open and his body became more alert. "That'd be her now," he said merrily. Everyone listened as the door creaked open, then the sound of rusted hinges squeaked as it shut.

"Herb? Herby? I'm back now. I got your medicine from the doctor. That woman at the store took all day to fill it and I swear I didn't have that much shopping to do. You'd think she would have sped it up when I told her I was in a hurry and I—"

Sharon Wellington stopped abruptly, holding a small white bag as she removed the light wrap she wore. "Oh, I didn't realize we had company."

She looked at Tisha and smiled sadly. "Well, how are you, honey?" She put the bag aside quickly and pulled Tisha into an embrace. Tisha stood to meet her.

Tisha hadn't expected such a friendly greeting, but as she walked into the woman's arms she immediately felt the tears sting just behind her eyes. The simple gesture helped ease the ache. This woman's friendship had been sincere since Tisha began her tenure at the school.

Stepping back from Mrs. Wellington, Tisha noticed how dramatically the older woman had aged in a mere thirty-two hours. Her hair, always so black, was now streaked with gray, and her eyes looked drawn and fatigued. What a toll recent events had taken.

"I'm all right, I guess. How are you?" Tisha asked. She moved back toward her seat but continued to stand.

"Well..." Mrs. Wellington was thoughtful a moment. She put her purse on the floor and then chanced a look at her husband, who was dozing, before she turned back to Tisha. "I could be better. But I have no idea to this day, Tisha, what in the world happened. I tried to call you but you haven't been answering your phone and I don't blame you. But in all my years, I've never witnessed anything like I did that day."

Mrs. Wellington sat down and motioned with a nod of her head for Tisha to do the same. She then looked at Chase, who sat quietly, and at the man standing near him. "I'm sorry, Mr. Alton, and your friend?" —she nodded to Leland— "I didn't mean to ramble on without greeting you both. Hello."

"Mrs. Wellington, it's all right. This is my..." Tisha hesitated. She didn't want to alarm the couple. "This is Leland McGehee. He's a... a lawyer."

Mrs. Wellington smiled at Chase, who stood to take the woman's hand, followed by Leland.

"Mrs. Wellington," Leland said.

"Well..." Mrs. Wellington began as she removed the wrap from her shoulders, "I guess you want to know what I know. The police have asked me question after question. It's like they didn't write anything down the first time I told them."

"It's a way of tiring you, Mrs. Wellington, so perhaps you'll misquote something you originally said," Leland put in.

She raised her eyebrows in astonishment. "Oh?" She wiped an imaginary piece of lint from her skirt. "Well, I could have told them I was tired before they started, so once would've sufficed. Honestly, that day is an entire blur.

I can see why you and Ms. Robinson didn't get along—you have the patience of a saint, dear. Even I sometimes find my patience with the children wearing thin - but not to the extent of... " She shook her head.

"I know," Tisha offered. "I understand."

"I can't believe it." Mrs. Wellington covered her face with her hands as tears sprang to her eyes. "Have you heard anything about the dear child?" Tisha shook her head, "She's not... is she?" Mrs. Wellington looked at the three of them in alarm.

"No... we don't know. Chase has a friend who's a doctor, but even he couldn't get any information on her condition. Her case is very guarded because of the situation: they won't let anyone other than immediate family, and I guess the police, know what's going on," replied Tisha.

"Did the police do anything other than ask you repeated questions, Mrs. Wellington? Did they say anything that you later pondered, or that struck you as odd?" Leland asked.

"Not really, but they were very evasive. I asked them questions but they haven't told me a single thing. I don't know what to do."

"You've done everything you can do, Mrs. Wellington: the rest is up to the investigators," Leland informed her. You don't have to answer any more questions without a lawyer present, however. That is your right, and I advise you to get legal counsel."

"Legal counsel? Will I have to go to court?" Mrs. Wellington asked anxiously.

"We ain't got that kind of money for no lawyer," Herbert Wellington put in.

Tisha turned toward the man, whom everyone had thought was asleep. He was still in a lounging pose, but his eyes were alert.

"I can... help you out," Chase offered.

"Absolutely not," Leland said firmly.

Tisha was startled by Leland's tone. The lawyer was looking at Chase as if he'd lost his mind.

"That's called a conflict of interest." Leland turned back to Mr. and Mrs. Wellington. "I have someone I'll recommend, but Chase" — he shot a look at his client — "really can't offer any assistance. It would seem like a bribe, and anyway I can't represent the both of you. I'm sorry. I was wondering, though: did you find the school negligent in any way? Being a new school, was there anything, other than Ms. Robinson's employment, of course, that seem to squirrel school resources or procedures? If there were some type of lawsuit against the school, you see, I could act legally on behalf of a group of people."

Mrs. Wellington looked thoughtful. "Well, I did always wonder if our principal hired people the right way. I never saw an HR department, and some of the teacher's aides… well, some looked like he just got 'em off the street and cleaned 'em up - like this was their first job. Considering my age, and the terrible ageism in schools today, I was glad to be hired, too," she added.

"What do you mean Mrs. Wellington? You're a wonderful teacher," Tisha protested.

"I know, honey - I'm talking about age, though. And it is hard for us older folks to do more and more of these jobs. I'm no spring chicken."

Tisha nodded her understanding, but truly she couldn't fathom anyone not wanting to employ such a reservoir of knowledge: Sharon was more than double her age. Still, something about Leland's comment pricked Tisha's own memory.

"Chris Jeeter, the principal told me once that he was so glad he hadn't waited for my paperwork and was glad he hired me on the spot," she recalled thoughtfully. "He then assured me that he did eventually get it. Maybe he didn't get Andrea's?"

Leland took a deep breath. "Maybe - or maybe he did get it and she simply doesn't have a criminal record. They didn't take time to background check some of the volunteers at that foster care facility."

Tisha was stunned.

"Mrs. Wellington," Leland began, "Could you provide the police with this statement about the school's HR policies? I'll make a note of that. It's important that you continue to give the authorities your account of what happened, without any of our input. I'm sorry, but Chase – I mean, Mr. Alton here - just can't help pay your legal fees. You're not in any danger, so you don't need representation at this time. Does this make sense to you both?"

Tisha looked back and forth between the three of them: Mr. and Mrs. Wellington and Leland. Mrs. Wellington nodded, but Tisha could tell she still seemed worried. She kept looking at her husband with concern, who despite nodding off intermittently was currently awake.

"You're saying we're on our own?" Herbert put in.

"No, you're not on your own," Leland replied. "We all want the same thing here: Andrea Robinson brought to justice and Tisha cleared of any wrongdoing. It's really Marina Stamos that we need to look out for. For one thing, we need her to convalesce in order to talk to the police. But we must work to attain that result separately, without any joint funds or resources. After all, Tisha is the person who had the actual altercation - and the possible previous encounter - with Andrea."

Leland stood to leave, holding his legal pad. "As I said, I will give you the contact information of someone else who can help you. Once an investigation is done, we'll see if anyone was hired without proper background checks and clearances to work with children. That sort of evidence would prove that the school put all its good teachers in danger unnecessarily. Whatever the case, it's a troublesome thought all around."

Tisha was glad this was over, although no real helpful information had been revealed. They all said their goodbyes and Mrs. Wellington hugged Tisha again. She told her she'd be praying for her. Tisha hoped nervously that the woman's prayers would be enough to restore and clear her name and deliver her from this entire chaotic scene.

TWENTY-SIX

A FTER SEEING MR. AND MRS. Wellington, Tisha was thoroughly exhausted. Nothing new or helpful had come of the visit: just yet another rehashing of the day. She was tired and weary, and it seemed as if things were only just beginning. They'd picked Thomas up from his grandmother's, and now he restlessly flipped from channel to channel to find a radio station to his liking.

Chase was silent as he drove to the house, not sure of what to say or do or how to eclipse the event from their minds. They needed a diversion: something else to think about. As poor as his suggestion was, he offered it anyway: "How about we go get some ice cream and things to make sundaes?" He looked hopefully at Thomas, who slowly brightened, then at Tisha.

"Yeah, ice cream, ice cream!" Thomas chanted at Tisha, who merely nodded. "I like nuts and butterscotch syrup on my ice cream," he continued eagerly. "What kind do you like, Tisha?"

Tisha looked at his angelic, energetic face, trying her best to brighten her own for his sake. She rarely ate ice cream in the winter back home, but this was Macon and considerably warmer. Not wanting to dampen the effort to lighten the mood, she allowed a smile to flicker across her face.

"Oh, I like everything: M&M's and Oreo cookies and

chocolate syrup – oh, and we can't forget the whipped cream and cherries."

"Yeah, cherries!" Thomas squealed as Chase pulled up to the local market. They all left the truck with just a little more optimism than they'd gotten in with.

Grabbing a cart, Chase moved through the aisles, filled as ever with way too many choices. He looked at Tisha, listless and quiet as she followed by his side. Thomas skipped happily ahead. Every now and then he placed an item or two in the cart: two bottles of chocolate syrup, waffle cones, several kinds of sprinkles – most of which Chase removed immediately, looking at his son disapprovingly.

"Wanna watch a movie tonight?" Chase asked Tisha, and nudged her with his elbow. When she looked at him, confused, he snaked an arm around her waist and started to pull her closer to him; but remembered her injured side and paused. "How's your side?" he asked cautiously. Dr. Byers had looked Tisha over earlier that week and made a report that confirmed the struggle with symptoms Tisha had described to him.

Tisha smiled at Chase, remembering his concern when Dr. Byers had taken a look at her bruises. Her leg was still sore and reddened, but her side was all right. Compared with her emotional state, though, the physical pain was nothing.

"I'm all right," she responded. Chase raised an eyebrow. "Really," she insisted. "Hey, wanna watch a movie?"

Chase looked at her. "I just asked you that," he said.

"Really?" Tisha replied. "Well, all right, sure."

Chase bent and kissed her on her lips.

"Ohh, yuck!" Thomas wrinkled his nose, rolled his eyes and scurried quickly to the candy aisle.

Tisha leaned into Chase, resting her hands on his chest, winding her arms around his neck and pressing his head closer to hers. "I'm gonna go pick that movie. What kind do you like? Not too much action - I've had enough of that to last a lifetime," she smiled.

"For you, I'd watch a romantic comedy just to see you smile," Chase said, and Tisha laughed and walked away down the aisle to the front of the store. "Oh, and don't forget to pick something animated for the minion, too."

Tish searched for the new movies display rack she'd seen when they first entered. Despite her rough few days, and not having the kids at work to take her mind off everything, she had this time with her one little man and one large man - and that felt good. She browsed the display for a romantic comedy. She smiled at how old-school Chase was: he still liked picking movies from the display at the store, even though he owned every conceivable on-demand and streaming gadget back at home. *Well, that will be our back-up*, she thought to herself. She really wasn't finding anything that interested her.

A newspaper cover just beside the movie display rack suddenly caught her eye. There was her school's name, in big, bold black letters. Tisha grabbed a copy of the paper. There in the lower right-hand corner was the principal's face: a smiling photo of Chris Jeeter.

"Hi, Miss Jameson." Tisha closed the paper with a start. She looked down and smiled.

"Oh hi, Sylvia. How are you, sweetheart?" Tisha said, recognizing a student from the school: not one of hers but from the class next door.

"Fine," the little girl sang.

"Sylvia? Honey? Oh, there you are. Come on, Mommy's ready to—"

The mother appeared at the end of the aisle with her cart, but stopped abruptly as her eyes locked on Tisha. "Sylvia! Come away, come over here right this minute!"

"Mommy, I was just—" the child said impatiently.

Her mother cut her off. "That's enough - *now!*"

"Uh, hello, Mrs. Anderson," Tisha said, trying to be cordial to the woman. Mrs. Anderson's alarm that her child was talking to a teacher implicated in the terrible near-tragic incident at the school told Tisha all she needed to know. Despite their familiarity, the woman now didn't see her at all. Tisha could tell Mrs. Anderson saw only a child abuser. Even if she wasn't sure of the real truth, she'd made up her mind already.

"Sylvia, you stay right over here," Mrs. Anderson said sternly to the child, as she closed the few feet of distance to stand before Tisha. If Tisha hadn't been angered at what she knew was about to come, she would've laughed out-right at this woman pantomime-stomping her way over to her.

The mother looked at Tisha with a penetrating, fiery gaze, and kept her voice low to speak so only Tisha could hear. "You" — she pointed a finger at Tisha — "stay away from my daughter. They should lock you and that other teacher up and throw away the key."

With that she turned, grabbing her daughter by the hand. "Come on, sweetheart, we gotta go so let's run along now."

Tisha watched open-mouthed as they left. The little girl turned and managed to wave good-bye as her mother forcefully pulled her along. Tisha waved to be polite, though she felt anything but.

"Hey, what's up?" Chase rolled the cart up to Tisha as Thomas hung acrobat-like on the front end. He hopped down and began to place items on the register scanner nearby.

Tisha shoved the newspaper at him. "I'll wait in the truck," she said dully.

TWENTY-SEVEN

AS SHE'D SEEN, REPORTS WERE now out that Tisha Jameson had been placed on administrative leave. Thanks to Leland's threat and written statement about defamation, all the reports emphasized that she was not a suspect in the ongoing investigation, but Tisha noted with disgust that they'd included such a clarification only as an afterthought. Nothing they said had improved her mood.

She wasn't able to teach; she wasn't even permitted to enter the school. To that end, guards now patrolled the building during school hours. Regardless of reparations in the press coverage, it wasn't enough. She'd done nothing wrong, she considered for the thousandth time. Why hadn't that been enough to warrant her return to her job? Being classified as a criminal, subjected to constant scrutiny and suspicious looks wherever she went, had caused Tisha to slip into a depressed funk.

In frustration, Tisha slammed a textbook shut, then shot Thomas an apologetic look when his head jerked up in surprise. At Chase's insistence, Thomas was permitted a few days of staying home from school, just until things died down. With more gentleness, Tisha set her pen aside. Lessons and ideas, for the kids she wasn't permitted to teach, came to her easily with so much time on her hands. In her lesson plan book she was already up to Cinco de Mayo. At this rate, she'd have written a holiday play incorporating every tradition from Hanukkah to Kwanzaa by the time she was allowed back to the classroom.

Thomas turned his page of completed problems over to her triumphantly. Tisha smiled briefly, glanced at them and could instantly tell they were all correct. Despite all the ideas coming to her, she was learning after only a few days of homeschooling that it just wasn't for her. It wasn't the same. Thomas was a great student and she enjoyed teaching him, but he was just one child and she was used to about twenty more. She missed them all: so very different, with all their personalities and issues, learning styles and competing needs. The classroom setting invigorated her.

She looked at her watch and noticed it was close to dinnertime. Lately they had begun their lessons at weird hours. She had no motivation to stick to a set schedule, and unsurprising for a seven-year-old, neither did Thomas. So they learned when they felt like it, which was seldom.

"Hey there, how about some Chinese food?"

Tisha stood as Chase entered the room. He winked at her and moved forward to give her a kiss. "That sounds nice," she smiled.

"I'll be back," he said and left.

———◆———

Chase had been at his desk, working, but he was so distracted that he was forced to take a break. He mostly wrote and did his recorded pieces for the studio while Thomas was away at school. He was under a rolling deadline for his sports commentary and also had to track the submission status of all the articles he wrote for various sports magazines.

For Tisha's situation, he was running out of options. His most appealing idea so far – that is, purchasing three one-way plane tickets to a distant island country - had been met with only halfhearted enthusiasm by Tisha and flatly prohibited by Leland.

Poor Tisha, meanwhile, had been racking her brain to come up with home-based activities. She and Thomas had done the whole gamut: finger painting, building an Indian hut, making clay pots and baking them in Chase's kitchen oven. By now, Thomas had even grown tired of the 24-hour cartoon channel; and as this was the extent of Chase's recreational creativity, this development represented a serious problem.

For most of the day Chase had remained in his office. Tisha was a great cook and she made their meals. Angie thus had less and less work to do: as well as preparing food, Tisha cleaned the kitchen immaculately. They were almost like a family.

Almost.

She didn't bother him in his office during the daytime hours, when Thomas would usually be at school. Despite all that she was going through, she was diligent. At some point, Chase reflected, she just fit in his house and his life, like a...

Wife. Chase slammed on the brake of his truck as the light turned red, clearly missing that it had been yellow for several seconds. He hadn't thought about anyone in that way for years, and he certainly hadn't thought about marrying again... until now.

He loved eating with her and he enjoyed her cooking: even more savory and spontaneous than the food Angie prepared. Angie was actually a pastry chef, and while her desserts were decadent, her regular meals were a tad too health-conscious. Although he loved her food, he felt no romantic attachment to his young housekeeper. Over two years of Angie working for him, he hadn't felt a thing.

To his dismay, Tisha had become withdrawn and restless, and the incident with that school mother days ago at the supermarket, which she had finally decided to clue him in on, had further depressed her. To him and Thomas, though, she was a champ.

The Golden Dragon restaurant was crowded with people from a local high school, plus a team of kids in basketball jerseys and sweatpants, all waiting anxiously in line for a table large enough to accommodate them. Chase watched them briefly, certain from their boisterous happiness that they'd been victorious in their latest game. As he often did, Chase thought about enrolling Thomas in a sport. Even though Thomas was big for his age, Chase wouldn't allow any thoughts of football to dance in his son's head. Basketball seemed pretty mellow, and even t-ball or baseball might be a good fit. As smart as his straight-A son was, though, not one single ounce of coordination with any type of ball looked like it had made it into his DNA. Thomas just wasn't the athletic sort, but Chase honestly did not care one way or the other.

Whatever Thomas decided — chess club, honor society, track and field - Chase would support him in all his aspirations. He resolved never to pressure him into something that just didn't seem to fit, simply because it was what he as a parent wanted. It would be awful if he had any ideas of living vicariously through Thomas, or if he harbored aspirations that the sport Thomas chose would pay megabucks if picked up after high school.

Nearing the small bar area, Chase stood under the sign that said PLACE ORDER HERE. An older man expertly passed drinks to the numerous seated customers and, without looking up, asked Chase for his order. Chase dutifully recited it and waited patiently. Smells of chicken, hot peppers and all things steamed and fried with their pungent dipping sauces wafted past Chase's nose.

Chase looked up to the television hanging in the corner and noticed that the news was on. He strained to hear it. The volume wasn't super high… but to his surprise, a hush seemed to come over those seated around him. Chase half-wondered nervously whether all eyes might zero in on him when the camera panned to a picture of the Glen Dale Elementary School. He read the closed captioning text and wished he didn't have to know any updates whatsoever. It only confirmed that he should hire a private investigator to find Andrea Robinson and end Tisha's misery so they could all get on with their lives.

The newscaster was continuing the broadcast:

No new reports have developed on the whereabouts of Andrea Robinson, wanted for the brutal attack on a child who attends the Glen Dale School in Macon County. We can confirm that Tisha Jameson, another teacher at the school, is said to have been cleared of all charges, but was with the child when she was rushed to the hospital. However, this network has also learned of another incident involving Ms. Jameson some years ago in her home state of Virginia, where a child subsequently died from brutal injuries. Prominent attorney Leland McGehee made a statement earlier in the week, assuring Ms. Jameson's innocence and accusing the county police department of inaccuracy and hasty handling of this case. Jameson has recently been seen with former LA Chargers football player Chase Alton, who now resides in Macon and has a seven-year-old son. In other news...

"Ha, ha, ha." The deep laugh of someone seated at the bar echoed around the room. Chase looked over and immediately recognized Thomas's friend's father, Jeb George, just feet away. Chase turned back to wait, wishing he'd chosen any restaurant but this one. *But wait: Macon was now his home too!* Plus, the reports had just said Tisha was innocent - yet had still alluded to her darn past. What a backhanded way they depicted her. Still, Chase maintained that he did not care what people thought. He continued to look straight ahead, staring but unseeing. He certainly did not have time for a drunk like Jeb George.

Jeb had lost custody of his son to his wife, and if his wife was anything like Teresa had been, Chase guessed he had

plenty reasons to drink. The two men might even have had
something in common, perhaps sharing commiserations
over their respective failed marriage attempts; but the man
was drunk, and Chase really didn't go in for that scene at
all.

Chase dismissed Jeb and pretended he hadn't heard the
laughter. If the man was smart, he'd keep his comments to
himself and not give Chase cause to shut him up.

"Imagine that, will you, a teacher? Are you kiddin' me?"
Jeb continued, and looked around at the people next to
him as if trying to engage them in his commentary on the
news segment. He lifted his drink as if toasting a great revelation. "Got yourself a mess there again, do you, Chase?"
Jeb continued.

"Shut up, will you, Jeb?" put in the bartender as he shot
an apologetic look in Chase's direction.

"Oh man, well, look here, if it ain't the devil himself." Jeb
leaned behind those seated between them to look Chase's
way. Drunkenly, Jeb slid off the stool, somehow still man-
aging to hold on to his half-finished beer, and made his
way to Chase's end of the bar. "You sure do know how to
pick 'em..."

He pointed a shaky, slender finger at Chase before continuing. "I tell you what..." Quickly he righted himself as
he began to sway; the glass he held sloshed amber liquid to
the floor. Jeb burped and swiped a hand across his mouth.
"Excuse me... why Chase, look, why don't you get yourself
an ugly bee-otch next time? Seems the beautiful women
run you into the ground." Jeb grinned at his own wit,
then sobered briefly. "I tell you what, though, you sure do
know how to pick 'em. That indie flick chick, what's her
name? Terese? Teresa? Your first wife, you know? Anyways,
she was a looker. And now this, this... Ms..."

Chase's jaw twitched angrily as Jeb continued. "Jameson,
that's right... Tisha... ah... man, got a fine, tight little ass on
her, don't she? You send her my way if things don't work

out 'tween you two. I'll take her off your hands when she gets outta jail." Jeb chuckled.

A red mist descended on Chase's vision and before he knew it, his fist had connected with Jeb's jaw. "You wanna shut your mouth, or you need some help?" Chase asked.

Jeb struggled to get up. "Leave it be, Jeb," called someone, but still he reared up and pelted Chase in the gut with his fist.

"I was just complimenting Alton here on his taste in women—now is that any way to treat a person?" Jeb asked indignantly, rubbing his jaw.

Even through his rage, Chase admired the fact that Jeb could fight despite his scrawny appearance. He gave as good as he got… but Chase wanted an end. He hadn't fought in years but none of his skill had left him. Though his hand twitched for a pounding, that wasn't who he was. Chase backed away regretting the first punch and knowing if he didn't leave, more blows would ensue.

"Forget my order. I'm out," Chase called over his shoulder as he made his way out of the restaurant.

Chase was at his truck in record time, and as he reached out to open the driver's door, his mood worsened.

"Chase, honey, I need to talk to you." There, blocking him, stood Teresa.

TWENTY-EIGHT

———◆———

CHASE WAS MAD AS HE drove home from the restaurant, his hand throbbing. Regardless of whose fault it was, Chase had once again found himself smack dab in the middle of a mess. And Tisha. Chase hurt for her, knowing she blamed herself and thought she was some type of jinx, prone to danger and mayhem; and now here he was, causing more of both in their lives. He knew the ordeal was taking a toll on her and she hadn't asked for any of it.

And then there was Teresa. Tonight she had all but ambushed him to ask – no, plead - for more money, and Chase had confirmed once again that she wouldn't get a dime out of him. He was thankful that Thomas wasn't around to witness his anger. This time, he'd managed to get into his truck quickly enough to leave her there in the parking lot without incident.

While Chase was married to Teresa, her actions, constant reckless behavior and very existence always gave the press something to talk about. It was never about him, even back then, but still they had hounded him: "Mr. Alton, how do you feel about your wife's accident?" "Mr. Alton, did your poor performance in the game today have anything to do with your wife leaving?" "Mr. Alton, are you really questioning the paternity of the child your wife is carrying?" "Mr. Alton, do you know the supposed father of your wife's baby?" "Mr. Alton, why'd you turn down a $ 15-million contract with the Washington Redskins?"

The questions would continue as reporters shoved microphones, digital recorders and cell phones in his face while surrounding him like a swarm of bees any time he made his way to his car or to the gym. Wherever he went, there they were too. The press waited with endless patience, taunting Chase and daring him to react with some smart retort, some comment or better yet, a physical lashing: maybe he could be goaded into shoving one of their camera men, or better for them, shoving a female reporter just to get on with his life. That would give them even more to report; more to dog him about.

Chase hadn't once taken the bait in all those years, yet now here he was, confronted with one small-town drunk, and he couldn't keep his fists to himself. *Pathetic.*

Chase drove toward home replaying the last thirty minutes, and as he neared his house, he realized he still hadn't purchased anything to eat. Going someplace else at this hour was out of the question. There had to be some frozen pizza or something he could make in that big refrigerator of his. If he explained what happened to Tish, surely she'd help. She'd understand.

Sitting there for a moment in the wide driveway, Chase looked at his half-million-dollar home. It was certainly modest compared to what he could afford, but a functional house nonetheless. He then thought of what was on the other side of the door and instantly brightened. Tisha was the sort of woman he would enjoy coming home to: she was the only upside to all the present madness. Seeing Tisha's face when she greeted him every time he opened the door, just the thought of her there even, was like a soothing calm after a disastrous storm.

Chase walked slowly to the front door. He himself had been the child of a single parent for most of his life; and even when his father was alive, everyone had been out working most of the time. Chase often arrived home from school to find their tiny apartment empty. His mother would call him like clockwork every day at five minutes after three to ensure he was where he was supposed to be. Chase would first complete his chores, then his homework. Alone.

"Hi," Tisha said as she noticed Chase standing at the entrance of the kitchen, watching her play a game with Thomas.

"Hi," Chase replied, relieved to be back. Tisha always said her hellos with surprising enthusiasm, and her warm greeting made it seem like he'd been gone for longer than thirty minutes: as if she'd missed him for even that short amount of time.

"Hey, where's dat grub?" Thomas said, laughing at his words and looking at Chase's empty hands.

Chase looked at the floor. "I didn't get it. I, uh…"

"Ah man! I got the munchies like a mug," Thomas whined, then smiled as if he'd said something his dad and Tisha would think was cool.

"Stop whining, Thomas, I've told you about that." Chase looked Thomas in the eye. "And where'd you learn that from?"

"Jason," Thomas muttered. It was his turn to look shamefaced.

"Jason, huh? Well, I don't want you hanging out with him anymore. You got it? I mean it, Thomas!"

"Why not? I'm bored!" Thomas replied incredulously.

"'Cause I said so. Go to your room. Now."

Chase moved aside a few inches so Thomas could shove past him. They heard Thomas's feet stomp quickly up the stairs and the door to his room slam shut.

"Chase?" came Tisha's quiet, steady voice.

"What?"

"Look at me. What is the matter with you?"

"Nothing!" Chase headed for the den, not meeting her eyes.

Tisha remained in the kitchen. She went to the pantry to look for something to cook while she took a few minutes to think. She knew both Chase and Thomas would also need time to calm down before she went to talk to either of them.

She took a deep breath. Being cooped up was getting to everybody… and it was all her fault.

Tisha's pantry foraging produced a can of peaches, a box of Hungry Jack and a very small bag of chopped nuts. "Not quite what I'm going for here," she muttered, and proceeded to check the freezer and fridge. There she found a frozen steak, which didn't go at all with the meal she had in mind. She continued to hunt, lifting packages and rummaging through the items. Finally, her eyes landed on a bag of frozen strawberries and one of blueberries. "Perfect," she murmured. She set both packages of berries in the microwave and set it to defrost.

She took a deep preparatory breath and started down the hall to the den. She saw Chase on the phone. However much she wanted to find out the reason for Chase's mood, he was clearly occupied. She'd go smooth things over with Thomas first, she decided.

From the door of Thomas's room, Tisha studied him for a moment. The boy was stomping around, apparently looking for something, and once he found it settled down on his bed with a dramatic flop. He shoved books off his bed angrily and they landed with a mean thud on the floor.

"Hey," Tisha said as she entered the room.

Thomas looked up momentarily and replied with a noncommittal "Hi."

Tisha looked around. The chair at Thomas's desk was piled with clothes and toys. In the corner lay a shiny scooter, with blue wheels glinting in the light. His shelves were lined with books, toys, a rock collection and a bunch of other colorful items.

Tisha stepped over the clothes that littered the floor

and took a seat on the bed. She took another deep breath before she began.

"You know, we're all a little crazy because of Ms. Robinson and this whole mess, but... well, your father didn't mean to yell at you. Everybody's just on edge."

Thomas sat up and looked at her skeptically. He rolled his eyes at Tisha. "That's not it."

"Sure it is," she replied, surprised. "We're all very frustrated."

Thomas took an exasperated breath. "It's because of Teresa."

"Teresa?" Tisha asked.

"She's my Mom."

"Yes, I—I know that," Tisha stammered, slightly bothered because she realized that maybe she really didn't know. She didn't know that Teresa played a part in anything affecting them or Chase at all.

"It's because she wants custo—" Thomas faltered.

"Custody," Tisha offered.

"Yeah, that."

"Well, uh. If that's the case, how do you feel about it?" Tisha asked.

Thomas shrugged. "Who cares? She doesn't love me."

You care, Tisha thought to herself, though she knew Thomas tried to act as if he didn't. "That's not true," Tisha said, trying to keep a neutral tone. "Who told you that? Of course she loves you." *How could anyone not love you, you sweet child?* she wondered to herself.

"She left us. She never came back. Now she wants to be in our family again..." Thomas lifted a shoulder and dropped it in defeat. "I heard Dad talking about it to Uncle Lee."

How confused he was, Tisha realized. It was apparent he had eavesdropped, but no one had discussed it with him.

"Maybe she just wants to see you, is all. You know, like..." Tisha searched for an example. When it came to her, as poor as it was, she used it anyway. "Jason — your friend. He's able to spend time with both his parents, and they're divorced, right?"

Thomas tilted his head to one side as if considering the idea. He immediately dismissed it. "Yeah, but he spends only some time with his dad," he concluded miserably. "He lives with his mom. That's what they're going to make me do. Go live with her in stupid *California*." Thomas made a face.

"How do you know? Did you ask your dad?" What a foolish woman Teresa Alton had been, and apparently still was. Such a woman didn't deserve such a smart boy.

"I don't want to live with her. I want to stay with Dad." Thomas looked up hopefully then, and blinked as if a great idea had just come to mind. He looked at Tisha. "Hey, maybe they wouldn't make me go if you and Dad got married! Then *we* could be a family."

"I, uh...wow." She hadn't been prepared for that one, and she hated the hopefulness she saw in his eyes – but Thomas's hope clearly diminished when she didn't answer right away. "Thomas, sweetheart..." she began.

"Don't you love me?" he questioned her.

"Oh yes. Of course I do, Thomas. I love you very much," *There's no question I do. I think I love Chase too,* her mind whispered silently. *But does your father love me?* she wanted to ask aloud.

"What's the big deal then?" Thomas asked impatiently.

"Well, your father and I, sweetheart... we have to love each other too, first. We both love you very much and we want what's best for you, but your father and I are really just friends – uh... whew."

Tisha grew hot and fanned herself. This kid was so serious. She couldn't deny that she was staying with Chase, though, and by all outward appearances, that must look pretty darn serious to Thomas. She should have thought about how awkward an impression that would be on him, considering the three of them hadn't ever even discussed the matter of her staying there.

"Why not?" Thomas whined. "Why does everything have to take so long? You've been just friends for months, now you're staying here with us and we all get along really great. Isn't that long enough to know whether you like each other or not?"

"Uh..." Tisha felt as if she were on the witness stand, her hand on a stack of Bibles, facing a jury of seven-year-olds who wouldn't understand adult matters. She knew of no way to put in seven-year-old terms all that she wanted to express. Like and love were being used interchangeably here, and she wished she could articulate the difference between the two.

"Well, I have to talk to your father..." - *which I should have done first,* she added to herself. "I think that you should ask him about your mom. But no matter what, Thomas, your dad will be in your life forever: she can't take you away from him. I don't have all the answers, but listen to me..." She took his chin gently in her hand and tilted his head up until his eyes met hers. "Your father loves you so much, and I do too."

Tisha remembered that day on the playground and how she'd sent him away to keep him from getting hurt. Sure, she'd needed help and he had been able go to get it, but regardless of her needs, her primary concern had been his safety. She'd die before letting Andrea do to Thomas what she'd done to Marina. The little boy was a hero in her mind and he meant to the world to her. Tisha loved children, period, but Thomas had carved out a special place within her heart.

"Teresa is your mother and I know she loves you too," Tisha added aloud. When he nodded, she stood slowly. She moved toward the door. "Now, clean up this room, please. I'm going to talk to your father." *Lord willing.* "Then I'm going to make your favorite for dinner," she added, trying to change the subject.

Thomas looked up at her, intrigued. "My favorite's pancakes, it's dinner time."

"I know," she winked, and left the way she came.

———————

Chase flipped angrily through the mail sitting on his desk. There were two letters from his magazine editor but he quickly tossed them aside. He didn't want to deal with anything right now, certainly not work. What he needed was something to pound, strike or punch. He rolled his neck in a circular motion to ease the tense knots, but even that was futile.

He heard Tisha enter quietly. She shut the door to the den, and when he felt cool hands on his neck he tensed for a mere second and then relaxed as they rubbed in a circular motion. Instead of sending chills throughout his body, those hands had the power to calm his temper and bring to life a yearning he hadn't had in years. He closed his eyes and let her fingers stroke his neck as a sigh escaped him.

"I'm sorry," he muttered when he felt Tisha move around the chair to stand beside him.

"I don't accept your apology, Chase."

"What?" Chase replied as he opened his eyes.

"You need to apologize to Thomas. There was no reason to get mad at him."

"Well, he did whine, and I don't want him hanging out with Jason," Chase defended.

"Why not? What happened?" Tisha stepped between Chase's legs to sit on his knee.

"If he's anything like his father, he's probably a jerk too."

"You still didn't tell me what happened tonight," Tisha prodded.

"I decked him," Chase answered heavily. Tisha looked at him questioningly. "Jason's father, Jeb George... he deserved it." Chase looked away. "He said something that I didn't like," Chase added, by way of explanation.

"Well, okay, what did he say?"

"Nothing."

"It had to be something," Tisha replied heatedly.

"Can we just drop it, please?"

"Fine." She threw up her hands in resignation. "I wanted to talk to you about something else anyway." She moved away from him and looked around the room, not quite knowing how to begin. Slowly she paced back to him, her hands clasped together.

"Thomas mentioned that you and Teresa have talked about him visiting with her." She trod lightly, realizing this wasn't the best time, but also that there might never be a good time. His present grim attitude seemed to be about more than what had happened at the school. Just maybe Teresa was involved, too. After all, the woman had been there when Tisha arrived the other night; but Chase hadn't broached the subject, so Tisha had decided not to either.

She took a seat on the high-backed leather chair facing his desk. Once seated, she looked at him and touched his hand. Chase was clearly upset. Tisha was upset too. Upset by the fact that he apparently couldn't confide in her; upset that she'd had to learn the news about Teresa from Thomas instead of from Chase. The man should have talked about the issue with his son by now, instead of letting the boy muddle together his own half-baked conclusions.

Tisha pressed on: "I know your ex-wife makes you angry and that you'd rather not deal with her antics, but I do think you should talk to Thomas. Right now he's speculating about what she wants to do, scared that she wants custody of him, convinced that he's going to be dragged back to California and away from you."

Chase withdrew his hand from hers as if she'd bitten him. Leaning back in his chair, he casually rested his left ankle across his right knee and folded his arms across his chest. "So, a day of peril and a week spent at my house and suddenly you and my son have some inside communication. You're now thick as thieves, huh? He confides in you and tells you all his secrets nowadays, does he?"

Tisha visibly stiffened. "You know that's not true. We shared a traumatic event, but don't make it seem like that's what this is about. We have grown close, Thomas and I, and if he's shared anything at all with me, it's because you've been pushing him away. If you must know, this is the first time he's told me anything about his mother and how he feels."

She took a deep breath and continued. "I realize we're all on edge, cooped up here together, but there's something more going on with you, I know it. If it's Teresa, then why can't you tell me? And don't shift this to take jabs at me or Thomas. I can handle it, Chase, but your son doesn't understand what the big deal is or where it's all coming from. Anyway, I think it's time for me to go home."

"What do you want from me, Tisha?" Chase replied tersely. "And why go home? Why are you so stubborn? There is a confirmed child abuser on the loose, but you'd rather return to your home with zero security than stay here safe with me?"

"Of course not. Chase, do you tell Thomas that you love him?" Tisha asked, dismissing her threat to leave and bracing herself for the explosion behind her question.

Chase gaped. "How can you ask me that? You know I love my son."

"That's not what I asked you," Tisha said.

Chase was silent for a moment. "I tell him every night that I love him."

"Chase, honey, does he hear you? Or do you tell him as he's drifting off to sleep?"

Chase looked back at Tisha.

"There's no question in my mind that you love him, Chase," she continued. "I just want you to go up there, talk to him and explain to him what Teresa wants. If you can tell him without getting angry, then explain why you think she's not telling the truth. Isn't that what you told me: that she pretends she wants to see him but doesn't follow through? Just *talk* to him and caution him about getting his hopes up about her. Let him know how you're going to handle the situation. All he wants is for you to talk about it to him, to clue him in and ask his opinion on the matter. He has some say too, regardless of his age. Any insight you can give is certainly better than letting him think the worst and fill in his own horrible details. And a mother's love, Chase… it's different at this age. He needs that."

"I won't let her hurt him," Chase muttered, and looked away.

"Like she hurt you?" Tisha whispered.

His head snapped up quickly to look at her. "How did you get to know so damn much?"

But, irritatingly, he knew she was right. He stood to pace.

"You ever been through a divorce before? You ever raise a child on your own with no clue how to do it?"

"No." Tisha looked away. She wished she had been there from the beginning for the both of them. Staying with them was so easy, because being there soothed the desperate need to feel a part of their family. "Sorry. I don't know what that's like."

"Great, then don't tell me what I should do about it. I'll handle it like I've always handled it and we'll be fine, thank you very much. I am all he needs right now. I suffice: I'm *it*."

"You do suffice, you *are* it, Chase. That's, uh, fine."

"That's not what I meant," Chase replied. "And another thing, why do you really care? *She* never did."

"I understand, but I'm not your ex-wife and don't you ever compare her to me again. I don't deserve that."

Tisha felt angry, and she felt sad. Chase obviously still

harbored a lot of hurt around his ex-wife's abandonment of himself and his son. She looked at the door and reached for the knob when he rushed over and pulled her from it.

"Please don't go. I'm sorry."

TWENTY-NINE

TO CHASE'S RELIEF, TISHA STOPPED. It scared him to think about her infiltrating his life so easily and burrowing deep into his heart, because that's what she'd been doing from the first day he met her.

"It's hard for me to find the right words. The words I'm using are driving you away, and that's not what I want."

Chase took her hand. It was cold and stiff in his own. He hated to think that anything he said could have her packing her bags and leaving him and Thomas for good. He'd had the best time with her this entire week, even in such dire circumstances.

"I'm sorry for what I said. I'm sorry you're in this mess, because I'm starting to love you, and I'm worried that when I know you're safe and Andrea Robinson is going to jail, you'll leave. Though we've been thrown together, I'm so glad you've been here. I enjoy your company every single day, I enjoy your cooking… I enjoy *you.*"

Chase was undeterred by her raised eyebrow. He felt out of breath laying so much on the line. He hadn't been prepared to say all that he did, but there it was: the truth. The utterly scary, heartfelt but simpler-kept-in-than-out truth.

Chase towered over her and she looked so small and delicate but she was anything but. He sorely regretted ever thoughtlessly comparing her to his ex-wife. She didn't resemble Teresa in any form, and he was sorry.

"Please don't leave us until Robinson is in jail, Tisha, please. I'd never forgive myself if…"

Tisha nodded. He hugged her close and squeezed her tight and before he knew he was kissing her, again and again until the anger and tension that emanated from each of them was diminished.

"You'll talk to Thomas? Chase, please…"

Chase raised his head and nodded. "Yes, I'll do whatever you ask me," Chase said and leaned in to kiss her again.

"… and me too, you'll tell me about Teresa and let me know how you feel – and soon?" she added. When she framed his face with her hands, he stilled, closed his eyes and nodded.

"Yes. There really is nothing to tell you about her except that I do not love her. I don't even *like* her. I tolerate her antics and she asks for money whenever she sees me. It's over between us."

"Was that so hard?" she said with a small smile.

"No, but I see my attempt to make you forget things doesn't work. I promise, and I am sorry," he said.

Tisha nodded. "Oh, it works," she smiled. "It works very well, but the issue is that my relationships with both the men in this house are growing more and more important to me. I don't want whatever I bring to strain any of that, and I want you to always communicate with me and with your son."

"I'm trying to communicate silently right now," he joked.

They kissed again, then at last Tisha broke away. "I'm gonna make dinner and then we can talk some more but if we carry on like this, there will be no dinner."

"You can be my dinner." He nibbled playfully at her ear.

She smiled again and chuckled. "In your dreams, pal."

Chase's phone rang. He pulled it from his pocket and threw it onto the couch across the room.

"You should get that. Dinner will be ready in thirty minutes - I'm really hungry now. Bye," Tisha said and before he could protest, she pecked him one more time on the lips and zipped back through the door and up the stairs to the kitchen.

Chase took a deep breath. He knew he should go talk to Thomas - and he would, eventually. He retrieved his phone and saw that the missed call was from the very woman who'd almost cost him Tisha via his thoughtless comparison.

While he was holding the phone, it rang again, and this time he answered it without hesitation.

"Hey Prescott, what's up?"

"Hey Chase, what's up with you? You all right?"

"Oh, just ex stuff," sighed Chase. "All good though. What can I do for you?" Chase didn't mind talking to Prescott Thompson. His editor boss and friend would give him something else to think about. Maybe Prescott had an assignment or something that Chase could think about. Any distraction would be welcome: after holding Tish in his arms as he had just moments ago, he was on the look-out for any excuse not to cart her off without delay and bind her future to his forever. All the tension that had left his body so easily came flooding back at the thoughts he was having. Scary.

He was brought back to earth with a jolt as he realized he hadn't heard a word of the assignment Prescott had just described.

"...a good story, wish he wasn't so washed up and delu-sional, but do some research – sure you'll be fine..."

"Mmm-hmm," Chase replied, trying desperately to regain the thread of the conversation.

"Great then, you can take it? I thought you might be tied up, but that's cool, I'll e-mail you your tickets and you can– "

"Wait, what?" Chase was caught off-guard. "I mean, I am tied up - I didn't know you meant *now* - I thought you meant, uh, after the season had started – that's not for another month!"

"No, man, I need you in Los Angeles to do the interview this week. The guy said he only wants to talk to you, and anyway, I can't get away right now."

Chase was annoyed. He wasn't following Prescott's requests properly, because of the thoughts of Tisha and the M word that kept intruding.

"You said you could take two days here and there now that your boy's getting older," Prescott replied impatiently. "You've been saying he could stay with his grandmother."

"Yeah, I mean, yes, I did say that, but –

"So what's the problem?"

"Well, Pres, I'm sorry… I'm just really tied up right now, that's all."

"Listen, Chase, you know that I'd put someone else on this if I could, but everyone else is already covering something. This Los Angeles guy respects you, and we might lose the interview if you don't do it. Anyway, just two days is all I'm asking: you get in, you get out, I'll clean up the run, just get the information for me: something to work with."

"I said I can't get away—I—"

"Listen, Chase, when things were going on with you and Teresa I let you out of a lot of stuff, especially for someone who had just started the career as a writer and commentator." His editor's tone grew steely. "My magazine isn't some little gazette, you know, and I just can't this time. You're the only person I got, and I need this story. It's my turn to ask a favor."

"Who's it on?" Chase asked wearily.

"Rose."

"Are you serious?" Chase exploded. "That man just got traded before the season started and he didn't do anything on the team he was on before he went to the Sharks. He's not doing anything now."

"I know, that's why I want *you* on it," Prescott said urgently. "You can get to the core of what his problem is. You're deep, and he respects you."

"Oh please, Pres." Chase felt deflated. He couldn't deny it: when he'd first started writing for the largest serious sports magazine in the world, there had been many months when he'd asked for favors, and Prescott Thompson, Editor in Chief, had done everything in his power to accommodate the young upstart's requests without hesitation. Time and again, Chase had asked not to be sent anywhere out of town while going through his divorce from Teresa, and he'd had to ask again when Thomas was an infant. Since then, Chase's articles had developed a large following as he became a household name of football. He knew that he was in no position to bargain.

Chase pinched the bridge of his nose in utter frustration. He didn't want to leave Tisha, not with things as they were; but he owed Prescott bigtime. "I'll see what I can do," he said finally.

"I'll email you your tickets. You leave before Monday night's game," his boss finished. The receiver clicked.

Chase groaned. Sitting down at his computer, he got down to the business of pulling together everything he could on the background and statistics of the no-good, possibly morally bankrupt player he was being sent to interview, ensuring he was up to date.

When the phone on Chase's desk rang, he grabbed it quickly.

"Yo man, what's up?" the voice on the other end said.

"Hey, I'm glad you called. Listen, man, can you find someone for me? Also, I need you to look out for someone, just while I'm out of town for a couple days. My main objective is to find this woman who hurt my... my friend."

"A woman hurt your friend? That's deep, man. Sure, just say the word and I'm there. You know that."

"Get here by Sunday, then. I've got to go on a trip for work and I want you to watch her for me. I'll e-mail you the details and any schedule stuff. For the most part she and Thomas should be laying low - she'll keep him with her. I want you around if they want to go out: I don't want them treated like prisoners here."

"Yo, sounds serious."

"Yeah," Chase agreed. It was serious. He was in love with Tisha.

"Okay, holler at you."

"Later." Chase replaced the receiver in its cradle.

He stood, stretched and headed for the kitchen, where the smell of crisp fried meat and all sorts of other delectable things wafted past his nose. When Chase got there, he stood watching Tisha and Thomas, their heads together and engrossed in what they were doing, unaware of his presence. Chase watched as Tisha guided Thomas's hand to ladle spoonfuls of what looked like pancake batter onto the hot griddle.

"There you go, perfect. Now put the halved strawberries for the eyes and blueberries in the shape of a smile and then—" She looked up and noticed Chase standing in the doorway.

Thomas looked up too. "Yo, Dad, we're going to have pancakes for dinner! Pretty cool, huh?" he said cheerfully.

Tisha looked back at Thomas in disbelief. "Man, look at you two," she said. "Typical men: one minute all in a huff, and the next it's like nothing's happened at all. Hmph!"

"Don't hold grudges, Tisha, they just don't work," smiled Chase as he entered the kitchen.

"Okay, Thomas," she instructed, ignoring his remark, "when the bubbles around the edges start to pop, it'll be time to turn it over." She glanced at Chase. "Uh, make yourself useful and set the table. How many pancakes do you want?"

"Fifteen," Chase said without missing a beat, eliciting a

chuckle from his son and a look that could kill from Tisha. He laughed too.

"Dad, can you really eat fifteen pancakes? You'll get a stomachache!"

"Yeah, you're probably right," Chase said, pretending to reconsider. "I'll take three," he amended.

"Well thanks, that we can do," Tisha replied.

Chase helped set the table and settled down to enjoy another delicious meal with his son and the woman who was taking up residence in his heart, and whom he hoped would choose to stay even after this nightmare was over.

He dreaded telling her about the trip he had to take for an assignment out of town but he hoped she understood. Truth be told, he was truly concerned about leaving at all.

THIRTY

THE TIME TO LEAVE CAME around super quickly. Despite their small tiff, about Teresa and his lack of communication with his son, they moved past it and things were pleasant again, like a family.

Chase was in his room packing a few last-minute items into his travel bag when Thomas entered the room. He climbed up onto Chase's bed and sat silently.

"What's up, sport?"

"Nothing much," Thomas replied dully.

Chase shoved aside the duffel bag and sat down beside him. "Listen, son, I'm sorry I've got to go away. But guess what? I got a bodyguard for you and Tisha, so I know you guys will be safe."

"A bodyguard?" Thomas said in awe. "You mean like on TV?"

Chase nodded, smiling. "Something like that. His name's Devon. You won't even know he's there. He's just gonna look out for you and Tisha while I'm gone. He'll watch the house, just to make sure all is safe. I don't want you stuck here. I'll only be gone one night, so I'll be back day after tomorrow."

"Does Tisha know?"

Chase nodded. He'd told her last night, providing full details of the plan so she wouldn't be alarmed. Tisha hadn't liked the idea much, but she'd accepted it on the understanding that it was only temporary.

Thomas seemed to take the news about the bodyguard just fine, and Chase took a deep breath of relief. His son was likely excited about the drama indicated by the mere presence of bodyguards, even as he also deducted that all was completely safe with them around. Chase knew that it remained a serious matter, however. The part he wasn't ready to talk about with Thomas yet was his ex-wife; but he'd promised Tisha he'd talk to him, so...

"You know, Thomas, your mother... She said that she'd like to see you sometime. I think it's a good idea." A pack of lies, but Chase didn't know what else to say to encourage the boy. "Is that all right with you? How do you feel about that?"

"Okay, I guess."

"Well, do you want to see her?" *Just say no, son, and I won't let her near you,* Chase thought silently to himself.

"I won't have to go stay with her, will I?"

"No way," Chase said with conviction. "Just, you know, visits and things," he added. He didn't actually know what would happen, because Teresa hadn't actually arranged anything. Everything out of her mouth was a lie, so he reminded himself that this might be one too.

"I just want you to know that sometimes she... says something and then she doesn't follow through. Just remember that it's not because she doesn't love you. It's just that she's..." Chase struggled for the right words. How could he tell Thomas not to get his hopes up for something that might never happen?

"You mean she's not a very good promise-keeper, Dad?"

Chase looked at his son. "Well, yeah. Yes, I guess that's what I mean. Remember what I told you, though: that alone doesn't make a person bad."

Thomas shrugged. "I understand. It's okay."

Glad you think so, Chase thought. "But don't worry, okay?" he added encouragingly.

"I'm not, Dad." Thomas placed his hand on his father's shoulder, as if Chase were the one needing comfort. Chase almost laughed. He patted the small hand on his shoulder and smiled at Thomas. "Take care of Tisha for me, will you son?"

"I will. I love her," he said simply. "I bet she's a good promise-keeper. Hey - Dad?"

"Yeah, son."

"You think you and Tisha will get married?"

"Uh, I-I don't know." That one came out of nowhere and socked Chase right in the chest.

"I think she loves you," Thomas continued.

"Well, how do you know? Did she say that?" He hoped beyond hope she loved him. There was no question she loved his son.

"Well, she said she loved *me*. I think she loves you, too."

"Thomas, you know that *I* love you, right?" Chase asked.

"Sure, Dad. I love you too," Thomas replied.

Chase went on. "So, if I were to be with Tisha for the long term, it would be okay with you? Would that be all right?"

It amazed him how the thought of a long-term relationship and even the 'm word' no longer caused him panic. It actually felt good to think about rebuilding his family in that way, and to think about himself and Tisha as a couple...

Thomas shrugged. "I think she'd make a good mom, you know?" he said matter-of-factly, then hopped off the bed and trotted out of the room.

"Yeah." Chase smiled at his son's back. He felt as if a huge burden had been lifted off him. He fell backwards onto the bed and stared at the ceiling. "I think she'd make a great mom, too," Chase whispered.

THRTY-ONE

———◆———

TISHA SAT AT THE SMALL kitchen table as Angie made dinner. Initially, she had thought Chase's brief absence on this business trip would be a good thing. She needed the time to sort out her feelings: just maybe she'd know what she should do by the time he got back. However, just hours after he'd left for the airport and Thomas's grandmother had come to pick him up for the day, the house felt empty and silent. She might as well have been living alone all over again.

The more she thought about being there, the more she thought being with Chase was simply some sort of delusional need she'd conjured up. Every day that brought no word on Andrea Robinson, she felt more and more like she should just go home.

Tisha looked up from her mug of hot tea and Angie refilled it again. "Thank you, Angie, but you don't have to serve me."

"It's not a problem," Angie said.

Tisha nodded. "Do you mind if I ask how long you've worked for Chase?"

"No, I don't mind," Angie responded. "A couple of years, after I returned from Paris. I knew of Mrs. - uh, Teresa, but she hasn't ever lived here, she just always came over a lot. Can I just tell you I don't like her at all. You're way nicer."

Angie looked toward Tisha for any reaction before continuing:"She's selfish, and I've never believed anything she's said. I think she left Thomas when he was about two..."

Tisha nodded sadly. She didn't mind at all the talk of Teresa, she truly wanted to know. She'd amazed herself with her own restraint when it came to asking Chase about her. He'd already told her about how painful his marriage had been, and that was mostly what kept her from asking. She knew he hated to discuss it at all. She also knew how long Thomas had been without a loving mother. It amazed her that he was still so considerate and kind despite her absence.

Tisha looked over at Angie, smiling as she willed herself back to the present. "You've been to Paris? What did... uh, what were you doing there?"

Angie took a deep breath. "I was at a very prominent culinary academy there, learning to be a chef."

"You're a chef? How come you're not working at a restaurant there? Why'd you come back?" Tisha asked. It had never occurred to her that Angie had studied cooking professionally. Then again, her abundant know-how around the kitchen, not to mention her amazing pastry and desserts, hinted that there was more to Angie than met the eye.

"I had a scholarship there, and I came back because of my... my sister's kids. She died and I came back to raise them."

Tisha set down her mug and regarded Angie. "Wow, I had no idea. That's something. Chase never mentioned you having kids."

Angie nodded. "I took this job to make ends meet. I never used to talk about them, they were babies when I got them. I just kept to myself, did my work and left."

Tisha nodded in understanding. "What did your sister die of?"

"She was killed in a car accident," Angie said, "along with our mom and dad."

"Oh my God, Angie, I'm so sorry. I had no idea."

"It's all right, time lessens the pain. I'm okay. There's something I'd like to tell you, though."

"Of course, anything," Tisha assured her.

"I, ah... there's a reporter that keeps calling here, but I won't let him talk to any of you. It's not my business, and maybe I shouldn't, but... I know him. He's the... same reporter who did the story on my family when my sister died."

"Oh well, wow - I thank you for that, actually. I don't care to talk to any reporters. Why do you particularly dislike him?"

Angie hesitated. "My sister was... an alcoholic, but she'd been clean for almost a year. I know she wouldn't drink," Angie said hurriedly. "The reporter said he'd tell what happened, that he'd give us a good slant, tell the story from my perspective."

"Did he do that?" Tisha asked.

Angie shook her head. "He lied. He painted my sister as a horrible person, a no-good drunk, when really she'd been sober and trying to get her life and her family together. The story ran and it was just, uh, just hard. It made it harder for me to get custody of the twins, too, but I did it. I've managed the best I can."

"I'm sure you have. I'm so sorry you had to go through that." Tisha looked at the woman across from her. "I don't need any further reason not to trust this man than your word. I would think twice before talking to a reporter anyway, but I definitely won't even consider it now that you've told me about your history with this one."

"He's very persistent, Tisha. He called again earlier today."

Tisha nodded. "It'll be all right. I understand what you're saying. I have a bodyguard. Have you seen him?"

Angie smiled. "Yes, I did."

"It's really weird," Tisha said. As she stood, she moved to stand beside Angie. Standing on her tiptoes, she pushed back the curtains and looked out the window, where a car with dark tinted windows was parked. Tisha let the curtains fall and turned to Angie. She rinsed her mug out and shrugged. "Different, I guess," she said.

After washing her hands, Tisha asked Angie, "You ready to learn to fry my momma's recipe for good old-fashioned extra crispy chicken?"

Angie nodded enthusiastically and was rolling up her sleeves when the door suddenly banged open. Devon the bodyguard stood there, and Tisha saw Teresa just behind him.

"You wanna talk to her?" Devon asked, jerking a thumb over his shoulder.

Tisha's gaze landed on the cause of some of her problems with Chase. "Teresa," she said cordially.

"Still here, are ya?" Teresa attempted to move forward but was halted by a strong arm. "Oh, come on now. Why don't you just... go somewhere, you big bully? Chase never hired *me* a damn watchdog," Teresa said as she cut her eyes at the big man. "And give me my purse back."

Devon was busy looking through it. "Hey," Teresa screamed and reached for something that Devon had removed from her purse.

"When you leave, you can have it back."

"Next time I'll bring my glock then, haha."

Devon gave the woman the purse back but kept the item that looked like a small purple box: almost like a makeup compact. Teresa certainly looked like she used enough of that stuff, if that was indeed what it was.

"That's a Taser," Angie spoke up.

Tisha raised her eyebrows in surprise.

"Yeah, so I can *zzzip zzzip* you for taking my man," Teresa hissed.

Tisha supposed she should feel safer, but it hadn't ever occurred to her what the thing was. She didn't own any weaponry of her own. Now that she'd been assaulted, perhaps she should take a page out of Teresa's book. If she got a Taser or more security, maybe she could go back to her own home. She wished she were a little more progressive, but with such a wonderful family, two big brothers and a house most often full of people, Tisha had never felt the need to be prepared... or a need to feel scared of everything. Not until her encounter with Andrea Robinson.

What could she do without her Taser? Tisha wondered. The thought made her feel only moderately better. "It's all right, Devon. Thank you," Tisha said, and then regarded Teresa.

"You still here?" Teresa repeated, putting a hand on her hip.

"I don't recall mentioning leaving."

"You might not have mentioned it, you might not even know it, but you will be, and soon. You should be ready to pack your bags when Chase gets back."

"That so?" Tisha looked at Angie, who stood alarmed and awkward, not knowing what to do. Angie's stance was stiff, her eyes moving back and forth between the two as if they would throw punches at any moment.

"Angie, I can, uh, show you this recipe some other time. Why don't you take the rest of the day off? I'll finish dinner and uh, it's fine. I'm good."

"Are you sure, Tisha?" Angie hesitated.

Teresa rounded on Angie. "Oh, you call her Tisha, do you? Well, you will never call her Mrs. Alton. You got that? I guess you like her 'cause she's not as demanding as I would've been, huh? I don't know why Chase hired you—"

"That's enough, Teresa. If you've got problems with me, talk to me. I'll see ya later, Angie."

Tisha watched Angie hesitate, her uncertainty evident as her eyes traveled between Tisha and Teresa. Eventually, Angie grabbed her coat. She delivered a mean look to Teresa as she backed away to the exit, saying a hasty goodbye and acknowledging Devon, who stood, still visible in the hallway, as she left.

"Now that we got rid of *that*..." Teresa nodded toward the door, "I can break some news to you. I've been meaning to get around to telling you, and now is just as good a time as any."

"And that would be?" Tisha raised an eyebrow.

"Chase and I share something special," Teresa declared.

Tisha watched the way the woman paced, the way she fidgeted with her hands. It looked so real, and maybe it was, but she wanted - she needed to believe it was all an act. Chase had told her that Teresa was an aspiring actress, after all.

"We share a child," Teresa finished meaningfully.

"A child you never wanted," Tisha corrected. "You think I don't know? You think Chase didn't tell me that you didn't fight one bit for Thomas? That you haven't even visited him to spend time with him?"

Tisha made a face. "Chase has seven years of blood, sweat and tears on you; and I can't forget *love*. It's so important - it's more important than any other thing."

Tisha had pictured this very scenario endless times, and as a result had many ready arguments lined up. She wouldn't let this woman get to her. *Poor Thomas, to have such a shrew for a mother.* In this silly charade, Thomas was Tisha's only concern. Regardless of what happened between her and Chase, she knew that Thomas deserved and needed a mother's love. If Tisha weren't going to be it, then she was sad about that, but someone needed to remind Teresa of what she had in Thomas, and how wrong she had been to neglect him.

"L-O-V-E," Tisha spelled out. "Something you couldn't, or wouldn't, give with your selfish self. You have a beautiful little boy, and Chase has defended you to him, but you know, I ask myself why over and over again. You aren't worth it."

"Don't you talk to me that way. You don't know a thing

about my life," Teresa leaned closer to Tisha. "You think you got it all. Living up here with my man. He's always going to be *my* man, you understand? And just what makes you think he could ever put up with you and all your drama? Ain't that much love in the world. You think I got problems – *please.*"

Teresa threw her hand in a wave toward Tisha. "This situation you got yourself into, it gets old. Can't even leave the damn house without someone coming up to you guys asking a bunch of questions about your problems. And look what he's already had to get for you." Teresa ticked things off on her fingers. "Paying for a lawyer to represent you; a bodyguard to watch you; and his doctor friend to come in and look you over. The sooner you're better off, the sooner he can get you out of his life. He's counting the days."

Tisha opened her mouth, then closed it again. Teresa continued her diatribe.

"Chase has been in the spotlight before and he didn't like it then, he certainly won't like it now. He doesn't need to deal with that again. He'll kick you to the curb before he lets both himself and Thomas be brought under that kind of scrutiny. It'll get old and he'll dump you. He loves me, he will always love me."

Teresa rubbed her body dramatically, emphasizing the parts that she thought Chase might love.

"I had his child and I am Thomas's mother. I'm gonna have another child with him, mark my words. I'm gonna share his bed. He slept with you yet?"

Tisha looked up sharply at that comment, but remained silent. Teresa smirked. "That ought to tell you something. No normal man turns down a chance for sex."

Tisha laughed bitterly. This woman was good. But it would take more than that to get at her. She was tough. She wouldn't let what was being said rattle her or make her doubt Chase.

She took a deep breath, putting aside the issues concerning her and Chase and reflecting on what had been said about Thomas.

"What's happened between Chase and me is none of your business," Tisha began with dignity. "But the one thing that is most certainly your business is your love for Thomas. Why don't you show him and everyone else that you're his mother? A mother who visits him, a mother who tells him she loves him and takes him places and spends time with him. That boy is special, but if you're bent on playing these little games, Chase and I won't let you use Thomas in any way, shape, or form to get what you want. You can forget that right this minute. If you and Chase are supposed to be together" — Tisha cringed inside even considering any of the things Teresa had said — "I guess only time will tell. Just know that I don't personally believe a single word that comes out of your mouth."

"You calling me a liar?" Teresa replied indignantly and stepped toward Tisha in a threatening way that caused Tisha to move back cautiously.

Devon cleared his throat.

Thomas rushed into the room toward Tisha, his jeans covered in dirt and his face bright with pride. "Tisha, guess what? Grandma and I went to the park and I hit a ball way out — "

He turned to acknowledge the other person in the room, belatedly realizing it was his mother. "Uh, hey... Mom."

"Hiya, Tommy." Teresa ran a hand over her hair. "What's going on?"

Thomas shrugged. "Nothin'," he replied, looking away.

Tisha looked on. She wanted to excuse herself, but it was clear to her Teresa wouldn't be staying. Her once confident, mean demeanor seemed to deflate when she saw her son. Tisha read the look of uncertainty mingled with panic on Teresa's face and saw how she looked repeatedly to the door. Just seconds ago, Teresa's face had been filled with certainty about her future with Chase, but with Thomas's entrance, all of that vanished.

"Well, you look so big. I was planning on buying you some toys, but I wasn't sure what you had already. I know your dad buys you everything you want."

"I got a lot of stuff," Thomas replied guardedly.

Tisha turned and rolled her eyes. Unbeknownst to Teresa, she could never buy Thomas's affections. Secretly, Tisha wished Teresa would leave; at the same time, she did sincerely wish that Thomas would eventually come to know and spend time with his mother. Tisha knew that she was a big enough person to let what was right override her desires where Teresa was concerned.

"Thomas, why don't you show your mom some of the stuff you have in your room, then she can decide what to get you?" Tisha said as she looked at Thomas. She nodded encouragingly at him until he nodded slowly too, catching her drift.

"Well, okay…"

"Listen, I'd love to, but I'm going to have to go. I've, er, got some errands to run," Teresa said hurriedly, making for the door. But when your dad comes back I'll come see ya, okay?"

"Teresa."

Without anybody except Devon noticing, Sandra Alton, Chase's mother, had entered and was standing just inside the kitchen. Teresa didn't even bother acknowledging the older woman as she scooted hurriedly past her and out the door.

The silence in the air was palpable, and Tisha wasn't sure how exactly to proceed. Chase's mother scrutinized her as if she were an intruder, and Thomas acted as if the last ten minutes hadn't happened at all. Tisha took a deep breath and managed a weak smile. "Thomas, are you going to introduce me to your grandmother?"

They'd left early that morning, before Tisha had had a

chance to meet the elder Mrs. Alton, and in some respects Tisha had been glad. Now, however, there was no hiding, and Tisha was confronted with a situation that could make or break her reputation with Chase's nearest and dearest.

"Oh, yeah, Grandmom, this is Tisha, she's my teacher… and she's dad's girlfriend," Thomas said knowingly.

"Hello," Tisha tried to sound friendly but didn't know how she sat with the woman quite yet. Maybe Chase's mother had wished Chase and his ex-wife would get back together. Maybe Teresa and Mrs. Alton had been close at one time and any new person for her son was unconscionable. Even as she considered all these possibilities, Tisha knew they were unlikely. If Teresa and Sandra Alton were friends, Teresa wouldn't have swept past her so abruptly without acknowledgement.

Wiping her hands on a paper towel, Tisha moved forward and shook the woman's hand. "It's a pleasure to meet you." She hoped she sounded warm and friendly. She had really looked forward to meeting the woman who had raised such a terrific man.

"The pleasure is mine," Mrs. Alton said. She was tall, with her son's kind eyes. "I've heard so much about you, it's about time I met you. I'm sorry my son didn't introduce us sooner."

"Yes, well, that's all right… uh, things have been hectic. I — "

"Tisha," Thomas protested, "I was trying to tell you about the ball that I hit way into left field…"

He trailed off when Tisha shot him a look.

"Yes, I know, honey. Just a minute and you can tell me all about it. I can't wait, though." She winked and Thomas was painfully quiet. "You were saying, Mrs. Alton?" she encouraged.

"Oh no, *you* were saying. I was listening," Mrs. Alton replied neutrally.

"Well… Oh, that's right: I was just saying that Chase

wanted us all to go out together sometime soon, he mentioned that. He had to go out of town on assignment for a day or two, as you know," Tisha said quickly, "so it's just Thomas and myself here at the moment. Can I offer you something to drink? Would you like some hot tea, perhaps?"

"Well, all right. I'd like that."

Tisha nodded, relieved that so far things seemed to be going fairly well. "All right, it will just take a few minutes. Please have a seat if you'd like."

Mrs. Alton obligingly took a seat in the chair at the small kitchen table. Tisha took her jacket and Sandra smiled in silent thanks as she situated herself more comfortably.

"So, Thomas," Tisha said, "please tell me about this ball you hit that would bring even Jackie Robinson to tears."

Mrs. Alton watched in surprise as Thomas let out a hoot of laughter. "Thomas, you know who Jackie Robinson is?" the older woman said, startled.

"Sure, Grandmom. Mrs. Jameson taught us about him when it was Black History Month. He's the first African-American to play for a major-league baseball team," —Thomas looked at Tisha proudly and continued rattling off some facts.

When he finished, Mrs. Alton looked at Tisha, astonished. "Wow," she said to Thomas. "That's something."

Tisha smiled at Thomas. "Now, tell me, tell me, tell me," she said eagerly. Tisha felt as if she had impressed Chase's mother, at least a little bit. It wasn't her primary intention, but if the woman now viewed her even a little more favorably, Tisha was happy.

Tisha's attention was rapt as Thomas recounted his outing with his grandmother, his epic hit and the home run that would undoubtedly have resulted, had it been a real game.

"That's so wonderful, Thomas. That deserves a celebration. Mrs. Alton, Thomas and I would love it if you stayed for dinner – wouldn't we, Thomas?"

Thomas looked at his grandmother. "Yeah, Grandmom. Tisha can really cook, just as good as Angie."

"Oh, I don't know about that, Thomas…" she began modestly.

"Really," Mrs. Alton said, "I'd like to stay. What's your specialty?"

"Well, I don't really have one. I was going to teach Angie my mother's recipe for fried chicken. She just finished peeling the potatoes. Uh, if that won't be too heavy for you, I'll stick to the chicken, but I can bake it with a little barbeque sauce instead if you like?"

Tisha realized she was gesturing a lot with her hands and made an effort to stop. She always waved them around whenever she was the slightest bit nervous.

"Heaven knows I haven't had fried chicken in a long time. That would be wonderful. Thank you," Mrs. Alton replied earnestly.

"Of course," Tisha said, and began to retrieve the ingredients for the chicken while she, Thomas and his grandmother chatted amicably.

Tisha was surprised at how well they got along, and Mrs. Alton even helped with some of the smaller things while they worked together in the kitchen, courteous and aware of each other, as if their cooking together were an every-day routine. Her energy, even after spending most of the day with Thomas at the park, was unyielding.

As Thomas helped to set the small space at the island, everyone sat down. After Thomas said grace, Tisha watched as the woman bit into her first bite of chicken. She chewed thoughtfully and Tisha pretended not to watch her even as she held her breath. So much rested on one tiny bite. Then Sandra Alton graced Tisha with an exuberant smile.

"This is wonderful," Mrs. Alton said.

"Thank you," Tisha replied, and immediately relaxed. She dug into her own food then, and made small talk as they all shared dinner.

Tisha knew once Thomas had left to go play in his room that the real inquiries would start. Sandra Alton was a very nice woman, and she and Thomas seemed to get along well. It was apparent that they were close. Still, Chase hadn't talked about his mother much, and now Tisha wondered why. She didn't have to wait long for an answer.

"Chase and I have just started to reconnect in the last year," Mrs. Alton began.

Tisha nodded. She reached for their dishes and stepped down from the high stool. "I see," was all that she offered in response.

"No, I don't think you do."

"Well, Mrs. Alton, it's really... none of my business. I'm not a nosy person," Tisha replied, immediately wishing she'd said anything but 'nosy'.

"And I'm not about to tell just anyone my personal information. So if I'm choosing to tell you, then it's not because I think you're nosy," Mrs. Alton replied.

"I'm sorry."

Mrs. Alton took a deep breath and continued. "I saw a lot today that showed the kind of person you are. I really learned a lot about you in just a few short hours."

Tisha was surprised to hear that the older woman had been watching her — contemplating her character, it seemed. Tisha had done the same, of course, but she'd never admit it so overtly. Mrs. Alton continued. "I saw how you tried to encourage Thomas to connect with his mother despite her selfishness. That was, well, very big of you. Someone else might have defamed her in front of him based on how she acts – however accurate their assessment of her actions may be. She doesn't deserve such a wonderful child."

Tisha nodded in agreement, but remained quiet. She leaned in clasping her hands on the tabletop as she listened intently.

"I also saw your praise of Thomas when he relayed his accomplishments today at the park, and then I saw you unafraid to deliver a small dose of discipline when he showed a little impatience and interrupted you as you were talking."

"You're very observant," Tisha replied, for lack of anything else to say. "Here I just wanted to enjoy my fried chicken."

Both of them laughed, then Mrs. Alton sobered.

"Teresa is a big part of the reason my son and I are just now reacquainting ourselves with each other. It did also have to do with his childrearing philosophy, of course. He wanted to raise Thomas as he saw fit, without any input and more importantly without any help from me." Sandra pursed her lips.

"You have to believe that Chase only wanted to prove that he could do a good job all on his own. It's obvious that every child-rearing skill he had in the first place came from what you did for him as a boy, and then as a man," Tisha put in.

"Yes, yes, I know that—now," his mother replied. "But it was hard in the beginning. I wanted so badly to help, and I tried. Oh, and Chase did have a very hard streak at one time. When Thomas was born and it was clear straightaway that Teresa didn't want that type of responsibility, Chase really changed. I can't blame Teresa exclusively for our rift, but she certainly didn't help matters."

Mrs. Alton picked at her napkin, shredding it into tiny pieces on the table. "I don't particularly like Teresa, and that's putting it mildly, but I do like you. I feel like I know you from the way Thomas behaves, and from what I've seen today, I know you're very special."

Tisha raised her eyebrows in surprise and felt tears sting her eyes. "Who wouldn't love your grandson, Mrs. Alton?"

Sandra Alton nodded. "And my son?" she prodded, unashamed.

Tisha unclasped her hands then, hesitating. "I don't know, Mrs. Alton. This situation with the school has thrown us together, but I... I really don't know where we stand."

"Sure you do," Sandra replied. "You don't have to know his feelings to be sure of your own. From my experience, a person always knows how they feel about another; but you want to wait to be sure he reciprocates your feelings, am I right? I understand, and I won't press you."

"Has Chase mentioned me to you?" Tisha blurted out. When Sandra stammered, Tisha had her answer. "It's all right, don't answer that. I don't want to know. I'm sorry I put you on the spot. When he comes back, I'll certainly know where we stand."

Tisha turned at Mrs. Alton's look of sympathy. She didn't know, and she shouldn't guess, what the other woman thought. Tisha reached for the stopper and secured it over the sink drain. She squirted in a few drops of dishwashing liquid as she turned the hot water faucet on full blast. She set dishes inside and concentrated on the water filling up the sink, her back still to Mrs. Alton. If only it were so easy, Tisha thought, to rinse away her troubles like the leftover food particles on the dishes. She'd be in great shape - if only.

"The meal was wonderful," Mrs. Alton said, breaking into her thoughts. "Where I come from, though, the chef doesn't clean up."

Tisha shook her head. "It's all right. It helps me think."

Tisha didn't want to shun the woman's help, so belatedly she said, "Why don't I wash and you can dry and put the dishes away?"

Mrs. Alton nodded. Tisha pushed away thoughts of Chase. "Chase will be back tomorrow evening. Would you like to stay the night and spend tomorrow with Thomas and I?" Tisha asked. "We have our own bodyguard," she added, laughing.

"Yes, I'd like that very much." Mrs. Alton nodded and

the two women resumed their tasks together as they exchanged light banter, discussing everything - except Tisha's feelings for the man she had indeed come to love.

THIRTY-TWO

———◆———

T HE LOS ANGELES INTERNATIONAL AIRPORT was too crowded. People kissed each other goodbye; others complained to the customer service representatives in an array of languages about delayed or canceled flights at the information desk. Nearby, what seemed at first glance like a maternity ward, but was only one of the crowded gates, was packed full of crying babies and dissatisfied, tem-per-tantrum-throwing toddlers.

To top it all off, Dean Jameson was stuck. Stuck at the airport, stuck with no cash, and just plain old stuck. He searched through his pockets one more time, to ensure he hadn't overlooked the credit card he always, -or almost always, it would appear- kept for emergencies.

Any old credit card would suffice, for that matter: anything to thrust at the impatient customer service representative who had managed to screw up his ticket. Someone had taken his cash, his credit cards, his plane ticket, and left him only with his identification. That small mercy was of abso-lutely no use to him right now: he was simply steaming mad that he couldn't get where he needed to be. A stupid ID couldn't buy a plane ticket, it couldn't figure out who stole his money, and it certainly couldn't magically trans-form into a 747 and get him home to Virginia.

He was stuck in California. Sure, it was sunny and lovely, but it was also home to unfortunate wildfires and the Kardashians, as well as plenty of other collagen-loaded, wealthy superstars. He had yet to see any, and he didn't care if he did or not… except maybe Halle Berry. Dean smiled in spite of himself.

Now, though, there were more pressing matters on his mind. For one, how the heck was he going to get home? Of all the places in the world for him to be stuck, it *would* be one of the farthest places from his home in the country. Why couldn't he have gotten stuck in Atlanta? Or on the road somewhere in Virginia? It just had to be stinking rich California. *Great.*

Dean was there to attend yet another conference on the country's most prestigious eye surgeons' views on the field and its projected progression over the next ten years. While mildly interested in learning about the latest technological advances in eye medicine, Dean hadn't expected to become a victim of theft during the trip.

Other than this annoying incident, the trip had been good. He'd relaxed, slept a little later than his hectically tight schedule in Virginia permitted; yet still felt no better than when he left. His main reason for attending hadn't been fulfilled. He'd come in hopes of finding some area of the field that really got his blood up and his soul stirred again, with noble thoughts of helping people to see properly. He knew he'd been graced with a precious gift in his profession, but of late, his ambition and his passion had just seemed to wane.

He stood looking back and forth between his watch and the airport screen displaying the times of flights. There were none leaving to Virginia, so Dean looked for the next closest destination, until he realized dejectedly that looking for a flight out was useless when he had no money to pay for a ticket.

To top everything off, his cell phone was dead.

"Excuse me, I'm sorry," he said to a teenager, who stood leaning against a wall scrolling on his phone. "My phone is dead, can I just borrow your charger? I've gotta make one phone call."

"Sure, man."

The young man dug through his backpack's numerous pockets and pulled out the familiar white cord. He put it into a plug near the base of a column and handed over the other end. Tisha was at Chase's and he didn't know the number there; Jina and Tony were probably on their way to Macon to see Tisha; and his mother... he hated to bother her with his carelessness. Dean was so irritated that he still couldn't pinpoint exactly when he'd allowed someone to get close enough to him to steal just about every dime. Could it have been before he left Atlanta, or even when he arrived there? He hadn't needed to pay for anything since arriving in California, and the last time he remembered pulling out his wallet to pay for something had been back in Georgia.

As soon as his phone flickered to life, Dean dialed his childhood home and the line clicked over, answered by a voice Dean didn't immediately recognize. "Hello, Jameson residence."

"Who's this?" Dean asked.

"Who's *this*?" was returned, and Dean rolled his eyes, now recognizing the silky voice. How could he not recognize the dulcet tones of Chyna Lockhart-Williams?

"Chyna, it's me, Dean," he replied more softly. She drove him crazy. "Is Mom there?" He knew Alfreah was like a mother to Chyna too. She'd spent so much time over at their house as a child that Dean's mother might as well have been her own.

"Dean, she's not here. They went for a walk this morning."

"You let them go for a walk? By themselves?" he replied incredulously.

"They are adults, Dean," Chyna replied. "If it makes you feel any better, I just checked on them and waved to them, but I'm not going to be a third wheel and intrude on the time she has with him. She's a capable woman, you know."

"Whatever," Dean said dismissively.

"What's the matter with you? Where are you?"

"I'm stuck," he said tersely.

"Stuck where?"

"California," he mumbled.

"Well, what happened?"

Dean sighed. "Someone stole my money."

"Oh no," Chyna replied, sounding sincere. Dean heard the shuffling in the background and the click of what sounded like computer keys as he listened intently. "Dean, I can try to get you a flight, but you may have to lay over," she offered.

"No, no, that's all right, I'll try Jojo and see what I can do."

"I'm offering to help you, so don't insult me. You've probably already tried Jojo, and if he wasn't there then, I'm certain he's not there now."

"How the heck do you know?" He heard her blow heavily into the phone. What was between them was about more than some silly plane ticket. Their history went back years: almost fifteen to be exact, to the night of senior prom.

"There's a flight right now. It's going to Atlanta, but the next flight to Dulles is an hour later. Is that enough time to get the next flight?"

"What? How - ? Uh, ok," Dean relented. "You didn't know how to turn on a computer when I last saw you. Your hotshot senator of a husband buy that for you?"

"Shut up. I'm separated. I've learned to do a lot of things on my own, and the things I want I buy for myself. That's all that matters."

Unexpectedly, the hope that had stirred in Dean's heart diminished at Chyna's revelation. She was just *separated.* Not divorced, not sending her former hubby the papers to sign, just *separated*. They could get back together at any time, he reckoned, and that part really bothered him. It had been years since he'd seen her. Dean had avoided going over to the house so he wouldn't have to see her: so he wouldn't have to be reminded how much he might still be in love with her.

"Dean," Chyna said impatiently. "The flight has two seats left; it leaves in twenty minutes. Do you want it or not?"

"Yes, yes I want it." It pained him to ask for help from anyone, especially her. "Uh, thank you, Chyna."

THIRTY-THREE

ISHA, THOMAS AND HIS GRANDMOTHER had a lovely evening. It started with a trip to the Tubman Museum. There were some of the loveliest, most comprehensive artifacts and historical information on African-Americans there. Tisha looked through her phone at all the pictures that she, Thomas and Mrs. Alton had taken and couldn't wait to show them to Chase. The day was so fun; the only thing that was missing, of course, was Chase.

Despite it being only two days, she'd really missed him, more than she ever expected she would. She looked up from her phone and sighed. She made a mental note to suggest the museum visit as a field trip to Principal Jeeter. *If I ever get my job back,* she thought sadly.

When she arrived at his house, she let herself inside with the spare key that Chase had given her. She looked back out at driveway, excited to see his truck there – but she was surprised to see that Devon's car wasn't. That seemed odd to her: the bodyguard had followed them to the museum, and she'd spotted him at different moments throughout the day. She looked up and down the street again, but shrugged, trying to ignore it as nothing. Maybe now that Chase was home, Devon had already taken off.

She was also surprised to see her own car. *Look at you, old thing – you look good.* It was parked on the street, looking cleaner and shinier than ever.

Still somewhat nervous, Tisha dismissed her thoughts. She was alone, but Chase was inside, and Mrs. Alton had insisted Thomas go home with her too, for a little time together. Tisha shook her head. *In all this time, you haven't seen nor heard from Mrs. Robinson, yet you still act like a scaredy-cat. Why on earth are you such a wimp?* She wanted to protest, but her subconscious was right: it was time for her to go home. She needed to stop letting Chase take care of everything and just… woman up. She chuckled at her thoughts. Giving herself a little shake, Tisha walked in.

The first thing she noticed upon entering the house was music, playing in some distant room. It was something soft and slow, but she couldn't make out the lyrics. Smells wafted past her nose, making her stomach growl with hunger. Angie must have cooked before she left.

Tisha looked into the dining room, intrigued to see two candles burning and two place settings. A lovely centerpiece of a single rose complemented the lighted taper candles. How on earth did he know she'd arrived? A romantic night that she and Chase hadn't actually had since… well, ever?

She grew excited. Perhaps she should take a quick shower and put on something nice? Then she smirked: she didn't have anything nice to wear. She didn't own a short cocktail dress, nor frilly anything.

She tried not to let her own lack of preparedness dampen her spirits. *The man is putting on the moves, the least you can do is be grateful. He let you stay in his house, he fixed your stupid car that really was nothing but scrap metal with a fuzzy engine, he got you a bodyguard and a lawyer - and now here you are, mentally lamenting about your lack of proper attire.*

Tisha laughed aloud in disbelief looking at the spread. As she leaned in to smell the rose, she suddenly noticed a lipstick print on one of the glasses, and the dregs of a drink. On the chair, she saw a woman's jacket. Lifting it,

Tisha smelled the remnants of cheap perfume, a kind that smelled familiar: like the kind Teresa wore.

Tisha didn't want to think the worst. She promised herself she wouldn't... but as fast as her thoughts had rushed to one positive conclusion, what she was seeing took them rapidly in the opposite direction.

She took a deep breath and set off up the stairs.

Reaching Chase's bedroom door, she heard the shower running. Tisha was too modest to go inside, but as she pushed the door to the room open slightly, the water stopped abruptly. She was about to go to her own room to find something nice to wear when the bathroom door swung open and Teresa came out, wearing a lacy black robe.

"Oh, Angie, can you do some laundry for - "

Tisha moved back and Teresa all but leered at her. She was holding a small pile of clothes, together with what Tisha recognized as someone's personal underthings. Just then, Chase exited the bathroom, also in a robe. Teresa quickly turned, holding her robe to her, and hurried to the dresser to pick up a litter of foil packets, shoving them into her pocket and looking sheepish.

"Tisha, Tisha, listen to me... this isn't—" Chase secured the towel more firmly around his lower torso and moved toward her.

"This isn't what? Sure it is. It's exactly what it looks like, babe - why you lying, honey?" Teresa drawled.

She moved forward, and Tisha saw Chase's eyes turn darker than she had ever seen them. She was actually frightened, but she was so confused about everything...

"He didn't want to tell you," Teresa smirked. "You're in a vulnerable state right now, so he lied."

"I didn't *lie* - how di you even get in here without Devon seeing you? Tisha, you can ask Devon..."

"Well, *somebody* lied. And she can't ask Devon nothing, I already told her that you were *mine*." Teresa turned to

Tisha, who felt like she was paralyzed.

"Didn't I? I told you the other day that Chase was mine, but instead of being smart and packing your bags right then, you had to find out the hard way." Teresa moved closer, but Chase pulled her back so roughly, Tisha thought he might have hurt her. Instead, she laid back on the bed dramatically, laughing loudly and almost crazily to herself.

"You shut up, Teresa. Shut *up*," Chase demanded. "Tisha, listen to me, you have to believe me. Let's go downstairs and talk. Okay? Talk to me..."

He moved closer but she took a step back. He was bare chested; the only thing covering him was the towel. Tisha felt sick. Rather than stay there another minute, she turned and ran so fast she tripped on the bottom stair. She righted herself and heard Chase calling after, but she kept moving as quickly as she could. Over Chase's yells, she heard Teresa's laughter, drowning out anything he was trying to say to get her to stay.

Chase could not believe what had just happened. He hurriedly pulled on a pair of jeans and the first shirt he could grab. He was so mad could he barely think straight; but he spoke calmly, even though his heart felt as if someone had just stabbed him repeatedly.

"If anything happens to her because of you and your crazy games, you'll regret your very existence. I'll see to it that you can't get another acting job in this country, and you'll never see Thomas again - if indeed you ever wanted to see him in the first place. This is it: the very last piece of my patience."

"You don't mean that—" Teresa began, and jumped when Chase yelled back at her.

"Don't tell me what I mean," he shouted. His hands balled into fists. Everything lining the top shelf crashed to the floor and a large hole was knocked out of the wall that supported it.

"You love her, do you? You can't love her, she's not for you. I am, I had your child," Teresa reminded him weakly.

"I do love her," he thundered. "I love her more than I ever loved you. I will always love her. Do you understand? Her, not you, not ever. Get out of my house, while you can still walk."

"I'll hurt her, you know. I can hurt her good," Teresa murmured.

Chase looked at her with disbelief. "Are you threatening me—threatening me, using her? You're even further out your mind than I thought, Teresa. If you touch her, I'll kill you. Get out - get out *now!*" Chase picked up her clothes and threw them at her. "Get up, Teresa. I'm not playing."

She scrambled up, clutching her items to her chest, and started down the stairs. He followed her, grabbed his keys and was out the door moments after her.

Tisha's car was already gone. He could hardly think, but if something happened to her he would never forgive himself. He called Devon as soon as he got back into the house and explained the situation. He waited and paced. He would need to ask if Devon could return, to help find her, but he needed to be thoughtful and respect her need for distance.

This was the one time he'd figured out that he loved someone truly - and before he could tell her as much, his ex-wife had swooped in and ruined his chances, just like she'd ruined his life the first time all those years ago.

THIRTY-FOUR

—◆—

TISHA WAS MADDER THAN SHE could ever remember being in her life, and to supplement that, she was hurt too. She shook her head as her foot pressed the gas. No, she wasn't even all that hurt; anger was the dominant emotion. Yes. Mad. Spitting mad! The only thing she could see was them, the two of them, together.

Tisha relaxed her foot against the pedal to reduce her speed. Her car... whatever the mechanics had done, it felt like an entirely different automobile. It moved faster, it accelerated and it revved. Her car never revved! Even as she enjoyed her car's new responsiveness, she wished she could take it all back: give the entire thing back to him. She would take back her old lemon, even with all its problems: the cost wasn't worth it. Here she was in another mess, only this time it involved her heart - and it was the worst feeling ever.

Tish turned off the main highway to the first rest station she saw. She collected her thoughts, and eventually she pointed her car in the direction of home. Not her apartment, not where she played house, not where the man she loved was rekindling things with his ex-wife, but back to *her* home: Virginia.

She got only a mile or two before she felt like crying. She couldn't do this - it was madness. She needed a few minutes to herself. If she went to Virginia, it would be only moments before the questions would start, and she'd eventually have to explain in full just why she had decided to come back so unexpectedly. No – that was out. Her apartment wasn't that appealing, either, with its falling-apart, low-grade everything. Even Andrea Robinson seemed a welcome distraction from that.

I hope you are there, you—you—I'm ready for you. No one had seen the woman, and Tisha almost hoped she'd run into her. It was her turn to feel lost. She'd lost her job, even though she'd done nothing but fight for what was right. Until this entire mess was cleared up, she couldn't expect to find another job, because no one in their right mind would hire her.

Tisha parked her car. She was determined to remain alert. No-one would catch her off guard or hurt her. She had enough energy and anger stored up inside to fight an army.

She watched as an ambulance zoomed past her house. As her eyes traveled down the street, she suddenly thought of Mrs. Wellington, who lived just a few blocks away.

The woman hadn't reached out to her for a while - but who could blame her? She was older, looking forward to retirement, and this was the one incident that had marred her autumn years as she tried to take care of her frail husband and ride off into the sunset.

Tisha felt sad and alone. No one had called her in these two long weeks she'd been off, come to think of it - not even Chris Jeeter. She should take a moment to visit them instead, Tisha thought, chiding herself. She was playing for time, she knew, because she just didn't want to enter her place. Not alone.

Then she remembered her bodyguard. He could go in there for her! Wasn't that what he was supposed to do? Tisha thought of Chase's towel-clad torso and quickly went off that idea. She'd go visit Mrs. Wellington instead. If her friend wasn't home, she'd wait, even if she had to sit in her car all night. Ultimately, Tisha admitted to herself, she was afraid. *So what?* That's what she'd do.

She decided she'd walk to the Wellingtons'. Her thoughts were running amuck and the fact that she'd be safer in her car never entered her mind. The happenings of the last hour had muddled her, leaving everything unclear. She felt discombobulated, confused, angry and very alone.

She'd left her family and friends behind. She had thought this new life was what she wanted, what she needed. When her job had led her to Chase and Thomas, it had seemed worth the move. She was in love with Chase, but he had a dramatic problem she couldn't compete with: a wily ex-wife. No matter what happened with Thomas, after all, Teresa would always be Thomas's mother, and come what may Tisha would have to find a way to put up with that.

As Tisha neared Mrs. Wellington's tiny little house, she smelled the smoke from the end of the street. She would recognize smoke anywhere. The smell of it, the milky—gray on top, the thick black closest to the roof of the house, concealing the fact that a building was there at all. It was an acrid, pungent smell that took her breath away and made her sick.

She couldn't stand the smell: burnt, charred. Even when her brothers burned bacon in the house, just that little bit was enough to cause her to gag and bring tears to her eyes. She placed a hand on her stomach as the lights of the ambulance screeched to a halt directly in front of Mrs. Wellington's place. The houses were close together, and Tisha prayed that the house the EMTs were rushing into wasn't the Wellingtons'.

On leaden legs, Tisha moved through the gathering crowd until she saw someone being loaded onto a stretcher. Her throat closed because of all the smoke and her eyes burned.

She tried to get closer in order to see more when she was grabbed from behind. "I'm not going to hurt you, but you're not to go in there." The voice was cold, chilling, and Tisha stiffened. "Get off me!" Tisha yelled heatedly. She turned and for a moment she thought it was Chase, but quickly recognized Devon, her bodyguard.

When Tisha saw that one of the bodies was closed up in a black bag, her knees buckled and her stomach pitched. She stomped on the toe of the man who held her captive and managed to break free. She ran to the ambulance and saw that a woman was being loaded into the back.

"Mrs. Wellington? Mrs. Wellington?" Tisha yelled. "Is that Sharon Wellington, please?"

"Are you family?" The EMT looked at Tisha and with a hand stopped her from getting closer.

"No, but I'm a close family friend," Tisha cried as she climbed into the ambulance.

"Herby? Oh Tisha, is that you, honey? Where's my Herbert?"

"I don't know—I—" Tisha looked up at the EMT, who shook his head apologetically. Tisha knew what that meant. Tisha looked back at Mrs. Wellington, noticed her nose was black with smoke and saw the EMTs tenderly wrapping her burned arms and legs.

"It's so painful," Tisha heard Mrs. Wellington say quietly.

"I know, I'm sorry, I'm so sorry, Mrs. Wellington. Just try to rest, just let the doctors take care of you, please," Tisha pleaded. She sent up a silent prayer while the EMTs attended to her friend's wounds. The steady rocking of the ambulance gave her a headache, but it carried them to the hospital.

THIRTY-FIVE

———◆———

WITH A SENSE OF DÉJÀ vu, Chase entered the North Macon Hospital for the second time in just a few short weeks. He didn't know what he'd encounter, but he knew it wouldn't be good. He found Tisha in a chair, staring off into space, and he instantly knew she was in pain, not physically but emotionally. It was the kind of pain that often plagued her precious heart.

Chase nodded to Devon, standing against the far wall. After they talked briefly, Chase knew exactly where Tisha was headed and the details surrounding her transit to the hospital. Devon had connections in every police department around the country, it seemed, and he'd told Chase that the Wellingtons' home was a deliberate attack: arson. So far, though, they didn't have any information on motive or anything else. Chase could only hope that Sharon Wellington hadn't been targeted as a result of her work at the school and friendship with Tisha, yet he knew there wasn't likely another explanation.

Once he reached her, Chase knelt in front of Tisha. Curious eyes were upon him from various others waiting in the area, but he didn't care about any of them. His concern was Tisha - it would always be Tisha. Not knowing what to say, he knew nonetheless that something was better than nothing.

"I'm sorry about the Wellingtons, Tisha."

He wasn't sure if she would put anything together about

Andrea Robinson's involvement, but it didn't matter: she'd still take it hard.

"It's my fault," she said, her eyes glassy and barely registering him at all.

When it did finally seem as if she'd noticed Chase, she looked at him briefly and turned away.

"I can't think about you right now. Why don't you leave me alone, please?" Tisha pleaded, her voice shaky and barely above a whisper.

"Don't do this. Please don't do this. I'm so sorry. I'm sorry, but I need you to believe in me — in us."

"There is no us," she retorted. "It's just an illusion: my *de*lusion. And, and… oh, I can't even think about you right now. This is bigger than your small, pathetic ex problems. You know why this is happening?" Tisha shook her head and covered her ears momentarily. "I need some aspirin…"

"I'll get it," Chase stood.

"*No. You.*" Tisha pointed a finger at him and didn't wait for an answer. "It's because *you* didn't handle your business where your ex is concerned. You think it's going to magically go away, but it isn't. It just grows bigger and bigger. Things aren't resolved by themselves, Chase. But I know, who invited my input, right? You and Thomas will handle this. This is your business, nothing of concern to me. Well, handle it then! Handle it by yourself, 'cause you don't need me. Right?"

Chase listened until Tisha was through. He didn't want to interrupt her for fear she'd get even angrier.

"Ms. Jameson?"

Abruptly, Tisha looked away from Chase and stood, wobbly on her feet, when her name was called.

"First of all," the doctor began, and cast his eyes to the floor as if humiliated, "I'm sorry for the way I treated you when you were brought in with the child. I…"

Chase looked incredulously at the man, now knowing that he was the one who Tisha had encountered weeks ago. He felt ready to punch him. Instead, before Chase could act, the doctor continued:

"All right, so firstly, I'm sorry. Second, your friend Mrs. Wellington has second-degree burns and is in critical condition. We've notified the burn unit and they will take her down there shortly. We're hopeful. It's amazing that with all she's been through, she is still very talkative, alert, and concerned about her husband, who..." He trailed off uncomfortably.

"They shared over forty years, Doctor. Didn't you think she'd be concerned?" Tisha replied in exasperation.

"Yes, yes. Of course – I - I didn't mean that she shouldn't be—" the doctor stammered.

"Will she make it?" Tisha asked, though her mind told her that she didn't want to know.

"I'm not entirely certain. It's more than just her burns: it's her long road to recovery, possible operations… With her husband gone, I just don't know how much she'll be able to take. Only time will tell. I'll let you go see her and talk to her, but only for a little bit. We've given her something for the pain," the doctor said, pointing Tisha toward the burn unit.

Chase remained where he stood, looking after them as they walked. Tisha looked back at him once; then, without any further acknowledgements, she turned and kept pace with the doctor as she disappeared behind the partition.

———◆———

Having spent almost six hours at the hospital, Chase was no better off than when he'd first arrived there. He'd finally left knowing that at least she had the bodyguard there to protect her: it was clear she didn't want Chase himself there at all.

Chase heard the car pull up in the driveway. Despite the lateness of the hour, a jovial Thomas skipped inside as he opened the door. Chase stuck his head out to wave to Mrs. Alton as she backed her car down the driveway.

After shutting the door, Chase centered on Thomas and the items he carried: a big greeting card, almost as tall as the boy was, and a small stuffed animal nestled in the crook of his elbow. Chase put on a face and tried to sound happy, realizing now why Thomas had asked his grandmother to bring him back for the night.

"Hey, Thomas." Chase turned to lock the door behind him. He dreaded the questions about Tisha, but knew they would come any moment now. "Looks like you had a good time at your Grandma's," Chase said, gesturing to the big card that Thomas held.

"Sure, Dad." Chase helped Thomas out of his jacket, which proved difficult when his son wouldn't let go of his treasured items for even a moment. Thomas looked around and cocked his head, as if listening. Cautiously, he moved a few steps to peek into the kitchen, then down the hall to check the den. When he looked back at Chase, his little face was a study in disappointment and a flurry of questions.

Chase knew what was coming, so he spoke up. "Listen, Thomas…"

"Where's Tisha?" Thomas interrupted.

"She'll… be gone for a few days," Chase said hurriedly. "Uh… she… she'll be… back in a few days," he repeated. "Why don't we warm up some dinner?"

"I already ate at Grandmom's house. Why didn't Tisha say good-bye?" Thomas insisted. Chase saw the look in his son's eyes: wary and skeptical, as if Thomas would believe nothing that came out of Chase's mouth.

"She'll be back, son," he maintained. "Now, let's see what you got there. You make that at your grandmother's house?" Chase gestured toward the card.

"It's for Tisha," Thomas said.

Chase rubbed his forehead and sighed audibly. There

was no end. "Well, can I see it?" Chase asked and held out a hand. He studied the drawings of the people on the paper. There were a pair of figures that looked like he and Thomas, and then a woman with glasses he knew immediately to be Tisha. They looked like a family, Chase thought sadly. Below the contented figures, in colorful, crooked letters were the words: HAPPY BIRTHDAY.

Chase slowly closed the card. He felt more deflated than he thought possible. With a sinking feeling in the pit of his stomach, he asked, "When's Tisha's birthday?" and felt like a fool even as he asked it for not knowing the answer already.

"Tomorrow... or today?" Thomas looked down at his watch: his time-telling skills were still sketchy at best. "It's past twelve. That means it's the next day, right, Dad? SO her birthday's today!"

Thomas looked up at Chase. "Didn't you know? Didn't Tisha like the dinner Angie made for y'all? Angie did a lot. She even made a birthday cake. She let me put the letters on it. Didn't you get her message?"

"No... no, son I didn't," Chase said despondently.

"I bought her a bear, too. Think she'll like it?" Thomas added brightly, holding up the small teddy bear that he'd purchased.

"Yes, Thomas, I think she'll love it," Chase said, shoving his hands into his pockets. "Listen, it's way past your bedtime." *Things will look better in the morning,* he thought glumly.

"Can we call Tisha and tell her happy birthday first?" Thomas asked.

"It's late, Thomas. We'll do a little something when she comes back, I promise, but she's probably pretty tired. Okay?"

Chase was grateful when Thomas nodded, however slowly and sadly, and turned without further comment to mount the stairs.

After settling Thomas into bed, Chase couldn't figure out what he wanted to do with himself. He didn't immediately feel tired. Hesitantly, he stood at the door of his own room, knowing he'd never get any sleep in that bed. Rage shook inside him all over again when he saw the rumpled sheets, a pair of his underwear on the floor, and condoms littering the bureau. If he could burn just that one room, he would. Teresa was more conniving and clever than Chase had ever seen in their marriage, all because she felt threatened. *As well she might*, he thought: because he was going to get Tisha back. He just wasn't sure how yet.

Closing the door to the bedroom, Chase went to his office in the den. Sitting down heavily, he pulled out his phone, skipped over two messages from Prescott, and then the voice of Tisha's sister Jina:

"Hey, Chase, my sister is too stubborn to likely tell you it's her birthday today but hey, it's her birthday. We're coming for a visit and I thought we'd all go out this evening, with you and Thomas of course. Was hoping you could occupy her till we're there. All right, talk later. Bye.

The next message played: "Chase, it's Angie, I'm whispering in case Tisha is nearby - you might want to take your phone off speaker if she is. I forgot to tell you—tomorrow's Tisha's birthday. I made a cake, it's in the high cabinet, so be careful. I put a candle in it already and if you get home, stick it in the fridge for a bit - but it's chocolate and should be fine in the cake stand. I didn't know if you knew, she didn't tell anybody, and I don't know how old she is, but oh well. I hope I did everything to your liking - hope everything goes well and that the dinner set up was appropriate. Good luck."

Click. The messages ended. With one mad shove, everything on Chase's desk went crashing to the floor. He was angry – and worse still, he was angry with no one but himself. He'd been carelessly nonchalant, and thought that just because Tisha was so different, she'd put up with everything and anything that was thrown at her. Chase had been aware of his ex, but not really paying attention to the danger she presented, so now he'd lost Tisha as a result. He could just have told her that he loved her so there'd be no doubt in her mind. Instead, she'd now been amply supplied with images that belied everything he should have already said to her.

Chase went to the guest bedroom and stood at the door looking in. Tisha's presence was everywhere. Her books and notepads were scattered among the array of colored pens she liked to use to write her lesson plans. He moved inside and saw scholastic order forms, tons of children's books spilling out of her embroidered tote bag, and a pair of glasses she called her 'kid-proof' glasses: large and gaudy, with ugly brown frames that held the lenses. Chase remembered how they hid her beautiful eyes; he remembered that first day he'd met her. She wore these during school, since her other ones had proved too delicate. Chase smiled as he picked them up. Tisha had explained how she'd dropped them once, and when a small Mary-Jane-clad foot had stepped on them and they'd remained intact, that's how they got their name.

Chase continued to regard the small space she used as a desk. She had brought a few pictures of her family with her - some without frames. She used a paper clip to attach them to books, which served as temporary display stands. Chase picked up a book illustrated by someone named Pinkney.

Tisha's makeup and perfume were on the vanity, alongside various powders, lotions and gels. As Chase got nearer to the bed, he tripped over something soft and furry. Reaching down, he picked up one of Tisha's slippers. It was in the shape of some fuzzy character Chase couldn't remember the name of, but one that Thomas would surely recognize.

Chase set the slipper gently next to its mate. He removed

his shoes, crawled under the covers and buried his face in the pillow Tisha had used. Her hair always smelled like peaches, sometimes strawberries too. Her perfume was soft and subtle, not blunt and overpowering, and when he had wrapped his arms around her for a much-needed hug, her body had been warm and her skin silky. Most importantly, she'd hugged him back. Having her in his life had been like a tease: he had just a glimpse of what things could be like before she was gone.

Turning to rest on his stomach, Chase pulled the covers up over his head, yet still there was no escape from thoughts of her. He vowed to give Tisha the time she said she needed to sort out her feelings. Chase knew, though, that eventually he'd go after her and bring her back to Macon. He'd give her a couple days away from him and Thomas, to consider how what Teresa had done was just a lie - a set-up. Then, when he went to get her, he was sure he'd know if she really and truly wanted to be with him - because he now knew, as a result of today, exactly what he felt for her. Even though he felt there was something mutual between them, it scared him to consider that even that could be a lie.

Restless, Chase got up and went to the den, to see if the sectional sofa could serve as a makeshift bed for the foreseeable future.

THRITY-SIX

———◆———

TISHA HAD BEEN AT HER parents' Virginia home all of forty-eight hours, and already it was just like she had never left. When her brother and sister had arrived and heard about what happened to Mrs. Wellington, they'd promptly dragged her back to her childhood home. She had little will to fight them off and had felt so defeated, she'd made only a half-hearted attempt.

Alfreah Jameson had taken one look at Tisha and nearly fainted. All the expensive foundation, concealers and eye creams on her face couldn't hide the tired eyes, nor the nice clothes hide what her mother protested was weight loss. Mrs. Jameson had barely glanced at Tisha before rattling off a diatribe of exasperation and chants to the Lord for assistance with her youngest child. When she'd finally finished, Alfreah had made Tisha her famous soup and a grilled cheese sandwich; and when Tisha feigned being stuffed, Alfreah had banished her off to bed.

As Tisha sat up in bed, she wondered briefly why she had tried to go to sleep in the first place. When her head had hit the pillow, she had closed her eyes, only to open them minutes later to toss and turn the night away.

Tisha found herself feeling unfamiliar in her own home. She missed reading Thomas a story, not to mention kissing Chase goodnight. The simplicity of those nightly rituals just could not be replicated – let alone the safety she felt at his house and in his arms.

The color scheme Tisha's mom had picked out for the room was bright and fresh. With matching curtains in shades of pale blue and mauve, along with new maple furniture, the room seemed inviting: Tisha's mother had managed to keep the colors Tisha loved while refurnishing the room since Tisha had left. It still wasn't the same, however. It would never again be hers, and things would never be the same. Tisha knew that even if the furnishings *had* been hers, personally picked out, they still couldn't compete with the human beings she'd left behind. Here, she felt alone and purposeless.

And yes, she admitted begrudgingly: deep inside, Tisha knew that Chase hadn't slept with his ex-wife. Nevertheless, she surmised that Chase wasn't totally hers, and would never be hers with Teresa's constant presence in the background, paired with Chase's unwillingness to confront the problem.

Added to that, however, was an unyielding guilt over the ordeal with Mrs. Wellington. Tisha blamed herself harder than ever for the evil, harm and hurt that had happened to another human being: this time, her friend. Tisha's very existence was trouble, and she refused to let anyone tell her otherwise. Her curse was so deep, she was certain that it had followed her out of Virginia all the way south to Macon, Georgia. Tisha had coped with the feelings of guilt in order to get through her days, but deep down, she believed that no one would've been harmed if it weren't for her.

Holding the phone between her ear and shoulder, Tisha listened as the rings hummed in her ear. Just seconds ago, her fingers had punched the number she now knew by heart. A nurse Tisha had met at the North Macon hospital had shown such kindness that Tisha now sought her out to help with updates on Mrs. Wellington.

"Nurse Barbara, please," Tisha said when the line was

finally picked up. Tisha was informed that the condition of her friend, Sharon Wellington, hadn't been upgraded as of yet - but thankfully it hadn't been downgraded either. After thanking the nurse, Tisha hung up.

She'd hated to leave Georgia at all and had promised everyone there that she would only be away for a few days. Until then, there was nothing Tisha felt she could do except pray.

The phone rang again just seconds after Tisha had hung up. "Hello?" Tisha said, not knowing who was calling and hoping that just maybe it was Chase.

"Tisha, it's Leland McGehee. I'm sorry, I found your home number - did you leave your cell phone in Georgia?" The lawyer's deep voice filtered over the line.

Tisha looked around. The truth was, she'd left a lot of things. Her phone was probably somewhere with her in Virginia, but she didn't have the energy to find it right at that moment.

"Oh yes, I guess I must have done. Good morning, Leland," Tisha replied. She sat up a bit straighter, hoping nothing bad had happened.

"I just wanted to let you know we got word that you can return to work after the holiday."

"When is that?" Tisha asked dumbly.

"Next Monday," Leland supplied. "Everything's in order. I'll be in touch about some specifics when you return, but I hoped to brighten your Sunday just a little, in any case."

"Well, thank you, Leland. I appreciate your calling. Um… Leland?"

"Yes?"

"Is there… any news about the investigation into the fire at Mrs. Wellington's place?"

There was a long pause. "Afraid not. There is proof that the blaze was started deliberately, but no-one knows by whom. I'm told they may have some prints, but it's early right now. Don't worry, they will find the people responsible for hurting your friends," he assured her. "When witnesses are affected, though, it does 'up' the urgency; so perhaps this will light a fire under our investigation… no pun intended. I'm sorry."

Tisha nodded. "It's okay. Uh, thank you so much, Leland, for everything," she murmured.

"Of course."

Tisha said her goodbyes and hung up the phone. She had badly wanted to ask about Chase, but she'd refrained – and she was rapidly learning that Leland would offer no extra information without being asked directly.

Tisha didn't know what she had expected, but it certainly hadn't been to get her job back. She had been excited about going back to work, but uncertainty about what awaited her there outweighed her optimism for a successful reentry. She should be happy – she *needed* to be happy, yet she felt ungrateful, because the fact remained that she wasn't in the best of moods.

Just as Tisha had arrived back at home, then, it was time to go once again. She thought of her mother, whom she had been the most glad to see. Tisha and Alfreah Jameson had always been as close as any mother and daughter could be, and no-one would've rested until Alfreah Jameson had confirmed with her own eyes that her youngest child was well and safe.

Tisha had lived with her parents for so long, and her dramatic move to Macon symbolized so much: her first time out of their house, away, on her own. Even when she went off to college, she'd lived off campus with her family the whole time and had got along just fine. In the last year, her father had become ill, so Tisha had decided to stay and help her parents without so much as a second thought. Her father's illness gave her a strong reason to stay, even when she should really have moved out long before. That said, Jojo and Dean lived less than thirty minutes away, and Dean often stayed over on the weekends to help in any way he could with their father. Alfreah Jameson would never ask for help outright, though - not of any of her children, at least - and so Tisha had stayed with them just a few more years.

After the incident with Melinda, Tisha had finally been certain that she couldn't continue to live at her family home. She felt as if she couldn't stand to live anywhere in the entire state of Virginia anymore; so, with her mother's assurances that she and her father would be all right, they had begun the search for a carer for Mr. Jameson. For the most part, the nurses had worked out wonderfully, and Tisha no longer felt bad about leaving her mother and father alone.

Tisha smiled sadly, remembering her mother's incredulity when she'd told the entire family that she'd accepted a new job and was moving to Georgia, within the month. At first, no one believed Tisha, but as the arrangements she made were gradually confirmed, she had left just as she had planned. The move had been bold: probably the biggest decision Tisha had made in her entire life. And every day since making that announcement, she'd still questioned whether or not it had been the right choice. Each time she questioned her decision, though, Tisha knew it had been the right thing for her to do, despite everything.

Padding her way to the bathroom, Tisha paused at her mother's room and peeked in. "Hey, Momma."

Alfreah Jameson sat on the side of the bed, her fingers busy removing the rollers that kept her springy graying hair in its curls. She was the same height as Tisha, and her skin was a creamy russet. Her eyes were the color of wool, and she moved with purpose and efficiency even though she had some arthritis in her hip joints. Nonetheless, Mrs. Jameson was energetic and cheery. The first few years after Tisha's father's diagnosis of Alzheimer's had been difficult, but Alfreah had managed to deal with it. In recent years, she had found a calling with church activities and a second career through helping others. Now, Alfreah looked up toward the door where Tisha stood.

"Hi, pumpkin. How did you sleep?"

"Good," Tisha lied. "Well... pretty good," Tisha corrected herself, when Alfreah raised a skeptical eyebrow at her.

"Are you having any more headaches?" Mrs. Jameson asked.

Tisha shook her head. She'd had a headache for the last three days, but it had eased somewhat: enough that she could pretend for her mother's sake that she was all right.

"Where you going all dressed up?" Tisha asked, trying to change the subject.

"Church, of course, honey," Mrs. Jameson replied.

Tisha scratched her head. "Today's Sunday," she replied dazedly.

"It's Easter Sunday, honey," Mrs. Jameson replied gently.

Tisha nodded in surprise, realizing that of course Easter was the holiday Leland had alluded to. Tisha rarely found herself not knowing what the date was, and here she was, not only unaware of the date but of the holiday as well. For the past two weeks, they all just seemed to blend together.

Moreover, Tisha realized sadly that she hadn't scribbled the date on a paper, talked about the weather with her students, or had someone change the day on the calendar that sat at the front of her classroom during circle time. Tisha was painfully reminded once again of what she had lost. Her motivation for getting up each morning was more than a job: it was a joy, something she looked forward to every single day.

Tisha looked back at her mother, willing away her wandering thoughts. "Well, give me a minute to get dressed - I'll go with you." She hadn't been to church since she had left, but with nothing else to do, she decided that adult Sunday school and a sermon from the pastor would occupy her time better than sulking around the house. She also remembered the many old friends of hers who still attended the local church. Touching base with them would no doubt lift her spirits, at least somewhat, and take her mind off her own troubles.

"All right, honey," Mrs. Jameson replied. "Are you sure you're up to it?" She moved to the door to stand in front of Tisha and took her daughter's face in her hands. "Maybe you could even sing for the congregation?" she prodded.

Tisha tried to look optimistic. "I haven't sung since I moved to Georgia, Momma. I don't... I don't think I'm up to it," she said, beginning to rethink going to church after all. But her mother had looked so hopeful... Tisha stuck with her original decision to attend.

"You think about it, baby. Singing will make you feel better," Mrs. Jameson said.

"Yes, Momma." Tisha smiled as best she could. Nothing would make her feel better... except a carefree courtship with Chase, seeing Thomas, having Andrea Robinson caught and in jail – oh, and Tisha wanted her good name restored. More than anything, she wished Mr. Herbert Wellington could return to be with his wife. Aware that she had to hurry to make it to church, she walked briskly down the hall to shower.

THIRTY-SEVEN

A FEW DAYS HAD STRETCHED INTO a long, unrelenting and tortuous week. Chase spent most of them with Thomas, trying to fill his evenings with something to occupy his mind and his time. With Angie off for the week, Chase and Thomas spent a few nights with Grandmom. Chase's attempt to get his son's mind off Tisha had worked - at least he thought they had, until a single question from Thomas showed unequivocally that all the reading, outings and all his other distractions had been for naught:

"When will Tisha come back? How come we can't call her? She'd never leave without telling me good-bye."

Of course, Chase realized: such was the consistency of Thomas's thoughts. He never forgot about her, he never got over her and Chase knew his son never would.

After dinner one night, Thomas and Chase had talked about it and devised a plan to get back the woman they both loved. "You gotta buy her a big gift, Dad," Thomas had said. Chase knew it wasn't really the way to get her back, but he surmised it certainly couldn't hurt. After much brainstorming and traipsing through malls, even stopping by a jeweler, they ended up on a new car lot. If Thomas wanted 'big' – which, unbeknownst to Thomas, also meant 'really expensive' - this gift was big indeed. Short of a new house, their purchase ended up being the biggest thing Chase could get her. She'd question his sanity when she saw it, but he could always return it if he had to. He would try anything at this point, because he felt that he had few other options.

With a sleeping Thomas over his shoulder, Chase entered his mother's home. Mrs. Alton lived just 22 miles from him, in a town called Warner Robins. Her house was small, just two bedrooms, but she'd picked it out herself. Chase had tried to get her something bigger when they'd moved East, but again and again she'd declined. "For what?" she had said. "More house, more to clean."

"Hey, there," Sandra greeted them at the entrance.

Chase smiled at his mother. "Hi."

When Chase was a child, she had been slimmer, but that was because she'd been working two jobs to support them after Chase's father had been shot. He liked her a little heavier-set, as some might call her: she looked healthier now, seemed more like a grandmother with meat on her bones. She looked *capable*, Chase thought.

His mother's skin was vibrant and healthy, the color of walnut shells; and her days were just as occupied now as if she still worked two jobs. From her full-fledged certification as a Literacy Volunteer of America to her reading circle for tots at the local library, Sandra Alton had filled her life with all sorts of extracurricular activities she found thoroughly enjoyable. In amongst all these, Chase regretted not coming to see her more. Only in the last year had they been able to find a common ground, and that was only because of Thomas.

"Hey, Grandma." A drowsy Thomas waved, his eyes opening a little as Sandra followed closely behind Chase to the guest bedroom.

"Hi, honey," Mrs. Alton replied as she brushed his cheek with a kiss.

In the bedroom, Mrs. Alton pulled back the covers as Chase placed Thomas carefully in the center of the big bed. She helped him into a pajama top while Chase pulled off his sneakers and socks. Together they covered him up, and Mrs. Alton kissed him good night.

Down in the kitchen, she handed Chase a mug of coffee. After sipping from her own, she set the cup down and looked at him.

"So, what are you going to do?"

Chase shrugged. "What? I'm just going out of town," he said casually, not wanting to elaborate on where he was going - not until he had solid confirmation that the woman he couldn't live without would agree to return with him. He wanted to keep things under wraps and not get his hopes up, due to the uncertainty of what awaited him in Virginia.

"To Virginia?" Mrs. Alton asked.

Chase looked up, shocked. "How'd you know?"

"I have my ways," Mrs. Alton replied mysteriously.

Chase shook his head back and forth. "Thomas talks too much," he chuckled wryly.

"You be quiet - he certainly does not," his mother upbraided him. "If I had to wait on you to tell me something... well, I'd be dead already. My only child is in love and I shouldn't know? Why, oh why - ?"

"I just didn't - "

"I know," Mrs. Alton interrupted. "You didn't want to make a big deal out of it, because you weren't sure yourself." She raised an eyebrow. "Or maybe you were just denying it. I know you very well, Chase Michael Alton. I know you better than you think I do."

"I've changed a lot, Momma," Chase countered.

"Well, hallelujah." Mrs. Alton raised her hands up in mock praise, then, more quietly: "Sorry, but I know that too."

Chase laughed.

Mrs. Alton turned her cup in her hands as she took a deep breath. "You did a good job."

Chase rolled his eyes. "He's only seven..."

"Shh! Let me finish, please."

"Sorry," Chase muttered.

"You've proven to me and to Thomas that you're more than capable of being a parent. More importantly, you proved to yourself that you're capable of being a *great* parent. Seven years, ten years or twenty: it don't matter, honey. I'm so proud of you and you've done well with your son... so far. Your father would be proud too, Chase."

Placing a hand on her hip, she continued. "Now, how about this girl? It's not good for a grandmother's ego to keep hearing about some other woman from her only grandchild."

Chase smiled. It was evident Thomas had informed his grandmother about Tisha – and his reports must've been favorable. He was glad.

His eyes took on a faraway look, as mention of Tisha brought back every memory he had of her. "I miss her, Ma. I... really miss a woman, for the first time in my life." Chase put his mug to his lips and took a sip.

"Have you slept with her yet?" Sandra asked seriously.

Chase choked. Quickly he set down the mug, coughed repeatedly to clear his throat and looked at his mother with incredulity. "What?"

"You heard me," Sandra replied. She put her mug in the sink and rinsed it out before drying her hands on a dish towel. She waved her hand at his look of shock. "Many a man claims he can't live without sex. If you haven't slept with her..." She shrugged her shoulders. "Well, that says something to me."

"I haven't slept with her," Chase whispered. This was his mother he was talking to, for goodness' sakes. He was mortified, that much was true. But he was interested in hearing more of her philosophy on the matter, in spite of himself.

"Good, I'm glad. It must be love." She rolled her eyes exaggeratedly toward the ceiling. "You and Teresa couldn't wait to get each other's clothes off. Don't look all embarrassed. You know I'm telling the truth. And look what happened to that."

"She had issues," Chase protested, his cheeks burning.

His mother snorted. "And you didn't? We've all got issues."

"You're no longer mad at me about our breakup?" Chase raised an eyebrow skeptically. He remembered a time when Sandra Alton had wanted to see them together. She insisted they go to counseling before they got divorced; but it was hard to feel at all culpable when dealing with his then-wife. Then again, his mother could only see one side, and that made it harder. Chase had been willing to try something - anything - in order to see if and how his marriage could be turned around. Teresa, on the other hand, wanted to hear none of it. She wasn't actually interested in marriage or in trying to make things work: she only wanted the money, without the responsibility or attachments of motherhood.

"I was never mad at you, Chase." After a long pause, Sandra continued. "You had a baby and I didn't want little Thomas coming into a broken home, that's all. Part of my misunderstanding was your fault, though. You closed up and didn't tell me what kind of woman your wife really was. You know what she used to do when you were still together?" Chase shook his head, and Sandra proceeded. "She's quite the actress, as you know. She'd come over here and bawl her eyes out. She'd tell me how you wouldn't try to work with her, how you didn't want to seek counseling and a whole truckload of lies."

"But you believed her," Chase countered. And she had. She had believed his wife over her own son, and that had hurt.

"I'm sorry, honey." She looked away and Chase could see that she struggled not to cry. "I just wanted you to be happy."

"Momma, I'm sorry, but I really don't want to talk about

her. I don't..."

"I know, and I'm sorry I brought it up. I'm all right," Sandra held up a hand, waving Chase away when he made a move to comfort her. "It's in the past, I know. I'm sorry."

"It's in the past, but not as much as I'd like it to be, Momma," Chase relented, realizing he needed to be more forthcoming about his plans and thoughts. He should start talking to his mother more often.

"What do you mean? What did she do?" Sandra reached for a tissue, held it to her nose and looked at him intently.

Chase took a deep breath and dove right in. He relayed the events leading up to his forthcoming trip to Virginia. How Teresa was the primary reason for the current rift between he and Tisha. How her conniving actions had been a catalyst in an already tense situation and had set everything off. How Teresa had expertly and dramatically ruined all of his efforts with a cunning trick, and now Tisha had returned to her family home in Virginia.

"Honestly, I don't blame Tisha for getting fed-up and feeling like she had to compete," Chase said dejectedly. "I should've handled things better."

Sandra listened patiently to Chase's rundown of his crazy week. She nodded in understanding. "Oh Chase, I'm sorry."

"It's all right." He didn't know what else to say.

"No, it's not all right," Sandra responded sharply. "Teresa is going to get herself in a whirl of trouble one day, and I'd pay a pretty penny to be there when it all catches up with her. Look, sweetheart. At that time, you kept a lot from me about her and you'd only talk to Lee, but eventually I began to understand her lies and see who she was for myself." She took a deep breath.

"I'm trying to say that you've got to clue us in about what's going on with you. We want to help you, and we can, but only if you let us. It hurt me when you shut me out of your life then. I'm sure it hurt Tisha when you wouldn't talk to her, too - and now what? No matter how much you thought you were doing the right thing, it takes its toll after a while." She smiled. "I've been praying that you get a woman before Thomas gets to be just as big and as stubborn as you are. One day, the two of you will decide you don't quite see eye to eye – and when that day comes you'll need a referee."

Chase smiled back, although he concentrated on his mother's words rather than her humor. "I didn't want to shut her out. I just didn't want to add any more to the things she's already going through. Also, I didn't know just how crazy Teresa was," he admitted ruefully.

"And that's big of you to protect her - but at the same time, people need to feel needed, Chase," his mother interrupted.

"I want to stick with her through this," Chase returned. "None of this is her fault, Momma. She didn't ask for any of this. I feel so helpless, and she's miserable. And when she's miserable, I am too." Chase's eyes focused down into the dregs of his coffee. "I just don't know what to do, or how to help her…"

"Be there."

Chase stopped talking and looked up. "What?"

Mrs. Alton reached for his hand. "The only thing you can do is to be there for her. Support her. Secondly, be there with *all* of yourself. Not with half a mind on her and the other half worrying about Teresa. You know she won't take Thomas away from you, by the way. A child to her ain't nothing but work."

She exhaled in exasperation. "Teresa never wanted kids. It interfered with her master plan, and while that's tragic by itself, it's a fact. She's a fool, Chase. I can't understand any mother not wanting to take part in raising her own son, but the reality is that it happens each and every day. It saddens me. Honey, Leland told me she hasn't talked to him about arranging visits, and yet you still worry. That

devilish woman pushes your buttons and you subcon-
sciously..." Mrs. Alton paused and emphasized the word
when it looked as if Chase would take offense. "... *subcon-
sciously*, honey, you let her. No woman can put up with
that. No woman should put up with the stains and residue
left by another woman. Of *course* I want you to be happy.
I thought she, Teresa, had made you happy: at least at the
beginning she seemed to... Now, please go get your girl,
honey."

"She's real sweet, Momma."

"I know. She's got to be to put up with you."

Chase feigned offense, then became solemn. "In the
news, you know, they made her out to be horrific at first,
because they didn't have the facts - and she took it so
hard... but you didn't believe that stuff about her, did you?"

"Do you think I'd leave my grandson with her if I
thought she'd hurt him, or anyone for that matter?" Mrs.
Alton looked insulted.

Chase nodded. "No, I'm just saying..."

"I know what you're saying."

Chase only smiled. He chanced a look at his watch. He
wanted to be in Virginia by morning, but he was glad for
this time with his mother. She was always right, and he
missed the closeness they'd once shared.

"When did you get to be so smart?" Chase looked at her
as he put his mug down on the counter.

Mrs. Alton set her face with a look of impatience. "I was
always smart. You, sonny, just cleaned out your ears and
started listening to me."

"Thank you, Momma. I love you." So much had been
cleared up between them, all in just a little over an hour. If
only they had taken the time to talk things out long ago.

"I love you too, honey." Mrs. Alton reached out to hug
her only child. "I wish your father could see you now."
Sandra framed Chase's face between her hands. "You're
still my son... no matter how much all this hair hides you

from me. Get a haircut, will you, before you go down to
Virginia?" She looked up at his growing Afro. "No need to
scare the poor girl while you're pleading for her forgiveness. And do something about this - tone it down just a
little, would you?" She smiled as she tugged on the hairs
of his chin.

Chase kissed her on the cheek. "Take care of Thomas
for me. I'll only be gone a day or two." Chase spoke opti-
mistically, hoping it wouldn't be any longer than necessary
before he had Tisha by his side.

Mrs. Alton nodded. "Given that steel wall you'd erected
around your heart, son, it's a wonder she found a chisel
sharp enough to get through it. With the way my grandson
carries on about her, she really must be something special."

"She is," Chase replied as he headed through the door,
smiling. "I love her." If only he could tell Tisha that as easily as he told everyone else.

Chase turned and gave his mother a departing look as if
to say, *wish me luck.*

THIRTY-EIGHT

———◆———

WHEN CHASE LEFT HIS MOTHER'S, the night was pitch black and the hour after midnight. Streetlights cast shadows over the car. He drove with the radio at a low volume as he concentrated on the road and sorted out the many thoughts that took up space in his mind. He made stops only for restroom breaks and maybe a snack here and there, but nothing elaborate and never for more time than it took to refill the gas tank and stretch his legs.

Chase hadn't been on a road trip in years, not even with Thomas, and he was reminded now of the few trips he'd taken with his Mom and Dad as a boy. Despite his unfamiliarity with the vehicle he was driving, he was beginning to get a feel for the late model Audi. *Tisha might hate it, though.* This was such a bold move... but he reminded himself briskly that he could always take it back. Truly, he hoped desperately that he wouldn't end up taking himself and the new car back to Macon without Tisha. Chase knew he'd be crushed if that happened, and so would Thomas when he told him.

As he drove, Chase mentally prepared the case for the car, and the many features he would bring to Tisha's attention. It wasn't the most expensive car he could've purchased, but after extensive research on the Internet and Thomas's endless input – mostly advice on the best color - it seemed it would be a good fit for her. Hey: *Thomas had been the one to pick it out.* Chase snapped his fingers at that one. *How can she say no to that?!* The car wasn't too small nor too big. It was sporty, fast and just the color of Tisha's old car. She needed a new car, anyway: the old one was a candidate for the junkyard. *How could she possibly say no?*

The sun was high in the sky, peeking through a mass of clouds, and rain misted his windshield - barely enough to warrant the use of wipers. The onboard GPS guided him through the back roads of suburban Virginia, and soon Chase slowed the car to a crawl, scrutinizing addresses and quaint single-family ranch-style homes.

When he arrived, he sat in the car for a few minutes. He hoped the extra few cars weren't an indication that Jojo or Dean were on the premises. Chase was in the mood to fight for Tisha, and while he had no plans to leave without her by his side, he really hoped he didn't have to take on both of them to do so.

Chase jumped when his phone started buzzing in its clip on the air vent. Chase recognized the number and reached out to touch the 'talk' button.

"Hey, son," he greeted warmly.

"Are you there yet? Did you see her?" the deepening but still small voice on the other end of the line asked impatiently.

"Hello to you too, son," Chase laughed. "Where's your grandma?"

"She's making breakfast. Where's Tisha?" Thomas countered.

"I'm here but I haven't seen her yet, okay? I'll call you when you can speak to her."

"What's taking so long? Are you lost?" Thomas questioned.

Chase nearly laughed out loud. He wasn't lost – in fact he'd made it there without a single wrong turn. Despite his son's annoyed tone, Chase was rather proud of himself.

"I gotta go, son. I'll call you soon, I promise."

"*Dad!*" Thomas yelled.

"I'll call you soon, Thomas," Chase said patiently. He was just as frustrated as his antsy son, but he didn't want to convey that to Thomas. "Bye." Chase hung up, pulled the phone from its holder and put it in his pocket.

When he got out, Chase took a moment to take in the place Tisha used to call home. He saw the red mailbox, shaped like a log cabin with a small red wooden bird on top of the chimney, and the shiny brass letter J nailed to the front. She'd described spending most of her life in this house, attending the High School just down the street.

Chase hunched his shoulders against the cool March mist. He glanced across the street. There sat a parked car, with tinted windows ensuring that no-one could see inside. When the car's lights blinked twice, Chase nodded in response. Sure enough, it was Devon. Chase wasn't sure how his longtime friend ran his business. He knew he had a fleet of men and women working for him, but for security reasons Devon made sure Chase never knew who was posted where at any given time. Regardless, his friend had impeccable skills: always ready and alert.

The skies overhead had darkened to a gray cloud cover, trying to push the sun away. Chase hoped the worsening weather wasn't an omen about how his meeting with Tisha would go.

When Chase reached the doorstep, his stomach growled noisily as the smell of something delicious wafted by. He collected his thoughts and admired the abundance of potted plants framing the steps. Underfoot, a straw mat decorated with flowers bore the word WELCOME in bold black letters. The mat was battered and worn at the edges, probably because it had indeed performed its duty of welcoming so many. The four brass numbers hung loosely and a little crooked on the door. At last, he knocked, praying that anyone but Jojo would answer the door.

A woman answered. She opened the door slowly and

gave Chase a smile. "Hi. Can I help you?"

"Uh, hi," Chase said, nonplussed. He'd been expecting either Dean or an older woman he'd seen only in pictures: Tisha's mother. The woman before him looked about Tisha's age, wide-eyed, wearing a dark-colored outfit with a jacket and numerous pockets. Chase cleared his throat. "I'm looking for Tisha Jameson. I'm Chase…"

"Oh, yes—hi," she replied warmly, as if she knew him. "Come in, Tish is here. I'm Chyna, a friend of the family's and Mr. Jameson's caregiver." She nodded toward an elderly man just beyond the doorway who sat in a wheelchair.

Chase stepped carefully over the threshold. He wiped his feet on the small square of carpet inside the door.

"T.T., you have a visitor," Chyna yelled. She took the handlebars of the wheelchair where Mr. Jameson was looking very warm in a wool-like throw, his head covered in a Kangol cap. Chyna began backing him through the door before Chase could offer to help. She moved quickly and expertly down the step, obviously in no need of his assistance.

"Oh, thank you, but we're experts at this. This is Mr. Jameson, Senior, by the way," Chyna said, laying her slender hand on the older man's shoulder. "Tisha should be in the kitchen. Can you please tell T.T.… ah, Tisha," Chyna explained when Chase returned her look with one of befuddlement, "that we've gone out for our morning walk?"

Chase nodded. "It's drizzling a little," he offered, not knowing what else to say. She already stood outside and could probably feel the light mist on her face. She smiled at him as an umbrella seemed to materialize from her hands.

"No matter, but thank you - it'll clear up in a bit. We'll be fine. See you when we get back, I hope." Chyna waved good-bye cheerfully as she pivoted with the wheelchair singlehandedly and pushed it down the walk.

Chase didn't know whether he should've attempted to introduce himself to Mr. Jameson or simply leave it alone. And Chyna had said she hoped she'd see him when they returned. He hoped so too. Meanwhile, he turned to follow his nose and his racing heart to the kitchen.

Just a few feet away and down the hall, Chase saw Tisha standing with her back to him at the stove. Whatever it was he'd smelled, it was sizzling in the pan she attended to. Her feet were clad in high heels, and a paisley-printed wrap skirt was tied at her waist in a delicate bow. His eyes traced the flowing material down to where it stopped, just above her knees. She wore a red sweater with the sleeves pushed up, and either her hair was shorter than he remembered or had she changed her hairstyle. This version was twisted into short skinny coils, silky and almost wet-looking, as if they held some sort of gel. This looked like her real hair: it was very short.

He'd never seen her in anything other than a pair of nice slacks or jeans and the darker wig that she wore because she said she was ashamed to show her hair and scalp. Here at her own house, though, she was relaxed, natural and no less beautiful. It didn't matter to him what she wore, anyway, because it was *her* and he missed her terribly. She was absolutely breathtaking. As she moved gracefully back and forth before the counter, her heels tapped the floor lightly and her shapely legs beckoned his attention.

Chase was startled from his thoughts when the back door to the kitchen slammed and a tall, dark-skinned guy entered. His deep voice reverberated over the sizzling of the frying food: "Look at you, girl!"

The man removed his coat and threw it carelessly over the back of a chair at the small kitchen table as if he owned the place. He called Tisha by the same nickname that the Chyna woman had used, then rushed forward, pulling Tisha into his arms and lifting her off her feet, hugging and kissing her as if she were his long-lost love.

Distracted, by her old school-friend, Tisha was wrapped up by the man and her breath caught, realizing with a jolt that Chase was there in her kitchen. He was standing tall and imposing, looking a little annoyed.

"Rahfe!" she said, catching her breath. "Put me down, Rahfe. Uh, Chase? Hey, hello."

Tisha turned her attention back to her high-school friend Rahfe Sidwell. Rahfe had been Tisha's date to the senior prom and for many years had harbored a crush on her that never seemed to fade, even after she'd told him plenty of times that she wasn't interested in him as anything more than a friend. Things had never gotten serious between them, but Rahfe had made it abundantly clear that he liked Tisha as much more than a friend.

"How are you?" Not ready to deal with Chase yet, Tisha addressed her friend instead. She tried to sound friendly and at ease, though with Chase's menacing-but-actually-quite-amusing gaze focused on Rahfe, it was proving rather difficult.

"Hey man, girl, how am I?" Rahfe responded. "That's the best you can do? Girl, you better give me some sugar."

Tisha smiled hesitantly and quickly pecked her old friend on the cheek, then hurriedly took a step back. "Uh, you look well," Tisha offered. God, she felt awkward, and Chase's intense and heated glare didn't help matters.

"You look fine, as ever," Rahfe replied.

Tisha laughed nervously and decided Chase probably wasn't going anywhere, although from the looks of it neither was Rahfe. "Rahfe, this is my… uh, friend, Chase. Chase: my friend, Rahfe, from high school."

Chase acknowledged Rahfe in pretty much the same manner that Rahfe had acknowledged him: with a closed-off nod that suggested both of them wanted the other to leave. "How's it going?"

With Tisha smiling at them both, Rahfe moved over to Chase, who courteously stuck out a hand for him to shake.

"Nice meeting you. Hey Tisha, I was hoping to talk to you for a few minutes but, ah, it looks like you and Rahfe are... close?"

"Um, no, just..." Before she could finish, Rahfe spoke loudly over her.

"Oh, Tisha and I, she's my girl," Rahfe said, beaming at Tisha. "We went to the prom together. Asked her to marry me when I was ten years old. I even gave her a ring made out of Reynolds wrap and the girl wouldn't hear a word of it. Huh, Tisha?"

Tisha laughed nervously, and was caught off guard as Rahfe pulled her close again. He was almost as tall as Chase but definitely less athletic. Rahfe had always had a healthy appetite, and over the years it had begun to show in his midsection. Regardless, Rahfe Sidwell was a sweet man and meant well, even if he was a bit too frisky for her liking.

"Why didn't you marry me, girl? I'm lost without you," Rahfe pleaded as he always did when he visited her. As always, it sounded as though he was only half joking.

"Your girl is out there, Rahfe - keep looking." She had no idea what else to say.

It was a minute before he caught on to what Chase had said about wanting to talk to her, but Rahfe eventually got the silent hint and said his goodbyes.

"Oh hey, before I go, Cheyenne said she'd come by any minute," Rahfe said, looking at his watch. "She said she saw you at church and you rocked the house like you always do when you sang. My girl got a voice like the angels in heaven," Rahfe added as he gave Chase a broad wink.

Tisha smiled. She had sung, and it had made her feel better, just as her mother said it would. Her pipes were a little rusty and out of practice, but it hadn't taken long for them to warm up.

"Thank you, Rahfe— I—" Tisha looked past Rahfe as the door swung open once again. "Oh my goodness!" Tisha squealed.

"Hey, girlfriend!"

Chase looked up slowly. This was obviously not the time to talk to Tisha, although she did shoot him an apologetic look as another childhood friend, Rahfe's sister Cheyenne, entered holding a newborn baby.

"Look at you," Tisha crooned, and without a second thought or even asking for permission, she seized the small bundle from the woman's arms. "Oh my God. Cheyenne, she's beautiful." Carefully but confidently, Tisha removed the layer of blankets to reveal a baby girl in a pink dress, her masses of curly black hair tamed unsuccessfully by an elastic bow about her head. "Hello, little Tina."

Tisha looked up at Cheyenne. "She's gotten so big. She's wonderful. Hey, where's Malcolm?" Tisha asked, knowing the couple were never far from each other unless they absolutely had to be. Cheyenne and Malcolm had attended school with Tisha, graduating the same year: high-school sweethearts who'd gone on to get married, almost three years ago already.

As Chase watched, Tisha turned and handed the baby back to her friend. She wondered what Chase thought seeing her with the baby. She looked up and when his eyes pierced hers, she quickly looked away. Every time she held any baby, a maternal feeling came over her and she felt a yearning for motherhood. She was feeling awfully nostalgic, what with all her friends visiting her and displaying how they had moved on with their lives and building their families. Meanwhile, she felt perpetually stuck in her own life; and the feelings she had toward Chase were so confusing. His imposing presence and looks of love right at this moment didn't exactly help to curb her inner longing.

For just a moment, she wondered what being a mother

felt like, what having a husband felt like… and what the future held for her and Chase.

Tisha looked up abruptly when Cheyenne apparently had addressed Chase more than twice, only to receive a blank stare in return. He finally focused and acknowledged her friend, smiling with embarrassment as he took her proffered hand and shook it, before shoving them back into his pockets like an awkward teen. "I'm sorry. I'm Chase Alton."

"Nice to meet you, Chase," Cheyenne replied, and then returned to Tisha. "We just wanted to stop by. I had to step out at church 'cause Ms. Tina here was fussy. When I came back, the church was tore up. I knew you would do it - I wish I could've stayed to listen, Tisha. You always sang so beautifully."

"Like the angels, I tell ya," Rahfe supplied.

Tisha nodded modestly, listening with only half an ear as she held the child in her arms. She loved babies, toddlers and children, period.

"We should be going…" Cheyenne landed her hand in a loud smack against Rahfe's chest. "Quit it," she admonished her brother, who quickly composed himself and obediently quit gazing hungrily at Tisha.

"Say goodbye before you leave town, will ya?" Cheyenne implored Tisha.

Tisha nodded. "I will, I promise." Carefully, Tisha tucked the baby back into her blankets. She kissed the baby's head and gave her a soft little nuzzle, before reluctantly handing her back to her mother. As Cheyenne left, Rahfe grabbed his jacket and leaned to give Tisha just one more peck on the cheek as he, too, moved for the door.

"Nice to meet you," Rahfe directed at Chase as he closed the door behind him.

Tisha had noticed the faraway gaze Chase's eyes had taken on as she held the baby. She wondered if his thoughts had been near her own, but quickly dismissed such imaginings, as they didn't look like they were coming true anytime soon. Not to mention that she felt like she should at least act like she was still mad at Chase, for the scene Teresa had caused just a few days ago.

Even though Tisha knew the truth in her heart, and even though it was really difficult to be mad at someone who looked so good, she would try as hard as she could for as long as she could. She moved back to the stove, where she smirked at the few pieces of black chicken. She lifted them from the cold oil and placed them away from the other golden pieces she'd fried earlier, before the flurry of interruptions had taken her attention from her task. She turned the burner back on and slipped in the remaining pieces left to fry, determined to concentrate on her task and listen to what Chase had to say now that they were alone.

"How are you, Chase?

She turned as he came further into the kitchen.

"I'm good. This place was pretty easy to find, although there's a lot of construction… but, uh, I'm so glad to see you," he stuttered. "Um, a lady I met when I entered - Chyna? She said she was going to take your father for their morning walk, though it's drizzling outside… I think they're probably already back…"

God, he looked good: slightly different, but oh, so good. Tisha had also noticed that he looked as tired and weary as she felt. His hair was buzzed shorter than usual, and his once thick beard was now a tamed goatee. And how could she have forgotten his eyelashes? So thick, long and abundant, just like the ones he'd given his son. He wore a leather city jacket that ended mid-thigh and a sweater the color of cinnamon sticks, with a wide white line across the chest. His long legs were clad in a pair of camel-brown jeans and his feet in a pair of black Skechers.

At the stove, Tisha turned over each piece of chicken to let it brown on the other side.

"How's Thomas?" she asked, trying to find a neutral

topic, anything that would give her a few moments to sort out her jumbled feelings at seeing him again. She picked up a dishrag and wiped the countertop beside the stove.

"He's mad at you," Chase replied seriously. He smiled as the dishrag she held flopped to the floor and she whirled around to face him.

"Why?" Tisha asked indignantly. Keeping her eyes on Chase, she bent to retrieve the dishrag. She set it aside and concentrated on rinsing the dishes, frantically reviewing her memories of her last few times with Thomas, to figure out what she could possibly have done to upset him.

"You left without saying good-bye," Chase replied, still mock-serious but with a playful glint in his eye. "You said you'd teach him how to color Easter eggs and you didn't."

Tisha smiled, her automatic guilt subsiding. "I'm still planning to do that. I just... I'll make it up to him."

She turned back the stove and retrieved the last pieces of chicken. She deposited them on the paper towels to drain, then turned off the burner before continuing to wipe down the surfaces.

"I missed you very much," he said, moving closer. "I bought you a gift."

She had missed him too, and his revelation made Tisha sigh aloud. Tisha turned on the water faucet so it blasted loud enough to drown out the loud flutter of her heart. She hadn't been expecting him to come to see her, but she was giddy he had. A secret part of her certainly wished he'd come the very day after she'd left and demanded she go back to Macon with him. Now he was really here, standing just feet away from her, and a war of emotions conflicted inside her.

"Did you hear what I said?" Chase moved to stand behind her.

Tisha turned around to stare up at him. "Yes, I heard you."

"Well, where are we, Tisha? How do we get past this?"

He lifted his hands to the tense cords of her neck and rubbed each side in a circular motion with his thumbs.

"I know where we stand, Chase. But, I mean, what about her? Do you love her? - Teresa?" Tisha questioned. She knew the answer, but she needed to hear him say it.

"No," Chase replied firmly.

"Did you fix whatever it was with her, so you can get on with your life?" Tisha questioned. Although she had her hopes, she didn't really know what banishing Teresa would entail.

"Yes."

"Okay, well… what did you do?"

"She'll be arrested for trespassing if she comes within fifty feet of me or Thomas - or you."

Tisha's mouth dropped open in astonishment. "Are you serious?" She hadn't doubted that something could be arranged, but nothing so drastic had occurred to her as a viable option.

Chase nodded earnestly. "Very serious."

"Well… th-that's certainly progress," Tisha said. She needed time to digest what had been revealed. *It was up to her now.* The ball was in her court, yet still doubt tried to rear its ugly head where Chase's feelings about her were concerned. It didn't take long for Tisha to recall Teresa's many comments that had prompted her doubts in the first place.

"She said that you couldn't love anyone else but her. You wouldn't talk to me, and you shut me out. That hurt, and I…" Tears began to form in Tisha's eyes and emotion clogged her throat.

"Lies… She's a liar." Chase took a deep breath before continuing. "Listen, I shut you out because… I didn't want to risk being hurt again. You got to something inside of me and it scared me to want to try something with you… when it hadn't worked one time already. But I did: willingly, unwillingly, whatever the case may be, we were thrown together through a fluke and tragedy. In that time, I let go and I let you in. I need you. I'm not in love with her. I'll never be in love with her — ever. Please say you believe me; please say you'll come back to Macon so we can sort this out. Please."

Chase closed the distance between them completely and wrapped her arms around his waist.

Tisha felt those familiar feelings that she had so missed: protection, closeness and love. Seconds passed as she gazed up into his eyes, reacquainting herself with him, his feel, and his smell. Inside his leather jacket, the sweater, soft as cashmere, molded to his strong frame. She had missed the way he held her.

"I miss holding you in my arms, and I miss seeing you every single day. I miss you and Thomas laughing and play-ing down the hall, and you teaching him and encouraging him to learn, to be kind and do good things and be a good person. You're beautiful, Tisha."

Tisha lowered her head, her mind on autopilot search-ing for flaws that would render his love for her impossible. Her fingers flew to her head. "My hair is very thin," she blurted. "It's not- "

"It's beautiful," Chase declared. "Why do you hide it?"

"It only grows in small patches, from the burn," she con-fessed self-consciously. She had worn her wig to church, as she'd always done; but all her pretty scarves and caps were down in Macon and she hadn't been able to find a single one to wear as she cooked in the warm home kitchen. Her friends had seen her head uncovered, but Chase hadn't ever seen her like this.

To her surprise, he leaned down and tenderly kissed the spots that had been burned bald and sensitive. She cried as his hands moved over them and he continued to stare into her eyes as if his feelings had never wavered.

"Everything you said about Thomas and me, about talking to him, was right," he said softly. "I didn't want to see. I didn't want to acknowledge that I needed help."

"I wasn't trying to be right, Chase. You didn't need any help. I just gave some input, but you would've been fine without it. I didn't mean to make it seem like you weren't capable. I wanted you guys to have a relationship that was open and affectionate…"

"I know that now," Chase interrupted. "Whatever I was doing before was just a guise, to keep myself from feelings of incompetency as a parent."

"You are so competent, Chase," she assured him. "You're a wonderful father." She wondered how he could doubt himself when Thomas was the best little boy anyone could ask for. No one could expect to take the credit for that but him, certainly not Teresa.

"Okay, but I, uh…"

When Tisha put her fingers to his lips, Chase kissed each of them separately, but then he reached up and pulled her hand down gently. "Let me finish," he requested.

"No," Tisha protested. She stood on tiptoe, and her steady gaze traveled slowly from Chase's lips back up to his eyes. She didn't need to communicate in words what she had wanted, needed from him. The silence lengthened as he finally touched his lips to hers.

THIRTY-NINE

"TISHA, I LOVE YOU," CHASE managed between kisses.

Startled then, Tisha stopped kissing him. "What?" She looked up at him confused.

"I said I love you. I don't know why it took me so long to say it. I think I've known it for a while now."

Chase watched a tear fall down her cheek and he quickly wiped it away with his thumb. "Don't cry. Please don't cry." Chase was momentarily doubtful. "You had to know – didn't you?"

Tisha nodded slowly. "I wasn't sure. I wanted so badly to know, but I was afraid."

Chase nodded at her confession. When she stood on her toes for more of his kisses, he gladly obliged.

They kissed each other, losing all track of time and place, until the old side screen door squeaked open and banged shut.

Chase lifted his head abruptly and turned. The sound was so sudden, it might as well have been a bullhorn. Tisha turned to hide her face.

"Oh heavens, I'm sorry... I..." Alfreah Jameson said as she entered through the - obviously much-used - kitchen entrance. Chase smiled, abashedly wiping his lips even as they still tingled and tried to find the words to introduce himself to the woman he instantly knew to be Tisha's mother.

Tisha spoke up quickly: "That's all right, Momma." She moved to take the bags her mother held and placed the items on the table. She kissed her mother's cheek.

"Okay, thank ya baby. Uh, hello."

"Hi, hello, Mrs. Jameson," Chase said to the short, gray-haired woman. He bent down awkwardly and hugged her shoulders.

"Momma, this is Chase Alton. Chase, my momma, Alfreah Jameson."

"Pleasure to meet you, Mrs. Jameson," Chase said. He smiled, unsure of what to do next, and feeling embarrassed by the thoughts running through his head about this very woman's daughter.

"Chase, something occurred between you and my daughter to send her back here to Virginia. I'm thankful that she's been a welcome guest at your home, but it seems to me that some unresolved issues you have caused her emotional distress. You know anything about that?" Alfreah placed a hand on her hip.

"Momma, I'm not emotionally distressed," Tisha said, mortified. Her siblings talked too much, she considered impatiently, and that was enough to cause anyone distress, emotional or otherwise. Chase, however, cut in.

"Uh, yes ma'am. I assure you those issues are no longer relevant and we're working on them together. I love your daughter so very much," Chase said, realizing he now knew where Jojo and Dean got their intimidation tactics from. "And I'm sorry, very sorry. I would never intentionally do anything to hurt your daughter. She means the world to me."

Tisha smiled, and so did Chase. At his honest and straightforward words, he saw Mrs. Jameson's subtle shift and softening eyes almost instantaneously. Alfreah Jameson was good at the killing look, but Chase was relieved, there didn't actually seem to be a mean bone in her body.

"Well, it's nice to meet you. I hope that you're a man of your word. I love all of my children very much."

"Yes," Chase nodded enthusiastically. He reached inside his pocket and pulled out a small, shiny box. "This is just a little nice-to-meet-you... ah, something... gift," Chase tilted the box as if looking at it would help him better determine what to call it. "A small gift. I thought about bringing flowers, that seems customary, but I'd like to find out what your favorite sort is first."

"Well, goodness, how thoughtful! Thank you." Mrs. Jameson accepted the small box he placed in her hand and carefully removed the lid. Nestled in tissue paper was a small porcelain figurine that Mrs. Jameson lifted admiringly. "It's so beautiful."

Tisha moved over for a closer look as her mother held the figure in her hand. Four small birds sat on a bed of grass while two larger birds perched atop a tree as if looking down on their young. The birds were all brown with large, dark eyes. The tree looked like a thick oak with delicate branches. It was hand-painted and looked expensive. "It is beautiful," Tisha agreed, eyeing him.

"Yes, goodness, Chase, thank you. This is very thoughtful." Mrs. Jameson smiled then winked at Chase. To Tisha she said, "I'm going to lie down, honey." She turned to Chase. "Chase, this is beautiful, I do thank you. I'm keeping an eye on you two, though," she said playfully. "Tisha, honey, wake me later so I can fry the chicken for this evening's meeting." Mrs. Jameson looked toward the stove and sniffed.

"I fried it for you, Momma."

"Now, I told you that I would get to it - why did you worry yourself so? You're supposed to be resting. How's your headache?"

Chase's brow furrowed. "You've been having headaches?" he asked as he moved to stand by Tisha's side. "Sit down here," he said, directing her to a chair at the table.

"Momma, I'm fine. Chase, quit it."

"You're fine, you're fine. Got a head thicker than a bowling ball. Doesn't she, Chase?"

"Yes, ma'am, she does," Chase replied. He laughed at Tisha's look of incredulity at his siding with her mother. He felt Mrs. Jameson would be an ally as far as her youngest daughter was concerned, and Chase was looking forward to a teammate that cared about Tisha as much as he did.

"My head is fine and I'm all right," Tisha snapped.

"Mmmhmm," Mrs. Jameson chortled. "Chase, would you like something to drink? Forgive my daughter's manners, she's not well."

"Momma!"

Chase merely laughed. Mrs. Jameson wouldn't swat at a fly if it buzzed in her ear. "No, I'm fine. Thank you."

"All right, well, see to my daughter, would you?" Mrs. Jameson looked at Chase.

"Yes, Mrs. Jameson."

"Call me Ms. Alfreah, that's fine." She patted Chase on the shoulder and turned to the stairs.

Tisha watched as her mother climbed the stairs. She turned back to Chase. "I've had a slight headache for the past few days – I'm not recovering from a triple bypass," Tisha protested. "So quit fussing."

"I'm just trying to see about you, T.T."

"And you better quit calling me that."

Chase merely laughed, but his light joking banter quickly subsided as he moved to pull her back into his arms again. "Come here." He proceeded to nibble her lips.

"I'm mad at you," she teased.

"Why?"

"Where's *my* present?" Tisha asked, as she began to pat the pockets on Chase's chest and then, as if frisking him, patted his sides. "Nothing?"

"I have a present for you," he replied. "Want to see it?"

Tisha rolled her eyes but laughed.

Just then Chyna stuck her head into the kitchen and smiled at them. Chase smiled back.

"Hi, you guys - I'm going to go. I readied your father for his nap, and your mother just came up there so she knows he's there. I'm going to be off tomorrow," Chyna said, looking at Chase, then back at Tisha. "I'm not interrupting something, am I?" Chyna asked. "In case I don't see you I just wanted to say goodbye."

Tisha shook her head and moved away from Chase. "I'm thinking about leaving tomorrow, Chyna, but I will call you, okay?" Tisha rushed over to hug her friend. Chase listened to their goodbyes with half an ear. Tisha was coming home to Georgia, but maybe one day they'd come back to visit - maybe even as husband and wife. He was beginning to have hope about a serious relationship for the first time since he'd been divorced.

"Hey, whose new Audi outside?" Dean said as he came around the corner. He wore a pair of jeans, a sweatshirt and a tool belt around his waist. "Alton," Dean said courteously.

"Dean," Chase acknowledged him back.

Chase watched Dean, who was watching Chyna. Though he did acknowledge her presence, Chase could tell there was something there.

"Since when did you start working on Sundays?" Dean looked at Chyna. "Anyway, I'm talking about the new car outside. You know: big red bow on the front and thirty-day tags?"

Almost in unison, every head in the room turned to look out of the small window to the street. Nonchalant, Dean moved to the fridge and got himself a soda as Tisha took off for the door. She turned quickly back to Chase. "You didn't," she said breathlessly, before rushing out of the side door.

Chase followed her, wondering what she'd think.

"Chase! This is *not* my present..." Tisha gasped in disbelief. When Chase nodded, she said, "I can't accept this... a car?!"

"Why can't you?' he returned, watching as she ran her hand over the door in awe. He could tell how much she liked it.

"I just can't. It's too expensive!" she protested. "Wow, it's pretty," she laughed. "It's a sports car… is it used?"

"You mean to tell me if it were used, you'd accept it? Heck no, it ain't used." He shook his head in disbelief. Her philosophy astounded him.

Chase walked over to the car, clicked the door open with the key fob and stood back with a mock bow, waving her inside.

After adjusting her seat and the mirror several times, she rested her hands on the steering wheel and looked around. She liked the smell of it. She liked the burgundy interior, and her eyes quickly scanned the back through the rear-view mirror. Truth be told, it was perfect. It wasn't so big that she couldn't park it without scratching a neighboring car, and it wasn't so small that someone could push her off the road just as easily. But…

"Chase, I won't accept this. It's too expensive. You can't just buy me something to… to…"

"Whoa, that's not what I was trying to do." He came around the car and slid in next to her. "You know I'd never try to buy your forgiveness."

"That's not what I was going to say." She looked at him. Chase relaxed.

"I was going to say that you should consult me before you go off and buy such a big item, especially for me. What if – what if I don't like leather seats?"

"Your other car was leather," he pointed out.

Tisha looked away. "What if I don't like the color?"

"Your other car was this color," he returned evenly, "but if you don't like it we'll get a different one."

He made it too easy for her. And, after all, she *did* like it.

"Besides, if you don't like it, not only will Thomas be

mad because you didn't make Easter eggs with him, he also will be mad because you didn't like the car he picked out for you," Chase added with an air of finality.

"You don't mean that. Did he really pick this out?" Man, she missed that little boy.

Chase nodded.

She put her hands back on the steering wheel and stared out the front windshield. "I do need a car, but – "

Chase looked around as the phone rang. "Perfect timing," he smiled as he handed the phone to her.

She took the phone. "Who is it?" she said to Chase, who gestured for her to put it to her ear.

"Hello?"

"Tisha," Thomas chanted.

"Hi, sweetheart." Tisha sighed and leaned her head against the car's headrest. "How are you?"

"Good. Do you like the car I picked?"

"Yes. I love it, Thomas." She rubbed a hand over the steering wheel. "I like it very much, honey. Thank you."

"You're welcome. When are you coming home?"

Tisha laughed. She looked at Chase, who visibly held his breath, then she said, "I'll be there sometime... tomorrow."

"Good," came the reply. "Love you."

She looked at Chase again. "I love you too, Thomas," she said, as she handed the phone back to Chase.

Chase talked to Thomas for only a moment longer. "So?" He asked her once he placed the phone back in his pocket.

"So what?"

Chase rolled his eyes. "You gonna keep the car or not?"

"I don't see why not. Thomas picked it out for me," she said with a wink. "Why shouldn't I keep it? Let's go for a test drive!" She fastened the seat belt across her lap and secured it into a comfortable position. Holding out her hand, she waited impatiently until Chase placed the key in her palm.

"Thank you, Chase," Tisha said seriously as she looked

at him.

Just as she inserted the key into the ignition, the front door opened and Chyna emerged. Chase was thoughtful a minute. He had witnessed something in Dean's eyes when Chyna had entered the room and recognized the way Dean had looked at Chyna as the way he himself looked at Tisha.

"Dean's in love with her." It was more of a statement than a question.

Tisha turned to Chase then and bestowed upon him the briefest but sweetest kiss. "Madly - he's just too stubborn to admit it."

As she kissed Chase a second time, any sympathy in Tisha's eyes for the would-be couple and their troubles was replaced by a devilish gleam.

"You better hold on tight," Tisha said as she revved the gas.

Chase was so excited. Tisha was coming *home*: to her new home, with him, near him, back to him - and Thomas, of course. He was relieved and excited: he'd done all that he could to get her back into his life, and now he was contemplating ways to make their time together more permanent still.

FORTY

$\longrightarrow$

THE DRIVE TO MACON WITH Tisha had been the most enjoyable long car drive Chase had ever experienced. Tisha did most of the driving despite his pleas to let him take the wheel, but he talked to her as she became accustomed to the car's drive, handling and maneuverability. Four hours passed quickly. When Chase saw the sign for Myrtle Beach, an idea popped into his head and he sat up in his seat.

"I want to drive now," Chase said firmly.

Tisha looked at Chase skeptically for a moment, her eyes instantly alight with suspicion. "You want to drive *my* car?" she said indignantly.

"Yes, I want to drive *your* car." Chase laughed at how quickly her initial protests about the gift had morphed into proud possessiveness in the last few hours.

"We're going to take a little detour," Chase declared, as Tisha pulled off at the next exit and into a gas station.

"Are you sure, Chase? Do we have time? Thomas sounded really bored. I miss him."

A sense of pride came over Chase, but he rolled his eyes skyward at her exaggerated look of disappointment. "The only time Thomas is not bored is when he's with you or sleeping. Sandra Alton doesn't quite replace Tisha Jameson. But he's fine, thank you very much." Chase said.

When they pulled into a rest stop, Chase made his way

around to the driver's side and stooped to kiss her lips. "I'm going to have you all to myself till tomorrow morning," he grinned.

Settling into the passenger seat, Tisha sat back, grabbed a bag of chips and asked: "So where are we going?"

Chase concentrated on the highway and turned off I-95, following the signs that led to a place he'd stayed at only once before, years ago, for work. While it wasn't some island in the Mediterranean, he remembered it as a perfect place to spend some real, uninterrupted quality time with the woman he loved.

———◆———

The suite Chase had requested at the Ocean View Hilton in Myrtle Beach, South Carolina, was absolutely lovely. Tisha went to the window as soon as she entered and gazed out in awe at all the water, twenty-five stories below, which stretched as far as her eyes could see. It was lit up and beautiful. The cold weather didn't detract from the inner warmth and serenity she felt.

After a few hours of shopping and sightseeing, Chase and Tisha were back at their room. It had two beds and another adjoining room, as well as a full kitchen with a stove, a small nook and a spacious bathroom with a bath and shower. It was still too cold for any kind of swimming, but they had at least looked at the beach, taken off their shoes and let the freezing water touch their toes before they came inside.

Chase carried in their two small duffle bags. Tish came back inside, feeling relieved and excited all at the same time. She watched Chase shrug out of his coat and place it over the chair. While she didn't think they had any real plans, he still seemed like he had something up his sleeve - though she had no idea what that was.

Tisha sat back on the room's comfortable couch and

inhaled deeply through her nose, and it was only then that she began to smell something awfully delicious – and, to her delight, awfully close. When her nose led her into the adjoining room, she discovered Chase lighting the many candles that littered a table, alongside numerous plates and silver domed chafing dishes. Looking up with a smile, he moved to reveal each dish in turn. Tisha's mouth watered as he revealed chicken, steak, crab and broiled lobster tails. Steam rose from every dish as he opened one after the other.

"When we got here, I thought I'd have some things sent up," he said smiling at her. He stuck out a hand and beckoned her closer.

Tisha moved closer, taking in all the wonderful details, even long-stemmed roses in a crystal vase. By their side sat an assortment of strawberries, peach slices, melon and cubed American and cheddar cheeses, arranged around a small fountain. There were also sides, including sourdough rolls, croissants and long elegant bread sticks. Chase picked up a strawberry, put it under the fountain's drizzle and touched it tenderly to Tisha's lips. "Chocolate?" she whispered as she took a bite. "So good. This is beautiful, Chase."

Setting aside the stack of food covers, Chase turned to her. "It's called room service," he said with a smile. Grabbing her around the waist, Chase groaned into the kiss as he held her close. "I wanted to make up your birthday to you. Let's sit down and eat, and we can chat about the future."

"The future? Really?" Tisha said as she stared at him.

Without saying anything more, he pulled out the chair for her and served her a sampling of everything. She was glad: she wanted to try everything. She dug in eagerly as if she hadn't eaten in days. She glanced over at him, noticing that he hadn't heaped his own plate with as much food as he'd given her. Setting her fork aside, she frowned, eyeing him suspiciously. His appetite never lagged. Tisha was alarmed: something seemed to be wrong.

Tisha set aside her fork and took a moment to wipe her mouth with the cloth napkin. "What's the matter?" she asked with concern when Chase looked up. "Something's the matter. You said that you'd start telling me..."

Tisha stopped talking when Chase stood. She watched him wipe his mouth and take a deep breath.

"I'm just nervous, I guess," he murmured.

"Nervous? Why?" she asked. He shrugged. "Are you nervous about us... about Andrea? Did you hear something about Mrs. Wellington?"

Chase shook his head. "No, Tisha. I'm not worried or nervous about anything except... uh..." He hesitated. "I wanted to tell you that when you left Macon so angry and hurt, I thought I'd lost you forever. I've never felt anything like that sense of urgency in any relationship to solidify the relationship once and for all, so there's no doubt between us." Her eyes followed him as if in a dream as he knelt in front of her.

"Oh, my God," Tisha exhaled deeply when Chase presented her with a tiny black box.

"I said that I love you and I meant that. That night, Tisha, that horrific night - everything I had planned was for you... us. I didn't even know it was your birthday, but that made what happened so much worse, and I'm so sorry." Chase took another deep breath as he realized his entire speech had been chopped up and repackaged to make him sound like a blundering idiot. Undeterred, he ploughed on.

"Tisha, I want to have more children, but only if it's with you. I want to wake up each morning and go to bed each night, but only with you next to me. I want to stand at the altar and wait, but only for you. Tisha Tyrell Jameson, will you marry me?"

An eternity passed, or what seemed like it to Chase. Then tears streamed down Tisha's face, and he hoped against hope that they were tears of joy. She had Chase worried, simply because it was taking so long for her to say anything.

"Are you sure?" Tisha wiped her eyes as a small but niggling doubt entered her mind.

"Tisha? I'm positive."

Chase looked away. He should've written the question down on a piece of paper and had her circle yes or no, because this - this was heart-stopping.

"I, uh … I can't yet. Not until Andrea is found, not until this is resolved – not until I know what -"

"Tisha, please, don't let this stop you from living your life," Chase pleaded.

"It's not, it's just that…" She stood up to pace, almost causing him to fall backwards. Instead, he took the seat she'd vacated and watched her.

Chase closed the box and put it back in his pocket. He wasn't sure how he felt. The anguish she felt was clearly real and it reached out to his heart, but right then the only thing he could feel was that all his efforts had been trampled.

However, despite feeling a bit shocked and a bit snubbed, he knew then how he had grown as a man, because he drew himself up to his full height and pulled Tisha into his arms.

"I'm so in love with you," Tisha whispered once wrapped in his embrace.

He was stunned at the words. She continued: "I'm afraid, too, though. How did you - how did you come to your decision? How do you know?"

She paused and nuzzled her face into his chest. "I'm sorry, you shocked me just now. I want to get married to you, of course I do. I don't know what to do, though. I feel overwhelmed…"

"Shh," Chase said, pulling her head back to his chest where she cried. He hadn't been expecting that. This wasn't how he imagined the proposal going at all - but she considered it, and for that he was acutely thankful.

"We won't talk about this anymore if it upsets you," he whispered.

"Please don't be mad."

"I'm not mad. I was actually thinking... will you sing to me?" Chase asked with a smile. Singing would take her mind off the proposal, he hoped, and he really did want to hear her sing. It was all he could think about, after her flirtatious friend had mentioned Tisha's turning out the church. If anything, Chase had grown still more intrigued by her since then. Her ability to sing was one more thing he should've known, he considered ruefully - like her birthday, like her favorite color, like a million more things he wanted to know about her.

He realized the unresolved issues, both there in Georgia and back in Virginia were keeping her from moving forward, and regretfully he considered that it may never be resolved. There was a distinct possibility that Andrea Robinson was gone forever. It had happened, and he believed Tisha would move forward one day; but until then, he wanted her in his life however possible - even if he had to put up with this phantom in their relationship. In any case, he had a plan: he was confident that he and Thomas could wear down her resolve.

"I don't know if I can sing to you, now, Chase... really?" Tisha laughed as she wiped away her tears. "Thank you for understanding." She reached up and kissed his lips, then stood back, smiling at him as she drew a deep breath.

"You bring me joy..." she began. Chase was instantly mesmerized by the Anita Baker classic. Tisha's voice was husky and deep, and her choice of song made her heartfelt thoughts that much easier to understand, erasing all doubt and confusion.

She sang as they held each other, swaying to a beat that existed only in their heads, and Tisha's words, soft, breathless and meaningful, were all he heard. He knew now that it wasn't the end for them, not by any means, and that he would be holding on to her for a very long time. In time, he knew she would let him do just that, officially, forever.

———◆———

Tisha fell asleep in Chase's arms, but when she awoke later she was in a soft bed with many pillows and it was pitch dark. She teetered between remembering singing to him and falling into a deep sleep. Chase was in the next room, he'd assured her, and anytime he was around, she felt safe. He was a gentleman and her life with him could begin, but not until they were out of danger. *Anita Baker…* that was all she remembered, that dream-inducing song, bringing with it blissfully happy thoughts that she loved someone and joy that he wanted her to be a part of his life long-term.

Right then, though, it was cold and she shivered. She drifted, floating somewhere, trying to get back to her dream-filled sleep. But it was dark and cold… *dark and scary.* A faint smell of smoke reached her nose as she was transported to another time and place. *Smoke: faint, gray, and if it wasn't too thick she could see through it…* She coughed and convulsed, drawing tighter and trying to escape, to wake up.

Smoke was the most hideous thing Tisha had ever smelled; it burned every part of her; her lungs, the membranes in her nose, and worst of all, it left her paralyzed with terror, gasping for breath. She smelled it now, strong, and when she had smelled it then it had been the same.

She and Dean were in the kitchen. The radio blasted on the counter and Tisha sat at the kitchen table where she did her homework every day after school. Tisha studied a problem for the tenth time, not understanding how to solve it, and waited impatiently for Chyna to hurry up with her own chores just a few doors down and come over to do homework together. Chyna had always had a crush on Dean.

Tisha turned her head and looked at her brother, who was preparing something at the stove - a B.L.T. it might have been. Her brother couldn't cook to save his life. He lifted a piece of black bacon and smiled at Tisha - then a loud BOOM thundered through the kitchen. Then she saw Dean struggle with fire that had somehow leaped onto him. Without thinking, Tisha was on him, thumping her brother's face and chest with her bare hands, but the raging fire abated only briefly. Dean was aware enough to use his own hands to smother the flames that had caught his face on fire. As the crackling at the stove continued, Tisha turned to shut it off, moments before a second pop filtered through the air. The skillet jumped and grease, hot, hot grease, spattered all over her face and scalp. Tisha screamed as she felt it burn the skin around her eyes, her forehead, and her hairline. She felt Dean's rough hands cover her face with a cold, wet towel, and her own skin sizzled in her ears.

Her eyes hurt but she managed to open them, and when she saw her brother's face, red and blistered, she knew that things would never be the same. Dean fainted.

The smoke continued to fill Tisha's nose, and images of Mrs. Wellington's face slipped in over Dean's. Tisha wondered how it had happened, how had her friend managed to get out, and what about her poor husband, Herby? Had she had to leave him to burn? Tisha hoped he hadn't suffered, even as she knew that he had. He hadn't been as agile as Mrs. Wellington had always implied. He moved slowly, an aging man, and if the fire had landed on him, he probably couldn't have escaped. *He'd burned to death.* The part of their fate that would plague Tisha forever was that *it was because of her.* Mrs. Wellington's husband had died and Mrs. Wellington herself faced a long recovery, without her husband.

"I'm sorry," Tisha whispered aloud. She couldn't wake up from the nightmare, and the acrid smell of smoke had brought everything back to her. Who was burning now?

Was that her fault, too?

Chase opened his eyes when he heard Tisha's cries. He was up immediately: the door that connected their room had remained open, and he was just feet away. He rushed in, turned on the lamp and saw Tisha thrashing. "Tisha?" It was early still, but Chase reached for her and pulled her closer to him, sitting on the bed and cradling her in his arms. He looked down at her anguished face to see the tears flow steadily down her cheeks and knew she was having a nightmare.

"Tisha?" Chase said, louder.

"God, I'm sorry. I'm so sorry he died," Tisha muttered, her small frame convulsing as her body was racked with sobs. He held her tighter.

"*Tisha!* Wake up, honey. No one here is dead, everyone's all right. Wake up!" Chase shook her lightly and sat up in the bed on his knees.

Tisha woke then. Her eyes adjusting to the darkness around her, she blinked rapidly but couldn't stop the tears. "Something's burning, oh God, he's burning. It's my fault. It's all my fault he died," she said, disoriented.

"Who?" Chase replied. "Nothing is your fault. No one's burning. No one died, baby," he soothed.

"Herby."

Chase knew immediately of whom Tisha spoke. He looked at her then. "This is not your fault, Tisha. This is the plot of an evil, evil person who wants to hurt you as well."

"Yes, me, it's about me, the issue is with *me*... I can't marry you until I know everyone will be all right. I can't," she sobbed.

Tisha was fully awake now and she pushed against Chase, but he held her tightly, purposefully. She continued despondently: "I wish she'd come and hurt me, because no one deserves this."

"Don't say that," Chase said forcefully. "No-one deserves this, and certainly not you."

Chase felt ill when he realized what her words had meant. Andrea Robinson wanted to hurt Tisha, but so far it was only a threat: no action, nothing, no sighting of her. Chase knew that despite his best efforts, it would be almost impossible to completely protect Tisha against someone who was so determined to inflict harm upon anyone at all - like the unsuspecting and unfortunate Wellingtons.

"She's not going to hurt you. She won't, I promise you she won't," Chase said, speaking as much to reassure himself as her.

"So long as you and Thomas are safe, I don't care what happens. You can't stop this stuff, you know."

Chase didn't want to hear any of that. He wondered where Tisha's unrelenting optimism had suddenly disappeared to. This wasn't the Tisha he knew. She must have had quite some horrible nightmare to suddenly feel so despondent, so pessimistic. Slowly Chase rocked her. He didn't have a counterstatement for the ones she'd made. He didn't know what to say or do, and deep down inside him, no matter how much he hated to admit it, he knew she was right.

"Nothing is going to happen to you," Chase whispered into her hair. After what felt like half an hour, he moved his head back cautiously to look down at her. Tisha's eyes had closed, her breathing was deep and even, and her eyelids pulsed steadily. Trying not to disturb her, he settled her back down. He reached for the light but thought better of it. He left it on and stayed with her, sitting on the bed and cradling her to him.

A long time later, maybe another hour, Chase still lay with his eyes open, staring at the ceiling. Her words had worried him, and he wondered if at some point Tisha had seen other things in her dream that she had kept from him to save him the worry. It was too late for that. Chase sat there and simply tended to her, rubbing her back and saying a prayer for peaceful sleep and for their future.

Regardless of what she'd seen, he resolved to counter her deadly vision with one of his own. For once, he'd have to have enough optimism for the both of them. It would require something he'd never had much of: something she had added to his life since he met her. More faith. More happy thoughts and greater expectations for a life and a wife, not just settling for his lot as a single father. He closed his eyes and made himself see his life with her and Thomas - and maybe even another child, if that was God's will. First, he saw her accepting his proposal.

When the room phone rang, its harsh tone crashed through the silence. Chase turned quickly to pick it up before it woke Tisha. He wondered momentarily who on earth would call their room rather than his cell phone, and at such an hour as well?

"Yes?" he whispered, as he turned to look at Tisha, who hadn't stirred.

"Mr. Alton, I'm sorry to disturb you. This is guest services," the manly voice said on the other end.

"Yes, what is it?" Chase asked tersely.

"There was an incident just a few doors down from you, earlier this morning. Some guests burned some food and there was a small fire, but we've contained it and we don't want anyone on your floor to be alarmed. There is some odor infiltrating adjacent rooms, and some of the guest have complained, but everything's under control and there's no need to vacate the building. Just so that you know."

"Yes, yes... thank you." Chase hung up, looked around and sniffed. Sure enough, the smell was there, but faint. Why, he wondered, hadn't he smelled it sooner?

He turned to look back at Tisha. Leaning over her, Chase brought his arms around her small frame and kissed her just shy of her ear as he whispered, "We're going to be all right."

FORTY-ONE

C HASE WATCHED THE ROAD AS Tisha slept. The morning had certainly pushed all thoughts of the previous rough night aside. Tisha apologized for putting a damper on what she assured him had been the best make-up-birthday ever. Chase assured her there was no need for apologies and they'd talked briefly about her nightmare, though Tisha had been reluctant to relive any of it.

Chase pressed a couple of buttons on his phone and it began to play Anita Baker's voice once more: her greatest hits, including the song Tisha had sung for him just the night before. Sure, their voices were different, but she'd meant each and every line just for him when she sang it, and it had sounded better to him than any Grammy-winning singer in the world.

For now, however, it was back to real life. Chase pulled up to his mother's house and turned to Tisha. He squeezed her leg. She sat up, stretched and yawned exaggeratedly.

"A huge yawn from my future wife," he smiled. "How are you?"

Tisha smiled. She didn't mind the new nickname: after all, she'd told him she wanted to marry him and she meant it. The only way to get rid of the nickname, she knew, was to say yes to the proposal, which she knew she would do any day now. She smiled and leaned over to kiss him with all the longing in her heart and thanked him for staying with her, comforting her and being there all through the night after her dream.

Tisha pushed the lever to readjust her seat to its upright position. Chase gave a hearty beep on the horn. In a matter of seconds, the front door swung open and Thomas barreled out of the house before Chase could even release his seat belt. Tisha exited the car and braced herself as Thomas bolted into her open arms.

Tisha had been looking forward to this: to Thomas welcoming her with such cheer and joy. She had missed him, and he showed no shame in expressing that he'd missed her too. What she didn't expect was the overwhelming joy it brought her. She looked down into his beautiful eyes. He was getting so tall, she noticed, so he didn't have to reach very far when unexpectedly he kissed her right on the lips.

"I missed you, sweetie-pie!" Tisha said, and tears stung her eyes but she didn't cry. She was just so happy, and to get this kind of welcome so soon after that proposal was like icing and cherries on a cake that was already completely delicious.

Thomas nodded. "I know. I missed you, too. Come see the present I made for you!" Thomas grabbed Tisha's hand and pulled her toward the house, then stopped abruptly and snapped his fingers. "Oh man, I forgot: it's at home."

"That's all right, sweetheart. I have one of you and your dad's biggest presents right here. I love my new car, Thomas, this is seriously the biggest present I have ever received."

Tisha felt somewhat silly, telling a seven-year-old that she loved the car he had picked out, but as she looked at Thomas and saw his little chest swell proudly, she didn't care how silly it may sound. Thomas turned to roll his eyes at his dad. "I *told* you, Dad," Thomas said impatiently.

Tisha hugged Thomas tight. She couldn't believe she'd been so fortunate as to meet both of them. These two men in her life were the only bright spot she'd encountered in years. She turned to stare at Chase across the top of her new car. Their eyes connected as she mouthed the words *I love you*. She thought about his proposal and wondered how in the world she could say what she did just the other night, putting a temporary hold on what was looking like her very beautiful future. She held on to her faith.

The bar was filled with smoke, noisy people who chatted and smacked their lips, and a television in every corner blasting the same basketball game a little too loudly. Through the thick curling puff she let out, she looked around the bar in disgust. She hated bars and she hated the people. The only thing she could get out of either was a wallet of cash, but even that had proven difficult tonight, even for her expert pick-pocket fingers, and even though she hadn't pick-pocked in years, there was a time when she didn't have to - when she used to have a very rich husband, only she'd messed that up, big time.

She hadn't gotten anything since that small heist in Stubbing her cigarette into the ashtray, she regarded the man sitting across from her. *He must be kidding*, she thought. "How much you talking?"

The man sighed impatiently, then threw out a figure. She looked away and feigned indifference. It was a start, but not enough. She needed more money, and her ex wasn't giving her any. "You know what, I could get all that and then some if I just remarried the sucker."

She looked away; remarrying wasn't something the "sucker" wanted to do, of course, and all her attempts to get rid of the other hussy hadn't worked either - even the last-ditch effort of pretending she'd been sleeping with him. The look on Miss Prissy's face was priceless, however, and she'd been proud of herself for the dramatic act. She *could* act: no one knew it, that was all. They just weren't giving her a chance.

That was almost two weeks ago, and she was still satisfied, however temporary it was. She'd pulled out all the stops, right down to the condoms - even remembered to park her car a few blocks away. She nearly broke her neck timing things just right, but she had managed it. And what was it all for, when the other day, she had watched from a secluded spot as those two had trotted right back home together, just as if nothing had happened?

She needed money, and this one across from her might be talking about something. She'd only reached out to him because she'd seen him in the paper and wanted to see if he could help her in return for her helping him.

"Are you sure you have evidence that Ms. Jameson did something to that little girl? It was in Virginia, right?"

She had him, she thought to herself. "Yes. If she hadn't been trying to get that little girl she would have been fine," she said coolly. She didn't actually have any proof, of course, but he didn't need to know that. One little wiggle of certain augmented parts and this stupid school principal might as well have been in love with her. And Chase had said they were a waste. They may have cost him a fortune, but they worked all the time. She smiled.

"Ms...."

"Malika - my stage name," she purred. "I'm an actress, you see, and I'm working on an indie film. I'll, uh, be going back to Virginia soon, that's how I, uh, met her. I'm working on a small, courtroom drama set in DC."

The man across from her nodded.

"Say, do you know where that woman is - the one that beat her up?" she asked casually.

"Yeah, that's Andrea, she's staying nearby," he answered.

"Oh, really? Like, in your bed?" She waited a beat and let her words register. The obvious flush on his face told her everything she needed to know. "Let me know if you want to, uh, switch. Black don't crack, you know. Hey, anyone ever tell you you're super cute?"

Inwardly, she was repulsed when she saw his chest inflate, but she leaned in. "I'm sure the two of us could have some fun."

"I really like Ms. Jameson. She's a very nice teacher, not to mention beautiful..." he trailed off absently.

The woman paused. "You're sweet on Ms. Jameson? – does she know? Look at you, you got a crush! You oughta tell her," she said eagerly.

"Her big boyfriend wouldn't like that too much."

"Well, she ain't married yet. Goodness! You seem so confident, Mr. Jeeter. That big ol' man ain't got nothing on you. You're an *intellectual,* you're smart. That man Chase Alton is a dumb jock."

The man looked nonplussed. "How do *you* know?"

"Oh I don't *know* – you know how people talk, that's all," she said hurriedly. "Listen, I just need a retainer… I gotta go. That Ms. Jameson's really scared of fire. She was burned way back when, so cause something, then you can swoop in and seal the deal, save her, and you'll be a hero. See?"

Thinking about this guy made her want to gag. Chase was big and solid and muscular – they'd made such a cute couple. This man was tall, thin and light skinned, with eyes like a roach. Even that Tisha Jameson wouldn't be interested in him, that much she knew: he was greasy, and he wasn't even that smart. Sure, she had had work done on her face, and just about every part of her body had been enhanced thanks to modern techniques; but come on, any old search engine could pull up a photo of NFL superstar Chase Alton's ex-wife! *What a dope.*

"I have it all," the principal was saying. "Just make the call anonymously. I won't pay a lot for that, but later, another something might warrant a greater sum. I might want you to torch the house... I was able to get someone to do the other house for me. Here – "

She reached across the table slowly to take the thick white envelope from his hand.

"What? The house where she's staying - with Mr. Alton? That's what you meant, didn't you? I, I just thought I should... try to isolate her."

"Well, perhaps you can call and ask him to meet you somewhere else. Then she'll be alone," he replied disinterestedly.

But Thomas might be there, she thought to herself. Remembering her act, she smiled widely. "Yes, you're right," she said, nodding. This man really did want to kill that silly little teacher. He was worse than she thought. "What are you gonna do about that other teacher woman?" she asked casually.

"I'll take care of her," he answered, "but I can't do both."

"OK. I gotta go."

She stood and pulled down her short skirt, clutching the thick envelope as if it would evaporate in her hand. He stood, too, and caught her arm.

"How will I know it's done?"

"Call me, baby, of course. Here's my card." She reached into her cleavage and her claw-like, onyx-colored nails pulled out a glossy black card, with her signature masks on it. She loved those cards. They gave her legitimacy, and while they featured a phone number that hadn't worked in years, this guy didn't have to know that. This dope probably wouldn't be able to track her at all, and if he did find her, she'd be safely back at home in California. The indie film out here was a bust: she simply needed money to get home and find some new opportunities. Macon, Georgia was *not* where it was at.

"I'll call you when it's done," she said. She slipped on her shades and walked out of the smoky bar.

FORTY-TWO

"CHASE, I'M GOING BACK TO my place – now get over it. We've had this discussion the entire week and I'm not backing down on this one."

Tisha continued to pull clothes from a large laundry basket sitting on the bed. Folding them neatly, she placed each one in her tote bag and took a moment to regard Chase.

She was relieved that the holiday week was coming to an end. Most years Tisha loved the short reprieve, but this year she was badly missing her classroom. She hadn't been there for quite some time now: an eternity, as far as she was concerned. She needed to get home to some semblance of normalcy; she needed to get back on schedule and into a routine. And for goodness sake, as much as she would miss Chase, she needed to go to bed at sensible hours instead of staying up and talking to him until the wee hours of the morning. She was likely putting on weight from all the fine cooking, too. Chase was glad he'd given Angie some time off, but Tisha liked the woman and they'd developed a fast friendship, often trading recipes.

Tisha wanted nothing more than to stay with Chase, and one day she knew she would be there permanently; but right now she had to focus on her own life and her own work. She'd been playing house long enough.

She smiled at Chase, hating that he was annoyed with her. "Absence makes the heart grow fonder?" she ventured, zipping the main compartment of her carryall. She turned to the vanity and closed the tops of various lotions, perfumes and sprays before placing them into the bag's side compartment.

"Chase, listen to me." Tisha placed the bag on the floor and climbed across the bed to where Chase sat. His eyes were cast to the ceiling and his body stiff and closed off. She knew that meant Chase would act as if he didn't hear the words she said. Still she pressed on:"I have a bodyguard that you hired for me, which must cost a fortune, but you," she tapped his chest, "you are always around, and nothing has happened to me yet. While I was mad at you" — Tisha had hated that time but brought it up only to illustrate her point— "I stayed at my apartment for a day or so without you - until the stupid cavalry came, of course - but I was *all right.*"

"I had updates on what was happening," Chase protested. "Your family came immediately, and… and anyone fool enough to mess with Jojo Jameson should be committed," he finished. Chase turned serious. "I worry about you."

"Please don't. Please don't worry about me," Tisha pleaded.

"Why not? You worry about people you love, Tisha: that's a prerequisite. Love them, worry about them. Not to mention, there are special circumstances involved here. You're the one who told me you're prone to danger," Chase reminded her.

"I was only kidding."

"No, you weren't."

Tisha sighed audibly. "I'm not staying, Chase. I need to get back to what I do, where I live, and where everything I need is. Not just stay where I've scraped together a few things to function for a little while." She gestured to the small space where her items for teaching were situated. She smiled for a brief moment. For the most part, it looked just like the mess she kept at home. Tisha turned back to

Chase and noticed the scowl. She frowned at him.

"What about when we're married?" he asked grumpily. "You're going to live here then, aren't you?"

"Of course - don't be dramatic, Chase. Anyway, by then I'll have everything I need picked out for my corner of the den downstairs."

"So you're going to marry me?"

"There's not a doubt in my mind, you know that. I just need time, that's all, and you know it."

Chase flopped back against the pillows and sighed in frustration. He recognized a losing battle when he saw it.

Tisha leaned down over Chase. Her hair fell across his face and he brushed it back gently to rest his hand on her cheek. "I can't bear the thought of anything happening to you," he said.

Tisha kissed him then. Somewhere along the line, Chase had changed. As hard a man as he tried to be, she'd softened his heart, and both he and Thomas opened her own heart, even wider than she ever thought could be possible.

"Nothing will happen to me," Tisha said, snuggling into his waiting embrace. His large arms and solid chest seemed to cocoon her like no-one else. She fit so perfectly.

Tisha remained there until it was time for her to go and face whatever demons were waiting for her at her apartment and at her work. Even as she drew closer to Chase, she dreaded whatever she would face. She had a funny feeling that perhaps one of those demons would be the school principal.

———◆———

Easter week was nothing but a distant memory when Tisha returned and immersed herself in her teaching. She was sorry she'd missed making Easter eggs with the kids to decorate the room and wearing her bunny hat, but overall Tisha felt somewhat optimistic. She'd been able to see

Marina Stamos, who was now protected by police guards. The little girl was doing considerably better, and Tisha thanked God that her injuries hadn't killed her, but her pre-existing intellectual disability made it hard to know what damage she'd sustained as far as her brain was concerned. She'd be a while recovering, but they all hoped she would eventually be able to identify her attacker. Andrea Robinson was the top name both Marina and Thomas had given so far. Tisha knew that she wouldn't feel totally carefree until Mrs. Wellington walked from the hospital on her own and Andrea Robinson was caught.

Surprisingly, however, Tisha's reentry had been a smooth one. Everyone was nice to her, including her fellow teachers, and her classroom was full of angelic children for the first few days of her return. Every one of them had welcomed her with a huge hug, and they'd chattered away to her like nothing unusual had ever happened. Some of them really didn't know what had happened: their young minds were too preoccupied to understand, and just a handful of parents - Chase included - still sheltered their kids from exposure to the TV news. The rest that did know only speculated and whispered to one another with no one really confirming or denying the swirl of stories that went around.

Each and every one of her students had also made her a beautiful card, and just as many for Mrs. Wellington. Tisha now had a stack of them to take as soon as she could get over to see the older woman, which she planned to do as soon as her school day was done. And Thomas, her heart, had organized the entire group to sing Happy Birthday to her. This is why Tisha lived: for work and for love of Chase. Both things gave her the purpose she needed.

Teacher after teacher stopped by to say a brief hello. Many of them Tisha wouldn't even have thought knew her name, but they were still kind enough to peek in her room for just a moment to welcome her back and give an encouraging word. A couple of them candidly told of having dealt with Andrea Robinson before - her short temper, her roughness with the children - but admitted they had never guessed that there was a more menacing issue at play. Tisha asked them to be sure they told the police and all assured her that they had.

No one could really believe that Andrea Robinson, or anyone for that matter, would be capable of such a horrifying act. Sadly, Tisha knew it was possible: she had seen much worse.

Tisha lifted a stack of books and put them in order. She turned a desk around and stepped up on the seat to take down the current month's calendar decorations. The kids had made big raindrops this week, and Tisha wanted to put them up. She carefully pulled staples from the board and dropped them into the trash can, then stapled up the new pieces strategically. When a knock sounded on the door, Tisha looked over, startled, and lost her balance. In a blur, she saw a figure rush forward to catch her as she fell into his open arms.

Placing a hand on her fluttering heart, Tisha exhaled and secured her glasses. "Mr. Jeeter, hello. Thank you."

"Tisha," Chris Jeeter said as he continued to hold her in his arms for longer than was comfortable. Tisha felt a little dizzy and instantly queasy, as if she were sick to her stomach. Seconds ticked by, until finally she said, "Uh, can you put me down now, please?"

"Yes, yes, of course," Chris replied, as he gently set Tisha on her feet. "That would have been a nasty fall if I hadn't caught you, young lady."

"Yes, uh, thank you," Tisha replied sincerely. Quickly, she busied herself with something else, this time being mindful to keep off any high places. She moved back to her desk at the front of the room, somewhat wary of him.

It was the first time since she'd been back that Chris Jeeter had come and said anything to her at all. Tisha had tried to touch base with him at the beginning, but it had been Leland that had passed her the word to report back to work and Leland who gave her info on the investigation. Chris Jeeter, she reflected, had been largely absent this entire time. When she'd called the school to speak with him, his secretary had invariably replied with "He's busy," or sometimes "He just stepped out."

Tisha wondered at the fact that, through all of this time, he'd never had the courtesy even to call her. Nothing. She'd had some instinctive reservations about trusting him even during the time of the play, but now she resolved not to trust him at all.

"Well, Tisha, listen, uh, I wanted to welcome you back," Mr. Jeeter gabbled. "True to form for one of my best teachers, here you are, right in the swing of things." Chris gave a broad smile and gestured to all the calendars, school books and many other little touches that Tisha had taken the time to add. "In your rightful place as one of the best teachers in this school," he repeated.

"Am I, Mr. Jeeter? One of the *best* teachers?" Tisha asked. She really and truly wanted to give him the benefit of the doubt. After all, he himself had surely faced much added scrutiny, media inquiries and calls from worried parents and teachers alike, but the fact that he had completely shunned her for all these weeks had her thinking about working for someone else entirely. She didn't want to, and in any case she likely wouldn't leave Thomas, but the man's lack of response to her had it all crossing her mind.

"Of course you are," Chris Jeeter said indulgently, giving her a knowing wink. "Why do you ask that?"

Tisha took a deep breath. "Mr. Jeeter, you must have known that I was innocent, right? That I could never harm a single hair of any of these kids? I had made complaints to you about Ms. Robinson. I even asked if you'd definitely done your due diligence with the background on her. Yet you didn't say a word about such facts or about my character during the whole media furor that we've all just been through. You didn't call me to offer... anything."

She was being careful: she didn't want to sound desperate or unable to handle the situation. In truth, it had been Chase who got her through. As it had all been happening, she hadn't really thought about Mr. Jeeter at all; but one word from him would still have made a positive difference. A single courteous call would have changed her entire estimation of him.

"Now just a minute, Tisha," Chris chided. "I always believed you'd never hurt the children, and I gave the police the log you kept on Andrea Robinson. And, well now, about saying outright that I hold you in the highest esteem as a teacher – you know I'm under a strict obligation here. I cannot play favorites. You are one of the best, but I had to be neutral in this situation. I could show no partiality to anyone."

Tisha stood her ground. "I never expected partiality, but I needed something, anything, to confirm that you didn't believe I'd harmed anyone. You never said once to the press that you didn't question my innocence."

"I never believed you would harm them! I... please forgive me. I would never believe such horrific things about you, never," Chris stammered, cornered. His voice grew husky as he reached out to lightly touch Tisha's face. His finger lightly grazed her cheek and slid down her face, pulling her lower lip down slightly.

Tisha reeled at first in disbelief at his intimate touch, then smacked his hand away and backed up. He'd crossed a line, and there was something in his eyes, something there that shouldn't have been. She looked to the door, regaining her thoughts and trying to stick to the matter at hand. For just a few seconds, thoughts of yelling for Devon crossed her mind. Her bodyguard would be standing just on the other side of her door. She knew that Chris knew that as well when his eyes followed hers.

Tisha looked back at Chris. *Her complaints,* Tisha remembered. She'd been outlining her complaints, and though slightly disturbed by his unexpected pass at her, she decided to pretend it simply hadn't happened. She composed herself and continued to speak about the facts that she wanted to present.

"What about the number of assistants this school needs, Mr. Jeeter?" she persisted. "It has been brought to your attention in countless staff meetings that this school needs more teacher's aides in the classroom and that the student-to-teacher ratio is too great, especially in the special needs classes."

"I can't create aides and teachers out of the air, Ms. Jameson," Mr. Jeeter protested. "The hiring practices are strict and competitive and they take a great deal of time to complete, and people are hard pressed to work with special needs populations. They require a great deal of… added patience."

"What?" Tisha looked at him more closely. This wasn't what she should be hearing from a principal. There were good teachers out there, this she knew. Perhaps his rates weren't competitive, or perhaps his self-righteous attitude deterred many – just as it currently put her off discussing anything further with him.

Tisha felt wary. She had spent much of her professional life ensuring things were above board and that everyone had what they needed. The needs for advocacy that she encountered were exhausting, and it was her very advocacy work that had ultimately brought her here to another district with still more problems to address.

"I just want to make sure, Mr. Jeeter, that this school is up to code," she continued. "I need to be certain that you have the number of personnel you need to care for this number of students. And when will the career center be open?"

"The career center?" He laughed derisively. "That takes

a lot of funding, Ms. Jameson, and I don't appreciate your suggesting that this school somehow lacks the proper support. I do everything I can to ensure we meet the proper standards."

He put his hands on his hips and got in her face. "Do you know how hard it is to be a principal? We have a hard job, Ms. Jameson, and it's a shame to be questioned by your own staff. The first few years of this school are vital to my professional success, and I *won't* be responsible for its failure."

"Its failure? Your success? You're exaggerating, aren't you? More to the point, is that what this school is to you: a make-or-break effort impacting you and you alone?"

In a rush, Tisha was reminded of the play and how Chris had wanted the local papers to cover the event, to portray the school in a positive light. Then there was the small article on him in the paper she'd spotted that time at the grocery store with Chase and Thomas. *Make me look good.* That's what he had said to her back then. Something was wrong here. Why hadn't Tisha seen sooner that this man was nothing but an opportunist? Maybe even someone willing to do things that weren't ethical in order to somehow make 'his' school a success.

The press, even with the Andrea Robinson situation, had portrayed him in a positive way, while smearing her name. Sadly, she now believed Chris Jeeter might actually have helped to fan the flames of gossip rather than defending her. The finger pointed at everyone but him - while her own name had been carelessly thrown around, dragged through the mud, even linked to some sort of seedy past. Nothing favorable about her had been printed or spoken, right up until Leland's prepared statement had been circulated. It was that statement that had caused people to look at other culprits and reminded the public about the police's shortcomings in evidence-gathering practices.

Tisha looked up at Chris. A war of thoughts had passed

through her mind so quickly: she must be getting paranoid. Tisha shook her head, quickly dismissing Chris Jeeter
as a suspect in any sort of wrongdoing. Her problems with
Andrea surely had nothing to do with him. The woman
had a vendetta against Tisha that went all the way back to
Virginia, and she hadn't known this man more than a few
months.

"I'm sorry, Ms. Jameson, that everyone can't be a saint
like you. A lot does rest on me regarding this school." Chris
waved his hands vaguely and looked about the room. "This
brand-new school here that I've decided to head up."

Tisha nodded, still trying to dismiss her thoughts about
the man. But she couldn't shake the feeling, and she began
to notice other things about him that she hadn't before:
his fidgety demeanor, the way he wrung his hands, the
way he rocked on his feet... were these signs that he was
concealing something? But she couldn't place it - and after
all, Chris Jeeter had done nothing to prove to her that he
had willfully neglected the needs of the school because he
was trying to cover something else up. Chris Jeeter was
misguided, selfish, a possible self-serving attention grabber
- but corrupt? Tisha tried to put aside her niggling doubt.
She didn't need to borrow trouble. She had enough of it
as it stood.

Tisha looked up again, ready to apologize for her accu-
satory statements; but Chris Jeeter had left, closing her
classroom door.

Tisha looked at her clock. Kids would pile in at any
moment and she was starving. When she opened her lunch
sack, though, a pungent stink from her egg salad reached
her nose, and she realized she'd forgotten to put it in the
teacher's lounge refrigerator. That smell was enough to
turn her stomach. Quickly, Tisha discarded the bag in the
trash and ran for the bathroom.

She felt ill. Hurriedly, she pushed open the door to the
small room and rushed into a stall. She pushed her hair

from around her face, lifted the toilet seat and heaved up her coffee from this morning: all she had had for the day. She felt queasy and feverish. As Tisha stood, she heard Devon call her name. "I'm all right," she yelled in response.

Using her foot, Tisha pressed the lever for the flush. She pulled her shirt back into place, composing herself, then opened the door and walked to the mirror. Glancing at herself in the mirror, Tisha washed her hands and wetted a napkin to wipe her mouth. She felt like she had to throw up again, and her stomach cramped – just as the door to another stall opened and a woman emerged who looked even taller than the last time Tisha had seen her. Cold, cold eyes stared at her. Tisha nearly fainted.

FORTY-THREE

———◆———

SHE SHOULD'VE FAINTED - THAT'S what Tisha knew she should've done. Faked some kind of attack, played dead: anything was better than standing on wobbly legs while a murderer, child abuser and whatever else Andrea Robinson was stared her in the face. Tisha was paralyzed with fear. Protection was a mere call away, if only she could yell. But sound died in her terrified throat, and she screamed only on the inside as the barrel of a gun pointed at her stomach. In that moment, Tisha also realized that something had been put into her coffee. She'd swallowed only a little because it had tasted odd. She'd thought the milk had curdled.

"Did you like that special brand of creamer I put in your coffee this morning?"

"What was it?" Tisha's stomach still cramped and it hurt slightly, but she was alert and didn't waver. She kept her eyes trained on the woman in front of her.

Andrea Robinson looked haggard. She wore raggedy, faded jeans and a tattered sweater. Her hair, a dusty black, looked thick and dirty, as if she'd been on the run since their last encounter. Her face was worse and crueler than before: hollow cheeks, a hard mean expression, emotionless eyes and pallid skin. Her eyes, always those of a madwoman, had nonetheless been kinder when Tisha had first met her.

But *forget all that*, Tisha's mind whispered hysterically; *if only she wasn't holding a gun*. But the woman was, and Tisha also noticed something silver on the end of it: something Clint Eastwood used in one of his movies — a concealer, was that the word? A silencer! That was it. Tisha forced herself to keep her eyes off the gun and on Andrea's face. Given just a little time, she was sure she'd be able to get Devon's attention and get out of there. The gun was an issue, but who had time to worry about such details?

"Took you long enough," Andrea drawled with a smirk. "Jeeter said it would work faster."

"What?"

"I said it took you long enough," the woman repeated coldly. "I been in here all freaking day. Your bodyguard would've had to get here pretty early to find me."

"Why don't you just tell me why you want to kill me so much?" Tisha asked quietly, trying to keep her voice calm. "I don't even know you, and I don't remember you..."

"Of course you don't, all you cared about was that stupid little girl," Andrea snapped.

"Melinda? Her name was Melinda. I was going to adopt her, I was... wait, whatever did *she* do to you? She was a child!"

"I lost my job, you closed down the house, and I lost my livelihood."

"You lost?" Tisha couldn't believe her ears. "You had your whole life - you could have found another job!"

"Well I *didn't* get another job," Andrea retorted angrily, "and it was those kids' fault."

"You can't blame an innocent child for- "Tisha started.

"You're not going to tell me what I'm going to do." Andrea stormed. "I didn't blame an *innocent* child. She got in my way, just like you - just like that other little dumb kid you just *had* to come rescue. This stuff is *your* fault, because you have a problem with minding your own damn business, right?"

Tisha shook her head. She wanted to tell the woman before her that she'd never had any prospects in the teaching profession, not because of interference from anyone but due to her overbearing attitude, together with her lack of personality, moral compass or sense of responsibility for her actions. But Tisha managed to keep this to herself.

"How did you know I would come to this restroom?" Tisha asked. She made a note never to come to the main bathroom again, just in case there were killers waiting around for her.

"I figured if you had to vomit, you'd get to the nearest place where you could do that."

"OK. Next time I'll get myself a trashcan."

"You think this is some kind of joke?" Andrea's fingers tightened on the gun.

Tisha shook her head slowly. She wiped her hands on her slacks as sweat began to pool in her armpits and – and… oh, for the love of God, she needed to throw up again. She wished she knew some way of making it projectile. She squeezed her hands into fists. If her stomach would just settle, she could think.

"I'm the one holding the gun and you're still just the same cocky bitch, aren't you? Man, you have some nerve. I would've liked to beat you up, see you die slowly, or even torch your place, but sometimes time just doesn't permit all that."

"Like you torched the Wellingtons? And, I have to know: did you kill Melinda a year ago, in Virginia?" Tisha asked urgently. She desperately hoped that Devon would come in, but of course it was a woman's bathroom: he had no idea what was taking place. Perhaps he simply thought that she'd been having a normal conversation with someone. Where in the world was Wonder Woman when you needed her?

"She fell on the playground," Andrea supplied, and shrugged, a wicked gleam in her eye.

"Don't lie to me." Tisha was angry and tired. She summoned whatever fight she had evaded when Melinda died: she had the woman now, and Melinda and Marina needed justice - not some wimp of a teacher with a heart for kids. She focused.

"What are you doing, channeling your imaginary friends?"

Tisha heard what was said but she continued to concentrate. She only had to distract her, to stay calm, thus she focused on the sound of her own breathing, her heart rate, the blood flowing through her veins, the tick of the clock, the constant trickle of the broken toilet in the stall where Andrea had hidden for the better part of the morning. All the sounds combined, ringing in her ears. And then the situation got worse.

"Hi, Ms. Jameson." Tisha looked toward the door as two little girls entered and as if in a dream, she saw the gun turn toward them.

That was enough. Tisha rushed forward. "Get out of here, get out of here, run. Devon!" she screamed, her eyes locked on Andrea's wrist. She grabbed it, flinging the force of her body against Andrea's chest. Caught off guard, Andrea was the first to hit the wall and Tisha pressed her against it with all of her might.

The two girls, covering their ears, rushed out quickly as Devon appeared in a blur. *He has a gun too* was Tisha's first thought - then a shot rang out, and Tisha realized it was from the hand she grasped. Through her fingers, Tisha felt Andrea's wrist contract a second time, and she pushed her arm down this time with all she had. Devon winced: he'd been shot - but she couldn't think, her hands were pressing, pressing down... and then Andrea went down. "Get down!" Tisha heard Devon yell, and as quickly as what he said registered, her own body went limp and her face hit the cold grimy tile of the bathroom floor. She lay still, heard two shots ring out and then... nothing.

She waited painfully as time seemed to pass, and then someone was pulling her away. Chris Jeeter appeared out of nowhere. "Tisha," he yelled, "Tisha, are you all right?"

Tisha heard him, realizing it was he who grabbed her and it was he who held her now.

"You bastard, you set me up! I know it was you. You set me up," Andrea screamed. She gritted her teeth at the pain in her arm and her leg where she'd been shot.

"Let go of me," Tisha said to Chris, who had managed to drag her out of the bathroom and into the hall. She turned to go back in to see about Devon when Chris grabbed her by the arm. "No! I won't let you. I won't let her hurt you."

She turned back to look at him as if he'd lost his mind, then down at the arm tightly holding her wrist. "I have to see if Devon is all right." She twisted until her wrist throbbed and finally managed to get away from him. She had barely a scratch - but the man who protected her had been shot.

She ran into the bathroom. Devon stood over Andrea Robinson, whose color had turned ghostly white. A pool of blood created a circle around her leg and the gun was across the floor opposite Andrea's body. Andrea's head rested awkwardly against the last stall door.

Devon stood, unfazed, as if he hadn't been shot at all, even as the blood ran in rivulets down his arm to drip on the floor. His other hand held the gun trained on Andrea.

"Devon, are you all right?" She rushed to him and, not knowing what else to do, she seized a wad of paper towels and pressed them against his injured arm.

"I'm all right," Devon said calmly. "I called the police."

"You did?"

"I thought you were taking an unreasonably long time, so I phoned for backup," Devon said. "I notified Chase too, just to be certain. Are you all right?"

Tisha nodded and looked at Andrea. "Yes, yes, of course. Th-thank you so much."

"Don't count your chickens just yet, I ain't dead," came a rasping voice from the ground. Andrea tried to sit up, and Devon's gun raised in anticipation as she moved. Andrea's eyes fixed on the gun and she was still again.

Tisha leaned closer. "Death would be too easy," she hissed. "You deserve to live out the rest of your natural life in jail, reminded of why you're locked behind four walls with bars."

When the police rushed in, Tisha looked to Devon with one last thankful nod before she rushed out.

———— ◆ ————

Tisha gave her statement quickly to the officers. She delivered all that she could in as much detail as she could muster, and when it looked as if the questions would start again, as they had a thousand times, Leland McGehee appeared out of nowhere to help her excuse herself.

"I know you're not going to question my client again without her lawyer present, are you, Officer?" Leland said, laying a warning hand on the officer's shoulder. Tisha rushed to his side, hoping Chase wasn't far away.

Leland nodded his head down the hall, but the only thing she saw was the commotion of other uniformed officers who held teachers back from looking on, and had already cordoned off the space with yellow police tape. Only when they dispersed did she finally spy Chase. One officer tried to hold him back, but Chase just kept moving, daring anyone to stop him. At long last, Tisha was able to sprint to his open arms.

FORTY-FOUR

TISHA COULD HARDLY SLEEP AND so she went into her living room where she found Chase still wide awake - still holding his silent vigil over her. It was only late evening but he'd stayed there, and that made her feel really good.

When he heard her approach, his attention diverted from the evening news on the television, which not surprisingly, was reporting the latest slice of news that involved her life. He held the remote up.

"You don't have to turn it off. I'm all right," she said quietly. Her attention was on the news too, now. As always, she wished it hadn't been her at all, but she was relieved that the story was finally complete.

"Are you sure?" Chase asked. He muted the television anyway and set the remote aside.

Tisha nodded and sat next to him on her couch. She tucked her legs under her and kissed him on the cheek. "How are you?" she said, noticing he wore a pair of nice jeans and a crisp white shirt but was otherwise very casual. He'd removed his shoes and his long legs and feet had white socks on them, somehow making him look less intimidating yet still larger than life on her little two-person couch. He looked good whatever he wore. She cuddled up next to him, his arm coming around her and pulling her tighter, just the way she liked it.

Chase looked at her incredulously, "You're asking how *I* am? Really?"

"I'm all right…"

"That's the second time you've said that, so I know something's wrong."

"I… think I made a mistake, Chase." Then the floodgates opened and tears came streaming down her face. Tisha stood and moved to the kitchen.

Chase was right behind her. "Whoa, why? You didn't make a mistake, you've done nothing wrong! Tisha, what is this about?"

"I made a mistake… in rejecting your proposal."

"Oh well, is that all?" he said, relieved. "Then yes, you made a mistake, I agree," he chuckled.

Tisha laughed but rolled her eyes at him. She pulled down the items she needed to make a cup of hot tea and turned to him.

"I felt so bad today. I had a stupid stomachache for one thing, thanks to that stuff that crazy woman put in my coffee, but I also felt bad that I was willing to give up on my life and the chance for a love of a lifetime just because some deranged woman was after me."

"Well, now wait a minute," Chase said thoughtfully. "I mean, she was *especially* crazy: not the type us regular people encounter very often. There's nothing wrong with being uncertain, Tisha. I don't blame you. In fact, I'm honored that you considered this so carefully."

"You are?"

Chase nodded and came closer. "You won't rush your decisions - you're not after anything I have."

"Just your heart."

"And you had that on day one," he replied softly. "You took my son's and then you took mine."

"Did I really?"

"Yes - but I'm talking about my materials, my protection, my name and status, comfort… They aren't much, I know, but just the fact that you're not so greedily ready to take all that I can give - I love you for that. Look, I've been with people who wanted everything I had outside of myself, things I worked really hard for; things they wanted to use up until I had nothing left, but never me. I love that you love just me and my son, and that you actually want to build a relationship and work through this thing called living: to just be regular, not some exciting Hollywood version of ourselves that we'd have to project. A reality show was likely in my future with Teresa. Do you know how ridiculous that could be?" Chase exclaimed.

"I understand," Tisha replied gently. "When I think about the girls that came into the bathroom today, well, sometimes I don't even want to bring a child into this world if it's so cruel. One of those girls could've been my daughter, Chase, they could've been hurt - and Marina, she could've been my daughter too. Life is so fragile."

What Chase had said was beautiful, and he was right about Tisha's motivations. She was really a very simple person from a nice family, and she simply wanted to be happy, drama free and not constantly under observation. She didn't care if the money and everything else he'd mentioned all dried up and went away. All those things only enhanced who he was and what he had to offer her.

"Yes, the world is cruel," Chase said as he wiped her tears. "And those kids could've been hurt, you're right - but they weren't, and Marina's going to be all right, and we will protect Thomas and our future children from whatever danger presents itself."

"I feel horrible, Chase, for feeling this way. Will you ask me to marry you again sometime soon?"

"I can ask you right now."

Tisha leaned away from him as he went down on his knee once more, right before her very eyes.

"I've carried this with me everywhere in hope," Chase said, pulling the tiny box from his pocket. "I believe in hope, Tisha. I believe in *you*. I never thought I'd get married again until you came into my life. I love you so much. Will you marry me?"

"Oh, Chase," she whispered. "*Yes*."

"Is that your final answer?" Chase quipped.

"Yes, yes and yes!"

The ring he presented looked even larger when placed on her slender finger, and it fit just right. "It's so beautiful," she breathed. "I love you."

"I love you, too." Chase said and stood up, reached for her and lifted her into his arms. She held onto him for the rest of the night, looking forward to the rest of their lives together.

———◆———

"Dad, you know how you said to tell you if anything at all seems… 'spicious?" Thomas struggled with the word as he and his dad rode to his grandmother's house.

"Suspicious, son?" Chase clarified, and when Thomas nodded, Chase prompted him to go on.

"Yeah, you said that we should tell you – like, it might not be anything, but you kinda just get this feeling, sometimes? Especially the bad feelings, you said to tell you the bad feelings mostly, and the good ones are pretty much okay… right?"

Chase nodded and listened more intently to his son. Since the incident with Ms. Robinson, Chase had vowed to turn a concentrated ear to everything his son said: to listen carefully and if need be investigate each and every one of Thomas's claims. Recently, Chase had been giving his son short pep talks about being upfront with things as soon as they happened, because in retrospect Andrea Robinson had shown signs of derangement long before that horrific day; and Chase had gently reminded Thomas that he should've said something much quicker about any incidents with her.

Now, Chase wished Thomas would skip to the point, rather than reviewing the word "suspicious". Still, Chase forced himself not to rush him. He listened patiently and encouraged him: "Sure, Thomas, I'm listening."

Thomas hesitated. "Well, like our school principal, Mr. Jeeter. He's nice and all, but, he's kinda weird."

"Weird how?" Chase was definitely listening now. Sure, he didn't like the man - but weird, as Thomas said, wasn't enough.

"He likes Tisha, I think."

Chase gripped the steering wheel but managed to remain calm. "Well, what makes you say that?"

"He's always looking at her."

Chase nodded and prepared to dismiss the comment. Men would always look at Tisha. She was breathtaking - but she was going to marry him, he reminded himself: she was already spoken for. Now, if Mr. Jeeter needed help remembering that - well, Chase would be more than happy to oblige. He kept his tone light as he continued. "Well okay, son, that doesn't sound terrible so far. How do you think he looks at her?"

"Like you, Dad," Thomas answered. "He looks at her like he's in love with her. That's kind of wrong, right?"

FORTY-FIVE

L ATER THAT EVENING, TISHA WAS making dinner when Chase let himself in. He smelled something heavenly. He and Tisha had a weekend to themselves ahead of them, at his insistence. Even though she welcomed Thomas being with them at every opportunity, Chase still thought they needed just one evening where he could have her all to himself.

Thomas's revelations had plagued Chase. As they continued the ride to Chase's mother's house, he'd pressed Thomas for exactly when he'd noticed Jeeter looking at Tisha. Thomas didn't really know, and Chase assured him it was nothing. The man was probably an okay person, he told his son, and urged Thomas not to think badly of Mr. Jeeter until Chase had a chance to do more research.

"So you think he's okay, do you, Dad?" had been Thomas's last question, and Chase had nodded. "I do, son. I think he's all right," he had lied.

"Hi," Tisha said brightly as he entered the kitchen, kissing him on the lips. He wanted her to be safe - that was the only reason he was annoyed, he told himself - but sadly, he suspected that the business with the school wasn't over yet. Now, though, with her kisses and the smells of her and the food all around, it was very hard for him to stay mad.

Tisha regarded him. "I know that look. What's the matter?"

"Something you want to tell me, about you and that sleaze-ball principal?" Chase said heatedly. Even in relaxed get-up, she was still sexy to him. Still, he was determined that her skintight jeans and oversized alma mater t-shirt would not deter him from having it out with her. He looked away to concentrate.

"As I recall, you were the one who went on and on about confiding in each other, and here you can't tell me that some fool is making eyes at you?" Chase snapped, crossing his arms over his chest.

"That's why I didn't tell you," Tisha sighed. "I know how you are - now you're all worked up. And nothing came of it, I assure you. I didn't make an issue of it."

"Still, Tisha, I'm upset that you didn't tell me. I can talk to Devon and get him to come back tomorrow, or I can talk to Jeeter. Which would you like?"

"You absolutely will not," Tisha protested. "The man was just shot, for goodness sake!"

"If he's not well, he has a team of folks - and anyway, it was a flesh wound," Chase said stubbornly.

"You're overreacting. The *principal*, Chase? He made a clumsy pass at me - that doesn't make him a candidate for murder."

"Yes, and just by looking at people, you suddenly know what they're capable of, right?" Chase snarled. "Did you have all this insight about Andrea Robinson? Huh?"

"Hey, that's not fair," Tisha said. From the look in his eyes, she knew he only cared for her safety.

"Listen to me," Chase continued in a more conciliatory tone. "I've got to go to North Carolina on Monday, to do another interview. I'll only be gone for the day. Why don't you come with me?"

"You know I have to teach next week," Tisha said.

"It's a day," Chase reasoned. "What do second-graders do that's so pressing, anyway?"

"Chase," Tisha said patiently, "you want me to come

with you because you think something's wrong, but it's not. Everything is fine. Look, Jina and Dean are coming down tomorrow night. We're all going to the pizza parlor, including Thomas and your mother – I already invited her – then Sunday we're going shopping for wedding stuff."

Chase nodded and pulled Tisha to him. "That's right, we're getting married. I forgot." He stuck out his tongue.

Tisha moved her head to look at him and punched him playfully in the chest when he laughed. "Have you come up with a date yet?"

"Me? The only thing I have to do is show up and test cake samples. You never said anything about helping to come up with a *date*," returned Chase. "Let's see, I think we should get married in… May."

Tisha nodded. "A year is good. Plenty of time to plan."

"Next year?" Chase shook his head. "I meant next month."

Tisha laughed incredulously, then sobered. She went back to the stove to stir the pot, her eyes boring into him. "Chase, we can't plan a wedding in a little over a *week*. That's impossible!"

"Not if we get married in jeans – in a shack."

Tisha laughed as Chase settled down. Removing his jacket, he washed his hands quickly and stuck his finger in the red sauce she stirred.

Tisha was preparing chicken *piccata* with sumptuous red wine sauce and freshly grated parmesan cheese melted just right to form the rich crust. A tossed salad and toasty garlic bread were the sides. He watched her from across the table as she said the grace and dug in. He loved her, he loved her cooking and he envisioned this becoming a nightly ritual in the near future. Chase still wasn't sold on that creep Chris Jeeter, but he let that go for the time being. Maybe he'd give the man a call, maybe he'd have to investigate him; but doing nothing was no longer in Chase's procedure manual. He would always protect what was now his, and he would take any threats seriously.

Chase reached across the table for Tisha's hand and kissed it. "This is so good. I love you."

"I love you too, future hubby," she smiled.

Chase was surprised, but he loved the sound of that. Yes, he would be a future husband to a future wife, and he recognized his good fortune in finding a love to last a lifetime. No-one, he felt, could take away that future.

They spent the rest of the evening finishing their dinner and cleaning up the kitchen – together, at Tisha's insistence - before discussing plans for their wedding, either next month or next year.

————◆————

Chris Jeeter was getting paranoid. Now that she'd been caught, Andrea Robinson was talking her head off and he was being implicated in everything. She made up things that weren't true, sure; but it was the true stuff that had him the most worried. That movie star wannabe - what was her name again? He needed to talk to her, and quickly. One last little event he needed to persuade her to do.

Time was running out. The only thing he'd wanted was for Tisha Jameson to help him, to make him look good to others. She *could* help him, of that he was sure; but now she'd stopped talking to him altogether. He had to convince her to help him. That's what he needed: her help. The actress lady was supposed to have scared Tisha, but she'd apparently left town and now everything was just a mess.

Chris paused the television when Tisha Jameson's picture came up again on the news. He studied her face. He loved her, why didn't she know? He had such a hard time showing restraint around her, but he was trying. She was so kind, and she always smelled like peaches, wildflowers, and everything sweet. Summer was coming after the chill of the winter. The spring would be short. How he loved the summer - and he loved her. He loved her dearly.

While he didn't want to hurt a hair on her precious head, his only alternative was a life in prison. It was her, he had convinced himself. It was her: *she* was telling on him – and unlike the deranged Andrea, they would believe Ms. Jameson. They'd believe what she said, now that she'd been put back into her rightful innocent place in the eyes of parents and their children. If he played his cards right, she might say good things about him and Andrea could go down alone, but he would need her cooperation. If she didn't help him – well, he'd just do away with her. He'd go ask her if she could, he'd just ask her once - and if she didn't, she'd beg him not to hurt her, to forgive her for her doing him in. But by then it'd be too late. He couldn't go back, but he'd at least have her grace him with a 'please': make her beg. For once, *he* would be the only one she called upon.

He looked for his gun - tore up his own place, but it was nowhere in sight. He hated when he lost things. "Where the hell is it?" he yelled aloud in frustration.

No one could've taken it. *No one except for her* — she took it. He needed to act more quickly than he realized. He scanned his calendar. Tomorrow: he could call her into his office tomorrow. He had called that actress several times and he did now once again, but the phone just rang and rang with no answer.

In a rage, Chris sent a bottle flying across his apartment. She'd taken his money and hadn't delivered anything. She said she would help - she didn't help. He couldn't reach her. She'd lied, just like every other woman in his life. He hated women. Chris threw a few more things and tore up her business card.

He could do it: he could pull off talking to Tisha by himself. It could go well for her, he reflected, or it could go very wrong. The outcome was in her hands.

———

Tisha was back at Chase's place and couldn't wait to tell him that not a single thing had happened all day. She'd brought Thomas home with her, they'd done homework, and as soon as Chase arrived she'd be going back to her own apartment for the night.

"It was fun with your family, Tisha. I like Dean a lot."

"Dean is so wonderful, isn't he? I love him," Tisha agreed. She warmed up some of the leftover chicken she made for Thomas and added a side of broccoli. Tisha wasn't hungry, so she ran through some of her notes for the coming week's lesson plans as the boy ate.

"Do you think when you and dad get married, you'll give me a little brother or sister?" Thomas asked between bites.

"Whoa, making a request huh?" Tisha laughed. "I guess we'll want to be married for a year or two before any of that."

"Then have children?" he pressed.

Tisha hesitated, unsure she should have this talk without Chase present, but she persisted anyway.

"Don't worry, uh, it's cool," Thomas continued. "And, hey, *you* have siblings - they're nice, right?"

"Oh yes, honey," Tisha replied. "I couldn't imagine my life without my sister and my two brothers. They *are* nice, but your father was an only child, and he seems fine."

"Yeah, I guess. I just think it sounds nice having another person to talk to."

"Yeah, it is nice to share," Tisha agreed cautiously. "We should talk about all this with your dad: see what he thinks."

"Yeah, okay." He continued eating.

Tisha rummaged through her purse, looking for a note she'd received earlier that day from Chris Jeeter. She hadn't thought anything of it, but she now remembered that it said to meet him after school. Oh well, she thought: she'd missed that, and a part of her was relieved. If he'd wanted to come talk to her, he could have, right after the last class ended. She really didn't want to talk to him, though, especially not alone. She'd told him that she was getting married and he hadn't looked happy about it. She crumpled the paper and put it away in her purse, which she placed on the floor.

"You finished, baby?" she asked absently.

"Yes, thank you," Thomas replied politely. "It was really good."

"I'm glad you liked it. I'll have to start building a list of things you like so I can make them for you."

"Oh, that would be cool," Thomas smiled.

"Yeah," Tisha answered. "It's not a big deal, though. I mean, you have a cook and all, right? Angie can make anything."

"Yes, she can make anything but she meal-plans for two weeks at a time!"

"Really? I'll have to get her teach me to do that!" Tisha exclaimed.

"Why?" Thomas asked. "It's better like you do it: like a real Mom. Besides, Angie has never, ever made pancakes for dinner. *That* was cool."

"Oh well okay… thank you." Tisha was overcome with the emotion she felt toward this little boy. She loved him so much. "I'm really looking forward to being here all the time, honey, when your dad and I get married. I'm excited about being like a mom to you."

"You *will* be a mom," he said firmly. "I'll call you Mom, is that okay?" Thomas stood and so did Tisha. She somehow felt nervous.

"Yes of course, honey. I'd like that."

"Great."

"You gonna do the rest of your homework now, then we'll watch a movie until your Dad comes?"

"Okay. When is he supposed to be here, anyway?"

"Soon, I think."

As Thomas left for his room, Tisha was about to start the dishes and clean the kitchen when the doorbell rang. She moved toward the door, but Thomas was there opening it before she could get to it.

"Oh, Thomas, did you look at the camera first - ?" The thoughts died on her lips as a familiar figure walked in.

"Yeah, it's just Mr. Jeeter," came Thomas's voice.

"Yes, hello, just me, paying a home visit," Chris Jeeter said, closing the door behind him.

FORTY-SIX

O VER THE LAST MINUTE, A new sense of urgency had come over Tisha. A feeling of panic descended on her, but she tamped it down. She remembered the note that this very man had left her… She hadn't ever seen him out of a suit, but there he stood in Chase's kitchen, sporting simple dark jeans and a black hoodie.

"Hello Chris," Tisha uttered. "This is unexpected: a house call? You must have really needed to talk to me this afternoon, huh?" She pulled Thomas back from the door. "Thomas was just gonna go up and do his homework – right, Thomas?"

"Okay," Thomas said, glancing at her as if she'd lost her mind but playing along. Just then, the phone rang.

Tisha located her purse just feet away from the hallway where Jeeter stood. As she retrieved her phone to answer it, she wished that she kept mace in her bag or better a taser, as Teresa did. She had nothing, even after all she'd been through. She felt so stupid.

"Hello? Oh, hey…"

"I got an alert on my phone from the video doorbell app - Is that, Jeeter? What is going on?"

"Oh, really? I heard that. Yeah, that's gonna be a little too long," Tisha tried to sound casual. "Mrs. Peterson, I assure you that she won't fall behind, she'll be just fine."

"Tisha baby, are you afraid?" came Chase's concerned

voice.

"Yeah," she said dragging out the words again, desperate to scream or yell but knowing that would be useless. Her throat felt clogged with fear. "Oh yes, Mrs. Peterson, I assure you I am, but listen, I'll see you really soon, okay?"

Tisha wanted to tell him she loved him, but she was afraid she'd scream or cry, so instead she quickly ended the call. A feeling of dread coursed through her, and as she turned to face Chris Jeeter again, he swung something very large and gray that silenced her next words and rendered everything black.

"Yes, hello, I need the police at my house *now*. I just called my fiancée and there is a strange man at my house. She is scared. My son is there too."

Chase sat there, about to go crazy. When his truck had overheated en route home, stopping on the shoulder had seemed like the wisest thing to do. With smoke starting to rise from the engine, Chase had pulled over and called a mechanic for fear it would explode. Sweat ran down his back.

"Yes, she and my son are there. Please hurry, the man may be dangerous."

Chase's other line was ringing and, at the risk of losing the call with the police altogether, he took the other call.

"Lee, talk to me. I'm just off I-75 but still an hour from Macon, and Tisha is in trouble. Jeeter is at my house. Are you nearby? Can you get there?

"No, you're closer than me," came Leland's reply. "Have you notified the police?"

"Yes, but tell me why you called, Lee - what is it?"

"It's Jeeter: they have a warrant out for his arrest, the list of grievances is a mile long: embezzlement, misuse of school funds... They've been following him, he'd been having an affair with Robinson. Meanwhile she's been talking away to the police, now that she's facing a long sentence. She said that Jeeter has been beside himself about Tisha, said he loves her, but seems to think she can somehow get him out of this recent predicament."

Chase rolled his eyes. He really hated it when Leland was still so formal and verbose when all he wanted to know was if Chris Jeeter might do Tisha harm.

"Is he a murderer?"

"It doesn't seem so, Chase, but I could reach out to the security detail, see if he's closer?" Leland offered.

"Yes, yes do that for me please," exclaimed Chase, only somewhat relieved. "Please just get someone there. Thomas is there too."

Chase didn't bother to say a cordial goodbye - he knew Leland would understand - but when he switched back, the other call had disconnected. He gritted his teeth in anguish.

Chase leapt out of his truck to see if he could help the idiot that was supposedly looking at the vehicle for him. The man had his head buried under the hood, acting as if he didn't know where to begin. Chase screamed over the roaring of cars, trucks and every other loud vehicle: "Can you or can't you fix my damn truck?"

"It'll cost you," the mechanic replied patiently.

The man had brought a tow truck, but something told Chase the man drove like he talked: slow. He could not risk it. "What if I drive it as it is? I gotta get home," he asked in desperation.

"Uh, not much, run a bit, I speck you gotta stop and let it cool..."

"Will it blow?" Chase asked tersely, moving to get back into the truck even as he asked.

"Nah, won't do that on ya," the man replied ponderously, lowering and fastening the hood. "These new babies got a little thang on 'em, keep them from..."

Chase was no longer paying attention. He merely glanced at the oncoming traffic, backing up only because the man in front of him didn't possess the good sense to get out of his way. Chase gunned the engine out into the lane, other cars' horns blaring and brakes squealing. He was gone: full speed ahead.

His fingers worked frantically to dial his home phone as he drove. He made himself a mental note to get Thomas a cell phone for his next birthday; any stupid rules about age appropriateness were no longer relevant. He needed to be able to get hold of someone that could help him. The phone rang on and on, and when no answer came, Chase tossed the phone in frustration onto the passenger seat.

———

Chris Jeeter lounged lazily on the sofa. His legs were crossed at the ankle in a rather feminine fashion as he flipped idly through one of the many sports magazines on the coffee table.

"Why did you tell on me, Ms. Jameson?" Chris asked when Tisha finally woke up. Her hands had been bound and her mouth taped.

"Umph," was all she could grunt in response.

He glanced up at her then, with that same lecherous look he'd had that day when he'd touched his finger to her cheek.

"Everything I ever did was for you," he continued. "I hired you even after I heard about your stupid incident – it was in the local papers – and still I gave you a chance. Now you've brought me all this negative publicity. You know that? I thought you were so special. Only you're a real slut. Getting to know that nice kid's parent, only to hook up with him! A big dumb jock at that." Jeeter tutted. "What a mess you've made, Tisha. Couldn't you have chosen some- one more intellectual, like me?"

Tisha shrunk as he stood, towering over her.

"I'd never hurt you, don't you know that by now? I had many chances to hurt you, but I didn't. I didn't let her hurt you either, did I?"

Tisha shook her head meekly. While she only guessed that he spoke of Andrea, he was clearly crazy.

"But you turned on me, everyone's after me. I only did what I did to make our school the best it could be," Jeeter said in a wounded tone.

Tisha listened as the man before her went on and on, speaking of the money he used, his affair with Andrea Robinson, and proclaiming all the while that he'd somehow done it all for her.

Tisha couldn't think. He scared her, and it was apparent that he too was crazy. Chris Jeeter was even crazier than Andrea, she surmised - as impossible as that might once have seemed.

She hadn't been paying attention, and without thinking she shook her head, not knowing what it was he had asked of her.

"You don't love me?" he yelled.

———◆———

Teresa needed to know if Thomas was at home, but she couldn't tell. She peered into all the windows, searching for signs of him, but she couldn't be sure whose the two cars were. As she made her way stealthily around the home once again, she saw movement in the lower window. It was a large window that gave her a clear view of the den, and she crouched low and saw a man - the man she'd stolen the money from, the one who wanted to get Tisha for something, Teresa really didn't remember now.

The man was standing over something - she couldn't see properly, the arm of the sofa blocked her view. He grabbed the something and pulled it up, and it was then that Teresa saw her: hands behind her back, mouth sealed with tape. Teresa couldn't believe her eyes. Sweat started to trickle down her back and bead on her brow.

She moved around to the front door and checked it: locked.

She really had no idea what to do. All Chase had to do was take her back, but no: instead he'd gone and taken up with this troublesome woman.

Teresa drew herself up to her full height. Removing her Taser from her purse, she held her bag close in the crook of her left arm, and shoved the device into the waistband of her skirt. She raised her hand and knocked on the door incessantly.

Inside, Jeeter was getting ready to move Tisha, but Teresa's knock sounded just as he was contemplating how to go about it.

"Umph, umph!" Tisha was instantly alert. She groaned with urgency and, to her surprise, Chris Jeeter ripped the tape painfully from her mouth.

"What?" he said impatiently.

"Let me get the door, please - please!" Tisha gasped. "Thomas will come down otherwise, and he'll know something is wrong so he'll let whomever it is inside. I can just go - I'll get rid of them, okay?"

"Don't mess up," he said doubtfully. He didn't take the straps off her hands, and she watched as he pulled a gun from his back and held it inside his hoodie.

Tisha nodded and moved to the door. Thankfully Thomas hadn't come down. He probably had his earphones in: he was likely into his video games, and for once in her life she was grateful for them.

Before she could open the door, Chris appeared once again at her side. He grabbed her chin and squeezed it painfully. "You get rid of them, now," he said quietly, in a warning tone.

Tisha winced, but nodded. She cracked the door and

opened it just a crack.

"Where is Chase? He know you got some man here?" came Teresa's voice. "What you guys doing in here, some hanky-panky or something?"

"Please, just go away,"

"No, you bit..."

"Please - *please*?" Tisha looked at the woman.

"You give him this... it's my letter." Teresa held something out and looked meaningfully at Tisha, who hesitated for just a moment before recognizing what was going on.

"Okay, okay," she said faintly. "I'll – I'll tell him you came by - I'll give him... the letter."

"Yeah, you tell him I'ma be back," came Teresa's reply. "You ain't gonna have my man, you got that?"

Before Tisha could grasp what was happening, Teresa tugged her purse tightly before turning and running down the steps, inside her car, she cranked her car's engine and drove away.

Tisha pushed her hands down almost stooping over in her efforts to hide the Taser. She really wasn't sure how she was going to use it, but her fingers gingerly touched the cold metal of the top and the raised buttons on the sides. To her surprise, Teresa had been nice enough to take the top off ahead of time. Tisha didn't have any idea how hard she had to squeeze it to use it... but when she turned, Chris reached forward, no longer holding the gun, so he could shut the door.

Seizing the moment's chance, she held up the device and drove it hard against his neck. The surprise forced him back momentarily, and with a colossal effort she worked her bound fingers over to the tiny buttons on the sides. Chris Jeeter's eyes bulged in startled horror. At first, she was taken aback by the blue current that even buzzed her own hands, but she did not let go despite wanting to, and despite being afraid she'd somehow injure herself with a shock while wielding it. It managed to deliver a short, powerful zap to his body.

Jeeter screamed but was otherwise rendered immobile. His body fell to the floor, convulsing. The gun fell out of his hoody and she moved quickly to kick it away, just like she'd seen Devon do with Andrea. Jeeter writhed in pain. When he made a move, she held it to him again and he was still.

Keeping her eyes on him, Tisha yelled for Thomas as loud as her lungs would permit and he came down in fright. She wanted to cry: those far-fetched video games were surely just like the scene he saw before him. A man on the floor, a gun off to the side... and he likely thought those games were just fiction.

"Come on honey, let's go. Let me get my keys, you - out, now, out the door. Out, to my car. *Go!*"

Thomas obeyed. Finally, Tisha heard sirens - and spied a noisy truck with a smoking engine. *Chase.* She took off in his direction, pulling Thomas with her.

The relief he felt was evident all over his face, and she was certain her face mirrored his. She and Thomas were safe. She dropped her purse and placed her bound arms a little awkwardly around his neck.

The police rushed in and moments later, a handcuffed Jeeter was brought out, looking weak and stunned. He was half-dragged, half-pushed to one of the many waiting police cruisers.

"How on earth did you take him down?" Chase asked.

Tisha shook her head in disbelief. When he saw that her hands were still bound, he quickly opened a small knife on his keychain and cut them away. He held her wrists, massaging them before wrapping her up in his arms again. "You will not believe me when I tell you," she said, and commenced to explain one of the most bizarre stories he'd ever heard. For once in her life, his ex-wife had done something right. And Tisha had been right, Chase couldn't believe any of it.

EPILOGUE

TERESA ALTON WAS IN JAIL, and Tisha was sad about that. Not sad for Teresa, but for Thomas. The woman had put herself there but it didn't make her son's fate any less terrible. She would only serve a few years, but her case had been quick as she'd taken a plea deal to get less time. That was months ago.

To Tisha's surprise, Chase's thoughts on Teresa had softened. After all, she had been the one to help Tisha get away but she'd also organized a hit, fake or not, to get Jeeter's money in the first place. That was still a conspiracy to commit murder, and no one could say for sure what Jeeter had planned if Tisha hadn't gotten the surprise gift of a Taser from Teresa.

Though the nightmare was over, Chase would never forgive her. Although they'd both took time to explain to Thomas what happened, Chase asked that he and Tisha never speak of his ex-wife again in their marriage, for as long as they could avoid having to deal with her.

Tisha was glad that the subject was off-limits, but one day she didn't doubt that it would come up again. As Thomas grew older, maybe he would even want to visit with his mother; but she really couldn't worry about that right now.

Chris Jeeter was in jail and Andrea Robinson was also in jail. Three lives changed, but three criminals forever behind bars for altering the lives of others.

Chase came up behind Tisha and looked at her in the mirror, his arms around her. They were house-hunting: moving to a new development just across town. Chase wanted to be in just before they were married so it wasn't his house, but their house. A new start. Given the trauma she'd been through with Jeeter, Tisha was relieved that Chase had agreed so readily to move.

He'd packed up Thomas and himself within a matter of weeks. Now the house was being built, but they were in the bedroom of one of the model units for the time being.

"You put all the bad guys away - now you just feed my child and I with love and delicious food, and that's all you have to do for the rest of your life."

Tisha smiled. "That sounds like so much fun."

After that difficult time at the school, Tisha was still teaching, but over the summer she planned to carefully evaluate whether or not she would be returning. She really wasn't sure. She knew she didn't have to work and that was a relief, but the question of what to do weighed on her.

"No bad thoughts, OK?" Chase chided playfully.

"I'm not, sorry."

"You know, I heard that Jojo and my housekeeper are dating," Chase said with a smile.

"Yes, I know, I think a little bird told me something about that too," Tisha replied with a wink. "Angie is a great person. I liked her instantly. I hope my brother is ready, though: she's tough. She'll be good for him, I hope. I'll say one thing, it'll either go well or it will be explosive."

"Hey, I'm rooting for it going well, because if he falls in love, he can stay out of his sister's hair and away from me," Chase laughed.

Tisha chuckled. "You survived both Jojo and Dean - you'll be fine."

"Speaking of Dean, what about him and Chyna?"

"Oh, yes, you remember Chyna? My dad's caretaker?"

"Oh yeah, he loves her huh?" Chase asked.

"You bet, it's just a matter of him realizing it," Tisha sighed. "Whatever the future holds for my wayward siblings, I am set for life. All I need is right here." She stood on tiptoe and pouted her lips for a kiss.

"Thank God," Chase said. He led her out of the beautiful model home but not before giving her the kisses he had come to supply on a daily basis.

Tisha smiled, taking notes all the while about the ideas that were running through her head. It would be so exciting to build a home and a life with Chase and Thomas. She couldn't wait.

They went downstairs, where Thomas was playing in the backyard and already making a friend, talking to a neighbor. She was glad he was so well-adjusted. Nothing seemed to faze him, everything just seemed to roll off his back. He was a wonderful child who had led her to an even more wonderful man.

Tisha simply watched, readying her mind and her heart for a bright future and all that awaited her.

ABOUT THE AUTHOR

Tracee Lydia Garner is a bestselling, award-winning author whose stories feature complex relationships and characters experiencing tough but realistic challenges in their quests for love. Born and raised in a Virginia suburb of the DC metro area, Tracee has a degree in Communications, works in health and human services by day and is a speaker-advocate for people with disabilities.

Tracee is a member of the Romance Writers Association (RWA); the Washington Romance Writers DC Chapter; Faith, Hope and Love, an online-only chapter of RWA. Visit Tracee at www.TraceeGarner.com

OTHER BOOK BY AUTHOR

A Current Affair
Book 2 – Jameson Family Series

COMING SOON

Dean Jameson

www.ingramcontent.com/pod-product-compliance
Lightning Source LLC
Chambersburg PA
CBHW030600180626
46816CB00005B/1619